All of Me Wants All of You

J.Z. HOWARD

All4U

Minneapolis, Minnesota

All of Me Wants All of You
Copyright 2014 by J.Z. Howard
Second edition

ISBN: 978-0-9914282-2-9
Library of Congress: 2014902025

Publisher: ALL4U

Cover design by Emily Shaffer Rodvold
Interior layout by Alan Pranke

PRINTED IN THE UNITED STATES OF AMERICA

Dedicated to all the brave souls who strive to become the best they can be.

CHAPTER 1

Kate Nelson glanced at the kitchen clock while unloading the dishwasher, chewing the inside of her cheek. In less than eight hours, she would be naked in bed with her husband. It was the afternoon of their twenty-fourth wedding anniversary and she had that all-too-common feeling in her neck and back muscles. The tendons were already tensing in dismay, and her mind was jumping into hyperspace thinking of ways to avoid the unavoidable. That morning she'd persuaded her husband to settle for body massages after their fancy dinner rather than intercourse. He'd agreed, but she was sure he wasn't happy about it.

"Hi, Mom, I'm home," Nicole announced, bouncing through the door in her black and gold cheerleading outfit.

"Why so early?"

"Gotta find my letter jacket and get over to the stadium for game practice. It's so chilly. I hate standing around shivering between touchdowns."

Her youngest daughter, a senior at Burnsville High School in suburban Minneapolis, rushed by Kate, kissing her on the cheek. Nicole ran back through the kitchen carrying her jacket. "Almost forgot, Mom … Happy Anniversary. Tell Daddy I wished him the same." She made straight for the door. "Hope you guys have a nice dinner out tonight."

"Thanks, Sweetie. Are you still planning to sleep over at Megan's tonight?"

"Yep." A car horn beeped outside. "And don't worry—there won't be any drinking at the party after the game."

"I sure hope not. Love you."

"Love you too. Bye!" Nicole zoomed out the door.

The house grew quiet again.

Kate rubbed her sore neck. *It's a good thing I started those new fitness classes.* She picked up the day's mail and sorted through it. Her eye caught sight of an opened package on Dean's desk. She knew it was none of her business, but curious, she slid a book out of the wrapping paper and glanced at the title: **Things Guys Think About Besides Sex.**

She carefully opened it. "Oh, my!" She flipped through the hundred or more pages—every page blank.

"Men! So it *is* the only thing on their minds." Unamused, she opened the inside cover and noticed an inscription:

Hey Deano,
Ha! Thought this would tickle your funny bone.
Your bud, Hal

She slid the book back into the wrapping paper so Dean wouldn't know it had been moved. She wondered why her husband's best friend would send him a gag gift like that. It was time to hurry off to her fitness class in St. Paul before tonight's fancy dinner for two … and being naked with her beloved husband.

L arissa Beaumont drove her Saturn to the tree-lined campus of MediMax Technologies and parked in the visitors' lot. She walked toward the main entrance of the company's glass office building, determined to get her son's part-time job back. Today's rescue mission involved fighting another of her son's battles, and Larissa knew full well that Cody should be standing up for himself, but he'd ignored her. She wished that somebody would've stood up for *her* and fought *her* battles when she was an orphan in the foster system.

Cody needs to be here and do his own dirty work. Like I had to.

The bright autumn colors of the trees surrounding the building lifted her mood. She practiced the mental discipline of seeing the positive side of life whenever negative thoughts harassed her. September's dropping temperatures signaled cooler nights for sleeping and fueled her optimism, as did the delights of the season like leisurely walks in the woods.

Larissa reached the main entrance and checked her lipstick in the glass doors—not too heavy, just right. She boldly grabbed the door handle and entered the building.

A well-dressed man in his thirties walking out the door looked her over. Even though her jacket masked her shapely figure, she could tell he saw through to the curves beneath. Her tight jeans did nothing to hide her slender legs. Regardless, she'd learned long ago to view this "male appreciation" from strangers with a comical eye rather than an annoying affront.

At the information desk she asked the attendant to point her in the direction of Human Resources. Propelled by her mission, Larissa headed down the hallway to introduce herself to the HR director. She marched to the department's lobby and approached the receptionist's desk. An empty chair greeted her.

Larissa spotted a nameplate beside an executive's polished mahogany door: **Dean Nelson, Director of Human Resources.** The partly opened door teased her to peek inside. Behind a traditional desk sat a nice-looking man in his fifties, writing with a fountain pen. His full head of sandy blond hair framed his rimless glasses, and a well-trimmed moustache augmented his Nordic face.

She stepped closer. . . .

Dean Nelson searched for loving words to write in the anniversary card to his wife. He felt the pressure of time running short. "To my one true love forever," he considered writing, but mentally scratched it out. *How I wish I could say that and mean it.*

On Dean's desk sat a framed portrait of the Nelson family—Kate arm-in-arm with him, their smiling daughters Lindsay and Nicole, and their yellow lab, Jester. Dean felt a surge of fatherly pride for his daughters. Kate's amiable smile and her curly auburn hair reminded him of their earlier years when excitement in their marriage had ruled the day, rather than the blah sensation he felt nowadays.

Next to the family portrait sat a large gift box wrapped with red ribbons. He'd purchased the anniversary gift for Kate earlier that day with some trepidation. It was a finely-crafted reproduction of Rodin's sculpture *Eternal Springtime* about fifteen inches tall. The two naked lovers kissed in a passionate embrace. He knew the gift was a calculated risk.

He tapped his pen, hunting for the right words. Decades ago they'd shared such an adventurous spirit; could he honestly write words reflecting the same now? His schedule demanded that he leave the office and run errands, then pick his wife up for their dinner downtown.

Dean heard a knock on his door. A woman's face appeared in the doorway.

"Mr. Nelson?" Her attractive smile sent a shock wave through him. "I couldn't find someone to direct me, so I hope I'm not intruding."

"That's all right." He found himself stammering a bit, "May I help you?"

"I understand you're the HR director who has reviewed my son's drug test results."

He sat back. "And you must be … ?"

Stepping in, she stretched out her hand to shake. "Cody Beaumont's mother, Larissa Beaumont. Until last week he was your part-time hire in the warehouse. His random drug test came back positive for marijuana."

It took Dean a moment to refocus. Touching her hand triggered warm energy within him. He shrugged off the peculiar feeling and snapped back into business mode. "Cody Beaumont? Yes, I do recall. But could we discuss this at some other time?"

She forced an unhappy smile.

"I see." Dean reached for a stack of file folders and pulled one out. "First, I'll need to check that he's signed a release." He opened the file. "Okay, here it is. Yes, we're authorized to share information and discuss his case. Before we go any further, however, I'm sorry, but I'll have to see some form of picture ID."

She opened her purse and handed him her driver's license.

He examined it closely: Age, 38. Height, 5' 9". Weight, 136 lbs. Eyes, green.

"My hope, sir, is that you'll be able to convince his manager to rehire him."

"Highly unlikely, but how about if we take a look at the facts? A lot depends on what his manager wrote in his file. Right now I really don't have the time though—" Dean saw her face fall. "Tell you what," he added, "give me a minute to study this. Have a seat."

That's when it hit him. The smooth way she settled into the chair and her poised posture accentuated her penetrating eyes, which reflected an inner attractiveness that matched her stunning outer features.

Pausing for a heartbeat, he cleared his throat and looked up. "Cody's test results are right here. I see he turned eighteen in June."

"Yes, the week after graduating from high school. The first thing he wanted was a job."

Dean scanned the multi-drug test report until he came to the signature at the bottom. "Unfortunately, Mr. Gomez, his warehouse manager, has already signed off on his termination. Sorry."

"Cody said as much. But he needs a second chance, Mr. Nelson. My son … he … he's just started community college, and his job here is important. It will keep him motivated to study and help him pay tuition and buy books, besides giving him the discipline he needs. Can you please ask his manager to reconsider?" Her eyes flickered with a plea for hope.

Dean paused. "Why didn't Cody come in today and speak for himself?"

She grimaced. "You've got me on that one. He's still young and hasn't learned to fight his own battles. But you're right; he should be here. Not me."

Dean noted her flustered tone then scanned the report again. Cody's THC level, the psychotropic ingredient in *cannabis sativa*, showed an increase since his hiring date weeks earlier. "Generally, a trace amount wouldn't prevent a college-aged student applying for a part-time warehouse job from being hired. The problem is it's gone up since then."

"What if Cody was retested?"

"It might be that an error occurred with the urinalysis. It's happened before." Dean knew false positives were possible, as they were with all drug tests. "I'll put in a call to Mr. Gomez. How's that? No promises."

"Great! Anything you suggest would be wonderful."

Amazed by her sheer persistence, he couldn't help checking her out again, comparing her to Kate. About ten years older, Kate matched this woman feature for feature. But his skin got prickly when he admitted to himself how Kate had let her sense of style and zest for life slip over the years.

"Your son didn't give us your phone number, Ms. Beaumont. I'll need that information and an email address. When would be a good time to reach you?"

"Just about any time between ten and four." She dug into her purse and handed him a business card. "Here's my work number and email." Her eyes met his. "I don't know how to thank you."

He glanced at the card: **Fitness & Flowers by Larissa**. The logo in pen and ink showed a curvy woman reaching elegantly toward the sky. "Assuming I get an okay from Mr. Gomez, Cody will have to provide another urine sample first thing Monday morning."

"Of course."

"I don't see anything here in the file about his father. Has he been notified?"

She looked away. "Cody's father has been absent from his life since his birth."

Dean adjusted his glasses. "Well, I hope Cody realizes what a lucky kid he is to have a mom who's willing to stick her neck out for him."

Larissa's shoulders arched upward. "I want to be honest with you. I love him dearly, Mr. Nelson, but he's been a party boy, and I don't know when he'll start getting serious about his future." She clenched her jaw. "I just want him to fulfill his potential, that's all. It's buried right now." She looked Dean in the eye then gazed down at the report. "Everything hangs on the new lab results, doesn't it?"

"Yes, and whether or not Mr. Gomez gives his okay. Also, Cody has to show up like he's supposed to for a retest and demonstrate a strong sense of responsibility on the job."

"Can we talk by phone as soon as the results come in?"

"It usually takes a day or so. Once Mr. Gomez and I discuss it, I'll be in touch."

She stood up to leave, reaching out her hand. Her caramel blonde hair tumbled over her shoulders. "Thank you for your help. And pardon me for taking so much of your time. You've been more than kind. I'll wait to hear from you."

"Like I said, no promises."

"I understand."

He noted her beautiful smile.

"Goodbye, Mr. Nelson. It's been a pleasure."

He watched her turn and walk out the door. Dean sensed her frustration. He glanced again at the framed portrait of his family on the desk. How he wished Kate's smile of fifteen years ago would be the same today. Noticing the time, he wished he felt more excited about picking her up for dinner. He loved her for so many reasons—her friendliness and readiness to encourage the best in everyone distinguished her—but he wondered when the last time was he'd had an intense, mouth-to-mouth, tongue-wrestling kiss with Kate.

The blah feeling overwhelmed him again. He glimpsed the svelte woman reaching for the sky on Ms. Beaumont's business card, whiffing the intriguing scent of her perfume and aching for something he couldn't quite name.

CHAPTER

Larissa banished her anxiety as she walked to her parked car. The sky seemed sunnier, and the warm autumn day cheered her. She appreciated the uplifting change. *More positive thoughts. Keep 'em coming. Thank you, Mr. Nelson.*

A new skip in her step accompanied the lingering impression of Mr. Nelson. He had grinned slightly when she'd handed him her business card. To his credit, he appeared open-minded and compassionate, and he was definitely handsome. She liked his hazel eyes and regretted that he was a married man, evident by the family portrait on his desk.

Fifteen minutes later, after driving across the Mississippi River from Minneapolis, she parked in the alley behind her fitness studio on Grand Avenue in St. Paul's commercial shopping district. Unlocking the shop's back door made her self-esteem soar. *My very own business!* She'd rented the former dance studio a year before and worked her butt off to build a paying clientele, currently sixteen regulars and counting. She loved teaching aerobic exercises and yoga, including fast-paced Zumba, to upbeat classical or blaring hip-hop music as a healthy way to help her clients tone up their sedentary bodies and de-stress their tense emotions.

For this afternoon's 4:30 fitness class, she chose Vivaldi's *Gloria* for warming up.

Larissa looked and, right on time, her clients began streaming through the door: Claire, a rather undernourished 45-something divorcee whose sorrow had deepened her insecurity; Jasmine, an African-American fashion model and wannabe actress who worked hard to keep in shape; Conrad, an accomplished dancer who loved the feminine companionship during workouts; Annabelle, an overweight healthcare executive whose goal of shedding thirty pounds meant walk-the-talk weight loss; and her newest client, Kate, a fiftyish lady from the suburbs who needed major loosening up. Larissa felt like a mother hen to this interesting bunch.

As the group was assembling, Larissa hollered, "Okay, everybody. Three minutes before we start. Let's warm up."

Larissa noted Kate's warm-up routine, particularly how she rubbed her neck and shoulders repeatedly. Kate muttered to Larissa, "I sure need your flexibility stretches and exercises today."

"You're making progress, Kate, but try relaxing more and not being so hard on yourself. Let your shoulders and neck get loose." Kate looked in shape, but muscle tension inhibited her body in other areas as well.

She recalled how Kate had seen a flyer for Fitness & Flowers at a local shop four weeks earlier and had signed up for workouts that day. "My shoulders are killing me," Kate had told her, "so getting rid of these neck aches would be super. Can you help?" Larissa had noted how she carried her weight well and was neither over- nor underweight, yet her posture slumped in contrast to her overall appealing figure and caring personality.

"I'm sure you'll benefit from our individualized classes," Larissa told Kate that day. "We also have a free women's empowerment support group on Fridays and weekends."

Annabelle paused during her leg stretches and spoke up, "I hope you're planning for us to do some Zumba, Larissa."

"Yeah," echoed Jasmine. "I could use some cardio."

"You're so flexible already, I'm jealous," said Claire.

Kate added, "If Zumba is your secret, Larissa, then I'm all for it. Your midriff and thighs are to die for."

They all laughed.

The back door swung open and Cody stepped in, surprising Larissa. "Hey, Mom. Sorry to interrupt. I got tied up on campus."

Larissa looked at her son, a handsome, tall, and charismatic young man full of mischief in a grown man's body. "Cody, I'm just starting class. Make it quick, real quick."

"I know I should've emptied the trash in the dumpster yesterday and cleaned out the flower cooler like you asked, but I'm here now. Any more chores on your list?"

"I hope there's homework on *your* list. Oh, and by the way, will you get busy and clean out your animal hospital? The scat from your injured rabbit is stinking up the place."

"No prob. I thought today would be a good time to release the little bugger anyway."

The crate for Cody's makeshift shelter for injured animals sat by the back door to the alley, as far away from clients as possible. He'd cared for traumatized rabbits, cats, turtles, birds, and dogs ever since he was nine years old, when his pet hamster had injured its paw.

She turned to her students and declared, "All right, everybody ... opening positions." Larissa began her instructions, stretching and twisting in her workout leotard, demonstrating poses and guiding her clients to Vivaldi's music.

After the 45-minute workout, Larissa was wiping her brow with a towel when she noticed Kate and Claire hugging by the front door. Claire looked at Kate, sporting a brighter smile than Larissa had ever seen. It gave her pleasure to see that. Claire waved goodbye, and Larissa approached Kate.

"Feeling more limber, Kate?"

"Much better, yes. Now, if these muscles would only stay this way."

"They're releasing endorphins right now. Repetitions and more repetitions will teach them to behave."

"Bless you, Larissa. My neck is beginning to feel looser, and that's a huge plus."

"By the way, it was great seeing you connecting with Claire just now. You're very kind with people, Kate."

"It's the least I could do. She's going through so much with her ex right now."

"Yes, Claire needs a friendly ear these days. It does my heart good to see relationships like that forming. You have a very gentle way about you."

"It shows?" Kate asked.

"It shows. And glows."

They laughed.

Kate smiled. "Time to go. See you next week." Glancing at the clock, she panicked. "Oh no! Gotta run! It's our anniversary, and my husband is picking me up for dinner. Bye!"

"How wonderful. Congratulations to you both."

Kate waved and rushed out the front door.

O utside Fitness & Flowers, Kate hurried to her late-model Lexus SUV. The crisp outdoor air cooled her sweaty brow. She looked back and noticed Larissa waving through the window, smiling.

Nothing had proven as effective to loosen her rigid muscles as Larissa's classes. The investment of time and energy to limber up was paying off. Watching Larissa lead exercises, following her fluid movements, responding to the way she quietly corrected mistakes with gentle pointers, all boosted Kate's motivation to improve herself.

As Kate got in her SUV, she noticed Claire leaning against her car, staring at the pavement. Kate frowned. "Claire, are you okay?"

"Oh hi, Kate. Yeah, I guess," Claire said. "I'm so sick of the divorce games my ex is playing. It's really getting to me. He just hung up on me."

Kate detected the toll on Claire's nerves as she walked closer. "Would it be all right if I prayed for you?"

"That's very kind," Claire answered, as Kate approached. "But please don't think you have to. Oh, never mind. That would mean so much, unless you're in a big hurry."

"Sshhhh." Kate put her hand on Claire's shoulder, sensing a sibling-like connection. Kate closed her eyes, fully aware of the urgency to meet her husband, and prayed softly, "Heavenly Father, lift my friend Claire out of her pit and touch her heart with Your love. Comfort her as only You can. Amen."

Claire blinked as Kate opened her eyes. "You actually prayed out loud!"

"Yes," Kate replied. A current of warm energy passed between them.

"Will you be all right now, Claire?"

"Of course. Please go. And … thank you."

Kate smiled, dashed to her car, turned the ignition key, and drove away to get ready for her dinner out.

Two hours later, Dean took Kate's arm as they walked into La Belle Vie restaurant. The elegant ambience impressed Kate, but she couldn't help thinking about her never-ending list of to-do's: answering text messages from her older daughter Lindsay in Iowa about college dorm life, counseling her younger daughter Nicole about the snarky fights she was having on Facebook with classmates, and keeping up with a bulging list of appointments and reminders. Dean had apologized for picking her up late. In all truth, she'd been running late herself, so Kate was grateful.

Always a gentleman, Dean held her chair as she sat down. The waiter handed them menus. She looked across the table at her husband. He placed a large gift box with red ribbons on the table next to the smaller gift and card she'd brought for him. "Dean, do you think we'll be having a romantic dinner like this in another twenty-four years?"

He looked far off and squinted. "Let's see, right now you're forty-nine and I'm fifty, so you'll be seventy-three and I'll be seventy-four." Peering at a distant horizon as if he were a ship's captain, he said, "I trust we will navigate whatever choppy waters are ahead and prevail."

She smiled. "Okay, I think you get what I'm saying, Skip." She kicked his leg under the table. She often called him Skip, a nickname he'd had since childhood. "I like the idea of us being together no matter what age we are."

"Yes, Katie," he said, using her favorite nickname. "Till death do us part."

She glanced at the menu. "I think I'm seafood hungry tonight. The pan-seared scallops look very tempting."

"And for me the top sirloin looks scrumptious."

They ordered calamari for an appetizer. She asked for a whisky manhattan on the rocks, and he ordered a fancy lemonade with a twist. Dean leaned over and kissed her hand. For a few heartbeats, Kate basked in the good fortune of having a husband who loved her and who also loved the Lord. "I'm just praising the Lord for you," she whispered. "How could I ever be so blessed?"

"God's the glue, isn't He? The center of everything we are."

She nodded and handed his anniversary card to him. It had a yin/yang pattern of two hearts entwined with the bold words on the cover *When Two Hearts Beat as One*. He read it aloud, "To Dean, my one and only. We live as one, we love as one. In Christ's love always, Katie."

He reached across the table and squeezed her hand, and kissed it again. Reaching for her gift, he opened the box she'd wrapped in bright aquamarine paper with pearl-colored ribbon. He took out a theatre brochure and peered inside it. "Hey, season tickets to the Guthrie. Way to go!"

She smiled. "We get to pick four plays for the current season. Look inside and see which ones you like." Dean read off the titles, and they talked through their choices.

When it came her turn to open his gift, she removed the card from the envelope marked KATIE and eyed the playful illustration. In a sailboat with a billowing heart-shaped sail, two lovers rode together, navigating arm-in-arm on the wide open seas. Inside she read the printed greeting, "Let's expand our horizons and live our marriage to the fullest." In his own words: *Dearest Katie, I truly hope and believe the best adventure is still ahead. To be closer to you is my deepest wish and desire. With all my love, Dean*

She reached across the table and intertwined her fingers with his, squeezing them tightly. "How special." His message thrilled her. She looked in his eyes and was surprised to see something—sadness? loneliness?—darken his gaze. *What could it be?* she wondered.

Dean handed her the large box with red ribbons. As she pulled back the paper, two naked lovers kissing passionately greeted her. Taken aback, she almost dropped the ceramic sculpture. Blushing, she stuffed it back in the box.

"What's wrong?"

"I ... I don't think it's ... it's quite what I expected."

"It's Rodin's *Eternal Springtime*, a famous piece of art. It visualizes what

I wrote in your card, 'To be closer to you is my deepest wish and desire.'"

Kate knew it was a gorgeous sculpture full of expressive yearning, but the lovers' embrace was unmistakably erotic. "Of course it's famous. I took art appreciation, you know. It's an excellent replica. I'm sure it will look nice wherever we find a place for it."

Dean looked hurt. She could almost hear him thinking, *Excellent replica?* "I was thinking," he said softly, "of our bedroom."

Now she was outright embarrassed. She could not imagine it anywhere except covered up in a closet. Her mind went blank with confusion. From feeling quietly elated, she now felt her head buzzing. A niggling reminder jabbed at her; she had put off calling the gas company to schedule the annual pre-winter tune-up for their furnace. *I need to stop procrastinating about simple chores.*

"Are you okay?" Dean asked.

"Yes, of course. Sorry." Her mind had gone blank. Empty. *Could it be the onset of menopause?* Her friend Ginny had insisted the start of menopause should no longer be thought of as "the change." Instead, for today's woman, it was a fresh opportunity to begin a second adulthood with benefits to explore and freedoms to enjoy.

"Are you off in La-la-land?" he asked.

"Never mind," she said, snapping back to the present. "I think I'll have the scallops."

When the waiter returned with their drinks and the calamari, they ordered their entrees. As the busboy refilled their water glasses, the activity allowed her to collect her wits. She decided to bring up Lindsay and her boyfriend Brandon to distract Dean from talking about the Rodin sculpture. "Lindsay texted today that Brandon's folks have been fighting again."

"What about this time?"

"His mother's alcoholic. He and Lindsay visited their family farm last weekend. His mom was acting up again, saying hurtful things about Brandon's dad."

"Treatment would help them both. Her to get sober, him to cope better."

Dean had worked as a professional addictions counselor for twelve years prior to switching to corporate HR and was himself a recovering alcoholic. Kate felt proud of him. Dean's successful sobriety the past fourteen years had calmed him, and his regular attendance at AA meetings inspired others who suffered from alcoholism or abusing drugs to stay clean.

"How's your lemonade?" Kate asked.

"Just right."

She wondered at times how he'd done it, denying himself the pleasures of alcohol. Thank goodness he seldom made a stink about her own drinking, like right now when she was thinking of ordering a second manhattan. What she honestly wanted was a double manhattan.

While eating, their conversation centered on parental and household concerns, like a new fence for the backyard. Kate splurged a bit and ordered two glasses of pinot noir with dinner. "It's so nice to have open-ended time together, Skip, like right now. I could sit here till midnight holding hands with you."

He winced slightly. "I hope by midnight we're doing more than that. Can't wait to get home and start our massages." He lifted his glass of lemonade. "Like my card said, Katie … 'the best adventure is still ahead.' To us."

They clinked glasses.

After they finished a delicious tiramisu, the nagging thought running through Kate's mind was, *What should I do about the sculpture?* She hoped it wasn't a not-so-subtle hint from Dean. Not tonight. What else, though, could two naked lovers mean?

Maybe the ghastly thing would find its way to the closet after all.

C H A P T E R

Friday night about 8:30, Larissa tried to relax at home. She needed a night alone, an evening off to watch a favorite old movie while sipping a glass of wine. A movie like *Hope Floats* or *Chocolat* or *Mama Mia!* would do nicely. Cody had borrowed the car to drive to his best friend Alex's house and hang out. Her fear was the two boys would get into trouble for smoking marijuana or drinking too much. Because it was the weekend, she knew better than to expect Cody's studies would trump X-Box game night. She opened the fridge and poured a glass of chardonnay. As she sipped, she recalled their conversation as he was about to leave the house.

"You know, I fought your battles for you today, Cody. I met with an executive at MediMax to ask if your manager would give you another chance."

Cody shrugged, indifferent to her running interference.

"You're very lucky if he gives it to you. If he does, you need to get over to the warehouse bright and early Monday morning for retesting."

"Another urine sample?" He seemed annoyed.

"Damn, Cody! You have to start taking this stuff seriously. Getting fired after six weeks at a new job with good pay is no way to start. It's your freshman year, so take it seriously."

"I know … I'm not in high school anymore."

"There's more than smoking pot at a campus football party or losing your job going on here. You need to get serious about your life. And if you smoke weed this weekend, it'll show up on the UA."

"Mom, if it makes you happy, I'll go there on Monday and pee in the guy's cup, and say all the right things, and do everything I can to get my job back, okay?"

She almost believed him.

He let his shoulders sag, dropping his churlish attitude. Kissing her cheek, he gave her a hug and she knew he meant it. "Love ya, Mom."

"Please make sure you're home by midnight. And no pot, okay? Love you, too."

That was half an hour ago. Now, while sipping chardonnay, Larissa gazed out her kitchen window. Her house was three blocks from her studio. She'd purchased the cozy two-story bungalow five years before, after her hopes for marriage with her fiancé Brad had been smashed. Looking out on the woodsy backyard, she felt gratitude for the home she'd refurbished with tasteful touches and style.

Entering the living room, she turned on the TV and decided to watch *Hope Floats*. She glanced at the framed portrait of Brad in his military uniform on the fireplace mantel. Brad's gentle smile looked back at her from under the bill of his Army officer's dress cap. Her Mr. Right, the man she'd truly loved: First Lieutenant Brad Eichhorn. The circumstances of his death flooded her. Just days before his furlough from Afghanistan prior to their wedding, a roadside bomb took out his entire unit. She would never know what he'd felt in those last minutes as he bled to death, but she believed he would have been thinking of her.

"I'm so glad I'll be your wife, Brad, and we'll have babies together," she'd told him on their last phone call. But his death had ended her chances of conceiving his child.

"Cut the shit," Larissa mumbled to herself. "You don't have to relive this. Just be thankful for all the great times we had."

Settling back in her easy chair, she took the TV remote in her hand and surrendered to her need to veg out. The thought of Brad's embrace the last time they'd made love tugged at her. She took control of her thoughts, practicing "thought catching," a mental technique she'd learned while meditating. She fast-forwarded the movie past the credits to Sandra Bullock's first encounter with Justin, her old high school flame who reminded Larissa of Brad. A lonely feeling crept up on her as she recalled Brad's tender lovemaking. Although very tender, their intimacy also felt lustful, edgy even—the way she enjoyed it sometimes.

The movie showed Birdie, Sandra Bullock's character, and Justin kissing and laughing in a kids' playground while goofing around like lovebirds. Larissa's own childhood had been a downward spiral of negative memories for the nine years she'd bounced between half a dozen miserable foster homes.

She picked up her cellphone and speed-dialed her foster family. As it rang, she thought of her saviors, dairy farmers Gladys and Jerry Beaumont and their three sons, Walter, Todd, and Russell. "Hi mom and dad," she said on their voicemail. "I'm feeling kinda homesick for you guys—and the boys, of course. No need to call back. Just letting you know I'm thinking of you and how much I love you."

Hanging up, she leaned back and relished the years growing up in Gladys and Jerry's loving care, and how they'd welcomed her until she knew she belonged. Memories of hanging around her three strapping step-brothers and the ways they made every day an adventure filled her with nostalgia.

Larissa watched Justin kissing Birdie. *What hope do I ever have for a kiss like that? Another Mr. Right must be out there somewhere. Would it be insanity at the age of thirty-eight to get married and have another baby?* She'd tried a couple of web-based dating services, looking but not finding, despite the advertising about happy singles finding marriageable matchups.

She hit the pause button, suddenly imagining herself in Dean Nelson's arms. *It's a shame he's already taken. What a catch!*

The thought of him close to her lingered.

Arriving home after dinner, Dean and Kate kicked off their dress-up clothes and changed into pajamas. Lifting his eyebrows as a signal, he whispered, "Ready to get started?"

"How about ten minutes?"

He nodded, wondering if they both meant the same thing. He suspected she'd meant mutual back rubs, but no more, as they'd agreed that morning. With Nicole sleeping over at Megan's and Lindsay at Drake University 250 miles away, he was hoping their privacy would encourage Kate to open up and let go.

"How about putting on some Mozart?" he said as he lit new candles around the bedroom.

"Great idea."

Dean waited for Kate to locate a special place in their bedroom for Rodin's sculpture, but the embracing lovers remained in the gift box on the kitchen table. Could the lovers' zealous lovemaking thaw Kate's resistance and bring the passionate heat back into their relationship?

In the dining room, Dean flipped through the day's mail. Jester walked up to Dean, wagging his tail. The dog seemed to sense Dean's perplexed mood. Dean reached down and petted his fur. As he sorted through the junk mail, Dean's mind jumped to the strong yearnings he felt. *It would be thrilling if Kate felt the loving connection tonight we once shared years ago.* Why her libido had hit the skids confounded him. Although his desire for her was still alive, it was flickering. Didn't she miss the pleasure and intimacy they both deserved?

"Dean, I need to call Nicole and see if she's doing okay, then we'll be ready."

"Call her now? She's doing fine, I'm sure." He hung his head in prayerful submission. *Am I too headstrong in this area of our lives, Lord? Am I being insensitive? Am I putting my own needs before Kate's?*

He opened his journal, the place where he recorded his struggles and the major events of his life. The spiral-bound notebook was the latest in a collection numbering dozens. For the past fifteen years, he'd felt caught in a tug-of-war over his and Kate's love life, feeling the pain of her avoidance and deliberate silence. He flipped to a recent jotting: *I feel cheated. I'm not getting any younger and this is dragging on too long. Married couples are meant to share openly and become one being. An active sex life is our gift to each other, but what fear—or shame—is driving her withdrawal? What has gone wrong with us?*

Dean understood their lackluster love life was missing intimacy as much as it was missing thrills and orgasms. Trust and openness had withered. And he appreciated how their individual needs for nonsexual affection mattered as well. He prayed: *Dear Lord, show us what Your will is for us. May tonight be the night our marriage heals. Amen.*

In the bathroom, he walked up to Kate as she spoke with Nicole on her smartphone. He began gently brushing her hair. In the mirror, he observed Kate's eyes—her pretty blue eyes. As she hung up and turned to him, the smell of alcohol on her breath hit him. It seemed more vodka-scented than wine-scented, and he guessed she'd quietly poured a secret glass for herself after they'd arrived home.

"Your ladyship," he whispered, "your lordship desires your presence." It grieved him how she drank on the sly, but confronting her tonight was ill-timed. "Our massages await, my dear, and my hands are eager to caress your silky skin. Let's away to bed!"

In the soft candlelight of their bedroom, Kate's naked body lay face down on the sheets. Dean rubbed lavender-scented oil into her skin with long, firm strokes. "You have such a lovely butt," he cooed. He recited a poetic description from the *Song of Songs*: "'How sweet is your love, my precious jewel, how your love entices me.'"

She purred in low, musky tones as he rubbed more oil into her skin.

He whispered another *Song of Songs* verse, "'You have ravished my heart, my bride; with a glance of your eyes you have wooed me.'"

She moaned in great pleasure. "How romantic hearing you say that."

Kneading her muscles gently, he lifted her head to kiss her. "Katie, my darling . . ."

She looked into his hazel-speckled eyes with a huge smile. "You're so wonderful to say those lovely words. Bless you!"

He smiled. They were connecting. He moved slowly, ever so gently, with patience. Her needs came first. No demands, no pressuring, no emphasis on sex, just winning her over with the soothing fragrance of lavender and his smile, and with words of sensuous love.

Softly, Kate stirred and uttered, "So lovely, absolutely lovely. Now lie back, Deano, and I'll begin your massage."

In the soft glow of the candlelight, Kate rubbed the lavender oil onto Dean's naked body with long strokes. The tactile sensuality of the oil spread along his back, easing his strong muscles. Her slippery hands moved in time to Mozart's *A Little Night Music* playing quietly in the background. He moaned with pleasure.

"A half an hour of that will do nicely," Dean murmured.

"Hush, dear. Let your mind and your muscles relax. Be still, my love."

Like most workdays, Dean had gone full steam since 7:00 a.m. As a great provider with a servant's heart, Kate knew he devoted himself to his employees and poured his energy into his career. His steadfast work ethic had led to pay raises and an agreeable lifestyle in their two-story colonial home on a tree-lined suburban street. At home, he'd fed the girls their baby food and helped dress them for preschool. He modeled the characteristics of a loving husband, even doing chores around the house other than the gardening—her forte.

She conveyed her affection and devotion lovingly through her hands and fingers, trusting that Dean felt her sincerity. Simply put, Kate loved Dean's generous, giving nature. His love made their marriage strong, vibrant, lasting, and admired by many. As a bonus, she enjoyed the freedom to volunteer as a short-term missionary and pursue worship activities such as choreographing holiday ceremonies at their church. Hearing him mutter poetic phrases from *Song of Songs* made her wonder, *Were the verses he quoted his way of saying, "Let's have sex?"* She wasn't sure, but she hoped not.

Hearing Mozart's serenade, Dean consciously let the music soften his yearnings for Kate and calm his doubts. While she rubbed scented oil along his skin with gentle strokes, his memory stubbornly recalled sessions in couples therapy years before that had failed to shed light on the mystery of their impasse.

"Talking with her about intimate details drives her away," he'd told the therapist. "So I've learned to back off." Kate had told the therapist, "Reaching that sexual high other women glorify may be fine for them— it's just not for me." Dean had looked at her and said, "What matters is our connection, Kate, our being vulnerable together and intimate. It's not just about sex." She'd rolled her eyes. "No, I think that's totally what it's about." He regretted how each of them had gradually compromised over the years to where he suspected masturbation was the only remaining outlet for either of them.

Kate rubbed the oil along Dean's legs, gently squeezing his tight calf muscles. Was he falling asleep? She expected his back rub would lead to his turning over and going to sleep. "How's that? Feel good?"

"Heavenly," he replied.

She gently stopped rubbing, half hoping Dean was drifting into a deep slumber. It was getting late. She leaned to snuff out the candles. Slowly, carefully, she moved off the bed, trying not to disturb him. But Dean stirred.

With a tiny moan, he said, "Stay a while. Let's cuddle."

"Why don't you just slip off to dreamland?"

"We're in no hurry. It's not that late."

He gently reached up, stroking her shoulders and neck. Her sore neck and shoulders felt a little less constricted after her fitness workout at Larissa's, but tensed again now. She let him knead the tendons and tissues with his mellow touch, but soon his hand was stroking her back and hips.

"We could do something else, Katie. Something we've been putting off."

Bingo. Just as she'd suspected. A flurry of thoughts flew through her mind. Where was this leading?

"What d'ya know … ?" He pointed to his groin. "Look …"

She averted her eyes from his growing erection. She wished Nicole could've been in the next bedroom as an excuse to tell him to stop. Sex had been easier in the early years of their marriage, and for a purpose: having children and creating a splendid family. Ever since … "It's hardly what we agreed, right?"

"Just relax." He tugged at her shoulders, bringing her closer to his body.

She resisted. "I thought this morning we said—"

"That was hours ago. I was hoping you might feel differently by now."

Her foggy judgment from the alcohol distressed her. Risking the frustrating effect it would have on him, she sprang up and left for the bathroom. In the silence, she heard him quietly groan in disappointment. What made her do it? Was it some trick of menopause? Was it stress? Was it the alcohol? Was it prudish modesty?

The crisis in their hotel room one year earlier in Honduras came rushing into Dean's mind. He'd arranged a special night together for just the two of them, apart from their fellow travelers on a humanitarian trip to Central America. He relived lying naked in bed next to Kate as candlelight caressed her curves. They hadn't made satisfying, passionate love in ages, and it was time. He'd been reading up on some techniques to arouse her, to pique her pleasure. The timing seemed perfect. That night his fingers found an area between her legs that elicited quiet moans.

"How does that feel, Katie?" Away from home with no kids to worry about, no to-do list, no reason to rush around getting things done, he'd anticipated the direct opposite of her sudden shriek of pain.

"Agghh!"

"Too much pressure?"

"It hurts. Go slower."

He'd messed up. He tried again, more gently, but she flinched and clamped her legs shut. He withdrew, vowing to learn more about the sensitive ways to please a woman.

What could've been a golden moment became one of sadness and grief. Waiting quietly for her to show some sign of willingness, to begin the dance of love, led only to more waiting. He'd smiled … waited … kissed her cheek … waited … kissed her lips … smiled …

That night in Honduras made him realize how broken things were between them. Alarms had gone off within him as their opportunity for intimacy slipped into indifference. He assumed his clumsy fingers had harmed her. "Actually, I'm not quite in the mood," she'd said. If his technique was not the main factor, then why was her libido in a deep freeze? Was he no longer attractive to her?

"What the hell is going on?" he'd demanded. "Why can't we just make love?"

Fear contorted her face. "Get away! You frighten me!"

"Frighten you? I'm your husband."

Pushing him backward, she shouted, "Not when you yell at me like that."

"Yell? I wasn't yelling. Okay, I'm sorry." He'd lowered his voice. "I just don't understand why we aren't making love."

"Having sex, you mean."

"No, making love. Am I that clumsy? Can't you find it in you to make love with me?"

"Oh, I see … now it's all *my* fault. You're the one who's obsessed."

"Obsessed? Are you nuts?"

"Sex, sex, sex. It's the only thing you ever think about. Don't think I don't know."

"Oh, so now you're a mind reader? Well, maybe if we got it on every couple of weeks—or couple of months, or *years*."

It might have gone on like that, except he finally turned away and she sobbed into the pillow. Golden moment ruined. Opportunity shattered.

Sequestered now in the bathroom, Kate sat on the toilet seat and pretended to pee, making noises like pulling the toilet paper off the roll. She prayed quickly: *Dear Lord, I need your help. Dean and I are miles apart. He reneged on his agreement, and I'm not exactly sure what he meant in his anniversary card by, "to be closer to you is my deepest wish and desire." Please make Your will clear. Amen.*

Had he really meant that god-awful statue as a gift? She disliked the battle they were having. She felt coerced. Sleeping in the same bed together and kissing was fine, but she would not be a pawn to his sex drive. Her modesty felt under attack.

She stifled a burp. The combination of whisky and wine, plus sips of vodka, made her head spin. Her eyelids felt heavy. She felt groggy and feared she'd been slurring her words. Had Dean noticed? She knew she couldn't keep Dean waiting in bed too long.

Oh, to drift off to sleep! I need to come up with a plan! Letting him have sex might settle him down, but was it worth the risk? Would it only encourage his wanting more, ever more, more often? *More, more, more! Is there never an end to it?*

Kate hesitated at the thought that her life might turn out like Claire's, Larissa's client. She did not relish having to wage divorce wars with Dean like Claire had to with her ex, if it ever came to that. All Kate needed to do was lubricate herself with KY jelly, go back to bed, and put on a performance for ten minutes, then forget it. Arguing was no use. Dean had often tried getting her in the mood in the past and had complained that she'd never found her "on" button.

Kate knew what her friend Ginny would say: "Get on with it!" Kate wished for a feeling from within to fire her up. Nothing. She sighed, trying to let her body relax. Her desire, weak as it was, tended to follow being aroused; arousal first, then desire (rarely). For Dean, his desire came first, then arousal (always).

"What's going on, Kate?" Dean demanded, standing in the doorway. "What's taking so long?"

She stood up from the toilet and saw he was wearing his pajama bottoms. "Just a minute." Her heart fluttered. The pressure was mounting; she could no longer delay. Fretting did no good. She reached for the KY jelly in the medicine cabinet.

"Congratulations, you've done it again." He stared holes through her.

She recoiled at his anger. She wanted to speak, but he spoke first. "What sick game are you playing? Don't you miss our making love?"

Stepping past her, he grabbed his toothbrush and knocked her arm rudely as he reached for the toothpaste. Behaving like a robot, he brushed his teeth.

She stood back, mute, trying to fathom what to do next. She truly wanted to somehow be the wife he wanted.

Defeat and desperation covered his face as he glanced at her in the mirror, rinsed his mouth, and spit violently into the sink. She gasped, believing he really meant to spit at her.

She ached to hold him, the man she loved dearly. He was a child of God who deserved love from his life mate. From her. How had it come to this? She longed to put her arms around him, to draw him to her. Very quietly she told him, "There'll be another time, Dean."

"Don't lie to me," he hollered, stomping away. "And stop lying to yourself!"

CHAPTER

On Thursday, Larissa waited in the lobby of MediMax's Human Resources department while Cody met with Mr. Nelson in his office. Fortunately, Cody had shown the responsibility to get tested that Monday morning after Mr. Nelson notified her. The autumn colors outside the floor-to-ceiling windows did little to calm Larissa. Even her plan later that day to walk in the woods and hear the fallen leaves crunching underfoot failed to lessen her anxiety.

She recalled the year Cody was born. He'd arrived in her life when she was a cosmetology student. In those days, sex was more of a game, and getting pregnant was a girl's fondest dream, or worst nightmare, or both. It happened during spring break on her trip to Florida. A local football hero and too many beers was all it took. First time; first pregnancy. She tried keeping her bulging waistline a secret from her foster parents and resisted her girlfriends' pleas to get an abortion. But with everyone's support once they found out, she went through with the pregnancy and learned how important she and the baby were to the people who cared.

After that, her opportunities for sex had nose-dived. During Cody's school years, she had remained sexually inactive until Brad entered her life. Well, almost. Just once, for one night only, she'd allowed herself a fling with a professional photographer who took catalog photos of her modeling lingerie for JC Penney's. Having sex was entirely consensual. The modeling payment of $2,500 had allowed her to keep up payments on her mortgage and utility bills. In thirty hectic minutes following the photo shoot, she got pregnant. Eleven weeks later, having told no one, she made the agonizing decision to get an abortion.

How ironic. Brad had been the one guy for whom she would've gladly carried a baby to full term—but he had died. Cody would surely have loved him as a dad and man of the house, but a nonexistent father was all he'd ever known. For that scar in her son's life, she felt corrosive self-blame.

Just then, Mr. Nelson's assistant, a young man with a preppy haircut and trendy dress shirt—the kind she hoped Cody would one day wear—answered a buzzer at his desk. He glanced at Larissa, nodded, and the office door opened. Out walked Cody, grinning, with Mr. Nelson behind him.

"Looks like I'll need that ride to work for the noon shift after all, Mom."

"Way to go!"

"You'd better get a move on, young man," Mr. Nelson said.

Larissa appreciated Mr. Nelson's earlier suggestion about meeting "man to man" with Cody. It spared both Cody and herself the awkward situation of parental supervision interfering with their meeting. She walked with Cody a few feet and asked quietly, "So tell me, what exactly happened in there?"

"Mr. Nelson went to bat for me," he said, smiling. "It was awesome how he talked on the phone to Mr. Gomez."

She heard an earful about Mr. Nelson's assurances to Cody's warehouse manager about the lowered level of THC in his retested UA—his urinalysis test. Turning to Mr. Nelson, she asked, "So his results did drop significantly?"

"Yes," Mr. Nelson said. "And company policy permits a new hire in his situation to return to work while serving a 30-day probationary period."

She looked at the sandy-haired executive, who seemed as pleased as she did.

"Cody," he said, "another infraction means certain termination, correct?"

Cody nodded. "Correct."

Her son's good fortune pleased her. Thinking about his deepest and longest-standing need, his need for a father figure, she wished, *If only a guy like Mr. Nelson could be that person.*

"I'm happy to have helped," Mr. Nelson added, looking directly at Cody. "I think it's fair to say we came to an understanding. Right, Cody?"

"Right, Mr. Nel ... er, Dean. A man-to-man understanding." They shook hands.

Mr. Nelson looked at Larissa. "Feel free to notify me if anything comes up."

Exuberant, Larissa smiled her biggest smile. "Well, then," she said to Cody, "let's get you over to the warehouse lickety-split so you can show Mr. Gomez the new you." She reached in her purse and handed him the car keys. "Bring the car out front, and I'll meet you in a couple of minutes."

Cody tore off. She and Mr. Nelson watched him run, both beaming. As she turned to thank him, he spoke first.

"That goes for you, too. The name's Dean."

"Well, Mr. Nel ... I mean, Dean, I don't know how to begin thanking you."

"I'm glad it worked out the way it did. Everything hinged on Cody's clean UA—and his taking responsibility, which he appears to have done."

"It's the wake-up call he needed." She looked into Dean's eyes and saw something she hadn't seen in a man's soul for years—generosity. The sparkle in his eyes told her this guy was a giver, an encourager. She felt a hint of heat warming her cheeks. Grateful feelings moved through her, and then a surge of desire, which she tried to mask.

At Dean's signal, they began walking to the main entrance.

"It means everything to me, Dean, that you've kept his job chances alive. I'm grateful beyond words." She wondered if he sensed the extra inflection in her voice.

"Now that he's over this speed bump, I think he'll do fine."

"I sure hope so. So much depends on his learning from this—his college classes, his own spending money, his future."

"If you see any drug-related behavior in the next few days, Ms. Beaumont, be sure and call him on it. It's important that he doesn't blow this chance."

"Of course. And please, do call me Larissa."

He looked at her and smiled. "Fine, Larissa."

The timbre in his voice when he said her name signaled a tiny new connection between them, she believed. The basis for their talking to one another might no longer be solely Cody's behavior. "The best way to reach me," she said, "is at my fitness studio."

"Fitness and Flowers, isn't it?"

"Yes ... by Larissa."

Dean looked fully into her green eyes. It came through loud and clear that he approved of her efforts and concerns as a mother, yet she hoped he was seeing beyond that. She knew he liked her looks, as most men did. She'd grown up with that appreciative gaze from many men and had long ago recognized it as typical, even to the point of laughing about it. *Men are so predictable!* Coming from Dean, however, it felt like a great compliment.

"Well," he said rather wistfully, "I've got a stack of personnel headaches to deal with. Let's cross our fingers that Cody has learned to grow up and fly straight."

Her gaze caught his, and she hesitated, wanting to reach out and hug him. She didn't quite know what made this man so appealing. For a guy in his fifties, his trim physique and broad shoulders and upright posture defied the stereotype of a middle-aged man with a beer belly bursting his shirt buttons. He could have passed every test necessary to grace the cover of a business magazine. She swore his hazel eyes were so transparent she could see through to his soul. It radiated kindness, gentleness, and strength. That was a lot to see in a fellow human being, and he delivered the goods.

She heard the sound of the Saturn's horn honking outside the main entrance. "Well, I'd better be going."

Cody drove the car to a jerky stop in the curved driveway. Larissa extended her hand and shook Dean's. She let her eyes speak for her. She guessed something special was going on in both their inner worlds. Walking away, she felt his eyes watching her. She hoped her dark slacks hugging her waist and fitted pink blouse held his gaze. Her shoulder-length, caramel-colored hair brushed her collar. She made a subtle move reminiscent of her days as a cocktail waitress—a tiny shimmy with her hips—relishing the pleasure she predicted he was deriving from her exit.

Outside, she felt the rush of being a queen in a man's world. She laughed to herself, feeling giddy. *Vive-la-différence* between men and women, she mused.

Cody shouted, "Hurry, Mom! We need to step on it!"

"Sure, alright," she replied. Hopping in, she said, "Away we go!" She looked in the side mirror at the place where Dean had stood, now obscured by sunlight bouncing off the building's windows. Perhaps he was back in his office, working hard at making an honest living and having moved on to more urgent matters.

"Mom, are you listening? I'm trying to ask you something."

Cody's voice zapped her back to the present. "Uh, sure, go ahead. I'm listening."

"Isn't Dean the coolest?"

Tickled by the power of a mature man in a growing boy's life—and her own life—she said, "Oh yes, I'd certainly agree with you there."

After his meeting with Cody and his chat with Larissa, Dean returned to his office. Closing the door, he plopped down at his desk. The voluptuous image of Larissa walking away was branded into his brain. He ignored the pile of personnel folders needing attention. The aftermath of his and Kate's failed lovemaking on Friday night sapped his willpower to work. Kate's avoidance replayed in his mind. Their conflict trumped what he'd hoped would be a memorable anniversary.

"You clam up and won't talk about it," he'd told Kate the next morning. "We've tried couples therapy, and it hasn't worked. What if you saw your own psychotherapist, Kate?"

Her response: silence.

Fed up, worn down, he looked out his office window and tapped his pen, questioning if it was time to see his own therapist. Marriage counseling two or three times over the years had failed. He recalled that one thing Kate had complained about to a female therapist was vaginal dryness. The therapist urged her to see her gynecologist about the soreness and infrequent intercourse. To be supportive, Dean had encouraged Kate. "Let me know what the gynecologist says about prescriptions and options for treatment." Eight weeks passed before he discovered Kate had never scheduled an appointment. When asked, she avoided explaining why.

He remembered asking, "Why did you say you'd see a gynecologist and then not go?"

"If that's how you're going to talk about it, let's drop it."

Since that time, niggling thoughts of divorce had begun harrassing Dean's mind.

He peered out the window of his office. The kind of desire he felt seemed so fundamental. In college he'd taken a course on the ancient Greeks. Their culture had openly revered love, sex, and beauty. Those three qualities combined in their deity, Eros. As they defined it, "erotic" meant enthusiastic openness to all of life's dimensions. When Dean married Kate, he'd assumed they would experience similar transcendent pleasure and fiery ecstasy, because marriage itself was forged on that foundation. Why lovers would not gratefully sizzle in the sacred flames of Eros baffled him. Had Kate been sexually abused as a child? He longed to give all of himself to Kate, and for her to give all of herself to him—to merge and become one in a shared, divine union.

Dean stood, put on his jacket, and left the office for the warehouse. He carried the more urgent HR files under his arm to discuss with Mr. Gomez. "I'll be back sometime after lunch, Dillon," he called to his assistant. Dillon showed a consistently strong work ethic for a thirty-something Gen Xer, yet he breezily joked with Dean like Robin bantering with Batman.

"Want me to transfer your calls, boss man?"

"No, I'll return them later. Unless you hear from Carl about the updates to the revised attitude surveys we've been sending out." Carl Langley,

Senior VP of Operations, delegated personnel issues involving morale to Dean for sensitive handling.

"Roger, boss." Dillon mock-saluted. "Standing by at your service."

Dean walked to his Honda Accord and drove east toward his company's warehouse located near the Mississippi River in an industrial area bordering St. Paul. Rolling down the windows, Dean allowed the rush of cool autumn air to blow on his skin. The azure blue sky made him question why all the technology and gadgets that Americans deemed necessary were holding people captive indoors, chained to screens and keyboards. Weren't the same digital gadgets meant to free people to spend more leisure time outdoors rather than entrapping them?

Dean let such thoughts float through his mind like fallen leaves drifting downstream on a lazy river. Sweeter thoughts came to mind about Lindsay and Nicole, his precious daughters. Lindsay was the more academic girl, Nicole the more athletic. Both had developed into fine young women.

Over a pop music station on the radio, he heard a singer's soulful plea for his lover to return his devotion. The plaintive loneliness in each word and chord resonated with Dean, reminding him that his longing for intimacy with Kate was an ancient lament as old as mankind's search for lasting love. Dean imagined Kate reaching for him and pulling him close, two disconnected people making love in the night.

How I wish Kate could hear this song!

Abruptly, a fantasy mirage of Larissa invaded his consciousness. He tried sweeping it from his mind but couldn't. His standards meant that straying was impossible, that his one-and-only faithful obedience to Katie had to remain firm.

At a stoplight, he reached for his Bible lying on the passenger seat. A note he'd stuck on the cover contained a verse he'd jotted down from Proverbs: **"Many are the plans in a man's heart, but it is the Lord's purpose that prevails."**

Time to lighten up and see the positive things in life, Deano. Be grateful. Believe. Stop obsessing. Better times are ahead. Have faith. If the Lord's purpose was that they reach new heights in their relationship, then his job was to trust. His hopes were so low, however, and getting dimmer.

A scruffy man by the stoplight held a cardboard sign with the scrawled words, **Veteran out of work. Please help buy my next meal.** The man ambled toward him. Dean took out a ten and two ones. He rolled down the window, handing the cash to the man just as the stoplight changed.

"Thanks, sir. It means a lot."

"It's the Lord's money. Thank Him. He loves you."

The man smiled and pointed his finger straight up. Dean nodded and stepped on the accelerator, reaching thirty-five miles an hour. He hoped the man felt a small blessing from God. If the guy had scammed him, he didn't care. Anyone who stood for hours holding a sign to solicit handouts was doing his own form of work.

After arriving at the warehouse, Dean made his way to Arnold Gomez's office, a functional room above the busy main floor where forklifts buzzed between industrial aisles of metal shelving. Mr. Gomez was a husky man in his mid-forties, of Chicano heritage. He sported a goatee and brushed-back black hair, allowing a full view of his pock-marked face. As director of warehouse operations, he supervised 380 workers.

While Arnold finished a phone call, Dean glimpsed the workers on the main floor, half-contemplating that Cody might be one of them.

"I'll keep my eye on him, Dean," Arnold said as they sat down. "Like so many part-time kids with college-itis, he shows up a little late sometimes. The work ethic of his generation … well, don't make me go there. If he doesn't show gumption this time, he's expendable."

"And if he changes, if you get better vibes?"

"Nothing would make me happier."

Arnold leaned back in his tall "executive" chair and held up his hand. "If you don't mind me asking, Dean, why are you putting so much into this kid? He's a part-timer. What's so special about him?"

Dean paused. He hadn't realized that he was coming off so involved. "Nothing's special about him."

Arnold frowned. "Doesn't look that way."

Arnold Gomez's instinctive insight played on Dean's mind as he drove back to the office. It signaled trouble. Dean hadn't realized he was tipping his hand. By pointing out his over-involvement, Arnold had done him a big favor. *Definitely something is going on. Dang it, I've gotta clear the air and put an end to this craziness.* Dean recalled that Larissa Beaumont's fitness studio was located on Grand Avenue. As he approached the next stoplight, he jerked the steering wheel and made a 180-degree U-turn, heading back across the river to St. Paul towards Larissa's studio.

The streets and avenues of Minneapolis' sister city had a stately character. They seemed friendlier to Dean than those of the bustling metro's "twin" to the west, and more pleasant to drive. Dean calculated that an extra forty-five minutes wouldn't make much difference to his expected return to the office. Functioning on pure impulse, he drove on, not exactly sure what he intended to do. The tall old trees lining the narrow streets towered above the slow-moving cars and trucks. The blazing sunshine dazzled his eyes, giving him a pseudo-psychedelic rush, not unlike the crazier times in his twenties when he'd been stoned on marijuana and cocaine.

He reached Grand Avenue in St. Paul's boutique commercial district and checked the street numbers of storefront shops until he located the quaint awning labeled *Fitness & Flowers by Larissa.* His heart raced. He sat immobilized. What could he say to make his visit to see her seem logical and justified? In his smitten state, nothing came to mind. He looked through the shop's display window. No fitness class was in progress, but an OPEN sign hung in the window. He might easily make up something about Cody's work status to tell her, but doing so would not explain his reason for driving the extra miles from Minneapolis.

Then it hit him. He and Kate loved the coffee beans from Sacred Grounds, a coffee shop two blocks away at Cromwell Street and Grand. It catered to customers who enjoyed contemporary gospel music and a wide range of faith-inspired art. The shop's fair-trade beans had a special taste. Dean drove the two blocks to Cromwell, double-parked the car, ran inside, bought a pound of Divine Delight beans, and drove back to Fitness & Flowers.

Carrying the sack of beans through the front door of Larissa's studio, he stopped short in the vestibule and observed her. She was alone, warming up to booming hip-hop music. A list of classes taped to the door indicated an intermediate class scheduled for this afternoon.

"Oh, my God . . ." Dean muttered softly to himself as he watched Larissa's torso bend, twist, and glide. The fluidity of her movements mezmerized him. The grace and sensuality of her lithe body amplified the intoxicating glimpses of her gyrating figure. Her beauty and athletic prowess intensified the fiery spell tingling his nerves.

I should turn around and hightail it back to the office right now. Right now!

Gazing at Larissa, however, he felt his promise of fidelity to Kate weaken. The pretext of buying coffee beans to visit Larissa's studio now seemed awkward and flimsy. But, right then, she spotted him and waved, so he walked inside.

"Dean!" she hollered in surprise. "Wow! I never expected to see you here. Welcome."

He stepped forward, holding up the sack of coffee beans. "I was in the neighborhood buying some coffee and remembered your address from your card. So I thought I'd drop by."

"It's great to see you." She strode across the hardwood floor straight up to him. Waving her arm in a wide circle, she announced, "Here it is, my dream … *and* my nightmare. But it's all mine. I hope you like it."

He laughed nervously. "Looks wonderful. You must be very proud. I'll bet you're giving the big fitness centers some tough competition."

She laughed. "Hardly. What my business offers is an entirely different experience. That's my marketing proposition. So far I'm making a pretty good go of it."

"You've certainly got gumption. That's what a small business owner needs." Offering her the beans, he said, "Care to try some of these? They're great." Realizing how corny this sounded, he dropped his voice and spoke in the manner of a TV commercial narrator, adding, "You might say these beans taste *heavenly*."

She groaned loudly.

"When you try them, let me know what you think."

"From Sacred Grounds? I've seen that place but never stopped in there." She hesitated. He could see she was thinking. "Tell you what," she said, taking the sack from him. "How about if I grind up some right now?"

Surprised but pleased, he nodded. His excuse about visiting her seemed to be working. But he felt his resolve to put an end to their flirtation dissolving.

Kate was running late as she hopped in her SUV. Starting the engine, she said through the open window to her friend, "The Christmas pageant this year is going to be over the top, Marlene. I'm so excited about our tryouts today."

"I think so, too, Kate. It's great we have so many talented kids to audition."

Kate waved to her companion, Marlene Wilkins, the pageant director and her co-choreographer of their upcoming church Christmas musical. "I'm in a rush, Marlene. Gotta shoot over to St. Paul in time for my fitness class."

"Okay, kiddo. I'll call you when there's a date for callbacks. Thanks for everything."

"Sounds good." Kate glanced at her watch. She stepped on the accelerator, hoping to get to Fitness & Flowers on time.

Dean watched Larissa walk over to the kitchenette where she poured a handful of the beans into a grinder and flipped the switch. While the grinder whined, he ran his eyes over her figure, prizing every curve and surface. He knew women had clever ways to enhance their cleavage, but she had no need to at all. In her skin-tight spandex, her tight butt and sleek legs looked fabulous. Every part of her seemed proportioned just right: waist, hips, and arms. A gorgeous body with a face to match.

Larissa said, "I've only got about twenty minutes before folks start coming in for class." Wiping perspiration from her forehead and neck, she asked, "Do you honestly think Cody is getting his act together? I sure hope so."

"I just talked to his manager a while ago. He confirmed that he's willing to give Cody another go."

"Great. Giving him a second chance was very kind, Dean."

He shrugged. Her sleeveless leotard allowed him to see more of her natural body.

The whining noise stopped. Larissa opened the top of the grinder. "Ummm," she purred, smelling the freshly ground beans. "Lovely. So lovely." She eyed the Divine Delight label and, mimicking his earlier tone, she shifted her voice into TV commercial mode: "You might even say 'divine.' Be sure and try some. Simply *heavenly!*"

They shared a hearty laugh.

Extending the open sack to Dean, she said, "Here, smell."

He stepped closer and bent his head down, putting his nose over the opening. She held it with a mischievous look. The aroma aroused his nostrils, and the close distance between their faces aroused the rest of him. The coffee reminded him of Kate.

The thought of Kate made him pause.

"Lovely, indeed," Dean said. "Divinely delightful, you might say." He lifted his head and looked into her emerald eyes.

There they stood—face to face, just inches apart, both smiling, sharing a moment of profound possibility. The silence stretched on. Larissa's eyes sent him a signal, an invitation. He swallowed hard. Was he dreaming? Squaring his shoulders, he cleared his throat. "You'll be happy to know that Mr. Gomez agrees it's up to Cody now to keep the good vibes flowing."

"Good vibes, yes," she said, keeping eye contact with him.

Dean felt captive under Larissa's spell. The desire in him ignited like a flame sparking dry kindling. Kate? She lived on a distant planet.

"That's so good to hear, Dean. You are really doing something in Cody's life that no man has ever done, and I can't say how happy that makes me. You're very special."

He felt as though he could reach out and pull her to him. He knew it was improbable. No, it was impossible. But the feeling kept his hopes alive.

Larissa felt enchanted looking into Dean's face, savoring the aroma of the coffee beans. Her eyes held his in a delicious state of anticipation. She wanted to reach out and pull him toward her. He stood an arm's length away, desire gleaming in his eyes. Her mind pleaded, *Please, make the first move.* Didn't he see the desire in her eyes? Or, was he thinking terrible things about her, a single woman flirting with a married man? *Please kiss me,* her inner voice cried.

His eyes spoke tenderly to her.

She fretted because he might walk out the door any minute and head back to his office. "So tell me," she asked, "have you heard the joke about folks calling the Twin Cities one name? You know, Minnehaha. 'Minne' for Minneapolis and 'Haha' for St. Paul?"

He laughed. "Yes, that's an old one. But nowadays St. Paul has stepped up and built the Science Museum, the Xcel Center, the Ordway, the History Center, and so many great places that weren't around twenty years ago."

"I get that. The old worn-out rivalry of our parents' generation is over."

"Right. We're enlightened nowadays."

As Dean talked, she took in his muscular body and manly face, his confident way of moving his hands for emphasis, his manner of speaking with authority and purpose. About a dozen years older than Brad, and only five or so pounds heavier through the middle, he looked fit and in overall good shape. He also made her feel like she had his full attention. And he laughed easily.

"But I really *do* like your side of the Twin Cities," he insisted. "I have a favorite saying about the two cities, if you're interested."

"You have a favorite saying, *really*? This I have to hear."

He straightened up as though standing at a microphone in front of a crowd. He cleared his throat in an exaggerated way and proclaimed, "My Twin Cities Tribute:

St. Paul has brick, Minneapolis has glass.

St. Paul has charm, Minneapolis has class.

St. Paul is the last great city of the East,

Minneapolis is the first great city of the West,

. . . and a river runs through it."

She loved it. She laughed. *They* laughed. "That was great."

"Where did you learn it?"

"I made it up."

"No way." She leaned back, wary. "You came up with it yourself?"

He nodded.

"Let me tell you, Dean, you *are* someone special."

She felt his appreciative gaze and detected a rising level of emotion, even arousal in his face. It made her think that his wife must be the luckiest person in the world. What woman wouldn't give her all for a husband like Dean Nelson?

Kate drove her SUV along busy Grand Avenue and passed Fitness & Flowers, looking for a parking space. No luck. Every spot was taken. She drove to the nearest side street, trying not to get flustered about finding a parking spot before her class started. In the past, "Hurry up and don't be late" would've run through her mind, but she consciously made an effort to "slow down and be on time."

Cruising cautiously along the next block of homes, Kate spied an open space by a driveway and parked. Grabbing her workout bag, she locked the car and walked toward Fitness & Flowers. As she reached the alley behind the row of storefront shops on Grand, she ran for Larissa's back door, fifty yards ahead. If she had been paying attention, she would have noticed Dean's Honda as she passed by it.

Like a flame sparking a fire, Larissa felt the heat in Dean's gaze. More precisely, she felt the heat of her own desire and wanted a man as likeable and sexy as Dean for herself.

"Well, I'd best be going, Larissa. The MediMax salt mine awaits my return."

She sputtered, "Thanks for … for dropping by." Her voice sounded low, husky. She sensed that he caught some of her sensual energy and carnal scent. It seemed his own sexual energy had been triggered. He leaned forward—she could have turned away or protested—and kissed her with gusto.

Exhilaration zapped through her. She kissed him back, squarely on the lips.

He smiled.

She smiled.

His eyes adored her.

Her eyes adored him.

In a blink, he started walking to the front door carrying the sack of coffee beans. Opening the door, he said, "Don't hesitate to call if you have any questions about Cody."

She stammered, "I … I will." It seemed a lame thing to say, but it was all she could muster. Dean waved goodbye, then the door shut behind him.

He stole a secret kiss—but never said a word!

Larissa envisioned the two of them embracing without clothes, touching one another skin to skin, heart to heart, soul to soul, pulsing with urgent energy. Her yearning for the elusive man of her dreams was reignited. Did such a guy exist? Would they ever find each other? Was Dean that man?

Clients began arriving. First to arrive was Kate, who entered through the back door.

"Hi there," Larissa greeted her. "How's that sore neck and those stiff shoulders, Kate?"

"They need a lot of loosening up, like always. Have you got some new stretches, Larissa? Anything new for today?"

"You've come to the right place."

Larissa's day shifted into high gear. Jasmine arrived, then Annabelle, next Conrad and Claire. She said hello to them all and asked about their day.

The aftermath of Dean's kiss exhilarated her. She tried to reconcile the extreme pleasure of his kiss with her jumbled emotions. She felt the crushing reality that Dean was taken, spoken for, off limits. *How I envy his wife!*

Kate pointed to the dozens of fresh flowers and greens covering Larissa's floral counter at the rear of her studio. "It looks like you've got a huge order to fill, Larissa."

"And how. That's not half of it," she replied. "I have a new corporate client, Target, and they need fifteen arrangements delivered tomorrow morning for each floor of their new administration building. Get this: the opening is at *noon* tomorrow."

Kate looked incredulous. "Oh, my! How will you get it all done by yourself?"

"Frankly, I don't know. Cody is coming over to help after class, I think, and everything will have to get done somehow."

"For nine years I've done seasonal floral work at Granger's. I love flowers and gardening, so I could pitch in."

Larissa looked astounded. "You do floral work? You'd help?" Kate's offer floored her. Granger's was the largest floral operation in the Twin Cities metro area, and Kate's experience would mean a lot. "Wow! What a help that would be."

"I'm quick and steady, and if you play classical music while we work, my rate drops from free to zero."

"Ha! That is so generous of you. I can really use your help. Thank you. I owe you one."

Kate nodded. "No problem. Tonight is Skip's poker night so I have a few hours to pitch in. Want me to stick around?"

"Would you? You are such an angel!" Larissa lifted her arms wide. She beamed with gratitude and hugged Kate, who headed to the dressing room to change. Larissa twirled joyously on her heel. "Okay, everybody," she announced, "let's start warming up!"

D ean's body buzzed as he drove back to the office. His armpits felt damp and his face felt flushed. He scarcely noticed other cars or vehicles. He felt giddy.

Larissa! I just kissed Larissa! And even better, she kissed me back!

Seeing brake lights ahead set off instant alarms. He slammed his brakes to prevent hitting the car ahead of him. "That's it! Snap out of it, Dean, or you'll get yourself killed!" he said aloud.

He jockeyed through traffic, concentrating on his driving. Since meeting Larissa the week before, his work productivity had tapered off, and Carl Langley's annual appraisal of Dean's performance was coming up in November. He couldn't afford a noticeable slump in his efforts to help meet the company's marketing objectives. It was clear he needed to keep playing a winning game at work as well as continuing to assess his marriage options. Yet, neither could he shake feeling like a man again, nor his scatterbrained exhilaration from Larissa's amorous attention.

BEEEEPP! BEEEEPP!

The horn blast from a large truck brought him back to the present; Dean's tires had swerved into the next lane. *Refocus, Dean! Refocus!*

The Scripture verse on the note stuck to his Bible resurfaced in his mind. *"Many are the plans in a man's heart, but it is the Lord's purpose that prevails."* That reminded him of a favorite verse from Psalms: *"Delight yourself in the Lord, and he will give you the desires of your heart."* Was the desire in his heart for Larissa part of the Lord's purpose?

He contemplated the hours ahead playing poker at his friend Hal's. Gambling with plastic chips playing nickle-ante poker was hardly the same as gambling with his wife's feelings while fooling around behind her back.

CHAPTER

Kate thought of the great fun she'd had with Larissa creating flower arrangements the evening before while she emptied the dryer. Working again arranging flowers had felt rejuvenating. "You have a flair for mixing colors and sizes," Larissa had told her. She and Larissa worked as a team using their decorative skills and collaborating on some dandy design touches. Cody had pitched in, wrapping the arrangements and loading them into a neighbor's van for delivery the next morning.

"I'm impressed how he's helping out," Kate said to Larissa, observing his careful handling of each arrangement.

"Me, too. When he puts his mind to something he does such a good job, there's no telling how far he can go." During a break, Cody had proudly showed Kate the injured cat he was nursing in his small animal rescue shelter. Having made a difference, Kate felt artistically affirmed and emotionally uplifted.

She carried the basket of folded linens upstairs, stumbling on the stairway. It was mid-afternoon, and she'd poured herself a vodka-Seven to celebrate. Actually, she'd poured two vodka-Sevens, and now she popped gum in her mouth to cover up any trace of alcohol on her breath. She still had to run to the supermarket and get supper started, and regretted how the alcohol swirling her senses made her feel tipsy. Chewing gum was "just in case" she ran into somebody she knew. Luckily, the deacons' meeting at Spirit Hills church that evening was still four hours away. Any trace would surely be gone by that time.

Too bad I'll have to miss Lindsay's homecoming. Why did the deacons' meeting have to be tonight?

Her habit of leaving her cellphone on "vibrate" meant that messages often went unheard until hours later. Lindsay's voicemail that morning said she'd be driving home from Des Moines that afternoon: "Surprise, Mom. I've finished my midterms a day early. See you for supper tonight and the long weekend. Love ya."

It was great news, really. More quality time with Lindsay and the family. But time was running short before her arrival, and the deacons' meeting would cut short dinnertime. She hiccupped. *No! Why did I ever pour those drinks?*

Kate stopped deliberately to steady herself and looked out the large bay window. The patio with its flower-decked rock garden was her favorite spot, and she'd managed to rake half of the fallen leaves in the spacious yard of their four-bedroom, two-story home. Reluctantly, she'd put aside trimming her cherished rose bushes until the chore of bagging leaves was complete.

Kate looked at the clock. It was after four o'clock, and she was behind on her to-do list. Lindsay might pull into the driveway any minute. She phoned Dean and left a voicemail: "Try to get home early, Skip. Lindsay's coming home, and I'd like us all to eat supper together."

Kate plunged into high gear. She took out four salmon filets from the freezer, loaded the dishwasher and started it, then scurried to the bathroom where she scrubbed the toilet and wiped out the bathtub. Zipping through chores lightened her mood. She felt euphoric appreciating how greatly God had blessed her family. Her thankful heart accompanied each action. She hurried to the hall closet where she reached for her jacket because the weather had turned cooler. A protrusion on the floor hit her toe.

"Holy shit!" she yelped. She looked down and there it was—the lovers sculpture, still in its box.

She didn't know which was worse—her shock at hearing herself curse or the reminder of the naked lovers. The box stared back at her. She wished she knew what to do with the sculpture, where to put it. *How I wish Dean had given me anything else. It belongs in a museum or an art gallery, certainly not a bedroom.* Fortunately, Dean had avoided nagging her about it … so far. She had to decide where to put it soon, as it was obviously important to him. *He deserves to see it somewhere in the house. Maybe the spare bedroom? Maybe tucked away behind a large plant?*

She passed through the kitchen and accidentally kicked over Jester's water dish, spilling water everywhere. Jester came running and licked her face as she mopped up the mess. "Yes, dearie, I love you, too." The gentlest of pets, in his eleventh year his rear legs were getting weaker, yet his affectionate nature never wavered.

Yanking on her jacket, Kate hurried off to the supermarket.

Forty-five minutes later, as she arrived home with her groceries in tow, Kate pondered the daily life of a twenty-first century wife. *Never a moment to just hang out and relax.* She'd no sooner unpacked the groceries and started chopping broccoli than Lindsay pulled into the driveway. Kate went to meet her at the door as she hopped out of her used Ford carrying a bulky bag of laundry.

"Hello, honey. It's so good to see you."

"You too, Mom." Lindsay hugged and kissed her. "It's been a hectic semester so far. Here's two months of laundry. Oh, and look who's here."

Lindsay reached down and petted Jester, now barking and wagging his tail. Lindsay looked perky and poised with her red hair pulled back into a ponytail. Kate felt pride in the family's brainiac—an A student who enjoyed her classes and books. Unlike Nicole, their tomboy cheerleader and teen fashionista who earned Bs and Cs, Lindsay put her studies first. Kate looked into Lindsay's winsome face, realizing how she'd grown.

"Look at you. You're an inch taller."

"How's everybody? How's Dad?"

"We're all doing great. Nicole called while I was shopping and said she can't wait to see you."

"That girl, I love her to pieces."

Kate kept thinking how healthy and wholesome Lindsay looked. In her junior year at Drake as a sociology and computer graphics double major, it was clear college suited her well. Lindsay gave her the rundown on the challenges in her classes. Kate waited for her to mention Brandon, wondering if she would drop hints about her boyfriend's requests to room together—the latest topic Lindsay kept alluding to in her texts. The possibility of them playing house was not at the top of Kate's approval list.

"By the way, Mom, Brandon and I are still talking about moving into an apartment to save money."

Kate cringed, trying to look indifferent while putting the broccoli on the stove to steam. She saw Lindsay notice her reaction, although she'd tried to hide it.

"Mom, it's not what you think. Don't go assuming so much, okay? You raised me right, and now you've got to trust me."

Kate bit her tongue and smiled. She felt twitches and pangs in her stomach. She did not want her daughter shacking up, but she didn't want to make a federal case of it either. That might backfire. No matter how worthy or respectable the young man was, Lindsay's sharing his bed was just not right.

"Well, Mom, I think I'll get my laundry started." Lindsay kissed Kate's cheek and walked over to the stairway with the laundry bag. "You know, times have changed in the past twenty years, Mom. Sometimes it's best to just go with the flow." With that, her daughter headed downstairs to the laundry room, leaving Kate to ponder her words.

Half an hour later, Dean walked through the door and exclaimed, "Hey, it's good to see Lindsay's car in the driveway!"

Kate smiled. "It's nice her midterms got done a day early, isn't it?" She didn't want to remind him about her having to attend the deacons' meeting. She could tell he was eager to greet Lindsay.

Dean gave Kate a quick hug then shouted down the stairwell, "Anybody home down there?"

Lindsay bounded up from the basement and threw her arms around him. "Great to see you, Daddy. I've missed you."

Maybe it was just her imagination, but it seemed to Kate that Lindsay's enthusiastic greeting for her dad outshone the one she'd received. Kate's mood soured. No, she told herself: Lindsay had just driven 250 miles for four straight hours and was feeling road-weary when she walked through the door to greet her. Since then, the girl had recharged her batteries.

"What's cookin', Kate?" Dean asked, sniffing the air. "Smells good!"

"Salmon filets, broccoli, mashed potatoes, and pecan pie for dessert."

"Wow, a feast." He hugged her again, this time a bear hug. "You are one great cook, Katie. I love that you think it's important for us to sit down together for family meals."

Dean certainly was behaving in fine form. Unusually so. Kate attributed it to Lindsay's arriving home on short notice. In his hand, he carried a sack of coffee beans. "I'll get the coffee ready for when we have pie," he said jovially.

She noticed the beans were from Sacred Grounds. She'd not told him about signing up for Fitness & Flowers' classes after visiting Sacred Grounds weeks ago. She was hoping he might notice the beginning signs of her improved fitness and flexibility without having to mention it, trusting he'd see on his own the difference in her figure and less-stressed demeanor.

Nicole arrived and announced at the top of her lungs, "I'm home!" Everyone "congratulated" her for stating the obvious. Dean lifted Nicole off the floor, spinning her around. Jester barked and barked.

Nicole shouted, "Oh, Daddy, it's so good to have Lindsay home, isn't it?"

He let her down and hugged her. "It sure is. That's my Nicky. You go, girl."

Nicole bounded over to Kate in cheerleading mode, throwing her arms around her and kissing Kate's cheek. "Mom, isn't it great? Us all being together again?"

For one joyous moment, Kate felt the intensity of love that Nicole had shown her father and Lindsay. Seeing the two girls back together, hugging and chatting away, did Kate's heart good. For the rest of the evening, it could have gone on like that—the four of them reunited, spending the evening over good food and sharing fun stories, laughing and kidding—but the deacons' meeting beckoned. She hurried serving dinner so she could head off to church, regretting how the quality of her family's togetherness and bonding would suffer when she left. After Kate gobbled down her meal, Dean looked as bummed out as she did when she put on her jacket to leave.

Dean told her, "Don't forget to remind everybody about Helping Hands, Healing Hearts tonight. We need more donations." He lifted her chin. "And we'll miss you. I'll miss you."

"Good reminder—thanks." Grabbing her car keys, Kate headed out the door. She drove away feeling sad, lamenting the irony of the deacons' meeting's service agenda that evening: reaching out to hurting souls.

L arissa prepared Cody's evening snack while waiting for him to come home after his noon-to-8:00 p.m. shift. Expecting him soon, she warmed a bowl of homemade vegetable soup and sliced pepper jack cheese and salami for a sandwich while she chatted on the phone.

"You can never be too cautious," she heard Russell say tenderly. The youngest of the three Beaumont boys, Russell was her favorite adoptive brother. "Please be extra careful any time you're alone in that house, Larissa."

"You're right, Russ. Thanks for the reminder." With the phone receiver cradled to her ear, she moved from window to window closing the curtains on the ground floor.

"A girl as pretty as you ... well, you know what I'm talking about, Sis."

"I do. I just wish things weren't like that. What a world we live in." His reminder recalled the time when a neighborhood prowler had stalked Larissa shortly after she'd moved to the Cities from the family dairy farm. The ghastly memory of an unemployed loner living on the next street who nearly raped her one summer evening attested to the dangers that vulnerable young women faced wherever they lived.

"I didn't like hearing that you heard strange noises the other night," Russell said.

"It bugged me, too." His concern for her welfare was touching. It was also a warning for her to stay vigilant. "Of course, it could've just been the neighbor's dog scratching around."

"Maybe. But if creeps like that sicko prowler can play tricks like that, so can anybody."

"You're so sweet, Russ, I love you for caring so much about me. Always the tender-hearted one."

"Thanks. I love you, too. And what about that rascal boy of yours? Is he learning anything in college yet?"

"He has a new job—how's that? And I'm crossing my fingers that his work attitude will transfer to his homework. Instead of YouTube videos and mindless cyber war games, I'm hoping he's focusing on building a future for himself."

"Mom told me he's moving boxes at the MediMax warehouse. Is he sticking with it?"

"I think so. He has so much potential, Russ. An executive at the company gave him a big pep talk, and it seems to have sunk in. I'm waiting to see signs of him showing more responsibility." The mere mention of "executive" gave her tingles. The floating feeling she'd had since Dean's kiss two days before still lingered.

"So I'm wondering, Sis, are you still staying as far away from a church as possible?"

"You had to bring that up, didn't you?"

"Are you?"

"And just where are you going with this? You know religion isn't my bag, Russell."

"Forget religion, Larissa. Spirituality. God. It's about God—and having a spiritual connection to divine power and peace. That's what I'm talking about. Everybody needs it."

"I get how you think that, Russ. We all went to church often enough, and for you, I know it meant something. But for me, well . . ."

"Well, what?"

"Well, God didn't exactly help me very much when I was a little girl, did He? And He doesn't seem to be helping much now, either. Going to mass with you boys and Mom and Dad was tolerable, but I'll never forget being an orphan. Now that I'm all grown up, I get to choose how I think for myself."

"Which means?"

"Which means, I've switched from stewing and moping about my ugly childhood to accepting it. What I think it comes down to is: I've decided I can never have the past I want, so I've given up the suffering I've felt wanting it to be better. Except I'm grateful for coming to the farm, of course, and being accepted by everyone there. But either I had to surrender to the things that happened when I was little and move on, or let them keep driving me crazier and crazier. So I've moved on."

Russell sighed. "There's still a ton of hurt, isn't there? I can hear it in your voice."

She loved Russell, but she'd had enough of this talk. "When I hear people speak about a 'God of love,' I turn pale." Her voice remained kind and soft. "You and I heard that preached every Sunday in church, but the best part for me was sitting next to *you*. Now you have a loving wife, but this God of yours hasn't brought *me* anybody to love. So when will this almighty loving God show up and be almighty for me?"

She thanked him for calling, and they exchanged warm goodbyes. *He didn't respond to my sitting next to him in church.* She wondered why they'd seemed so right for each other back in high school. As for another prowler, she resented having to be on the defensive.

Hardly a minute passed before a stubborn thought pricked her consciousness: the dreaded feeling that she'd grow old as a spinster. Regardless of how she wanted her life to turn out, no one else could live her life for her and it looked like God wasn't helping. Her life was her own project. She was doing the best she could, but where was Mr. Eligible Bachelor? She'd tried online dating services with no results, but it looked like she might have to give Internet dating another go.

She went to her easy chair. Larissa allowed herself to relax. She reached for her "destiny box" sitting on the shelf in the antique oak bookcase. As a child of eight, she'd decorated a cast-off cigar box to hold "scraps of hope," trying to make sense of her chaotic life. Lifting the lid made her feel nostalgic. She took out the tattered letter she kept on top of her keepsakes, opening it carefully, marveling at the faded pink ribbons she'd glued to the top of the box. The child-like handwriting was difficult to read, and smudges soiled the lined school paper.

Dear Larissa,

I hope you will read this letter years from now. I am deathly afraid of Mrs. Sweeney. If she sees me writing this, she will burn this letter and punish me in her hateful way. I hate her. I hate everything about her. I hate the wooden yardstick she uses to beat me with. She makes sure to never leave marks where anybody can see them so people from the county foster system will never find them. Every time she says, "It's for your own good, you wicked girl," I cringe.

I am writing you, my older self, because I must believe it will be different someday. I hope I can live better when I'm older. Then I will get even with the whole rotten disgusting foster care system. Mrs. Sweeney forbids me from asking questions about my mom or dad. One day I hope to find out where Mom went, and who she was. Dad too. I keep crying for someone to come rescue me . . ."

Larissa dropped the letter to her lap. She'd never found out anything about either of them. As a four year old, she recalled being torn from her mother's arms. The reality of standing beside Mrs. Sweeney on the stone steps of that government welfare building and seeing someone drive her mother away in that gray car was seared into her memory.

She closed her eyes and sank back into the soft chair. Not until the summer after she finished fourth grade did she get placed in a home with people who loved her—and ultimately adopted her. "You're our little pumpkin now," said her new adoptive mother, Gladys Beaumont, squeezing her tightly the first day she arrived. "Welcome to your new home, sweetie."

"An' I'll be your papa from now on," added Jerry Beaumont, her new adoptive father. Pointing to a trio of dirt-caked farm boys fresh from the cattle pens, he added, "An' these three hooligans are your new brothers." The farm family genuinely cared for her, and the security she had from a family who would stay beside her no matter what felt empowering. At last, at age ten, she belonged.

Larissa's fingers reached for the Purple Heart and silver locket in the box. She lifted each one, holding them gingerly, wishing as she'd wished so often to know more about her father (a decorated soldier?) and mother (a war widow?). These were the sole keepsakes passed down to her. A faded picture of a toddler's face filled the heart-shaped locket. Was it a photo of her at age three? Other than these meager clues, she knew nothing of her parents' identity and existence. The official answer she'd heard regarding her parents was, "The files are sealed, legally and forever. We can't tell you. It does no good to keep asking. Now shut up."

The foster agency's cruel silence had soured her. Despite the fact that the rules and laws of adoption had changed in following years, her case had taken place in the era when adoptions were closed and records had been destroyed. No legal or practical alternatives existed.

Larissa gazed at Brad's photo on the mantle. She closed her eyes and let herself feel again the touch of Brad's hands on her bare skin. She loved the blissful, pleasurable feeling of him penetrating her, filling her up inside. She remembered how he slowly brought her to a soaring climax, blasting through every limit. Ecstasy surged through her as they played erotic games and teased one another, until they'd both merged into one being, one ecstatically complete whole.

Larissa yearned to have a sexual partner again. A powerful impulse came over her. With Cody due home any minute, now was hardly a good time to be alone with her battery-operated boyfriend. She checked her cellphone and saw Cody had texted her while she'd been warming his snack in the kitchen. His text said he had dropped by Alex's and wouldn't be home till ten, another two hours. The idea of an orgy of self-love with a vibrator made her tingle. Solo sex with a mail order sex toy, now tucked away in her dresser drawer, was not sketchy or creepy; it was something every enlightened woman enjoyed.

Larissa headed upstairs to her bedroom, opened the bottom drawer of her dresser, and took out the box containing two vibrators. She loved the deep invasions inside her that Brad was so skilled at, feeling ravished by his love to the core of her being. Her desire now was for a slow, easy series of ripples of intense pleasure. Her self-pleasuring—she hated the word *masturbation*—might not match the deep, heart-expanding feeling of Brad's erection touching her deepest parts, but it still could partially satisfy her unmet longing.

She removed her jeans and flung them on the bed, then slipped off her panties. She reached for the KY jelly and the box. Two vibrators sat in their labeled slots: Hot Indigo and Lusty Lavender. She picked up the Hot

Indigo vibrator and twirled it, considering ways to use it. Its vivid color and twisted shape with bumps and ridges made her mind swirl. On her night stand she saw the framed photos of Cody: his smile while drawing a crayon picture in kindergarten; his grin while holding a Little League trophy; his mud-splattered clothes while feeding a suckling calf; him wearing a tux at seventeen while standing awkwardly beside his equally awkward date in his prom picture.

She sighed, then sank on the bed, hesitating.

She gazed at the vibrator in her hand as the urge for self-pleasuring drained away. Although a few minutes of stimulation would be enjoyable on a superficial level, the lack of connection at a deeply intimate level could not be satisfied. And that is what she truly needed.

She rested her head on the pillow for a few minutes then put on a nightgown and descended the stairs, stopping midway and gripping the handrail. Aching inside, she plopped down on the next stair-step, unable to stop tears of grief.

When the phone rang, Larissa abruptly snapped out of her sorrowful mood.

"Uh ... hi, Mom," Cody mumbled, his words heavily slurred. "You gotta take meee to the hossspital. I'm sssick."

She heard a loud belch. "You sound drunk."

"Nah ... I jussst puked an' puked. You gotta come taaake me to ER."

"You don't need the ER. I hope to hell you haven't been smoking pot. Have you?"

"But, Mom, you don't unnnderstand. Alex picked me uuup from work early, and we've finished offf a bottle of Southern Comfort and a 6-pack."

"Agh. So have him drive you home." She glanced at the clock. It was 9:05.

"No, Mom, youuu don't get it. He'ss drunk. We're both sick. Will you just commme get me?"

Thankfully, Cody was not at the warehouse, and he was only five blocks from home. "No! I'm not your chauffeur. Have you forgotten how to walk?"

"Mom, pleeease . . ."

"You can walk home and puke all you want on your way here."

"Uh, I think I'm gonna puke right now."

She cringed hearing his gurgles of vomit. She also heard girls giggling in the background. Over his objections, she raised her voice, "You are still living under this roof, Cody. So our house rules stand. You are my son, and we are a family. I need you sleeping here in your bed tonight so I won't have to pace the floor. We are a team, and we need to stick together. You can walk home from Alex's like you have hundreds of times. Am I making myself clear?"

"Fine. To hell with it."

The line went dead.

She looked up to the ceiling, sending out an SOS signal to the universe: *We need a lot of help down here. Is anybody up there paying attention?*

Larissa went to the kitchen and flipped on the outside porch light. She wanted the light to draw Cody inside, to signal she was waiting and his home was welcoming him. Unless he passed out or refused to leave Alex's, Cody could be walking through the back door in a half hour. He knew his way home, and he'd had enough sense to call her. She thought briefly about putting on her jacket, getting in the car, and meeting him halfway. *No.*

At least Cody had not screwed up on the job. How awful Dean Nelson's reaction would have been if he'd heard the ugly news about Cody goofing up again at the warehouse. She went to the closet, put on her jacket, and stepped outside into the crisp night air, waiting and looking up at the stars.

CHAPTER

D ean sat in his office eating a Subway Cold Cut Combo. It was mid-afternoon and he'd just sat through a two-hour operations meeting without lunch. An assignment for a new attitude survey had landed in his lap, one of Carl Langley's fourth-quarter requests of his executive team. Morale was questionable in some operating units, and Carl wanted to compile the who/what/why data. Dean's team had updated an "employee engagement" questionnaire and he needed to approve the final questions, a task he quietly enjoyed. A high-priority HR project like this required his undivided attention, and he wanted to stay on top of it.

While chewing his sandwich, Dean skimmed the local news section of the *Star Tribune*. One of his small pleasures was checking out human interest stories; it helped distract him from workplace pressures. A front-page report about a local prostitution ring sparked his curiosity.

"Police arrested forty-one men yesterday in a sting operation involving high-priced call girls from countries as far away as Romania for trysts in local four-star hotels. The men, mainly married professionals in the community with families . . ."

Dean's phone rang. He checked caller ID. As he lifted the receiver, he heard his older brother Mitch. "Hey, Deaner. Gotta sec?"

"Sure, Mitch. What's up?"

"When you send Mom her check this month, can you add a hundred bucks for her personal care assistant?"

"What for?"

"Roxanne is doing a great job and Mom loves her. Last week Mom's wheelchair needed a new battery, and guess who went straight out and bought one with her own money?"

"Wow, those things cost over fifty bucks. That was generous. Sure thing." Dean and Mitch had a mutually agreeable arrangement for handling their mother's Alzheimer's care and nursing home fees. Dean sent the necessary funds to Chicago to cover contractual costs, and Mitch did the hands-on visits and daily street-level duties.

"Great, I'll tell her. So, Deaner, I'm standing here in the supermarket checkout line and this chick on the magazine cover reminded me of you. She's this hot babe in a micro bikini. Get this. The caption says, 'Want a body built for sex? How to get yours.'" Mitch hooted. "So are you getting yours, Dean? Or are you still in the dumps and thinking of jumping ship?"

"I wish, Mitch. Neither, frankly. There isn't a whole lot to hoot about these days."

"So I'm wondering, why do you keep dragging your feet with Kate?"

"I don't think I am."

"Get off it. If she's holding out, then why not go out and get laid?"

"Easy for you to say. You're divorced and single again." Dean glanced at the prostitution sting news story. At his core, he secretly empathized with the well-off husbands like himself and understood them, even though he had never been with a prostitute, nor had he ever come close to seeking one. *I wonder how many of these guys are from sexless marriages?*

"But, Deaner, I think you're sitting on the fence. Think of me as your conscience telling you to shit or get off the pot."

"Look, Mitch, there's so much more to marriage than sex. On so many levels Kate and I are happy. Why spoil all that?"

"Hey, I'm just saying that focusing too much on 'it'—the 'it' that's always missing—is turning you into a major league, World Series sourpuss."

"Kate and I honestly love each other, Mitch, and ruining that seems too high of a price to pay." Dean wanted his marriage to work. Both he and Kate centered their lives on their faith, so why wasn't their marriage working? He'd prayed often for God to make a difference, and wondered if God had heard him. Were his prayers wrong? Unheard?

"Hey, Skip! Off in dreamland again? You haven't heard a word I just said, have you?"

"Sorry. Uh, I couldn't help checking out this article in the paper. Local guys getting arrested with high-priced hookers."

"Damn it. I hate it when you do that. Okay, so if not hookers, then why not go to a strip club or get a massage? Tell me how you're going to survive without getting any. I sure as hell know I can't. I'm not as pious as you."

"Enough already. You won't get an argument from me today. I'd love to trade places with you, honestly. There, I've said it." Dean had to wonder: *What makes the male of the species desire sexual adventure so strongly and take high-stakes risks? Are men, all men, highly sexed and genetically polygamous? Or, does marriage get inherently dry and dull after the honeymoon years and drive men to find satisfaction elsewhere?*

"Keep in mind you're getting over the hill fast," said Mitch. "Gotta go, Deaner. Groceries to pay for. See ya."

Dean looked at his watch and realized his 4:30 workout at the health club was less than an hour away. Mitch had hit a nerve about his aging: certainly Dean couldn't allow things to remain unchanged until their 25th anniversary, nor until his elder years when he might need Viagra but have no use for it. He gathered up edited copies of the employee engagement questionnaires under his arm, promising himself to study them at home. After leaving instructions with Dillon about calling a meeting of his troops the next morning, he walked out to his car.

Outdoors, he took big breaths of the refreshing fall air and felt reinvigorated. Some distance away, he saw a woman leaning on a car and then realized it was Larissa. His throat went dry. A jolt of electricity pulsed through him, the kind he had not felt since visiting her.

Larissa grinned broadly, and yelled, "Thank you. Thank you, Dean Nelson." She walked straight toward him. "I was crossing my fingers we might connect. And here you are. I think Cody is trying to turn over a new leaf. You've no idea how much all you've done means to us." She stopped an arm's length away, reached for his face, and kissed his cheek.

Dean felt a high-intensity laser bolt zip through him.

"You did it!" she exclaimed. "You did it!"

Taken aback, he stammered, "I did? Did what exactly?"

"Cody drank a little too much the other night but got up the next morning and went to work on time. Mr. Gomez noticed him doing a good job and said so. After that, he came home and did homework for two straight hours. How about that? He said he did it so he wouldn't disappoint you. He has a perfect record of not being late for work so far."

"*I* did that?"

"How can we repay you, Mr. Dean Nelson, Mr. HR Director? That's what I want to know."

"Repay me? I don't think—"

"Don't be so modest. I haven't seen Cody behave so grownup in ages, except for a slip or two which has to be expected. Something wonderful is happening since you talked to him."

Dean felt unsettled about their physical closeness in open public view. He looked around the parking lot to see if anyone was observing them. He noticed her lovely bare shoulders; in the warm weather, she was wearing a blouse with spaghetti straps. "Hearing all this good stuff is great, Larissa, but—"

Abruptly, she kissed him squarely on the lips. "You're Cody's hero. And now you're *my* hero, too."

He reeled from her surprising kiss. The feeling of direct contact from her lips felt affirming. A rapid clash of feelings stirred within him. He felt a spike in his hormones along with jabs of fear that somebody inside headquarters might be observing them. He could imagine the members of the Professional Ethics Board frowning on that kind of encounter.

"Tell you what." He stalled for time. "How about if we connect later? Um … I have a workout that gets over at 5:15. We could meet for a few minutes after that."

She paused. "Wow, that would be great, but I have to get back to St. Paul. There's a new floral order I need to put together and deliver that'll take a couple hours."

"Then I'm sorry. How about some other time?" He didn't really mean that, but his attitude survey project demanded his primary attention after the workout.

"Wait!" she said. "What about later this evening?"

Dean blinked, amazed at Larissa's persistence. "Well, there's an AA meeting that runs from 7:00 to 8:30 that I go to sometimes."

She asked about the location, and he warmed to the idea of skipping the meeting and using the time interval to meet with her. "I guess I could be free. Sure, why not?"

"Great. Cody and I can be done with supper about 7:00, and he promised he'd get busy on his homework. So I can meet you wherever you like."

Persistent and *relentless* and *seductive,* he thought.

"Just say where." A subtle smile shaped her lips, the kind that caught him in a trap he didn't want to escape.

The shape of her lips and the softness of her skin made him think, *she's a goddess!* Her eyes sparkled in a way he found irresistible. "Well, there's a Barnes and Noble in the Burnsville Mall. How about at their coffee shop?"

"Fine. Barnes and Noble, Burnsville Mall. Gotcha. I can be there by seven-thirty."

"Seven-thirty is good." He gave her his cellphone number in case of a mix-up, and she waved to him as she headed back to her car. He felt a new lightness in his feet as he walked to his Honda. She waved again as she drove off.

Like many AA-ers, Dean attended his home group regularly, but now and then he visited different meetings. Tonight would be one of those nights, except Kate wouldn't know he was meeting Larissa afterwards. He could still pop in at home for dinner and postpone going over his work files until later that evening. He just needed to tell Kate a tiny fib during dinner about attending the optional meeting, return home before nine o'clock, and nobody would be the wiser.

While driving to the health club, Dean couldn't help thinking of King David in the Old Testament. "A man after God's own heart," according to Scripture, the great king had lusted after Bathsheba and sinned sexually with her—a beautiful woman with a centerfold's body and allure. Despite the devastating negative consequences that followed David's sinful actions, he still retained his man-after-God's-own-heart status. Was he, Dean Nelson, a modern David after God's own heart, similarly tempted? Was Larissa his Bathsheba? Was he on the same sinful path? If so, could his dealings with Larissa ever be forgiven, as David's were?

"The marriage bed must be a place of mutuality—the husband seeking to satisfy his wife, the wife seeking to satisfy her husband." This scripture from First Corinthians came powerfully to his mind. God's will was for Kate and him to find the satisfaction the Lord intended. *So simple. God has actually* ordained *our making love!*

Sick with longing, love-starved and sex-starved, Dean wanted to give his love to Kate and to give that love generously, and to be loved in the same generous way. *But has our intimacy been in the deep freeze too long? Is it too late?* If Kate did not want what he had to give, then surely someone else would welcome it.

Halfway to the health club, Dean took his foot off the accelerator. Why was this routine workout interfering with what he really wanted right now? Letting Larissa drive away was a mistake.

In his mind, he saw a movie:

The irresistible power of Larissa's sensuous femininity dissolves Dean's rationality. Imagining her nude body ignites his desire. Making love with Larissa is all that matters. Reaching for his cellphone, he wonders, "Will she answer?"

He hears her voice when she picks up. His lips brush the phone's mouthpiece as he whispers, "I'm coming over."

"Now?"

"Yes, now. Is the coast clear?"

"Yes. I'm here at the studio."

"Okay. Fifteen minutes."

"Hurry. I can't wait."

Arriving at Fitness & Flowers, Dean pulls up to the curb and parks. He looks up and down the street, walks to the door, and enters the studio.

A sweet voice from the back says, "At last! Lock the door behind you."

He closes the door, locks it, and turns the Open sign to Closed.

She comes to him, arms open.

He approaches her, arms open.

They rush into each other's arms.

The movie stopped. Still at the steering wheel, Dean moaned. Disturbing thoughts of divorce crept into his consciousness—thoughts of escaping his vows and living free.

CHAPTER 7

Larissa's mind raced as she wandered the book aisles of the Barnes & Noble store waiting for Dean to show up. *What was I thinking? Stupid me, I've stepped over the line by talking him into meeting me.* She could not back out now. She told herself Dean could've said no, but he hadn't. She'd been firm with herself earlier in the day about keeping everything casual and loose, but then face to face with him in the parking lot her resolve had melted.

She kept replaying that compulsive kiss on his lips—so over the top and bold. *God, what an idiot I was. But he obviously liked it.*

Here she was, meeting a married man, a family man, and while it had something to do with Cody, it had a whole lot more to do with her. Larissa's entire being ached to be in Dean's presence, to feel his warm and marvelous glow envelop her.

Did she have a plan? If so, it was sketchy. Dean had a special power over her and she wanted to experience more of him, to taste more of his powers. In some strange way, her future seemed intertwined with his, and she had to explore where it might lead.

Larissa looked at her cell phone: 7:40. He was late. Would he blow her off? Would he leave her abandoned? There it was again. *That nasty old bugaboo. Abandoned.* Quickly her mind went into rewind and a play-by-play began of those gruesome childhood years in foster homes. *No!* She stopped herself, interrupting her thought stream. She refused to rehash Mrs. Sweeney's punishments and boldface lies. Glancing at the books in the self-improvement section, she recalled titles she'd read that had helped her learn to reframe her experience of the past, to replace stale and damaging self-talk, and to practice acceptance and surrender. She'd reset the course of her life based in part on the therapeutic ideas in such books.

She wandered to the cookbook aisle and came across a "food as sex" book. It was no stretch to imagine a fancy candlelit dinner with Dean in her dining room, serving something elegantly simple like lamb ravioli, salad, and gelato for dessert. Envisioning herself gazing into his eyes as soothing music played, she imagined their rendezvous as a movie:

> *Half purring, she whispers to Dean, "So, how about a little strip show while we eat?"*
>
> *"A strip show?" Dean's face brightens.*
>
> *"It's just us, Dean. We're alone."*
>
> *His eyes widen, as round as Frisbees. She giggles. A mischievous sparkle gleams in his eye. "So when does the show begin?"*
>
> *That's her cue. She stands and sheds her blouse slowly and deliberately, flinging it toward him with a risqué gesture. She notices his eyes looking at her with delight, and how some ravioli dribbles out of his mouth. It makes her giggle. They both laugh.*
>
> *She gives him a Victoria's Secret come-hither gaze. Reaching back, she unsnaps her bra. With small, smooth moves of her shoulders, it drops lower and lower. His eyes stay riveted on her exposed breasts as they move, shimmering and liberated. She relishes the joy he experiences watching her. It feels freeing and scary at the same time, exhilarating and taboo.*
>
> *He hollers, "Whoopee!"*
>
> *His praise spurs her on. She wiggles out of her jeans, down to her pink cotton panties. His eyes blaze with amazement.*

Her silent encouragement fires him up. He makes tiny moans. She twirls so he can see other parts of her body. Exhilarated, she bends and twists as if prancing on a stage.

He reaches for the exposed skin on her back, and his touch feels so tender and loving. He slowly removes his shirt. Her hands caress his naked muscles. One by one, he sheds his own clothes, performing his own strip tease.

She succumbs to a flood of rapturous emotions, pulls him close, and surrenders to him, throwing her head back in ecstasy as they embrace …

Dean walked in through the revolving front door of the store. The movie stopped. She stood, observing him. He halted, looked around, and appeared as though he might be wondering if she'd "forgotten" and had abandoned *him*.

Leaving him in suspense for a few heartbeats, she stepped out from her hideout and waved. "Over here, Dean."

His eyes lit up. "You made it."

Awkwardly, they made their way to the café and ordered decaf lattés. He pointed to a quiet table for two where they sat down. She'd purchased a thank you card while waiting and handed it to him, along with a surprise gift.

"You shouldn't have." He opened the card and smiled as he read it.

"It's the least I could do for all you've done for Cody. Go ahead, open the present."

He unwrapped the gift and exclaimed, "Ha!" He held up a one-pound package of Divine Delight coffee beans.

"I stopped by Sacred Grounds on the way here, thinking you'd like some more beans."

"Nice. Always a good idea to have plenty on hand." He looked at her appreciatively, reached across the table, and patted her hand.

A warm tingle shot up her arm. "It's my way of saying how much you mean to me because you've taken such an interest in Cody's life."

"Stop giving me so much credit. Give yourself the credit."

"Seriously, you've made a huge difference for him. For us. He realizes now that somebody like you—a man—believes in him. And a heck of a man at that."

He sat straighter, studying her face. "That's very sweet. But *you* were the one who had the guts to knock on my door and get things rolling."

"Yes, but this stage in his life is so critical. To have a man who knows what it means to grow up to be a man, someone who understands life like a man, to show him respect—well, it's priceless."

Dean sat back. "Tell me about his birth father, if I'm not prying." Dean appeared genuinely interested.

"He was this jock from Florida who flirted with me on spring break. He played college football, and we had sex one night on the beach. When I found out I was pregnant, I notified him but he blew me off. No matter how hard I tried, he wouldn't own up to it. He lived thousands of miles away, and I was just twenty. So my adoptive family rallied behind me. They helped me bring up Cody while he was an infant and toddler. Cody doesn't even think about his biological father any more."

Dean sat quietly, absorbing, reflecting. "Well, that's quite a story. I can see how he's had his ups and downs."

"There you have it, the Larissa-and-Cody saga." A lull followed. They'd talked enough about Cody, she thought. She feared she'd said too much. Would Dean stand up and leave? Inside, she died a little until he spoke.

"As long as Cody keeps showing a turnaround in attitude and behavior, his thirty days probation will come and go without a hitch."

Given the brief time Dean had agreed to meet, she wanted to move the conversation to a subject directly involving the two of them. She saw her chance, but did she dare risk it? "It's clear you see potential in Cody." She paused. "And what about his mother's potential?"

His eyes reacted to her seductive energy. Had she blown it? She smiled stiffly. He looked at her as if ready to say something confidential. She hoped for a sign, a gesture, anything that declared his romantic interest.

Taking a sip of his latte, he finally said, "If you'll excuse me, I need to use the restroom." Standing up, he added, "Pardon me, I'll be right back," and he walked away.

Had she offended him somehow? She tried letting her shoulders relax. Perhaps this wasn't such a good idea after all, feeling so attracted to him.

Although it appeared mutual, it muddled everything. Was something extraordinary going on between them, or was she imagining it?

She needed to clear her brain, to free up her feelings. She looked around the store and observed the shoppers. One of her favorite hobbies was people-watching, sort of like Humanity 101. A stubborn question fogged her thinking: Was Dean really coming back—or leaving her stranded?

She noticed a middle-aged man flipping through magazines in the For Men section. He glanced around cautiously, as if he was eyeballing some skimpily clad women. She laughed to herself. What made men so predictable? What primitive drive held them captive to the sight of a naked female? It amazed her how often women let this mighty power go unused, or even realized they had this vast power.

Is Dean coming back? Am I waiting like a fool?

A good-looking man walked past the magazine rack, stopping at a nearby bookshelf labeled "Spirituality and Religion." He opened a book that caught his attention. Tall, fit, urbane, and clean-shaven, he was younger than Dean by a dozen years. She noticed what looked like a brown burn mark on his jaw and neck.

Dean came walking back. "I don't know about you," he said, still standing, "but I've only got another thirty minutes or so."

Her cellphone showed it was nearing eight. "Me too."

He sat down and spoke quietly. "I hope I'm not being improper for asking … but is something special going on between us?"

She took a moment to breathe. "Yes, something special *is* going on, Dean."

He paused. "I thought so."

He reached out his hands and held hers. His eyes locked on hers, and she remained suspended in silence for the next few seconds in what seemed eternal time.

Her breathing became faster, heavier. "I'm not sure what's supposed to happen from here," she whispered.

"I'm not sure either. I haven't felt like this in ages, Larissa."

She wanted to kiss him so badly, to throw her arms around him and never let go. She wanted to forget his being married and all that went with it. His hands felt so warm, and she ached to be alone with him.

She glanced toward the man at the Spirituality and Religion bookshelf. Taking note of where Larissa was looking, Dean glanced too, and she saw his face instantly go pale. Dean turned his chair away, clearly having recognized the man.

"What is it?" Larissa asked. "You just went as white as a sheet."

Lowering his voice, he said, "I know the guy."

Intrigued, she asked, "You do? Who is he?"

Dean remained vague, mumbling something to himself. "I'd rather he didn't see us. Let's go." He turned farther away to conceal himself from the man's view.

She realized that Dean's discomfort signaled a close relationship between the two men. The mysterious Spirituality and Religion customer walked on and headed for the sales counter to buy the book. Larissa smiled, hoping to ease Dean's anxiety. It worked. He relaxed.

"Let me walk you to your car," he said softy.

They left by the opposite door where Mr. Spirituality and Religion was paying for his book. Dean held her arm gently as they walked to the parking lot. Night was falling and shadows blanketed the pavement as they crossed the lot. She accompanied him to his Honda, several spaces closer to the store than her Saturn, and stopped away from the store's lighting. Nobody was around.

Dean smiled at her, then suddenly his lips connected to hers.

She felt his fire. Her own fire ignited. She responded with abandon, their lips and tongues and arms and bodies united. Her feverish breathing came faster and harder, matching his own bursts of powerful breathing.

Gasping, she pulled back and cried, "Whew! The way you make me feel!"

"I love the way you make *me* feel!"

Another long kiss.

They stood entwined in one another's arms, blissfully joined. Larissa glanced in several directions to satisfy herself that nobody was observing them. The shadow they stood in afforded some cover of darkness. He took her hand and opened the passenger door, urging her inside.

Dean walked around to the other side of the car. As he passed by the car parked next to his, Dean glimpsed a bumper sticker:

NO Jesus, NO Peace

KNOW Jesus, KNOW Peace

Getting in the driver's side next to Larissa, he felt a twinge of hesitation. Uneasiness flickered in his stomach.

"What should I do with this?" she asked, holding up a book.

It was his Bible. "Here, let me have it." He took the Bible, along with some newspapers she handed him, and put them on the back seat. His sleeve snagged the sticky note on the cover of the Bible, popping it off. There in his hand was the verse from Proverbs: *"Many are the plans in a man's heart, but it is the Lord's purpose that prevails."*

He nestled closer to her, but his amorous energy dissolved. Now that privacy was theirs, a huge part of him wanted to reach out and embrace her. She cozied up to him, closed her eyes, and puckered her lips, purring. He hesitated. Her emerald eyes opened, inquisitive. He leaned in to kiss her, but then he sat back ramrod straight.

She stared at him, alarmed.

"Sorry ... something isn't right," he said.

"Not right? What do you mean?"

"It's not right. I shouldn't be doing this."

"You shouldn't? How come?" Her voice raised in pitch.

He looked down, speechless.

"But we're just getting going, Dean. Why are you acting like this?"

"Sorry." He choked out the words, "It's something I should only be doing with . . ."

"What kind of shit is this?" Her face flashed the look of a fool betrayed. "What the *hell*, Dean?"

"I hate saying it, but it has to end here, Larissa. It just does."

"End here?"

He sighed, saddened. "It's better if we don't go any further."

"Better? A moment ago … what could possibly … ? I don't get it. Why are you afraid?"

"As much as I want to, and I really do want to, it's not right."

"It sure feels right to me."

"God knows how great it would be. Please believe me, it's not because of you."

"What is it then? Damn! Just tell me!"

He shrugged. "I understand you're upset. I'm so sorry this is hurting you. I don't exactly have a speech prepared. I'm sorry."

"Why are you messing everything up? I thought we both wanted to?"

"Everything in me wants you, but I'm married." His voice sounded weaker. He tried looking her in the eye. "In God's eyes, what we're doing is not right."

"God has nothing to do with it! Why are you bringing God into this?"

She slapped him.

His hand went to his cheek. "Look, everything in me craves to feel your skin, your body, to run to a motel and jump into bed together. You're so beautiful. But it has to be my wife I do that with."

Furious, she shoved him hard. He banged his head on the doorpost. His glasses flew off.

Dazed, he groaned. "I'm sorry this is so painful. Forgive me."

"Forgive you! Damn it all, I want you, Dean! I don't give a shit what you think God says!"

He touched his nose; it was bleeding. He tried moving closer to comfort her, but she shoved him again, this time harder. He lurched backward, moaning in pain.

"I'm not trying to hurt you, Larissa." He picked up his broken glasses. "You have to believe me."

Larissa's mouth stopped working. She could not spit out another word. She pulled on the door handle and bolted out of the car. She wanted to yell at the top of her lungs, *Damn you!* She wanted him to love her, to make her whole with his love, to have her wishes come true. For once. But Dean just sat in the car with his head down, like he was paralyzed.

She ran to her car, opened the door, and jumped inside. Tears gushing, dumbstruck, she watched him stare straight ahead and start the engine. He drove off. No wave. Nothing.

How can this be happening? My life was feeling so good, but now … !

The hurt felt like sandpaper on her soul.

How could I be so gullible? I never saw it coming.

Her vision became blurry. She banged the dashboard with her fists, screaming, "NO! NO! NO!"

Nothing made sense. Nothing at all.

CHAPTER

"Hi, Honey. How was your meeting?"

"Okay," said Dean, coming inside. "Good to be home."

"If you're hungry, I can warm up some pecan pie."

"Sure. Thanks."

On evenings when Dean attended AA meetings, Kate took care to have something ready that he liked to eat when he got home. She sliced a generous piece of leftover pie and warmed it in the microwave. Most AA evenings she took advantage of the spare time while he was gone to do mini-projects. Tonight's unexpected meeting allowed her time to deal with the Rodin lovers sculpture. She'd located a place for it in the living room, tucked away in a formal space that doubled as an art gallery. Positioned by the bookcase, it stood next to a large-leaf schefflera that helped obscure it. From the doorway, it was barely noticeable.

While Dean changed into pajamas, she reviewed her plan: she would show him where she placed the sculpture, and in that way honor him and his anniversary gift. Kate said a little prayer and consciously relaxed her shoulders to get rid of her anxiety.

At least one worry was off her mind. Nicole's bedroom was down the hall, and this time her daughter's presence at home on a school night eliminated the possibility of "anything physical" happening after Dean saw the sculpture.

As Kate walked by Nicole's room, she observed her nonchalantly listening to an old pop song: "It felt so wrong, it felt so right . . ." crooned the song on Nicole's iPad—something about kissing a girl and liking it.

"No more of that tonight, honey," Kate said, raising her voice. "Is your homework done? Especially math? It's important, Nicole." No reply.

Rattled by her daughter's indifference, Kate wondered, *What world are these kids living in these days? What world am I in?* Plainly, the two worlds were not remotely the same. Kate attributed these tensions to typical teenage raging hormones. Might Nicole be upset over the rumor spread by a classmate about the cheerleading squad having sex with football players in the boys' locker room? Should Kate make a big deal of it, or let it go?

She shrugged off the uncomfortable sensation, went to the living room, and stood by the sculpture, waiting for Dean to walk in and notice where she'd put it. She felt determined to show him the loving affection and appreciation he deserved for giving her the gift, however distasteful she judged it to be. Both of their anniversary cards stood perched on the fireplace mantel where the family displayed greeting cards. The words in his card made a deeper impression this time because she'd taken a moment to tune in more closely to the feelings he'd expressed: "I truly hope and believe the best adventure is still ahead. To be closer to you is my deepest wish and desire."

If he meant for them to live adventurously, she knew she had done little about it. Was she mirroring the same commitment?

Dean stepped into the living room. She smiled, showing him with a playful Vanna White gesture where she'd placed the Rodin. That's when she saw something strange about him; he wasn't wearing glasses. In fact, a fresh red cut trickled blood down the bridge of his nose.

"Are you alright, Skip? I'll get a bandage."

"There's something I want you to hear, Katie." She heard a catch in his voice. Before she could speak, he cleared his throat and croaked, "There's a reason my glasses are missing. And a reason I have this cut."

"Wait. I'll go get a—"

He held up his hand like a traffic cop. "It's nothing. A woman I've been seeing recently shoved me tonight. My glasses flew off. That's why I have this cut."

She stood there. Had she heard him right?

She stammered, "What … what did you say? A woman you've been seeing … ?"

"Tonight I broke off seeing a woman I've been attracted to lately. The bad news is, my glasses are broken and the arguing got rather nasty. The good news is, it's over."

Stunned, Kate stood staring. "You … you've been seeing another woman?"

He nodded. "It ended tonight."

"I'm … I'm . . ." Words didn't come. *Not possible!*

"I was going to try and hide it. Pretend it never happened. But then I got to thinking … well, I think it's time we talked, Kate. I mean, talked about us, not her."

Hearing him say "her" made Kate feel sick. She wanted to smash her fists against his chest and face.

"We are living a joke, Katie." His voice sounded flat. "Our marriage is a joke."

She gasped. Her throat tightened and words escaped her.

Raising his voice, he repeated, "Did you hear me? Our marriage is a joke!"

"Lower your voice, Skip. You don't have to yell." *A joke?*

His voice got louder. "It's needed saying a long time, and I'm mad as hell about it."

"Dean Nelson! What's gotten into you? Shhhh! Nicole will hear."

"Never mind her. It's about time we had this out. How much longer can we go on fooling ourselves?"

"Fooling ourselves about what?"

"That we love each other, but we never make love."

She recoiled. "Am I really hearing this? I love you. You love me. We're married."

"Married? Is that what you call it? Words. They're just words."

"Lower your voice. Please."

She heard feet approaching in the hallway. Nicole poked her head around the corner. "What's all the shouting? Are you guys okay?"

"We're fine," Kate said, "just fine."

"No we're not!" yelled Dean. "We're fighting!"

Nicole cringed.

Kate took a step back. "I've never seen you act like this."

"Like I said, we are *not fine!*" exclaimed Dean. "We're trying to communicate. And it's about time." Quieter, more controlled, he looked at Nicole. "Now let us have some privacy!"

Nicole ran back to her room, banging her door shut.

"How could you?" hollered Kate. Glaring at Dean, she moved to go after Nicole, but he stuck out his arm and blocked her way.

"Are you nuts? You've gone and upset her. She needs me."

"She'll get over it. She'll survive. But will *we?*"

"What? Now just hold on a minute. What do you mean will *we* survive? I think *I'm* the one who should be asking that question."

"In case you haven't noticed, we live like roommates. You want less, I want more. In fact you want nothing. If it goes on like this much longer—"

"What are you saying? That we're getting divorced? Are you threatening?"

He shook his head. "Who said anything about divorce? Don't get ahead of me. Solutions, Kate, we need solutions."

"Solutions to what? To your being unfaithful? To your being horny?"

Dean shook his head, downcast. "Hear me out. We're living like we're in a chess match and we're both stuck. Nobody knows the next move. Stalemate. I want to know why you don't want sex anymore. If God thinks sex is okay, and He does, why don't you?"

"This isn't the time for that. Nicole needs me to go to her."

"STOP! STOP AVOIDING THE SUBJECT!"

Kate trembled. Dean's yelling … she couldn't believe how scary he was. His arm blocked her from moving. Was he going to hit her?

"I deserve to know, Kate. God ordains married people to enjoy sex, and sex feels good. That goes for any marriage. So why don't we do what feels good?"

Kate couldn't help thinking: *Sex feels good? Who is he kidding?*

"Stop avoiding, Kate. Just answer the question. Or does 'making love' sound better than 'having sex'? Is that too crude for you?"

She stared at him like he was a savage beast. Fear shot through her like a sharp spear. "Arguing is getting us nowhere. This is no time to talk about it. It's *you* who needs to do the explaining. *Who* was this other woman?"

"Answer me, Kate. No more dodging."

"Who, Dean?"

She felt cornered. She struck back. "Tell me about the other woman. *Who is she?*"

"It doesn't matter."

Kate stood her ground. "What's wrong, Skip? I love you, you love me—at least I thought you did."

"Ha! How about intimacy, Kate? Where's the intimacy? Scripture says we are to become 'one flesh.' That means being intimate, not strangers in the same bed."

Astounded, she stared at Dean. Her maternal instincts demanded that she go comfort Nicole. Her head began buzzing.

"We've tried therapy and marriage counseling and self-help books," he went on. "For what? Nothing. You just keep avoiding me. I want to know when it will stop. Will it ever? Do you still respect me? Am I no longer attractive? Why can't we just talk like grownups?"

Kate's eyes drilled holes into him. She hated him. Nicole needed her. Now.

"All the times I've been patient, waiting for something to change. Geez, Kate, do you have any idea how tough that is?"

Her ears nearly exploded. Truthfully, she didn't know how to answer him. She didn't know what she thought about any of it. Avoiding him? Well, his aggressive tone didn't help. It made matters worse. He was acting just like her father. Critical. Cutting. Cold.

"What is it about me you no longer like?" He waited for an answer. "Healthy couples make love every few weeks, even more than that. So I'm having a hard time believing we're normal."

"This is so tiresome. And what do you mean 'normal?'" She frowned. "Look, our daughter is in her bedroom freaking out. We can talk about this later. Then it will be *my* turn to interrogate *you*. Now get out of the way, you adulterer!"

She tried pushing past him.

"Adulterer? No, it was nothing like that. We never had our clothes off. We never had sex. It was over before it started."

"Who, Dean? *Who* is she?"

"Forget it. I'm not dragging her name into this. Besides—"

"Somebody younger? Prettier? Sexier?"

"Don't, Kate."

"Quit your excuses. Who, Dean?"

Dean grabbed her wrist. "I stopped because of you. Because of *us*."

She jerked her wrist free, shoving him away. She spun on her heel and hurried down the hallway, reaching Nicole's door. She felt hammering inside her head, and the mounting urgency to make sure her child was okay.

"Kate, we have to stop talking around the edges. If we don't talk about it, or you *won't* talk about it—"

Kate turned and spit out, "Forget it! I'm not listening!" She knocked on Nicole's door.

"We *could* be living an adventure, Kate. And I mean that in every way, not just in bed, but in so many ways. *If* we cooperated, *if* we both wanted it."

She knocked again. "Nicole, please open up." Kate tried the door. It was locked. "Nicole? Let me try and explain."

Nicole's voice came through the door. "There's nothing to explain, Mother. Whatever you and Dad are unhappy about, I don't want to hear it."

Dean began walking toward her. Kate feared he might become violent, but he brushed past her to their bedroom.

"Please, let me talk to you," Kate said to Nicole. "I know this is coming as a big shock."

"It's between you and Daddy. Stop trying to be SuperMom. We can talk in the morning."

"Promise?"

"Promise."

Kate fretted. What would the damage to Nicole be, the fallout? Would she keep their fight to herself, or would she tell Lindsay?

Kate turned as Dean rushed out of the bedroom carrying a pillow under his arm. That had to mean he was heading downstairs to the guest bedroom. In no mood for fighting, Kate ignored him, resigning herself to flop onto the bed and mull over her chaotic emotions. For the first time in many years, she realized—with relief actually—that she would sleep in their bed alone.

Crash! A loud smashing noise came from the living room.

Kate jumped. A feeling of dread gripped her. She tiptoed to the living room. There, all over the floor by the fireplace, lay the plaster shards of the shattered sculpture.

Dean was nowhere to be seen. From downstairs came the muffled sounds of his grumbling. Nicole peeked out of her bedroom door. Kate heard her pad down the hallway to the living room, where the two of them stared in shock at the plaster fragments littering the floor.

CHAPTER

While Annabelle did leg stretches on the ballet barre, stretching her heavy thighs in hopes of fitting into leaner jeans, Larissa prepared for her Friday morning women's group. Her humiliation from Dean's stunt the night before made her chest tighten. The image of Dean looking so tormented, like it was his duty to stop, made her exclaim aloud, "Bullshit!"

"Are you alright?" asked Annabelle, puffing heavily.

"Yes. Fine. Sorry about that."

The chemistry with Dean had seemed genuine. But the crude way he'd acted made her despise him. Larissa told herself his conduct had nothing to do with his desire for her, or her desire for him. She seethed. Then she did what came naturally—turned the blame against herself. *In all honesty, what was I doing chasing him?* Her flirting had been a bad idea; that much was clear. Despite his sexy attractiveness, a fling with a married man was just another dead end in her life, although it would've done wonders for her self-esteem for a while.

Jasmine arrived. She glided around energetically ala a Hollywood starlet, flitting about and checking out her curves in the wall mirrors. Claire arrived, looking more drawn than usual. The ladies loosely called their mini-group, Boosting Our Natural Femininity Into Repeatable Ecstasy, or BONFIRE. Any female client could join. Claire had come up with the moniker, and it had stuck. Larissa really liked the "fire" part of the name because of its passionate overtones. She offered the ninety-minute session as a bonus for regulars who showed an interest in nutrition, meditation, relaxation, mindfulness, and let's-get-real girl talk. She was hoping Kate would join their sisterhood soon.

"Okay, ladies, let's get started in two minutes."

Larissa went to tidy up the restroom in the rear. She checked the toilet paper roll. Cody had "forgotten" to change the empty roll. Maybe it was time to offer him an incentive; perhaps some pocket money would boost his understanding of how his few chores helped make the operation of her enterprise a success. The one reliable thing that he cared about consistently was his animal shelter. The crate by the rear door near the dressing room held his latest rescue animal, Mrs. McNamara's cat. He'd fashioned a splint for Trixie's tail after her neighbor had accidentally closed the bathroom door on it.

The four women—Annabelle, Claire, Jasmine, and Larissa—sat cross-legged on a circular rug. Larissa lit a candle, and everyone sat silently with her eyes closed for sixty seconds. Claire stated her goal: "To improve my muscle tone and flexibility in order to reawaken my sexuality and to bring my new sexier self into full bloom." Jasmine, the African-American fashion model with a splendid figure, stated hers: "To use the benefits of my outer disciplines from building my personal brand to strengthen my inner disciplines for the well-being of every person I encounter." Then Annabelle added: "To get healthier by losing thirty pounds and keep the weight off while contributing as a competent professional in the field of healthcare."

Larissa smiled proudly. "Wow! Well said, all of you. Working with you guys is such a treat." She handed each woman a freshly cut white carnation. "White is for purity, and with this flower, I want to honor the purity of your motivations to improve yourselves."

The women smiled.

A theme emerged as they talked, roughly put: "Let's enjoy being women." Larissa suggested that they give some attention to the benefits of deep breathing. "Our breath is the first thing to focus on. It is life itself. Relaxation is essential to inviting in sensuality and opening ourselves to pleasure." She led the women in a yoga-based relaxation exercise, encouraging them to relax with their eyes closed. For three quiet minutes they practiced focused breathing until Larissa directed them to sit up.

"Alright, let's do a review from last week. Before we can expect having a passionate relationship with anyone, we have to be in a passionate relationship with ourselves—and with life itself. When you allow joy and pleasure into your life, you move closer to being your truest self, the self others are attracted to. Letting yourself be open and more receptive to pleasure is not a luxury, it's a necessity which allows your life force to flow. Your true essence is more attractive than the person you work hard to convince the world you are."

She glanced at Claire. "Like the person your ex has always wanted you to be." Next, she made eye contact with Jasmine. "Or the woman you want everyone to think you are."

Claire spoke. "That all sounds very nice, but I'm at the butt end of a hideous divorce because he thinks I'm so unsexy, so unlovable. Menopause is right around the corner, and I'm living alone for the first time in nineteen years. What are *my* chances?"

"We've talked before about the power each of us has to redefine ourselves," said Larissa calmly. "Passion starts with our relationship with ourselves, with or without a partner. Giving abundant love to yourself frees you up to give more love more often—to a new or an old partner, to everyone, to life itself. When you no longer need sex or the attention of someone special to fulfill you, you're free to act without having to get anything, and your actions can *express* rather than *seek* the openness you desire and the love you deserve."

Abruptly, the front door flew open, and Kate burst inside. She was breathless, agitated, and fuming. "Sorry! I'm ready to explode. Forgive me for interrupting, but I don't think this can wait, Larissa."

Larissa welcomed her and gestured for her to sit in the circle. "Glad you're here. Feel free to join us."

"Sorry about being so rude." Kate motioned for Larissa to stand up. "Please?" She leaned in close and whispered hoarsely in Larissa's ear. "I'm terribly sorry to barge in like this. It's urgent. I have to talk to someone. Something awful happened last night, Larissa."

Keeping her voice low, Larissa asked, "Can't it wait until BONFIRE is over? You'll love what we're into. Get comfortable, grab a cushion, and make yourself at home."

"I hate to be such a bother, but can we go someplace private?"

Larissa winced. "Will one of you ladies take over for me?"

Jasmine raised her hand. "Let me, Larissa. I'll manage."

Larissa thanked Jasmine and encouraged the women to continue their relaxation exercises, then stepped over to the kitchenette area by the dressing room in the rear.

Kate followed. "It's all a big mess, Larissa. I tried calling my best friend to talk about it, but she wasn't around. So you came to mind. I had to come right over. I think I'm going crazy. Skip and I had an awful argument, and I think there's real trouble brewing."

Larissa nodded, rather impatiently, wondering how she could help.

"He acted very strange after coming home last night. He was late and got straight into his pajamas. When he walked into the living room, I noticed his nose was bloody. I thought, 'How strange!' So I asked him about it."

Larissa swallowed hard. "A bloody nose?"

Kate nodded. "All of a sudden we were fighting and shouting at each other. He'd told me he was going to an AA meeting, but he was seeing some other woman! He wouldn't come clean, so I yelled at him, 'Dean Nelson, what's gotten into you!?"

Stunned, Larissa said, "Did you say … Dean? Dean Nelson?"

"That's his name. Why?"

"But I thought his name was Skip?"

"It is. It's both. Skip is his nickname. So I began questioning him, and next do you know what he said?"

Freaking out, Larissa could hardly breathe. *It can't be!* "DEAN?"

"Yes, Dean," Kate said, puzzled, frowning. "Why is that a big deal? I call him Dean lots of times—especially when I'm angry."

Larissa couldn't stand it. She had to get away from Kate. She scrambled to the dressing room and shut the door. Her heart pounded. Her body shook. Her life seemed to collapse. She sank into a chair and held her head in her hands. *This has to be a mistake!*

Kate knocked on the door. "Are you alright? What did I say, Larissa?"

"Just give me a minute. I'll be fine."

"I didn't mean to ... let me in, Larissa."

"Be patient. Just be patient with me." Her throat croaked out the words as though somebody else was speaking. She noticed a new message signal on her cellphone sitting on the makeup table. She checked the number. It was Dean. Instinctively, she picked up the phone and listened. Every cell in her body shuddered.

"Hey Larissa, I'm not going to sugarcoat this. I'm so sorry. Try not to think of me as a jerk, okay? I had to stay faithful. If that sounds corny, sorry. I wish you the very best, because a woman as strong and beautiful as you deserves the best. The very best."

Larissa threw the phone down on the table. She shook her head in disbelief. How could something this crazy be happening? She paced in the tiny space.

More knocking. Larissa opened the door slightly.

"Larissa, please, are you alright?" Kate pushed on the door and barged inside. "How did I offend you? I'm so sorry. What did I say?"

Exasperated, Larissa made sure to close the door, then looked at her helplessly. How could she tell Kate? How could she avoid the truth? How could she spare her? She choked out the words, "Did you say he came home late from an AA meeting? That his nose was bleeding?"

"Yes. What of it?"

"Because I'm pretty sure I know where he was."

Kate's face went pale. "You do?"

"Please tell me you won't hate me. I had no idea. Truly."

"You're not making sense."

"Does your husband work at MediMax?"

"What has that got to do ... ? Okay, yes he does."

Bracing herself, stepping back farther, Larissa spoke as sympathetically as possible. "Your husband was not at an AA meeting. He was with *me* last night."

Stunned, Kate inhaled sharply and stared at her.

Larissa held her gaze, expecting to be attacked.

Betrayal etched Kate's face. She frowned at Larissa in utter shock. "How *could* you?"

"Like I said, I truly had no idea he was your husband."

The look of sheer disbelief in Kate's eyes never wavered. She swung her open hand and slapped Larissa. Larissa's fingers went to her burning cheek, but she made no gesture to defend herself.

Kate raised her hand to strike again, but stopped. "I'm not sure what's worse," she spit out. "Knowing he was carrying on behind my back or knowing it was *you*."

"Believe me, Kate, all I've ever heard you call him is Skip. I've only known him as Dean. Even if I had suspected, do you have any idea how many Nelsons there are in the phone book? Think of the odds. Astronomical!"

Kate stared at her. "I'm done here. I'm through. Never again." She turned toward the door.

"No, don't! Don't leave, Kate. Let's talk this through."

"The truth, Larissa. I mean it. I want the truth. You never had the vaguest inkling?"

"Never, ever. Honestly. How could I have known?"

Silence. Kate paused at the door, about to leave.

"Look, I was just enjoying his company. Nothing more."

"How far did it go? Tell me how far."

"Some flirting. Not even making out." Larissa refused to mention the kisses.

"I don't believe you. There had to be more."

A sudden knock on the door. "Mom?" Cody's voice came through the door. "Can you come out? Trixie needs help."

"Cody?"

"Yeah, it's me. Trixie's splint came off, and her tail is bleeding again. I need a towel—quick."

Larissa reached past Kate and cracked open the door, holding it partly ajar. "Not now, Cody. Later. Can't you see I'm busy?"

"But Mom, her cat really needs help and—"

Larissa shut the door.

Cody banged on the door, his voice rising, "This can't wait, Mom!"

"Just hold on a sec," she shouted. Hoping to gently temper Kate's hysteria, she asked, "What more can I say, Kate? It wasn't like a cheap romance novel. It was just a fleeting attraction."

Kate stamped her foot. "Shut up! That doesn't change *his* sneaking around and fawning over you." Kate's nostrils flared. "No one can compete with someone as young and pretty as you. Someone as gorgeous as you!"

"Kate, Kate … I assure you *nothing* happened. *He* nipped it in the bud. *He* stopped it. *He* did it for your sake. But it's over now. He ended it. It's done."

Kate blinked, dazed.

"He said he wants to invest in your marriage. In *you*."

Kate flung her hands high in the air. "How dare you! The idea of you talking about us with him makes me want to puke."

"Mom, hurry up!" shouted Cody through the door. The door handle rattled. "I really need some help out here."

"He's a good man, Kate. A decent man. He stepped over the line a bit, but then he had the good sense—the guts—to call it off. Cut him some slack."

Tears gushed down Kate's cheeks. She looked at Larissa blankly. Larissa reached for a towel to wipe Kate's wet face. Kate brushed her hand away. The towel dropped to the floor.

"Adultery. That's what it was."

The door flung open. Cody stepped inside. "Mom, will you just hand me a towel?"

"Okay, here." She picked up the towel off the floor and tossed it to him. Turning to Kate, she said, "No, Kate. It wasn't that. If my son—Cody here—hadn't lost his warehouse job at MediMax two weeks ago, Dean and I would never have met. He went to bat for Cody and helped him keep his job. I felt grateful, and it just evolved from there."

"You're not leaving anything out, are you?"

"I'm not."

Taken aback, Cody exclaimed, "Mom, are you guys talking about *Dean?*"

"Ask *him*," Larissa said to Kate, nodding to Cody. "Go ahead. Ask him if it's true your husband went to bat for him so he could keep his job."

"What's going on, Mom?" Cody looked in disbelief at Larissa. Suddenly his face registered understanding. His hand slapped his forehead. He stared at Larissa. *"MOM!"*

"Enough!" Kate shouted, cupping her hands over her ears. She rushed out of the room and strode angrily to the front door. "Never again. I'm never coming back!" The women in the circle stared, completely puzzled. Kate disappeared out the front door, slamming it behind her.

Larissa turned to Cody. "I'm so sorry you had to hear that."

His face blushing, Cody looked in stunned silence at Larissa, then ran out the back door.

"Stop, Cody! Let me explain."

The sound of the back door closing made her shiver. The faces of the women in the circle turned to her, alarmed. "Can we help you, Larissa?" asked Jasmine.

Larissa hurried to the back door, pushed it open, and shouted at Cody as he was reaching the street corner.

"Wait! Stop! I'm so sorry! You never should've heard that."

He stopped, turned to her. "But I *did*. I *did* hear it."

"It all started very innocently, believe me. We didn't go too far. Can you blame me for finding him attractive?" Cody just stared back at her and kicked at a pile of trash.

"Bye, Mom." He turned and disappeared.

Larissa stood immobilized. *What now? What have I done?!*

CHAPTER

Playing the par-four tenth hole, Dean got the strange sensation that he was truly enjoying himself. It was the weekend, and for two days he'd kept his distance from Kate in an effort to cool things down. A bright but not-too-hot sun brought out the fresh green of the grass and the sparkling blue of the picturesque pond alongside the fairway. Dean's longtime friend and closest buddy, Hal Ostrow, four years older but more athletic, was three shots ahead of him as they started the back nine at Rolling Acres Golf Club.

Dean sat back while riding with Hal in the golf cart, quite pleased that he was playing so well. When Hal took out his five iron for his second shot to the green, Dean noticed Hal's thinning hair and bald spot, but his swing embodied the grace of an Olympic athlete in top form. A brisk wind helped Hal's ball reach the edge of the green. In that splendid moment, surrounded by glorious nature, Dean thought: *What a great game. I love this game.*

Rolling Acres was Dean's playground, and being outdoors on a Saturday morning was the prescription he needed. Dean swung a three wood for his second shot and the ball cleared a sand trap, landing on the green but far from the pin. Hal chipped a beauty near the pin and nailed a six-footer for par. Dean missed a long putt and a ten-footer, settling for a bogie. "Way to go, partner," Dean slapped his pal's shoulder. "You're up five."

"Yes sir. Not so bad yourself, Skipper. Next hole let's both make a birdie."

As they headed for the eleventh tee, Dean felt grateful for the chance to shake off the unsavory shouting match with Kate two nights before. He'd slept downstairs since then, allowing both of them a timeout. He cringed, though, recalling how Nicole had come downstairs to see him the following morning.

"Are you sure everything's okay, Daddy? It sure didn't sound like it."

Dean felt ashamed and embarrassed. "I'm so sorry about telling you to go away, honey. And I hate that you had to hear all that shouting."

"Daddy, I know you didn't really mean to hurt my feelings."

He hugged her. "That's my girl. You're a big girl for not being furious with me for yelling at you like that. Mom and I still love each other, you know."

"Of course. I'm just sad you both got so upset."

"Be patient with us, okay?"

She flashed a quick smile. "Sure, Dad. I know you can't always agree on everything. I'll be fine." Nicole wished him a great weekend and scampered upstairs.

He knew his daughter's plans for that weekend centered on cheerleading practices for the upcoming hockey season. The Burnsville Blaze were a perennial hockey powerhouse in Minnesota. Dean had the highest hopes for her doing well and enjoying her last year in high school.

On the eighteenth green, Dean watched as Hal dropped a dandy fifteen-footer. "Nice putt!" hollered Dean. His fifth three-putt of the round finished their twosome.

They'd planned to have a late breakfast at their favorite pancake house with Pastor Harrington, and they were running a few minutes ahead of time. Reverend Trevor Harrington served as the pastor of missions at Spirit Hills Evangelical Fellowship, and he often chummed with Dean and Hal. Carrying their clubs from the cart, the two men walked to their cars for the ten-minute drive to the restaurant. Dean debated whether to tell Hal about his and Kate's fight. He'd hinted to Hal about their bedroom doldrums in the past, and Hal had provided an empathetic ear. Dean appreciated how Hal made sure not to pass on Dean's comments to his wife Ginny. But Dean held back this time, so they got in their respective cars and drove off.

Dean removed the small bandage covering the cut on his nose. It was healing over. Although a scab remained, he decided to leave it alone and let nature do the healing. His new pair of glasses was on order. He'd told Hal and coworkers at the office that he'd run into a tree branch while raking his yard.

Dean checked his cellphone for messages. A voicemail from Kate popped up from the day before, which he'd ignored. He listened to her agitated voice:

"Well, you've really done it this time, Skip. Or should I say Dean? Congratulations on making a fine mess of everything. It just so happens I've spoken with the woman you were hitting on. Does the name Larissa sound familiar? Yeah, that's right. My fitness instructor. Your mistress. How you ever managed to get involved with her I'll never know. She said it was all very innocent. Right! Our last name never registered with her. We have to get serious about this mess. As far as I'm concerned, you're done staying in your cave downstairs. Right now, in my book, you're toast!"

He hung up. *No way! Larissa?* He was shocked. His mind whirled. His pulse quickened.

He pulled the car over and leaned on the steering wheel. His heart pounded as he weighed the ramifications of the news. Before meeting Hal and Trevor to discuss Spirit Hills' activities, he had to clear away the fog clouding his brain. His first thought was to call Larissa to see if she was all right.

He dialed. Larissa answered. "Hi, it's Dean."

"Great," he heard her say.

He plunged ahead. "I just listened to my wife's voicemail. She told me about you. Uh ... I'm so sorry. What a bizarre mess."

No ranting or trash talk from Larissa. Her flat tone made for an awkward verbal duet. "And ... ?"

"I never had a clue," he went on.

"Not even a hint?"

"No. None." He waited for her to say more, but she merely let out a heavy sigh. "I know you think I'm a first-class jerk, Larissa, so I'm apologizing for that." He purposely left the pause open-ended.

"I was flabbergasted. I'll let Kate fill you in on the details. Another time would be better to talk. I need to go."

"Look, I was astounded to hear you already knew Kate."

A long pause. "It blew me away, too. I'm still digesting it."

"I am so very sorry."

Larissa scoffed. "Tell me, Dean—or should I say, 'Skip'?—is this the typical 'she doesn't *do it* anymore' situation?"

Dean winced.

"I'll take that as a 'yes.' Nice triangle: You avoided making love with me . . ." she laughed . . . "and I take it Kate avoids making love with you."

"I'd better go now."

"You poor boy. You poor sad boy."

"Uh . . . gotta go. Bye."

Hanging up, he glanced toward the heavens. *What a colossal mess!*

Shaky, Dean arrived at the pancake house. He noticed the crowded parking lot. Clusters of people stood milling around outside the entrance of the restaurant. He spotted Hal driving up and parking. Their friendship felt more like that of two soul brothers.

Hal got out of his car and approached Dean, who signaled for them to keep their distance from the crowd. "There's something I didn't want to bring up while we were golfing, Hal. I've moved out of the house and I'm checking into a motel for a few days."

Surprise animated Hal's face. "Out? Out of the house?"

"Yep. Early this morning. I packed two suitcases, my briefcase, and my laptop."

"A . . . a motel?"

Dean nodded. "The luggage is in my car, and I'm heading there to check in after I leave here. I need to hibernate in a quiet room on my own for a while. Maybe for a week."

"Slow down. A week?"

"Katie and I had a blowout a few nights ago. I've wanted to tell you about it. I think a few days apart will be good for both of us."

"Whoa, start at the beginning."

Dean launched into a narrative about the whole fiasco. He admitted that he had strayed (not mentioning Larissa's name), and that his behavior had been adulterous. "If not technically adulterous, then at least it was emotionally." He assured Hal he'd brought the matter to God in prayer. "But Katie and I never managed to get anywhere discussing it—or what brought it on."

"Sounds like a deep hole you've dug for yourselves."

"Very deep, I'd say. It's important to me that you understand my camping at the motel isn't because of kneejerk anger. It is a protest, though—that I won't kid you. It is a time to reflect and seek God's guidance. Things can't stay the way they are."

"I see," Hal answered quietly, acknowledging his distress.

Dean breathed heavily. "I'm frustrated, Hal, and I'm sick and tired of being the complainer, the accuser, of bringing up our differences but getting nowhere. I'm not trying to humiliate Kate or shame her, but it feels like I'm out of options. It's a timeout, a breather."

"What about the girls? How is this impacting them?"

"For now, they're dealing with it okay. I've been sleeping in the guest room since the fight, so it won't come as a surprise that I'm leaving. I'm open to hearing from Kate and the girls anytime. I'm not trying to cut off communication. I've just got to get my head around what's going on. It's something I feel really sad about, Hal."

"You're that miserable? Is Kate, too?"

"Only she can answer that. But I'm guessing it bothers her in her own way." That triggered a thought. "I have to say, though, going solo for a while feels pretty darn good."

Hal leaned forward and looked straight into Dean's eyes like a doctor.

Dean laughed. "It feels liberating, freeing. She'll have a chance to reflect as well. A few days apart in the grand scheme of things won't hurt. It's really for the best, I think."

Hal looked dubious. But he caught the spirit of Dean's perspective.

They heard a car horn honking. Their pastor, Trevor Harrington, pulled up in his classic MG. He waved and parked. It tickled Dean how much this man of the church enjoyed his sporty sky-blue refurbished coupe.

Fifteen minutes later, the three of them were sitting together in a large, private booth. "Let me run an idea by you, boys," Trevor said. "Do you think it's time that we lobby for *Song of Songs* to be the next Wednesday night Bible study series?"

Dean was skeptical. "The idea's been suggested before, but it's gone straight into a black hole."

"Too touchy, definitely too hot to handle," said Hal.

Dean looked at Trevor. His friend's hair looked like an ocean wave ready to break on shore, so striking was the dark hair that hung above his forehead. Healthy and rugged, Trevor adjusted his collar to cover the burned skin on his neck that ran up his left jaw and reached to his left ear. It showed whenever he turned a certain way, but after a while most people stopped noticing the brown marks. Dean recalled Trevor's story of how he'd been burned as a young boy by a blazing car tire hurled by angry protesters in Nairobi.

A waitress walked up. "Are you gents ready for some breakfast?"

Hal and Dean ordered eggs with buckwheat and potato pancakes, respectively. Trevor ordered a veggie omelet, hash browns, three slices of bacon, a tall glass of orange juice, and steaming hot coffee with a steady number of refills. Raised in Kenya for nineteen years by American missionary parents, and having just turned forty, Trevor had grown to love this kind of over-the-top American meal, along with cheeseburgers and pizza. "As long as I indulge only once or twice a month like this," he said, "the needle on my guilt meter doesn't go crazy."

Dean turned the conversation back to *Song of Songs*. "I think the poem's sensual imagery—let's call it what it is, sexual imagery—intrigues men more than women. My guess is, it probably frightens women. For so many centuries, they've been chastised by church leaders to remain 'pure.'"

Trevor nodded. "That's where the husbands group I meet with acknowledges friction, too. And it's where the resistance to our proposal may also come from—the women who follow church dogma. We've all heard it, the old 'sex is sin' thing."

"It's certainly very graphic," said Hal. "And that's our challenge."

"There's a husbands group you meet with?" asked Dean, jumping back to Trevor's comment.

"Yes. I help run a men's sexuality group," replied Trevor. "Based on things I've heard there, we may be speaking for a third of the husbands in evangelical churches."

"That many?" replied Dean. The idea that other husbands were dealing with similar struggles, facing a decline in their sex lives, felt earthshaking to him.

"Well," replied Hal, "haven't you said, Trev, that the husbands who've been married for quite a few years come right out and admit that sex is lacking in their lives?"

He nodded. "There's a lot of frustration, yes. As for the sensual imagery in *Song of Songs,* I think it could trigger a divide between wives and husbands."

Dean leaned forward. "Would any women even show up?"

"It has such rich poetry," said Hal, "there must be a few wives who feel the way we do."

"I know one couple a study like that could help invigorate," answered Dean.

Hal shot Dean a glance. "Let's propose it then."

"Great." Trevor was all for it.

Dean sat in his own world, thinking about the husbands' support group while Hal and Trevor moved on to golf scores. Dean pondered what would have happened if Trevor had discovered him with Larissa that night at Barnes & Noble. *God forbid,* he thought. Trevor, merely ten or twelve feet away, could have easily glanced in their direction and spotted Dean. As a friend of both his and Kate's, having traveled with them overseas on half a dozen mission trips, Trevor would've no doubt innocently mentioned seeing Dean at B&N the next time he'd seen Kate. On the other hand, observing a woman as attractive as Larissa, he might've suspected what was really taking place. *By some small miracle, I dodged a bullet.*

The table conversation shifted to Dean. Hal looked directly at him. "Those doldrums you mentioned for that couple who needs invigorating— do you want to say more?"

Dean went blank. Should he answer Hal or dodge the truth? He looked at Trevor. Over the years, both Hal and Trevor had listened with open minds about numerous topics, offering solid and sensitive feedback. So it was not unlike Dean to open up to Trevor—and Hal knew this.

"To be frank, Kate and I have hit some speed bumps in the bedroom. Actually, I feel totally fed up. That's the abridged version."

Trevor's face indicated surprise. "How so? Would counseling help?"

"Been there, done that."

"I can refer you, if you want. Either for both of you, or for you alone."

"I'll put it this way. For a lot of Christian wives, it's kids, kids, kids. Then one day it morphs to church, church, church. *Too busy, sorry, I'm living the Lord's abundant life. Not tonight, honey.* I think, for some wives, their families and homes and church life take over, and intimacy goes out the window. It's been that way for Kate and me."

"I see," said Trevor, nodding.

Dean shrugged. "Candidly? My energy around studying *Song of Songs* is motivated by our ongoing roadblock. How do I say it?" He hesitated. What came next would take guts to speak aloud. "I ... we ... oh crap ... I'm stuck in a sexless marriage. I hate to admit it, guys, but it's been that way for years. I know that must be hard to believe because we act so happy and all. Let's just say Kate gave it her best early on, and we have two lovely kids to show for it, but for a long time sex has been a disaster."

The men sat stone still. "Years?" both said in unison.

Dean could tell they thought he was exaggerating. "I'm not kidding, guys. It's a sex-starved marriage. Long term. Period. End of story."

Hal's eyes showed genuine sympathy. Trevor's face, etched in a frown, showed the gravity of Dean's disclosure.

"Let me say a couple more things," Dean went on. "First of all, I realize nobody can change somebody else. The same goes for Kate. If a change is supposed to occur, it must be the other person who does the changing, for his or her own good reasons. Also, I want to be upfront about something else: In the past month, I've strayed from our marriage."

The look on Trevor's face revealed amazement. Hal's showed grave concern.

"I hate to say it, but it's true. Early in our marriage, in the free-love days before the girls arrived, I strayed a bit and engaged in some heavy flirting and sex play. But since then, I've stayed entirely faithful to Kate until recently. In the past couple weeks, a very sexy woman appeared out of the blue. She came to my office one day about her son's employment—and, well, things sort of caught fire like putting a match to dry kindling. We never got naked or had sex, but sparks were flying, oh yes. I wanted what is no longer in my marriage from *her*. The good news is I broke it off a few days ago, before it turned into an all-out blaze."

"And the *bad* news?" asked Trevor.

"I lied to Kate and snuck behind her back to see this woman. My actions were deceptive and adulterous. No argument there. I played a secret game with temptation for a while, and I behaved in ways that stretched my vow to remain faithful. And to top off the disaster, unbeknownst to all of us, the woman turned out to be Kate's fitness instructor!"

The other men's mouths dropped.

"And the worst?" added Dean. "Besides hurting Kate, I displeased God."

Trevor blew a long blast of air from his lungs. Hal swallowed hard. No finger wagging, no condemnation; only empathy and concern. "I'd say," suggested Trevor, glancing at Hal, "that it's absolutely critical for us to pray about this."

Dean did not want to share any more about the pain he and Kate were experiencing, so he switched the subject back to *Song of Songs*. "As for our Bible study proposal—"

Hal interrupted. "Don't you want to tell us a little more about your plan to, you know, move into a motel?"

While Dean filled in Trevor about his plan to stay a few days at the local SleepWell Inn, Trevor questioned whether he'd thought through the unintended consequences. Dean bluntly replied, "No, it was a gut decision. I need a breather. As for the rest of our sad tale, I'd rather put it on hold for now. Let's see how the situation looks down the road a ways."

Hal continued, "Are you thinking of the D word? Has it gone that far?"

Dean shook his head. "It hasn't. But I can't pretend it has never crossed my mind. A few times, yes. Right now, though, it's off my radar."

Hal nodded. Trevor remained silent.

Dean barreled ahead. "I need your perspectives about our stalemate, guys. Because that's what it is."

"Interesting you should put it that way," replied Trevor. "I just picked up a book about eroticism in the Bible. It makes some unusual points that seem relevant here. The author says God Himself is erotic."

"Wow. Sounds like something we could use in our *Songs of Songs* proposal," said Hal.

Dean asked, "You mean to say somebody out there thinks God *approves* of passion instead of disapproves? That God thinks sensuality and spiritually aren't opposites, or in conflict?"

"Basically, yes. The author is a theologian who cites a number of biblical passages where historical interpretations by church elders have misconstrued God's view of human sexuality. His premise is: Whatever harms a person's sexuality also harms a person's spirituality, and vice versa."

"Boy, this is great," said Dean.

"I'll lend it to you."

Dean sensed a strong affirmative connection from both men, so he kept up the momentum. "How can something so foundational to marriage—intimacy between spouses—be neglected? It's illogical." His anger bubbled to the surface. "I feel stuck in an ugly web of Kate's rejections. It's almost like I'm living with an addict, guys. Her denial affects me the same way I've seen families being hurt by addicts and alcoholics in my old counseling practice—battered trust, continual frustration, even despair."

"You really have gotten up a head of steam about this, haven't you?" Trevor remarked.

"Damn right I have. If sexual intimacy isn't part of marriage, where God *wants* it to be—after all God prohibits it anywhere else—then where *does* it belong? I'm not a monk in a monastery, guys. I didn't sign up for a celibate life." He wondered if, and how often, wives struggled with the same issue and felt as powerless as he did. Should the day ever come as Kate's lover, he hoped to bring out her best for *her* sake, so she would break free to become more complete—her best self.

Trevor looked down at his plate then up at Dean. "I didn't sign up for celibacy either. But here I am, forty and single. Abstinence is my daily challenge. It goes with being a single Christian, especially clergy. Obeying

God's guidelines in this area is tricky and hasn't always been a bed of roses, let me tell you."

Dean sympathized. "So, where do you go for release?"

"A conversation stopper of the first order," quipped Hal.

They all laughed.

"Probably the same as you," Trevor continued. "A man has to do what a man has to do, alone on his own, if necessary. And not be ashamed about it."

"I'm with you one hundred percent," Dean said. "That's another thing nobody ever talks about. Not in church, that's for sure. When is it ever preached about?"

A quiet pall hung over the booth, and none of them made eye contact.

"Maybe it's some kind of test," ventured Hal. "Some kind of testing of character. Could God be asking you to blindly obey, like Abraham did when he faced the absurdity of sacrificing his son Isaac? Something extraordinary like that?"

Dean shrugged. "It could be, I guess." He looked at Trevor. Trevor looked at him. Their eyes displayed similar tensions. "To remain faithful 'till death do us part' during a long drought, during a famine, is definitely a test alright."

"A test of character and patience over passion," echoed Trevor. "Amen to that."

It was fairly well known that Trevor had come close to getting married some years earlier. Dean asked, "I've always wondered why you never got married, Trev. What's the story on that?"

"Simple, but sad. I loved a beautiful young woman who was raised in the African mission field like I was. The wedding fell through when she told me she couldn't bring herself to leave Africa and come live with me in the United States. I had to decide to stay there or come back here to finish seminary and begin the ministry I believed God was calling me to."

Dean noted how hurt, how adrift, Trevor seemed. He vowed to help him in whatever way he could.

Trevor looked directly at Dean. "So, have you examined your side of this loss-of-sex situation? What you might have done to bring it on?"

"Yes, and yes again. I once heard that men don't have a clue how to get women excited. If that's so, I wish Kate would tell me and not treat it so delicately. Naturally, when our lovemaking dropped to zero, I made some pretty direct comments. I think my frustration came out as hurtful pressure that made matters worse, making her feel guilty or defective. I was sick of walking the tightrope between low libido, hers, and strong libido, mine."

The three of them sat quietly as their waitress refilled their coffee mugs.

"It's important to remember," suggested Hal, "that marriage is like the sacred covenant God makes with His people. As often as we have broken our side of that covenant, God has been constant and faithful in keeping His side of the bargain, never calling it quits on us. Is that how you feel, Dean?"

"Hal the lawyer speaks," said Dean, sardonically. "Well, I haven't called it quits. Yet. But it's getting harder not to every day."

"Marriage is three-way," added Trevor. "Husband, wife, and the invisible, eternal presence of God. Beyond being legal, it's holy, it's moral, and it's carnal."

"I agree with all that," said Dean. "It's just so flipping hard to pull it off in practice. With Kate and me, it's going to take a big miracle."

"God is the miracle maker, Dean," said Trevor. "That's not just a platitude, it's true. He's the source of miracles, and I mean *big* miracles. We tend to only count the miracles recorded in the Bible, like walking on water and the Resurrection."

"Well, it sure is going to take a huge miracle for us to be healed. For our dying marriage to resurrect."

Trevor turned serious, even stern. "Do you really believe what you just said, Dean? Do you really believe that God *is* the God of big miracles—today, for you, for Kate, for anyone in these modern times who has faith?"

"I'm not sure what I believe anymore. I want to believe what you're saying, though."

"Then do it. Stop doubting, and believe." Trevor and Hal each placed hands on Dean's arm. Right then their meals arrived. Like the pleasure of the golf game, the smell of the hot food made Dean happy. "Meanwhile, lads," said Trevor, "I've got a Missions meeting to run in an hour, and I'm famished."

"Look, guys," said Dean, trying to put closure on the discussion. "I'm committed to focusing on the positives, not just on what's missing. Except for this one stubborn issue, which I'm sure Kate thinks I'm making a humongous fuss about, our lives add up to a pretty sound marriage. When it comes to teamwork, travel, parenting, finances, volunteering, household chores—you name it—we're basically in sync. And in love."

Trevor and Dean and Hal looked at one another, sensing a silent new connection, a fresh bond. Dean sensed each man in his own way felt a level of holy intimacy uniting them.

"Let's say a blessing for our meal," said Trevor, bowing his head.

The three men folded their hands …

CHAPTER

11

Tight-lipped and sullen, Kate took notes during the Mission committee's review of its annual goals. It was Saturday afternoon, and Pastor Harrington shared a passage translated from a letter by the pastor of a struggling church in Honduras, where the mission team had served:

> "We were greatly blessed by your visit when you served side-by-side with us, and, despite our wretched poverty, we never felt inferior or ashamed. At first we feared your abundant material resources were all you would bring. But instead, you brought love, and we always felt your deep, personal connection with us."

The Honduran pastor's words caught the group's attention. "Now get this," continued Trevor Harrington. "Here's how he closed."

> "The way Americans have exported their cultural stress to our little corner of the world, however, made us scratch

our heads. As blessed as we were by your gifts of labor, time, and funds, we pray with concerned hearts for God's peace to ease your overly stressed hearts."

"Those words sum up a lot," said Kate to the dozen lay volunteers around the table. "I feel like I'm the stress queen in *my* world."

"That sure says it for my world, too," affirmed Marlene Wilkins, the group's lay volunteer chairperson and a friend of Kate's.

Ginny Ostrow, seated next to Kate, whispered in her ear, "The lesson seems to be, 'We welcome you back with open arms, but please leave your stress at home.'" Ginny was Kate's longtime friend and one of the loveliest people she'd ever met. She and her husband Hal double-dated occasionally with Dean and Kate. They went to movies or out to dinner and enjoyed game nights at one another's homes, especially playing Scrabble. They had served on the Honduran team together as couples on a two-week gospel mission trip.

As the group members responded, Kate only half listened. She felt bothered that she'd neither seen nor heard from Dean since yesterday to discuss their plans for the weekend, and now half of Saturday was over. Although she understood why he avoided committee meetings on his days off, his absence from today's session concerned her.

"We'll have to remain vigilant about curbing the high levels of stress we bring with us," said Trevor. "But, aside from being more aware of our cultural baggage, I found Pastor Morella's comments about our humility encouraging. We know every human being is poor in the sense that each of us is simply incapable of being what God created us to be. So, for me, his comments are a reminder for us to be aware of our mutual brokenness as fellow pilgrims seeking wholeness in this fallen world."

Kate understood why Trevor said *we*, even though he'd spent half his life in Africa where everything moved slower, and time was less of an adversary. Despite his upbringing, Trevor considered himself an American because of the twenty years he'd lived in the United States since arriving for seminary training.

"How many times have we heard it?" asked Ginny. "We should never make the mistake of believing that a lack of material things is at the root of poverty. It is always about broken relationships—mine with you, neighbor with neighbor, ours with the planet, and ours with God."

Several people nodded.

"Unless we set aside our stress when we work with others, the Good News we hope to share may go largely unheard," added Marlene.

"Guilty as charged," Kate piped up again. "No denying it. My stress levels go with me wherever I go, like excess baggage." She noticed Trevor glance at her in an odd way.

To Kate's way of thinking, Trevor embodied the servant heart and sacrificial lifestyle of an apostle. Since his early youth, he'd served Christ's gospel firsthand in Africa. Above everything, he was the role model of an organized leader who exemplified boots-on-the-ground spirituality. His experience in foreign cultures and arsenal of practical travel skills helped teams of volunteers get through airports and border check points smoothly.

"I want to remind everybody," Kate announced, "that Dean's company is the collection site for recycled and reusable medical supplies we collect for Haiti. Just use a tag or a label to designate that donations are for the *Helping Hands, Healing Hearts* program. Feel free to contact him; he's the point person who can answer your questions."

Trevor went on to other topics. His voice dimmed to a hum as Kate's mind drifted. She pondered instead her frazzled life as a homemaker, mother, wife, *and* committed Christian. *So much to juggle.* She wondered if her busyness had led to avoiding her family—they wanted more and not less of her—while she invested her time and personal attention on so many activities. *Am I piling on? I guess I have been.* Was she avoiding intimate moments with her husband by using her service in the church as a cover?

An hour passed, and the committee meeting dismissed. Kate and Ginny chatted while walking out to the parking lot. A nurse by profession and a sincere listener, Ginny impressed Kate as even-tempered, soft-spoken, and a trustworthy confidant.

"You seem bummed out," Ginny said quietly.

Kate sighed, "You can say that again." She hesitated, but the empathetic look in Ginny's Scandinavian-blue eyes encouraged her to speak up.

"I guess I'm feeling pretty inadequate," Kate said. "Even though I'm doing everything right that I can think of, it's not really working."

"What do you mean?"

"I'm exhausted. Even this meeting today felt like overkill. I'm so darned busy, and nobody really appreciates it or cares."

"Sounds depressing. If now is not the best time to get into it, Kate, that's okay."

Kate choked up. "It's really getting to me."

As they approached their cars, Kate longed to let a volcano of words burst out. But could she tell Ginny how much her marriage was hurting? Did she dare verbalize even a hint of it?

"Anytime, anywhere, Kate. I'm there for you."

Kate understood she truly meant it.

"Will you call me?"

Kate actually hungered to call her, realizing how much she needed to be heard. She knew Ginny would be a lifeline. "I don't think either of us has the time right now for a play-by-play."

Ginny looked at her as if with the eyes of an angel. "Anytime, anywhere," she repeated, putting her angel arms around Kate and squeezing tightly.

Kate walked to her SUV, sensing the time was *now* and could not wait. *I'm always putting off important things and settling for silence. I'm sick of making up excuses.* "Hold it, Ginny! I've changed my mind. Are you up for a walk by the lake?"

Ginny nodded, smiling.

Twenty minutes later, they were talking as they walked on a footpath along the shoreline of Lake Minnetonka. "Women need to feel loved to have sex, and men need sex to feel loved," Ginny told Kate. "It's as simple as that."

"Nothing so complicated can be that simple, Ginny."

Kate loved this metro lake, a splendid work of nature's grand design. Although surrounded by stately homes, architect-designed cabins, pleasure boats, and shopping areas, the lake still retained its raw natural beauty. The women were walking under a cloudless sky, warmed by abundant sunshine and enjoying the crisp air. The lake's dark blue water splashed in choppy waves along the shore, and white caps appeared far out on the horizon.

"My main gripes about sex?" Kate said. "One, I hate talking about it. Two, it just doesn't feel pleasurable or fun. Three, it's not that I don't love

Dean or that he doesn't love me." She assumed that, after two days of uneasy detachment, Dean was off pouting somewhere on his own, refusing to say a word, trying to make some kind of statement. Surprisingly, an urgent surge of energy swelled up from deep within her. "Of course I feel loved! In so many ways we have a good marriage."

Ginny listened quietly, waiting for Kate to say more.

"I guess I'm not that gung-ho about being a good lover," Kate admitted. "After our girls were born, Dean and I decided not to have more children, so he agreed to a vasectomy. In my mind at least, that redefined our sex life and made 'doing it' less necessary—and frankly, more of a chore."

"A necessity? A chore? Kate! I've heard that a vasectomy *loosens* the restraints for most couples."

"Back then, Dean wanted us to learn some new sex techniques, even to play with some sex toys, and I just couldn't go along with that. He wanted sex to be an adventure … for both of us. He even said he wanted sex to be sacred—'shared sacred sensuality' is how he put it. That was a dozen years ago. But the more he pushed, the more I backed off. I didn't like feeling pressured. He wanted to liven things up, but anything we tried fell flat, according to him. I didn't like making love when it felt like following a recipe or instructions in a manual."

Ginny gazed out at the wind-whipped waves. "So what would you like it to be now?"

"I would like it to be blissful. I'd like to be blissfully absorbed in exciting waves of intimacy and togetherness, free of conflicts. But that doesn't seem possible. Too many things need to line up for that to happen, and it's sooooooo much work."

"Sex is work? The alternative seems to be resigning yourself to inadequate sex until death do you part. Are you really willing, Kate, for that to be as good as it gets?"

"Sounds depressing, doesn't it? Actually, inadequate sex is more than we have now, which is zero-point-zero."

Ginny put her arm around Kate. "From the articles I've read and the TV health shows, many husbands, and plenty of wives, say they can't go without it for very long."

"It's not a pretty picture, I know. For Dean it's a need. But what scares me is he seems to think this conflict is something I've made happen. Does he think I've created this situation on purpose?"

"He might. What's the stumbling block for you?"

That question stung. She wanted to skip to a new subject. Her modesty felt violated. "Could it have to do with a man's biology? You know, a male's genes? I've seen some science-type articles that say so."

"Maybe," said Ginny. "But if he's sexually energized all the time, wants frequent intercourse, and is doggedly demanding about it, that's another thing altogether."

"That's really not him, thank God. So where does that leave me?"

Ginny absorbed Kate's intensity quietly. "If you feel he loves you, then it should be easy, right? Love him the way God wants every couple to love each other. Simple."

"But it's *not* simple. That's the point. How I wish! But it's *not!*"

Ginny looked annoyed by Kate's forcefulness. "Then where is the blockage, Kate?"

Kate stopped walking. She looked at Ginny, then peered out at the waves which reflected her choppy emotions. "What in God's name is wrong with me?" she muttered aloud. "My head knows what to do, Ginny, but I just can't bring myself to do it. It's so sad."

"You sound like a victim. You're talking in circles, Kate. Listen to what you're saying. Over and over, the same thing. Stop and listen. Talk and make some sense."

"Gosh, Ginny … why are you so irritated all of a sudden?"

"You keep dancing around the edges. Get real."

Kate resumed walking. "You've made your point. And?"

"And you're coming up on fifty, right? This is basic stuff. Is it that you don't care? Or are you a prude?"

"Oh, great! Now I'm a prude. And I don't care. Thanks a lot." In truth, she felt like a prude.

"Kate, listen to me. You've been on the mommy track so long, the good-Christian-wife track so long. Have you lost your bearings? You think of yourself as a fine wife, I'm sure, and a good cook who bakes Dean's favorite pies and cookies. But look how you've bombed out as a lover."

"Are you saying I've deliberately—?"

"Shhhh! Listen. When was the last time you had an orgasm?"

Kate stopped dead in her tracks. "Is this some kind of inquisition?"

"Kate, Kate, Kate. We all know plenty of women have orgasms. And scads who don't."

"Do you, Ginny?"

"Dang right. I have them when I want them. Sometimes explosive ones."

Astounded, Kate tried to hide it. "So you'd say that you and Hal are good lovers?"

"We're good for each other, yes. Very good." Ginny paused. A lake gull soared overhead making a loud cry.

"Look, are you someone who thinks sex is dirty, Kate? It's obvious that certain women do. And because they've been preached to about it, they have trouble feeling pleasure. And the church hasn't helped, except to make people feel sinful and guilty. When it comes to love and sex, the church has dropped the ball." She glanced at Kate, who stared far across the lake. "As for orgasms, sometimes women have them on their own."

Kate sucked in her breath. "Geez, this is getting pretty far afield."

They continued walking.

"Think about it, Ginny. God has so much more to deal with than our little bedroom battles. It just feels like we *should* have sex, *should* make love, should, should, should. Give me a crossword or Sudoku puzzle before bedtime and I'm happier than a clam. All I ask is for a little peace and quiet to unwind the way I want to."

"Okay. Everybody deserves that. But if your relationship with Dean is shipwrecked, then your prioritizing God's big plans will also crash on the rocks."

Kate gathered her thoughts. "You're right. But we *are* called to higher things, aren't we? To a higher purpose? Something more noble than screwing like monkeys? That's what pigs and dogs do."

Ginny scowled. "Are you saying it's basically about lust?"

"We're Christians, Ginny, called to be holy and pure, not to act like hyenas and wild beasts. We're meant to be redeemed humans living on higher ground, holier ground, with our lives showing love and grace and service and sacrifice. That's who we are."

Ginny inhaled deeply. "Okay, maybe it's true we spend too much time on bodily matters and not enough on matters of faith. But wild beasts? Shouldn't humans accept and appreciate the physical gifts God gave us?"

"You sound like Dean. No, that's not where I'm headed. But, it's *my* issue to tackle, I know that. And the clock is ticking."

"I've heard you rave about your fitness lady, Kate. Do you think being gay is your hang-up?"

"*What?!*" Kate whipped around and stared at Ginny.

"The way you talk about her, it seems possible."

"*No!* That's a *crazy* idea!"

"Look, I'm not accusing you in any way. And speaking for myself, the idea of kissing a woman creeps me out. But if that's what's going on, then just say it."

Kate put her hands over her ears. "I would rather shoot myself. That's not what's going on at all!"

"Well then, let's take that one off the table."

Kate stammered and tears welled up in her eyes. "In fact, Ginny, she … Larissa … my fitness instructor … she … well, I just need to tell you. … Dean was … was seeing her on the sly. Thank God he had the moral fiber to stop seeing her before it went too far, but I'm devastated! Not only about Dean, but Larissa was like a sister I never had. I feel so betrayed!" Tears escaped and ran in rivulets down her cheeks.

"Dean? Seeing another woman? Are you *kidding?*" Ginny put her arm around Kate.

"No. I'm not kidding. I'm furious—and ashamed. Plus, I have no idea what to do about it!" She wiped away the tears with the back of her hand.

"You're dealing with a husband who's that frustrated?" Ginny looked at her with compassion.

Kate sighed. "So much of the time I think it's hopeless. He does too. I'm seeing that now, and I hate it, but I don't know what to do. For me, intimacy is more of a concept, more mental. For Dean, it's definitely not. For him, it's 'let's do it, and enjoy it.' The pleasure part scares me, frankly." She twisted her face. "Did I just say that?"

"You did."

"I guess it's true then. I'm afraid. Is that insane or what?"

"What scares you?"

Kate had to think. "It's nothing Dean does or doesn't do, I'd say. Not really. Maybe it goes back to when I was in high school, and what you said about the church condemning sex. I sat in church hearing that, and my mom and my aunt warned me constantly to protect my virginity. I ended up caring more about getting good grades than dating and making out."

"I think what you're talking about is a kind of poverty, a poverty of pleasure created by misguided myths and misconceptions that have trapped you."

Kate let that sink in. "I never had sisters growing up or a bunch of girlfriends. My girl cousins lived far away and were younger. Mom was no help, either. Did you grow up that way? With nobody to talk to about your first period? Or how to show you to put in a tampon?"

"Just the opposite. My girlfriends and I loved kibitzing about that stuff."

"How I wish I'd friends like that—someone to show me how to put my hair up in curlers and enjoy being a girl."

Kate understood that she and Dean were caught in a horrible downward spiral. "I don't think Larissa is at the root of it," she admitted. "It's something else." She chewed the inside of her cheek. "Pleasure of almost any kind feels foreign to me, Ginny." *Perhaps even threatening. That can't be right.*

She wished she could be more like Larissa, free and open about sex. No wonder Dean was attracted to her. "I tend to put off signs of affection from Dean because I'm worried about where they're all heading."

"Kate, pleasure is just the opposite. It's something soothing and comforting, or stimulating and exciting. Being afraid of pleasure is, well, debilitating. Have you thought about seeing a professional?"

Kate grimaced. "We've tried it a few times. You know ... better communication skills and feedback exercises for homework and all that. Pleasure seems fine up to a point for me, but too much of it, especially when it's with our clothes off, feels dangerous, risky. And that's when sex hurts, when I'm uptight."

Ginny frowned. "You're trapped. And Dean is trapped along with you."

"I have to admit he's suffered a lot, sad to say. I can't keep dragging him down, can I? He's already frustrated out of his skull. Can it be reversed? When I hear you talk about explosive orgasms, I go blank. I'm the guilty party. It makes me want to run away screaming."

"I feel for both of you. But can it hurt to see a professional again? What if it does help?"

Kate knew Ginny sensed her pain. Whatever the root of her troubles, nothing useful had ever been identified or resolved whenever she and Dean had seen professional therapists. *Truth is, I never cooperated much in those sessions!*

A flock of Canadian honkers flew across the sky heading south. Kate longed to join them and fly away, far far away. She shook her head skeptically. "I think Dean is looking for more, a whole lot more than therapy can deliver, and a whole lot more than *I* can deliver. How will I ever reach the level he expects?"

"How much do you want to?"

Kate had to ponder that one. The troublesome topic of menopause was something she and Ginny had covered in the past: the symptoms, the coping strategies, even the benefits. She and Ginny were in the same age bracket when it came to early perimenopausal dynamics. Ginny believed in enjoying the "springtime" of the second half of a woman's life. She'd once remarked, "These days, given that millions of women after menopause live another thirty or forty robust years, aging can be more of an opportunity than a liability."

Kate wasn't so sure. But Ginny and Hal had an active love life, and they both appeared satisfied. She feared things with Dean had been deteriorating too long, and that her stock of reliable excuses was running out.

"I wonder if hormonal changes are the root of my troubles, Ginny—if hormonal replacement therapy would help."

"Have you asked your gynecologist about it?"

"I have, but not recently." Often she'd noticed some dryness and tightness. *What* was *that elusive, mysterious something?* Nothing had relieved the awkward pressure she felt to perform in bed. And she still resisted experimenting with the varieties of ways to create arousal and desire, or the "creative" positions described in women's magazines. While she felt certain Dean wanted her to experiment—like a lady of the night, no less—sex had become just another item on her to-do list, and way down the list at that.

"All the fuss about sex makes me question the role of sex in America's cultural DNA," said Kate, "especially the low standards on TV and the Internet. It's intimidating living nowadays when couples want so much more from their relationships as never before, when their expectations seem so unreachable."

"You may have something there, Kate my dear, but this is about you and Dean."

"Back when we were still having sex, around the time Nicole and Lindsay were in grade school, I felt it was my duty to give in to Dean's wishes to 'do it.' I was afraid if I said no, he would feel disappointed and might leave me for some babe with a hot body and higher sex drive." Immediately Larissa came to mind. "When all I ever wanted was to feel … to feel the warm intimacy that brings us closer together, to feel completely special to him."

"Sounds fine to want to feel special. But has your own fear blocked you from feeling special? You need to get clear about that."

"I wasn't sure which he wanted more—me or sex. Maybe he actually wanted me so much I misinterpreted his desire for me as his need for sex."

"Intimacy feels sensual and sustainable and builds togetherness when you open yourself to sex as a way to make *him* feel special, when you want *him* the way he wants you."

Kate's mouth flew open. "Yes! That's it." She thought for a few seconds, considering the possibilities. "But how much do I *want* Dean? It always comes back to that, to my level of desire. I doubt if I can ever match his level, Ginny."

"Sit down and talk to him about it."

Talk to him about it reverberated in Kate's mind.

"You're afraid, aren't you?"

Kate's downcast gaze studied the asphalt path at their feet. Ginny was right, and once more the burden of guilt piled higher and heavier on Kate's shoulders. Guilt for not wanting sex and guilt for her unwillingness to talk with her husband about it. Where was the fear coming from? Why her dread?

"As for Dean's cheating," Kate croaked, "I see how my leaving him high and dry made him vulnerable."

"Way to go. That's a crucial insight," said Ginny. "I think Dean did the noble thing by calling a halt to it. That deserves some credit."

"Yeah, you're right." Her mind turned towards Dean's attraction to Larissa. She envied both of them. The ease they exhibited around expressing their sensuality and enjoyment of pleasure hit home. *No poverty of pleasure for them!*

Ginny squinted from the sun bouncing off the water. "Can we switch to something else for a minute? Hal has sworn he's going to beat you at Scrabble if it kills him. It would be nice to move on to picking a date for our next game night. He wants girls-versus-boys partners. So, how does next Saturday night work for you guys?"

"I'll check and shoot you an email. It's our turn to host."

"Gotcha. So it'll be our turn to bring treats. Sounds like a plan."

Kate saw they were approaching the boat dock where they'd begun their walk. "If I could just find a mentor, someone who knows how to bring out my femininity. Someone I could learn from who's in touch with her erotic side."

"Someone on the Internet? Or in the personal columns? It's interesting also to hear you use the word *erotic*. Hal told me Trevor is reading a book right now by a theologian who writes about sacred sexuality and something called erotic monogamy."

"Who would've ever imagined? Sacred? Erotic? Erotic monogamy?" Kate wondered, Did such a thing exist? And was it possible to find sexuality lessons from an expert?

They arrived back at their cars. Ginny stretched out her arms and hugged Kate, hard and long. "Pray for guidance, Kate. Let's see where this goes. Keep me in the loop, okay?"

Kate hugged her back, immensely grateful. Ginny's flannel jacket brushed against her cheek. A sudden gust of wind pressed them tightly together. Having a friend like Ginny listen and give her the support she needed, even when it had irked her, was a divine gift, and Kate loved her for it. "Thanks for everything, Gin."

Ginny looked at her teary face with sympathetic eyes. "Time to go. I'll pray for you and Dean, and I'll keep praying." She smiled, got in her car, and closed the door.

"Did you happen to get the title of that book?" asked Kate through the open car window.

"Not really. *God and the Erotic* ... or something like that. I'll email it to you."

Kate waved. Ginny waved back then drove away.

In a daze, Kate drove through the familiar manicured suburban neighborhoods, so distracted she missed the turn she usually took to her house. A list of errands crowded her mind. Besides stopping at the cleaners and supermarket, she needed to drive over to St. Paul after stopping off at home. She and Trevor had arranged to meet at Sacred Grounds to work on details for the annual Thanksgiving charity dinner at Spirit Hills. Secretly, she half-expected and hoped Dean might be there chatting with Trevor.

Let it go! she told herself. But while part of her was focused on her necessary errands, another part could not escape her troubles with Dean.

Dean's insistence on sleeping downstairs since their fight bothered her. His return to their bed was dragging on. All couples have their spats now and then, she told herself, even though she knew theirs went beyond that. More than a kiss-and-make-up treaty between them was necessary. It fell on her to bring up the issue.

I have to step up and take responsibility. Seriously. Very seriously.

The autumn temperature was dropping fast, and once she got home, she would have to get a jacket to wear over her lighter-weight woolen shirt. Cooler October weather lurked just around the corner, a reminder to haul out the winter gear. Reaching their street, she turned the SUV into their driveway and shut off the engine. The devotional book she'd been reading during her morning quiet times by Marianne Williamson came to life as the Quote for the Day echoed in her mind:

> *It is our light, not our darkness, that most frightens us. We ask ourselves, Who am I to be brilliant, gorgeous, talented, fabulous? Actually, who are you not to be? You are a child of God. Your playing small does not serve the world.*

Kate got out and walked into the house. *Yes, I guess I've been playing small—certainly in one respect.*

Jester greeted her. The house felt empty. She missed Dean's presence. In the kitchen, she found a note taped to the refrigerator door in Dean's handwriting:

Dearest Kate,
I've decided to stay in a motel for the next few days. . . .

CHAPTER 12

Larissa dodged shoppers hunched over in the cloudy October chill as she walked down Grand Avenue, recalling Cody's reaction to the news about her entanglement with Dean. They'd sat together in the kitchen the next day, talking awkwardly.

"Did you have any idea something was going on between us, Cody?" she had asked, running her hand through her hair.

"Not a clue. None."

"I hope you don't think I'm … I'm … you know, a slut."

"Not a chance, Mom. You're no such thing."

She stood up and began pacing. "Or that he and I went too far. Because we didn't."

"No, Mom. I don't think that either."

A dark frown clouded her face. "Honestly, maybe someday I'll understand it myself, Cody. I hope so." A kinder shift in tone sweetened her voice. "I hope you still think of him as a decent guy." She forced a smile.

"He's always been decent to me, Mom. Always. Though it was a shock. Who knows? Maybe this'll make you both better people in the long run."

"Did you really say that? You're able to see it that way?"

"Mom, take it easy. Stop pacing." Heartened, she'd observed the love in his eyes, brighter than ever. "I'm kinda sad for you, though," he added. "And for Dean."

She stopped pacing. "Really? Can you blame me for finding him attractive?"

"Not at all. And I'm not surprised he saw something special in you, either."

Relieved, she leaned against the cupboard. "Still, I was hoping ... even though I knew in my right mind it could never amount to anything ..." Her voice drifted off. "Oh, Cody, you'll never know how much I've wished you had a dad like him."

"Mom, you're reading my mind!"

They glanced at each other, united in spirit. Larissa sensed her son loved her more at that moment than he'd ever loved her before. Instead of scolding her as expected, he'd opened his arms to her. She stepped toward him, and he hugged her tight. She began weeping on his shoulder, long and cleansing tears.

Now, days later, Larissa headed into the blustery wind, acutely aware of the region's first blast of the long, cold season ahead. In the shivery air, the leaves swirled in a blur around her as her teeth chattered. The hostile weather mirrored the troublesome losses that were dragging down her hopes and dreams.

Kate had quit her workouts, deserting her own fitness goals and Larissa's friendship.

Dean had rejected her affections, leaving her hurt and dissatisfied.

Brad had died an unjust death sacrificing for his country, leaving her unmarried.

Her biological parents had abandoned her, leaving her to fend for herself.

These losses bruised her confidence much the same as the wind-blown leaves buffeted her shivering body. The night before, she had been jolted by another shock. Alarm filled her when she removed her bra before going to bed. The nipple of her left breast had felt tender to the touch, and it oozed a murky fluid that was neither blood nor milk. Doing an immediate self-exam, she discovered more of the strange fluid leaking out. Checking the other breast and finding it was normal, she recalled how her "girls" had nursed Cody until he'd turned ten months. In her mind, she heard Brad exclaim, "You've got all the right curves in all the right places, you sexy broad!" *Those were the days. How I miss him.* But her left breast had kept leaking, which gave her reason to worry. She'd called her doctor that morning and left a voicemail requesting an appointment.

Staggering against the frigid wind on the busy avenue, all that mattered at the moment to her was keeping warm. The harsh wind nearly blew off her cap as she passed by the Sacred Grounds coffee shop. She strode on, heading to her studio, carrying supplies she'd bought at the corner supermarket. On a whim, she stopped, turned around, walked back to the coffee shop, and stepped inside to escape the cold.

The smell of fresh-roasted coffee brightened her outlook. "I'll have a cup of Divine Delight," she said to the barista at the counter. Locating a seat in the crowded shop, she found a comfy booth by the window. She sat down and sipped the cup of steaming hot brew. The cozy warmth in the room calmed her. Outside, the swirling leaves blew against the window. The memory of Dean's first visit to her studio made her smile, now that she realized what a flimsy pretext he'd concocted. *That man!*

The pleasure and the pain of Dean's kisses the night of their rendezvous at Barnes & Noble alternated in her mind. The hope of love she'd ached for remained an empty, barren hole. She was still adjusting to his unforeseen ending of their flirtation and Kate's shocking revelation that he was her husband. The harsh way Cody had discovered their intrigue still bothered her, even though he'd responded supportively once they'd talked about it. Damage control might still be necessary with Cody, even now. She wondered how far his estimation of her character might have actually dropped.

From her purse, she removed one of her favorite feel-good books, **Eat Pray Love.** It always inspired her, and she wanted to relive Elizabeth Gilbert's adventures as an empowered woman. Larissa's own journey toward enlightenment hardly seemed as exciting as Gilbert's. *I certainly haven't traveled like she did, or met the man of my dreams yet. I've tried speaking directly to God like she did, but He's not there for me.*

Larissa opened Gilbert's book and reconnected with the woman she wanted so much to be like, boldly seeking happiness through pleasure (in Italy), through spiritual enlightenment (in India), and through the love of a good man (in Indonesia). Gilbert's quest resulted in both physical love with Felipe and divine love with God. *If it can happen for Gilbert, can it happen for me? Yet, if staying single is my destiny, I'll do my best to make the most of it.*

Her cellphone rang.

She closed her eyes and took deep breaths, rather than answer it. Feeling the warmth of the coffee cup in her hands and the sheer pleasure of being sheltered in the toasty warm room was more important. The phone stopped; then it rang again. Glancing at the caller ID, she answered it. "Hi, Mom. Good to hear your voice. How are things on the farm?"

"Peachy, sweetie," said Gladys Beaumont. "How's everything up there in the big metro?"

"Not so bad. Cody and I are looking forward to Jerry's birthday." Being interrupted felt a bit aggravating, but this was the mother who loved her.

Gladys laughed her high-pitched laugh. "Remember now, it's a surprise. So don't you go letting on, hear?"

"You know I won't, Mom. I'm sneakier than that." Imagining Jerry's wide smile and rascally eyes eased her blues. Visiting the Beaumont clan at their farm 145 miles away on the flat, grassy prairie of southern Minnesota always made for a pleasant trip, a nostalgic and welcome break in her routine. "I hope you've got some good ideas for a present I can get him, Mom."

"Sorry, honey. You know your papa. He never wants anything that fits into a box, a bottle, a bag, or a tube. He only wants you and that grandson of his to visit."

"I remember. Nothing in a box, bottle, bag, or tube."

"He's out feeding the stock right now, up to his knees in manure. So tell me about that boy of yours. Does he like his job? Is he paying his way yet? How are his classes?"

The chit-chat continued for a few minutes. Then, saying her goodbyes, Larissa sent best wishes to everyone, gave her beloved adoptive mother an "airmail kiss," and hung up.

Sunlight peeked through the window as she looked out at the chilly wind blowing oak and maple leaves across the street like over-sized cornflakes. *Winter will mean more overtime hours for Cody filling rush orders for the holidays. Yay!*

Larissa sat back and sipped coffee. *Another day without someone to love. What a struggle my life is.* She "caught" her negative thoughts and made conscious choices to replace them: *I'm thankful for my own home, my "forever family" on the farm, my growing list of clients, and Dean's influence on Cody.* Yes, that man's role in Cody's life seemed more like that of a father, a far cry from her son's jackass football sperm donor.

Wistfully, she imagined sharing her life with a new Mr. Wonderful, wherever he might be. It was easy picturing getting married to a reputable man and moving into a home together, and envisioning having another child. *Before reaching forty, I hope.* Still, if remaining single was her fate …

The coffee shop's door opened and the howling wind blew in. Larissa looked up. Walking inside was a fitness client she recognized—Kate. Larissa turned away and stared through the window, hoping to go unnoticed. She overheard Kate order a latté at the counter. Larissa made sure to hide her face, lifting **Eat Pray Love** higher. She glanced around the crowded room, noting customers working on their laptops and chatting in the homey setting, but she saw no open places to sit.

As Kate paid for her coffee, she scanned the room as if looking for someone. Larissa peeked over the top of her book. When Kate's head turned toward Larissa, her mouth dropped open. Larissa made a tiny wave. Kate lifted her nose in a snide gesture and turned away. Larissa clenched her teeth.

Kate walked through the congested room, keeping her head turned away from Larissa, roaming around but not seeing the person she was apparently looking for, nor finding a place to sit. Finally, she settled on a bench near Larissa, the only space available other than the empty seat in Larissa's booth. A silent standoff developed. Larissa found it rather laughable, actually. She noted the nearby customers immersed in their own endeavors and decided to lob a throwaway line. "Let me guess. I suppose you're thinking I'm fouling the air, right Kate?" She almost added, *me being the "other woman" and all.*

Kate folded her arms, looked away, and sipped her latté. Her attitude came across as, *Keep to your own business and stay out of mine.*

Larissa sat back, in no mood for a fight. It weighed on her how Kate had quit her workouts, both for Kate's sake and her own. Neither woman spoke for a full minute. Kate showed her back to Larissa, rubbed her neck and shoulders, tapped her fingers on the bench, and cleared her throat.

"Please respect my privacy," snapped Kate. "We have nothing to say to each other."

Larissa felt a challenge coming on. "Is that so?" She waved her hand in a welcoming gesture, pointing to the empty seat in her booth. "Care to sit?"

Kate looked down at her lap. A few seconds passed. Slowly, she stood, stepped over with her latté, and still standing, said, "Doesn't it bother you? Knowing you would've been a home-breaker?"

Larissa sat back. "No, because it would've been consensual."

"Oh, *that's* comforting."

Larissa pretended to go back to reading, but she set the book down. Mindful to keep her voice low, she added, "For a second there, I figured you were on a witch hunt. I guess I was right."

Kate hesitated. "If you thought a witch was trying to steal your husband, wouldn't you be, too?" She turned to sat back on the bench.

Larissa frowned. "Well now. I am soooo not going there. But I get where you're coming from, and I'm sorry you've been hurt. I truly am. Like I said, would you care to sit down?"

"In case you're interested," Kate sniffed, "It's gone from bad to worse. Dean has moved out over all this fuss and is camping out at some motel." She turned her back again to Larissa.

"I see. And you blame me, right?"

"You probably knew that already from talking to Dean," Kate said, facing away.

"No. We haven't talked at all."

"I'd like to believe you."

"You can. It's true."

"Tacky and tasteless. That's what it was."

"And frightening to you, I'm sure. Now you blame me, of course." A customer opened the shop's door, allowing a gust of wind inside that made both women shudder.

Kate stared at her. "So tell me: How did he come on to you? Was he the aggressor?"

Larissa lowered her voice to a whisper. "Look, let's not make a scene. Either sit here, or be on your way. This is not exactly polite conversation for either of us. It was never going to be like that, not like you think. It would've been much more than empty sex."

Kate rose and sat down in the booth, dropping her voice. "That makes it worse. I have to know. ... Were you really going to have sex with him?"

"Why don't you just go ahead and whack me and get it over with? That's what you want, isn't it?"

Kate sipped her coffee sloppily, spilling a few drops. "Ooohhh! Can't you see how difficult this is for me?"

Larissa nodded. "For a wife who feels betrayed, having to process this, yes I get that."

Kate stared back at her. "Then was he—or wasn't he—the aggressor?"

"Don't, Kate. Don't do this to yourself."

"How can you expect me to ever trust you again? Or him? I thought you and I were becoming good friends."

"We were. Definitely. And nothing about this has to spoil that." Larissa calmed her breathing. "Trust—trust matters enormously. It's something so delicate. And you have to believe me, I never knew Dean was your husband. Girl Scouts honor. Do you seriously think I would have gone out of my way to hurt you, Kate?"

Kate shifted uncomfortably, squirmed, looked up at the ceiling, sipped her latté. "I'm trying to understand what went on so I *can* trust. I've been racking my brain. Who was the real culprit?"

"There *is* no culprit. Give up that idea."

"Listen and listen good," Kate said, leaning toward her. "Dean cheated on me, regardless of how far it went. You may have seduced him, I don't know. Whatever. But, this *has* damaged my trusting you. And I don't like it."

"Neither do I."

K ate stood up and went to the counter for a refill. She needed space—some distance.

Could she ever be friends with Larissa again? How could she ever forgive her? *But am I being blinded by my freaked-out nerves and anger toward Dean, when it might be me who I'm really angriest at? He wouldn't have wandered if I'd been the lover he needed.* Larissa was Kate's friend after all, and she knew losing Larissa's friendship would only add to the self-inflicted losses she was facing. When the clerk turned to help her, Kate smiled stiffly and walked back to Larissa's booth.

"So many puzzle pieces are missing, don't you see? Would you help me connect the dots so I can understand better? And, I do have to know, … is he really off your radar, or are you still feeling the hots for him?"

"Yes, he is off my radar. No, I'm not. I mean that one hundred percent. I haven't seen him since the night he broke things off. It's over, Kate. Believe it. Can we *please* move on?"

Kate sat in silence.

Larissa reached across the table and gently touched Kate's hands. "You're all in knots, aren't you?" Kate did not pull away. She sensed Larissa saw her anguish. "This is about more than sex or adultery or romance. I think it's got something to do with the way you feel about yourself, Kate."

"Does it show? Is it so obvious?" She looked directly at Larissa. "I'm so unlike other women. I'm ashamed, embarrassed. I'm so unsexy, it drives me crazy. I hate thinking that something is lacking in our marriage."

"That's saying it honestly."

Kate spoke softly. "You, Larissa, are the sexiest woman I know."

Larissa rolled her eyes. "Well, uh, that's very kind of you, but I'm not sure—"

"You are. Don't deny it."

"Uh, and where are you headed with that?"

"It's more than the fitness classes and the yoga and the Zumba. You have something more. It shows in everything about you, in the way you see yourself, in the way you treat your body, in so many ways."

"Whatever you say. I guess I'm flattered."

"It's not flattery. It's the God's honest truth. You have something few women have."

Kate gazed out the window at the blowing leaves and fast-moving clouds.

"Would … would you help me?" Kate continued. "Would you show me how to be sexy? How to be the kind of woman you are?"

"*Me?* The kind of woman *I* am?" Larissa sat up straighter.

"I want to have what you have. Do you think you could show me how you learned to feel pleasure, to enjoy yourself, to relax, to like your body, to want sex?"

Kate could tell Larissa had never heard anything like this, that her idea seemed quirky—yet intriguing. It also pleased her they were talking like sisters.

"So are we friends again, Kate? Can I go so far as to say that?"

Kate ventured a slight smile. "I hate being enemies, even though I'm still pissed. But I suppose it's time to see past my anger and let it go."

Larissa glanced at the coffee in her coffee cup. "That's a relief. I'll never forget the way you pitched in to help me with those overnight floral arrangements for Target. What a great night that was! And maybe—who knows—we might be even better friends from now on. I hope so."

"Me too," Kate sighed. A moment passed. "Then how do we start? Where do we begin?"

"You're really serious?"

"Totally."

"Okay, well then, let's give it a try."

"Great! Thank you, thank you." Kate squeezed Larissa's hands.

Kate's phone signaled a new call. Larissa saw her glance at the caller. Kate answered. "Hi, there, Trevor. … Oh? No problem. I've been waiting here for you, but I've run into a friend. If you need more time, connecting in a couple of hours should still work fine. She and I have something to do anyway. … Where? Okay. I'll see you then. Bye." She clicked off the phone and looked back at Larissa.

Larissa swallowed more of her coffee and picked up the supermarket bag. "I've got these supplies to take to Fitness and Flowers. If you're interested, we could head over there right now and get started on your crazy idea. Let's see where all this takes us."

"Perfect! Let's go!"

CHAPTER 13

itting alone in Room 253 of the SleepWell Inn brought a fresh change of pace for Dean: time to think, new scenery, the luxury to take a long nap or hot bath, the freedom to ponder new possibilities and choices. He leaned back in the motel's standard-issue recliner with his feet propped up leisurely on the queen-sized bed. Reclining in this manner reminded him of the old days when he'd traveled on the road for week-long sales stints. The cheesy prairie landscape picture over the bed and the draperies with gold polka dots soothed his nerves.

He opened his journal and turned to that morning's comments:

Of course there's so much more to life than sex. I know this. And I realize that enlightened lovemaking is not the be all and end all. But I wonder. Nobody ever coached me on the finer points of lovemaking, of pleasing a woman. I suppose it's the same for hordes of men. What part of the missing spark for Kate is my own doing?

A pile of human sexuality books from the library and half-price bookstore lay spread out before Dean on the table. His research into healthy and dysfunctional human sexuality fueled his determination to investigate areas of improvement he could make. *How have I failed Kate romantically and sexually? How can I love Kate more without conditions or pressure?*

A male author in the Tantric tradition made the claim that "**. . . for centuries men have grown up essentially ignorant and grossly unaware of women's erogenous preferences and desires, lacking the basic techniques to elicit arousal. Often the onus has rested on women's shoulders for unsatisfying lovemaking, rather than on her male partner's missing technique and low threshold for patience.**" Dean read on about the delicate finger pressure an informed man could apply to a woman's genitals to satisfy her during a laid-back massage.

He reflected on times in the past when he could have used such a technique with Kate but hadn't. He'd feared she would flatly object. His ability to get an erection and his confidence to maintain it for twenty to thirty minutes were not troublesome issues. *But as valuable as a new technique may be, it does not seem to be the root of our problem, or the solution to it.*

He went over his ground rules for taking a few days off from the pressures at home: Work regular hours at the office, continue paying household bills, stay available to Kate and the girls, and pray, pray, pray. His note on the refrigerator had included these words:

. . . This timeout does not mean the worst, so don't take it that way. Please understand this is a mini-sabbatical meant to be valuable for both of us. I will stay faithful, not seeking or dating any woman or playing around, especially not making any contact with Larissa. I am doing this for us. Please believe me. I love you, Katie. Dean

A voicemail from Kate earlier in the week echoed in his mind: "You shouldn't have moved out without telling me. You didn't even give me a chance to discuss it. What a cheap trick!"

He had no reason to defend himself. His choice to step back was the first unilateral decision he'd made in twenty-four years, and he did not feel the necessity to apologize. *I want my actions to speak loudly, and this is a way to up the stakes.* Negotiating with an unwilling, tight-lipped spouse no longer was an option. The stronger the message his actions sent, the more she would have to weigh the consequences of inaction. The freedom of solitude he felt in the motel's recliner felt liberating; he had peace and quiet to reflect and rest.

Dean picked up a book by a female sexologist who'd identified certain trouble areas of a woman's sexual anxiety: arousal, impaired pleasure, and orgasm. In a study of nearly 2,000 women, the clinician cited that one-sixth of the participants affirmed the most common factor related to low desire was ongoing distress in their close relationships. *Okay, so why doesn't Kate tell me* what *is distressing her? I feel "ongoing distress" acutely myself!* He laughed to himself at the next thought that popped into his head: *Post-Romantic Stress Disorder.*

As he saw it, Kate viewed their predicament as a problem to ignore, while he viewed it as a mystery to solve. Like two weary boxers slugging away in a boxing ring, they were in a tit-for-tat downward spiral of negative actions and reactions.

He opened another book, an ob/gyn reference manual that referred to *vaginismus,* the subconscious fear of vaginal penetration resulting in pain. He wondered if this was another clue to the problem; was it a condition with a treatable diagnosis? A flicker of hope zipped through him. *What if Kate agreed to seek meaningful help?*

He picked up his phone, dialed Mitch in Chicago, chit-chatted for a few seconds, and said, "Overall, Mitch, Kate is basically saying, 'I expect you to be monogamous, but don't expect me to meet your sexual needs.'"

"Here we go again, Deaner. So why are you trying to be the nice guy all the time? She's giving you the shaft. Don't just stand there and take it."

"Right now I'm holding out for a *both/and* resolution that blames neither of us, not an *either/or* shame-based ultimatum."

"So you say. But why *do* you tolerate her crap? You're incredibly soft on her. Do the simple thing—get out and move on."

"Always the peacemaker, Mitch, that's me. But the bigger issue is, I still love that woman."

"Yeah, and so where does it get you? It's the same old song and dance you perfected as a kid. You would never get mad at Mom and Dad when they mistreated you, either. Why don't you just let your anger out?"

"Anger is a lousy aphrodisiac. Besides, Kate isn't a fighter like you. She's withdrawn and quiet, and anger would just turn her away even more."

"Deaner, stop procrastinating. Act on your feelings for once."

"Easy for you to say. For now, I've promised myself to stop coaxing, pleading, suggesting, insisting."

"You've caved in. Why do you think I divorced Denise? The pain, man, the pain. Somebody had to go first. I bit the bullet."

"But I want the outcome to be right for both of us. Badgering Kate and constantly seeing her as the problem … well, that's not getting either of us anywhere."

"*Your* energy without *her* energy will never solve the puzzle. So where *is* her energy? Why isn't she living up to her vows? Like I said, get out while you can. If you don't, then forget running to me for sympathy."

"What if there's a solution that's not centered in the bedroom, Mitch? Companies like MediMax go through reorganizations all the time, so why not marriages?"

"Lame analogy."

"If I am the loving husband I should be, then I should be caring about her as a total person, and focusing on the ninety-five percent of life we share that's nonsexual."

"Call me the day you make up your mind. Don't forget it's a two-way street."

Dean mumbled his thanks for Mitch's candor as they hung up, but he smarted from Mitch's advice. He glanced at the books on the table, then reached for his laptop and searched "sexless marriages." The dozens of listings floored him. One listing contained a forum of 42,568 members. Posts by sex-starved spouses, male and female, told wrenching accounts resembling his own:

> **Most people expect they will have sex when they get married, and when they don't, it's like they've been deceived. Sex is what makes a marriage a marriage and not**

just another friendship. When I've tried talking to my wife about it, she walks out of the room or turns her back on me. I love her, but I feel my marriage is not going to survive. I am scared. I am struggling with the temptation to leave. You can't dance a duet with a partner who won't dance!

Another website displayed a post from a wife, which read:

I have been married for 26 years to a kind man and a very good father. Sadly over the years, I've discovered he has an extremely low sex drive and refuses to talk about it or seek help of any kind. I have tried for years to change things, but it always stays the same. I would love to hear from anybody in a similar marriage, especially how you have coped. We have not had sex since my youngest was born, and she is turning fourteen in November.

So there are women who feel like I do.

Her anguish and her plight touched him deeply. Opening another blog, he was astounded by the sheer number of people posting their heartaches in public.

BUZZ! The hotel's phone on the bedside table rang.

BUZZ! The phone jarred him again. *I'm not answering it.*

BUZZ! The red light on the phone blinked. *Go away! Not now!*

Once more the phone jarred him, then finally stopped buzzing. He inhaled and exhaled.

Dean's cellphone began ringing. *Shit! Must be Kate. Forget it.*

He sat back, sagging against the chair, letting the phone ring. He was among a huge pool of people hurting like he was, tens of thousands like him out there corresponding coast to coast. As the cellphone kept ringing, he viewed a reply to *Frazzled*, one of 142 comments.

I've often heard it told that sex is not everything... until! Until it disappears in your marriage and becomes a problem. Then it becomes extremely important. No matter how much you love each other, something has to change or there won't be anything left to change.

The cellphone stopped. Dean stopped reading. The similarity of the bloggers' anguish made him pause. *I am not alone. Others are out there. Men and women. Someone must have an answer!*

A knock on the door interrupted him. His brain swirled.

"Who is it?"

"It's me, Dean," came a man's voice through the door. "Open up!"

Dean walked slowly to the door. "Who's there?"

"Open up and see."

Opening the door a crack, he blinked. "Trevor!"

"Hey, Dean. What took you so long? No, don't bother. C'mon, let's go for a ride."

"A ride? Where? What's going on?"

"I'm kidnapping you for your own good. And I need a favor. You're perfect for it."

"Where? Where did you say we're going?"

"I'll tell you while we're driving. We're headed somewhere special. Hey, guy, are you deaf? I've been in the lobby on the phone trying to get you."

Flummoxed, Dean decided resistance was futile. He grabbed his jacket and wallet, and followed Trevor outside to his car.

"So, Trev, have you come to talk me out of doing this motel thing?"

"Nope. Everything you're up to works for me."

Dean looked at him pointedly. "What then?"

"Like I said, let's enjoy a little ride."

As they got in the car, Dean explained that he was still working regular hours, continuing to pay household bills, and keeping up his end of things. Trevor quietly started his MG and they drove along streets covered in fallen leaves. Mentally, Dean kept searching his imagination, wondering what was up.

"So, Trevor, this secret mission is about what exactly?"

L arissa sat cross-legged on the floor next to Kate on the circular rug in her studio.

"My first goal?" Kate paused. "Let's see … to feel sexier. For Dean's sake as much as my own. Oh, and I want help with more outward things like sexier ways to wear makeup and how to do my hair and nails, and help shopping for new clothes and shoes. Basically, to feel more self-confident."

"Excellent." Larissa felt pride in Kate's assertiveness. She reached for a match and lit a candle.

"Before we get too far," said Kate, "let me ask. When you have sex, Larissa, do you enjoy it?"

"Making love? Yes. Very much."

"Often? Every time?"

"I don't know of anybody who enjoys it every time. But, yes, sex often feels great."

Kate looked away.

"Umm … so how would you rate your sexual IQ, Kate?"

"Ugh. Close to zero. I definitely need to learn some new attitudes. And I have some old baggage that keeps me stuck, I think."

"Sounds appropriate."

"Dean deserves better, too. We've lost our intimacy. And it's time I started doing my part of the heavy lifting. We need quality intimacy."

"Let's not call it lifting. Maybe 'letting go' is more like it."

"Sounds good to me." Kate smiled a tiny smile.

Larissa appreciated how Kate wanted to love Dean more, because he deserved it.

"I'm tired of playing small," Kate said. "I want my light to shine. Just because I grew up stuck in the Dark Ages doesn't mean I have to stay stuck there forever."

"That's the idea. Straighten your shoulders, Kate. Take a deep breath, then exhale slowly and say your intention aloud."

Kate breathed deeply. "I'm a child of God, which means I'm meant to be gorgeous and beautiful. It's my birthright. It's time I stopped hiding my light under a bushel."

Larissa clapped her hands. "Super! Here's a suggestion for you; start attending BONFIRE and join our sisterhood."

The "I'm-a-child-of-God" part pricked Larissa a bit. She'd seen the religious posters and art at Sacred Grounds and heard the gospel-based music there, and she knew how strongly Kate and Dean were invested in their faith. Accepting this as part of Kate's belief system was essential for Larissa to provide effective guidance for Kate, and she didn't want to spoil Kate's enthusiasm with her own skepticism.

"So let me ask, does Dean have a hint that you've decided to do this experiment?"

"No, not at all. I've really only just decided myself."

Larissa felt she was in a reality warp. Here she was, the third part of a crazy new triangle. The same three people, but every role was flipped around now.

Kate looked intently at her, waiting. "My hope is that my actions will speak for me."

"I like your honesty." Larissa felt powerfully moved by Kate's confiding at such a vulnerable level.

Kate's gratitude radiated. Her shoulders relaxed for the first time since she'd sat down on the floor and closed her eyes. Larissa touched her arm. "You realize, I'm sure, that you need to put every ounce of effort into changing those stale attitudes in order to succeed. And change may come slowly from your inner being, but it will come."

"Right. I need to be patient. I think one of the things holding me back is—what's the word?—okay, the stigma. I've always felt a stigma around sex. Any sex. All sex."

"Stigma. That's a biggie."

"It's not that I don't know the anatomy or the functions. I took health class like everybody else, but beyond that I go numb."

"Numb. Okay, let's talk about your own anatomy. What kind of numbness?"

"That's just it. I don't like talking about it. It makes me jittery."

"Well, we're here to do this work. When you pleasure yourself, what happens?"

Kate went silent, staring at the rug in front of her.

"You do masturbate, don't you?"

More silence. "Every so often." Kate paused. "Actually, not really."

"Why not?"

"It's dirty."

"My dear, we *do* have some work to do. What happens when you touch your clitoris? Does it feel good?"

Kate's cellphone rang. She reached for it automatically. It seemed obvious to Larissa that Kate welcomed the interruption as she grabbed the phone.

"Hey, Trevor, what's up? Uh-huh. Oh? You haven't?" Kate nodded, listening. "No, I'm busy with something else right now, but I can still meet you. Fine. Where?" Kate shook her head a couple more times. "Alright, I can get there in about twenty minutes. I'll look for you by the door. Sounds good. See you then."

Kate hung up. "Sorry about that. Larissa. I was going to meet someone earlier to discuss the floral plans for our upcoming Thanksgiving charity banquet, but he got held up in a meeting. I should run so I can scout out a few things at the florist's before I meet him." She reached for her purse.

Unexpectedly, a bright idea flashed in her eyes.

"Say, you know, we could use *your* help on this project, Larissa. I think it would be great for you to tag along. Why don't you ride with me?" Larissa felt Kate grab her arm.

"Uh, well, we still have more to discuss, and after that—"

"What a great idea! Yes, come with! It's perfect. Hurry, Larissa."

"Now?"

"Yes. Ooohh, boy. Are you gonna love this!"

"Love what?"

"A big new floral project that's perfect for you. Let's hurry."

"Where?"

"We have no time to waste. And this could really boost your business. I'm so happy for you. Let's split!"

Dean sat quietly in Trevor's MGB GT as they drove, still waiting to hear where Trevor was taking him.

"What I love about this baby is how great it handles on snow and ice," Trevor prattled on. "I still am able to find plenty of parts, and a mechanic friend of mine knows a slew of tricks about servicing it. I even do a few things under the hood myself."

"So where did you say we're going?"

"Great mileage, too, both city and highway."

Dean couldn't blame him for liking the vehicle. Impeccable inside and out, it broadcasted the owner's uniqueness to everyone. "You mentioned we're going somewhere special. That I was doing you a favor?"

"Another thing I like is the GT's capacity to travel long distances over the road, Deano. I love how solidly and securely it handles."

Dean gave up. He practiced an AA discipline he'd learned, letting go of attachment to outcomes. Having a fixed idea of an outcome often meant being disappointed, rather than remaining open and ready for the unexpected. He leaned back in the leather seat, allowing the comfortable ride to settle his curiosity. Another AA principle he practiced was that of acceptance: "Acceptance is the answer to *all* my problems today," said a passage in the Big Book. Accepting his alcoholism had been a crucial step in his staying sober and reaping the benefits of emotional calm and harmony. *Heck, I could apply this same principle to my marriage too. Let go of my anger and resentment and accept things exactly as they are.*

"You know, Dean, I've got to admit I've been envious of you and Kate at times. Until we talked at breakfast with Hal, I'd always thought you two were happy together."

"So we fooled you, huh?" Dean grunted. *"Looked* happy together is more like it. I've come up with a name for our keeping up appearances. I call it the Happy Couple Game."

"Well, you're both pretty good at it. So is your happiness all for show?"

"Quite a bit, yes. As a new husband, I learned early on from Kate's parents, who set the bar high as experts. They were all about looking good but fooling everybody."

"So you've been playing the Happy Couple Game since getting married? That long?"

"No, but in the last ten years or so, yes. It's insidious. It just crept in on its own—but don't we all wear masks? After the girls started middle school, it became clear that Kate and I were living more as roommates, like a brother and sister, and putting on happy faces in public."

Trevor's eyes left the road and he looked at Dean with sympathy. "Now there's something I happen to know about firsthand. Being single at my age is sort of a happy game of its own, and I sometimes play a kind of Happy Single Guy Game."

Dean paused. "Not having that one ultimate person in your life is a killer, huh?"

Trevor was silent.

"You should try being married and lonely at the same time then. Even with that one ultimate person as a spouse, marriage doesn't automatically solve everything."

Trevor glanced out the window. "I've questioned God quite a few times, whether His will for me is to stay single. In some ways I live like a monk. Maybe it's a calling I'm supposed to embrace, like the Apostle Paul did. Sometimes I wonder."

"So why *are* you single? A guy like you—women should be fawning all over you."

"Excellent question. You might say that when my plans to marry Stella in Africa after I finished seminary fell apart, it did me in. I thought Stella was 'the one.' God must have thought differently. Ever since then, 'the one' for me has never come along."

"Sad. I feel for you."

"Stella struggled with her decision to come back with me when I returned to Kenya to get married, but she finally decided her life was there, not here. That's when she called off the wedding."

"It must've hurt horribly."

Trevor nodded. "I've gradually come to accept it, difficult as it was. For some reason, no matter how much she and I loved each other, it just wasn't meant to be."

Dean sat quietly. He reached over and put his hand on Trevor's shoulder.

"Believe me," continued Trevor, "about my still being single, a lot has to do with the Apostle Paul. He stayed unmarried all his life, and look how much he did for the gospel. He even said that unmarried men can spend more time concerned about the affairs of the Lord, and 'he who refrains from marriage does better than he who marries.'"

"I've read the same thing. Tough message. Celibacy involves more than its share of sexual challenges, I'm sure."

"Let's just say God's highest purpose for sex is marriage. Outside of matrimony, it's a whole other bag. Very restrictive. In my case, it's probably the biggest issue I deal with. Although I'm not gay, I still have to work at not being viewed as gay."

Dean noted his angst. "It would've been okay for you to say you were gay, if you really were."

"Never have had homosexual feelings. But I can sense when certain people see me as gay. What else are people to think? I'm a single guy who's turned forty without a mate."

Dean listened without jumping in to fill the silence. The strong wind outside shook the windows, signaling colder temperatures. "So does that make you a modern-day Paul?"

"If the right woman ever came along, no. Believe me, I'm still waiting." Trevor cleared his throat. "I've always dreamed of getting married and having kids. Being a father is my secret dream. That would be over-the-top wonderful." Pointing to the brown scars on his neck and jaw, Trevor asked, "Tell me, do you think these burn marks prevent eligible ladies from showing interest?"

"Maybe. Maybe not. I don't think the right woman would be put off."

"They've made me doubt myself many times. Are you sure? Be honest."

Dean shrugged. "It could make some women shy away, I suppose." Dean wanted to say something positive but words didn't come. He didn't want to spout some glib cliché like, 'Trust God, and be patient.' As a discerning believer, he understood that being too quick to chirp the party line could be hurtful.

"One more challenge I've faced being single, Dean, is how to express a healthy sex drive appropriately. Sexual purity outside marriage has been tough. I think believers who see themselves made in God's image are to be as passionate as God himself is. The bad news? Healthy sexuality for all people has been frowned on as sinful by the church for centuries."

"You get my sympathy. Isn't that the premise of the book you mentioned, Trev?"

"Basically, yes. The author quotes scriptural passages that turn everything we've been told about sex on its head."

"So where does that leave you?"

"High and dry. One does one's best."

At the next freeway exit, Trevor turned on the frontage road and drove a couple more blocks. He braked at a neighborhood church and parked in the rear of the traditional brick edifice with Gothic-style windows and a tall bell tower.

"Is this the 'someplace special', Trev?"

"Come with me and see."

They walked inside and located a side room where Dean noticed a half dozen men sitting on metal folding chairs in a circle. Trevor greeted everyone, then pointed out two empty chairs where Dean and he could sit.

"Guys, this is my pal Dean." A chorus of hellos and how-are-yas greeted him. "Dean, this is the husbands' group I told you about." Their ages appeared to range from mid-thirties to late sixties, and each guy in the diverse group was welcoming and friendly.

A husky, well groomed man in his fifties named Mel said, "We once called ourselves the Sex-Starved Husbands Sub-Committee."

Laughter.

Trevor, although single, had a standing invitation to attend as a pastoral counselor. Similar to AA meetings and its guidelines, Dean learned everyone's identity was to remain anonymous and everything said confidential.

"What do you call yourselves now?" asked Dean.

"Loving Husbands Living Christ-like Marriages."

Dean wondered if he liked the first one better.

An accountant-type man, lean and lanky in his forties, stretched out his right hand. "Name's Colton. Nice to meet ya, Dean. Welcome."

Dean shook hands. Others in the circle spoke their names: "Kevin … Terrell … Emilio … Scott … Ralph."

Ralph spoke next. "Let me make clear that all of us aren't Christians. Guys like me. But seeing as I'm Mel's business partner, and stuck like he is, I come here because we all have the same goal—a better love-life with our wives."

"And that means no hookers, no extramarital affairs, no crazy acting out," chimed Scott.

Each man's marriage, Dean discovered, was chronically sexless. "Most of us can only guess why," said Kevin. "But we try to leave it up to God for things to work out."

"So, what brings you here, Dean?" asked Terrell.

"Well, I'm in the same fix as you guys. Basically, I want my marriage to live up to its fullest potential, and it's in the doldrums right now."

The men voiced their understanding and approval.

Terrell, an African American, continued: "My gripe is, we're in spiritually difficult marriages unfairly because God has stringent rules. His demands require us is to stay faithful to our wives. Period. But I sometimes feel branded as a pervert in her mind because she thinks I'm oversexed. She can't fathom why porn attracts me. But she doesn't put out. The pisser is, she expects me to not sneak looks at other women, so I'm always in a squeeze, and I hate it. No matter what, she expects me to be loyal."

The guys nodded.

"Porn is so hard to avoid," complained Scott. "I battle temptation and fight off cravings every day. Even last night I caved in against my promises not to. So, yeah, I'm the first to admit I'm struggling with sexy women exposing their hot bodies. It drives me batty."

Mel, who seemed like the unofficial leader, spoke up. "I'm freaked out over my failure to live holy and pure. Helen says it's my problem, not ours. We've tried watching some church videos that are supposed to unlock communication channels, but all it's done is lead to more misunderstandings."

Scott asked, "Does marriage automatically kill desire? Does it have to?"

Kevin said, "I think we all get Scott's point. Our wives should be upholding their vows to love and cherish us, just as we want to love and cherish them. A little variety and adventure between the sheets wouldn't hurt, but we get nothing."

Nods from Dean and several guys.

"In other cultures," said Trevor, "particularly in biblical times, men frequented brothels and had sex with concubines. King Solomon had 700 wives and 300 concubines."

Amazed at such a number, Dean glanced at the other men reacting as he was. He noted that Colton sensed the downbeat level of conversation.

"Let's pray right now, guys." Colton bowed his head. "Dear Lord, it's tough for us to understand Your will. We know You want us to be faithful in all circumstances, to be committed husbands and fathers *and* lovers. But where's the fairness? Is the problem marriage, or is it because Christianity gives our wives an out?"

Several amens followed.

Kevin sighed. "It seems there's an unspoken assumption in many circles that women are naturally passionless and passive. We men, meanwhile, have to work at taming our unruly, pagan desires. Does it really have to be that way?"

Dean was feeling his own sense of grievance. "I wonder if trying to be 'Christian Super-Moms or Wonder Women' is what kills libidos."

"When my wife and I were dating," Emilio responded, "she was all free and fun. But a couple of years after the wedding, she turned blasé and disinterested. What's up with that?"

Mel asked Trevor, "Any theological viewpoints to share?"

Trevor shifted in his chair. "Well, St. Augustine's hostility toward sexuality was well intentioned but it has done a lot of harm. He viewed sex as a necessary evil in order to have children. That's it. Augustine praised the celibate life of a monk as man's highest calling. And his claim that the flesh is wicked and the spirit is holy—and the two are forever incompatible—has persisted for hundreds of years."

"What about the Apostle Paul?" asked Ralph.

"Paul preached that the desires of the flesh are wrong and sinful too. He argued that sensuality and spirituality were at war against each other.

Throughout the ages, theologians have postulated that bodily pleasure and spirituality can't mix."

"But," cried Colton, "there have to be valid ways of integrating the two. I am *both* all the time every day. Can't these scripture passages be read differently?"

"There are many examples," said Trevor, "and I believe Protestant reformers like Martin Luther say so. He believed that 'sex was medicine for the soul,' and that sex was as important to life as eating and drinking, in addition to having children. Some theologians today claim we no longer need to be alienated from our erotic selves, that sex, love, and beauty are all God-given, all sacred."

Dean loved hearing all this. The exchange of ideas and perspectives made him wonder about women's feelings. "Shouldn't our wives be in groups like this talking about these issues, too? There must be wives who are struggling the way we are. Men can't be the only ones. I just read a blog by a woman who is struggling like we are. You know, guys, there are thousands out there in cyberspace, a whole world of people in our shoes, and I mean tens of thousands. We're not alone. Check it out."

"Maybe it's women's hormones," Terrell said. "Don't estrogen levels decrease over time?"

"They do," Colton replied. "And we guys are testosterone-driven. Maybe that's part of the puzzle."

"Well, as much as it bugs me," said Kevin, "I'm going to try and keep from thinking we've got it right and the women have got it wrong. There has to be a happy middle ground somewhere."

Dean chimed in, "I know at least one woman who likes sex. She's not like the women we're yapping about. Others like her must be out there."

"Is she married?" Terrell asked.

"No, come to think of it."

All laughed.

"Is she a Christian?" Colton asked.

"No, not that either."

"Well, there you go."

All laughed.

Kevin grumbled, "Hold it. What if becoming mothers is what does it?"

Mel raised his voice. "Hey, guys. Listen to this." He opened a psychology book about marriage and read aloud from a dog-eared page: "'So you want a better sex life and more intimacy? The key is to be more compassionate and less critical, to respond with more awareness to your partner's vulnerability which is often hidden under the protective armor of distractions and busyness. Try applying the principle of *purposeful emotional agreeability*.'"

"Sounds way out there," grumbled Scott. "What's emotional agreeability?"

"There's more. 'When you decide to purposefully agree emotionally with her, healing occurs in your relationship. You may disagree about any number of things, but as long as you believe she is special and act with purposeful emotional agreeability, she will feel treasured.'"

Several men murmured. Dean thought such an approach held out a glimmer of hope for a nonsexual approach to their impasse, from his obsessing about sexuality to a new possible freedom. He would try practicing this principle. *I need to quit complaining and live the other 95 percent of life. The idea of a non-bedroom approach may work. But does it mean giving up sex altogether?*

Dean looked at Trevor, thankful he'd brought him to this group. "Hey, guys, I would like to drop in again," Dean said as they disbanded. The men responded with encouraging words and gestures. Deep inside himself Dean sensed another awakening: Could the answer to "the mystery" be found in satisfaction with God Himself, in no longer seeking happiness from any human source, including Kate, but solely from God's presence and promises?

Back in Trevor's MG after the meeting, Dean sank into the leather seat, feeling refreshed. "Those guys were awesome, Trevor." A new context now framed his struggle.

"My gift to you, Deano. My gift of hope for you."

"I'll say!" Dean took a long, satisfying breath. "I feel less like the Lone Ranger. I don't mean to sound cynical, but maybe there's no such thing as hot sex in a long-term marriage."

"Maybe. Maybe not. At least you have some pals now to debate that with."

"Yes, thanks to you." Dean shook his head in amazement. "Well, thanks for kidnapping me today. I'm going back there for sure." He slapped Trevor's shoulder.

Trevor drove another few blocks then looked over at Dean with a slight squint. "If you don't mind, I'd like to ask you something. I value your opinion, Dean."

"Sure. Shoot."

"How do you see our ministries doing at Spirit Hills? I wonder sometimes what people really think."

"I'd say they're doing great. Are you worried about something?"

"Well, I'm wondering: Is the congregation a little too comfortable? I mean, where's the sacrifice? Do you see anyone really sacrificing to build the Kingdom? You know how our Lord suffered. Can you think of anyone *suffering* at Spirit Hills to share the gospel?"

Dean paused. "Not when you put it that way. No."

"There. That's my point."

"What's on your mind?"

"It gets to me. I've never seen more abundance than here in the U.S., especially in churches like Spirit Hills. Nothing compared to Africa's poverty. I think it's culturally difficult for Americans to set aside their comforts and live as risk-taking, sacrificing Christians. At least by biblical standards."

"I'd say you have a good point there."

"It's something I've been mulling over a while. Ministry has been my path in life. It was my father's path. Lately, I've been bouncing around the idea of striking out on my own, of doing something wild and daring like Jesus himself did. Maybe going into business or starting a nonprofit."

What Trevor was saying sounded intriguing. "Well, I'll be your sounding board, Trev. I'm interested, wherever these ideas take you."

"Something really bold, Dean. I just don't have a specific idea yet what it might be."

"It'll come to you. Give it time."

As they talked, Dean realized anew how talented, adventurous, and genuine he was. If anybody could pull off the things he was talking about,

Trevor could. "By the way," said Dean, "are you ever going to tell me about that favor you want me to do for you?"

"Yes. In fact this is good timing."

"So ... ? I'm waiting." Right then, Dean recognized a familiar street, River Bluff Drive. Instantly, it became obvious where they were headed. "Hold on. So we're headed to church? Do you mind telling me *now* what the big favor is?"

Trevor came clean. "Okay. Our outreach committee is hosting the upcoming All Souls Thanksgiving Dinner. I'm the event chair, and there's a ton of stuff to finalize before 450 hungry guests show up on our doorstep. I could really use your help."

"What kind of help?"

"You've been an emcee at crowd events before. Would you take that off my plate?"

Dean hesitated. "I get it. Taking me to that great men's group was a bribe. Ha!" He punched Trevor's arm good-naturedly. Trevor punched back.

"Right. Your helping me will let me stay focused on food prep and organizing the horde of volunteer servers. So, was the 'bribe' worth it?"

"Absolutely. Okay, it's a deal. I'll be glad to."

Seconds later, Trevor's MG pulled into the Spirit Hills parking lot. A shock wave appeared to destabilize Trevor. Something he saw through the windshield immediately riveted his attention. Dean glanced outside where he was looking and saw two familiar women walking toward the main entrance.

"Wow, who's that with Kate?" Trevor asked.

Dean gulped. He saw Kate and Larissa walking together. How could that be? "Uh ... her name is Larissa. I've no clue what she's doing here, though. Kate either. So do you know what's going on?"

"Sort of. Kate hinted she was bringing somebody along, so we agreed to meet here." Entranced, Trevor continued, "I asked Kate to help with the floral centerpieces and the decorations we'll need for the dinner. ... Who did you say she was again?"

Double trouble went through Dean's mind. He laughed to himself. Larissa's first impression on men was invariably jaw-dropping bedazzlement. "She's somebody you might like to meet," Dean said, amused. "And, I should tell you, or rather confess, she's the woman I spoke about at the pancake house—the one I was flirting with."

"What? Her?"

"Actually, yes, she's the one. But I put an end our seeing each other, remember? We've cleared the air between us, and neither one of us has designs on the other anymore. End of story. It's over."

"You mean that?"

"Yes, like I said, I mean it. But I have no idea why she's with Kate!"

Trevor put down his window and hollered, "Hey there, you two! Hold up!"

Dean and Trevor got out of the car. "So, Trev," Dean asked, "is this something you set up with Kate? Something you finagled to bring me and her together so we'd kiss and make up?"

"No. Where did you get that idea?" Trevor's eyes remained focused intently on Larissa.

Seconds later, the four of them stood huddled in the chilly air outside the main door, making introductions. Dean was totally baffled by the cordial way Kate and Larissa interacted.

Kate glared at Dean. He held her gaze with a neutral look, while feeling a tiny twinge of envy for Trevor as he and Larissa walked toward the entrance. He noticed them taking quick glimpses at each other. *No surprise!*

Out of nowhere, Kate swung her purse at Dean as they walked to the entrance. "We have to talk, Mr. *Dean* Nelson. And I mean right now." She stopped and stood her ground, letting Trevor and Larissa walk ahead.

Dean stopped. "Oh, do we? The note I left on the refrigerator said everything. We both could use a timeout, Kate."

She stomped her foot. "Your playing house at some flea-bitten motel is quite the stunt, and it's adolescent to the max. I won't stand for it. Just what are you trying to prove?"

"Sshhh! Stop making a scene. We can talk about this later." He gestured to Trevor and Larissa looking back at them squabbling. "Just let it go for now."

Lowering her voice, Kate growled, "Don't think for a minute you're off the hook. Helping Trevor plan this dinner may be more important right this minute, but running away from our problems is childish. And I won't let you get away with it."

He looked at her, remaining calm. "I love you, Kate. Remember that." He hoped saying it, and meaning it, would deflate her anger—if only just a little. She stomped ahead, not looking back.

"Like I said, Kate, I love you."

Purposeful emotional agreeability. Focus on the 95 percent. Use a non-bedroom approach ...

CHAPTER 14

This is the man I saw in the Spirituality and Religion section at Barnes and Noble! thought Larissa, looking at Trevor. Up close, walking beside her, he was even more handsome than she remembered. Six-feet-two in the flesh and oh so alive, Larissa shivered as he held the door for her, but it wasn't due to the chilly temperature. She guessed he had no idea about her former dalliance with Dean. Entering the church, she tried to both hide her own excitement and detect what she hoped might be a similar level of excitement in Trevor's eyes.

Several steps behind them followed Dean and Kate, quarreling. Suddenly, Kate dashed past them to talk to the person at the Information Desk, whether to ask a question or because Kate was irate, Larissa couldn't tell. Dean caught up with Larissa and Trevor as they walked on. "Larissa, for the sake of transparency and honesty," he began, clearing his throat apologetically, "I think you need to know I told Trevor in the car ... uh ... the basics about how we know each other."

Larissa's eyes bored into him like a power drill. *Did you really have to bring that up right now? Stupid Dean! Now Trevor knows I was the "other woman." Shit!* She cringed.

Much to her surprise, Trevor bowed in an exaggerated and formal way. "I trust both of you have reached a higher level of perspective and your character growth is the better for it." To Larissa, he nodded graciously. "Unless I'm mistaken, it looks as though you and Kate have gotten past the strife and are working things out. Correct?"

"I … I'd say so," said Larissa. "Yes, very much so."

"There it is," Trevor declared. He gestured down the hallway. "Shall we move along? Our tasks await us."

Both Dean and Larissa were amazed—and immensely relieved.

Not only was this guy forgiving, thought Larissa, but he had levity and a willingness to turn the whole embarrassing situation into something almost pleasant. He even took her elbow as they walked, playing the part of an old-fashioned chaperone. She glanced down and saw that he was not wearing a wedding ring. This fact and his behavior—the touch of this charming man's hand—eased her misgivings about any unsavory thoughts he might be thinking about her.

Larissa's qualms about entering a church were something else, however. Any church triggered her unease. They were all the same. She activated her mental guard against the myths and misconceptions of religion because, to her, religion was more a barrier to spirituality than a doorway. But for the moment, she was present for another reason; she couldn't pass up the revenue from dozens of floral centerpieces, and the bonus was walking next to this gorgeous man.

Trevor guided her farther inside the Spirit Hills edifice. She noticed how the building looked less like a traditional church and more like a corporate office center. Except for a large wooden cross hanging on the wall, only one stained-glass window—of Jesus and his disciples—met her eye. The carpet and walls, the windows and doors, all looked tastefully neutral.

Kate joined them as they walked past the Information Desk. "Here's the key for Fellowship Hall," she said. "We'll be able to get a good idea of the room layout and placement of tables." Still in a bickering mood, Kate turned to Dean and dropped back from Trevor and Larissa, keeping her voice low. Even so, Larissa overheard her grumble, "I'm hurt you didn't talk to me first before leaving that note, Skip. How could you have gone off like that and not told me first?"

Dean calmly patted her arm. "There's a time for talk, Kate, and there's a time for action. I took the action I believed was for the best." Their voices trailed off. . . .

The immense Fellowship Hall impressed Larissa as she and Trevor entered. She estimated it seated 500 people. Kate and Dean followed, and all four shed their jackets as they got down to business. Observing Trevor in his shirtsleeves, Larissa noted his muscular arms and fit torso. But a ghastly scar on his neck covered one side of his throat—ugly, brown wrinkled skin—and she looked away, then looked back. *Whoa! That looks like it's from a severe burn. Poor guy.*

She and Kate began locating where the forty tables would be placed and the ideal size and shape of the centerpieces. Trevor and Dean headed to Trevor's office to work on their projects. Larissa felt thrilled about meeting Trevor, but his ordained status as a professional clergyman disquieted her.

"Am I detecting a sparkle in your eye?" asked Kate.

"Trevor is one good-looking guy, you know."

"Amen to that."

"Where have you been hiding him? And what a snazzy blue sports car he was driving. My, my. Is it his?"

"Yes. It turns heads, doesn't it?"

"So does he."

"Am I detecting more than a little interest on your part?"

"Maybe. Maybe not." Larissa's impression of Trevor was that of a fine, date-worthy man—someone whose body mirrored an ancient Greek athlete's, except for the unsightly brown scars.

Kate rolled her eyes and smiled. "Maybe not? C'mon. Really? I'll remember that."

Larissa swallowed. A dating relationship seemed remote to ridiculous, never mind a long-term relationship. As a potential bedmate—*like it would ever come to pass!*—he seemed highly desirable, if she could overlook the scars, but he doubtless put God and religion first, a deal breaker.

"Larissa, are you there?" Kate was speaking. "Have you heard anything I've said?"

Larissa's mind switched gears. She and Kate launched into a discussion about the kind of flowers and vases they could use from the samples Kate showed her. "Yes, I think low round containers with frosted glass are great," Larissa said, returning to work mode. "If we go with orange and yellow chrysanthemums with sprigs of Baby's Breath, and harvest-style grain stalks around each base, then I'd say the centerpieces will declare the season nicely—and be cost effective."

"What were you just daydreaming about?" Kate didn't wait for an answer but stifled a giggle. "Are you smitten?"

"Smitten? No, of course not! I was distracted is all. It's been quite a while since I've darkened the door of a church. I was just letting it all sink in."

"Sure," Kate replied, winking. "Anything you say … uh-huh."

It didn't sound as if Kate was convinced. The truth was, Larissa felt she was already turning into an old maid, a spinster at the mercy of occasional insomnia and depressive moods, particularly as the final year of her thirties was upon her. Without another baby or a family to care for, without someone to love or to give her love to, her barren life reflected her darkest fear: *abandoned forever.*

For the next half hour, she and Kate collaborated like a finely tuned team. Kate's knowledge of the expected guests and the tastes of the volunteer committee, plus her discerning design sense for colors and styles, made Larissa appreciate her in a new way. Kate's passion for the purpose of the dinner, as depicted on the hanging banner that read *The Bread of Life is Christ,* impressed Larissa. Kate's fervor radiated. The astonishing thing was the way her enthusiasm washed over Larissa like warm sea water, soothing and calming her icy skepticism about religion. For one blissful moment, Larissa realized how much Kate loved Jesus, and she felt lifted out of her melancholy.

A masculine voice spoke from behind Larissa. "Dean and I are taking a break for a while."

Larissa spun on her heel to see Trevor, smiling. Words she wanted to say, as simple as "Hello," stuck in her throat.

"Time for you too?" he asked, nodding toward a sitting area. Kate had moved to a corner of the hall where she and Dean were conversing, clearly into their own thing. Larissa overheard Kate asking, ". . . So who's cooking for you? Are you eating well? Who's doing your laundry?"

"Sure," Larissa replied. "You know your way around here better than I do. Where to?"

He gestured to a nearby nook with a window seat. As they walked together, she sensed Trevor subtly maneuver to his "good side," where the brown burn scars were invisible. They stopped at a vending machine.

"Coke? Sprite? Mountain Dew? Fizzy water?"

"I'll have fizzy water," she said. He dropped in some quarters, selected a bottle of carbonated water for her and one for himself, then pointed to the window seat overlooking a large tree-lined pond. Her throat went dry and her heart beat faster. They sat down, looking out at the sun-bathed view punctuated by a flock of honking Canadian geese flying south in formation.

Up close, looking directly into his pleasing face, she observed no hint of his burned skin. His honey-brown eyes shined clear and strong. A sense of tranquility set her at ease. The honking sound of the geese faded away.

"I've always liked this time of year," she said, "when the seasons change dramatically."

"Yes, it's truly a sacred rite of passage, seeing God's hand in everything."

She hesitated. Was this some weird pick-up line meant to test whether she believed as he did? She shooed the thought away and assumed a less cynical view. "It certainly is beautiful. The change of seasons and variations of color are spectacular."

He smiled. The gentle glimmer in his eyes relaxed her.

"So, Trevor, you're from … ?"

"Africa. Kenya, to be exact."

She sat back, surprised. He appeared entirely American, whatever that meant. In the next few minutes, he spoke about his growing-up years, about his decision at eighteen to study theology in the United States, and his choice to stay and live in Minnesota after he graduated from seminary.

"Sounds very different from the way everybody I know grew up."

"Undoubtedly. Nothing like it here. But it's given me a broader, more global perspective, which serves my work well."

"Do your parents still live in Africa?"

"Yes, they've made a lifelong commitment there."

"Such dedication!" As different as anyone she'd ever met, she viewed Trevor's upbringing and early home life as a fascinating adventure one reads about in magazines or sees on TV shows such as *National Geographic* or the *History Channel*. But like her early uncommon upbringing as an orphan and her adoptive childhood woes, his early life also had kept him an outsider from the culture they both lived in today.

"In a funny sort of way," Larissa said, "my own childhood was rather like living on a different continent." She gave details about her years struggling in the foster system and finally being adopted. She felt grateful that his eyes showed understanding.

"That makes us two peas in a pod," he declared. "Two travelers through life, starting out on unusual and unique paths, whose paths have now crossed."

She waited for him to spout some wise phrase from the Bible, to talk about some Christian or Hebrew hero whose life had begun unusually. Trevor talked normally, however, just as Kate and Dean did, and every other sentence wasn't about God this or God that.

"I've never talked to anybody from Africa before," she went on. *Why did I say that? What a lame thing to say.* She'd wanted to fill the silence. Sitting together without talking felt awkward, but apparently not for him. Did she dare ask him about his scar? She imagined he would quickly brush her off, saying he'd suffered a farm accident as a boy or some such tale.

"What was it like growing up there?"

"We were stationed near Nairobi, a place with very few trees and hardly any water. Very dry. Our mission was to bring the gospel to the tribal groups in the surrounding hundred-mile area. None of the tribes had Bibles, so we did our best to teach the gospel in their local language against stiff odds. Whenever possible, we brought food rations and modern technology, like pumps to tap drinking water, hoping to improve their health and living conditions."

She shuddered a bit. "Sounds awful. I could never have done it. Ooofff! But the results sound impressive."

"At times I thought that way, too." He turned his head and pointed to the burn scar on his neck. "You might be wondering about this. I've never met anybody who hasn't."

Was he reading her mind? "Uh, well, I had noticed it, yes. But please don't think you have to say anything about it."

"I don't mind. I prefer to get it out of the way, actually." Trevor spoke about the time his family had visited Nairobi when he was a boy, during the chaos of an attempted coup. "It was a hot August day, and the city was overrun with army troops trying to capture the president and take over the government. We had come to offer Bibles to people in the slums, but the whole place was in an uproar. The soldiers were looting and raping more than they were carrying out orders. Meanwhile, protesters everywhere were burning tires and throwing rocks at the troops and police, and my family and I inhaled smoke while trying to calm everybody. That was when a blazing tire hurled in the air landed on me. The pain was so terrible I thought I'd die. But my father pulled it off me with his bare hands. I fainted and came to hours later, and ever since have had these scars."

Larissa gasped. "How horrible!"

"It was, yes indeed. Then came seven skin-graft surgeries, thanks to a gracious doctor in Nairobi who saved my life."

"How old were you?"

"Twelve."

"It must've been God-awful painful." *Did I just use God's name in vain?*

Trevor nodded.

The main thing she couldn't stop thinking about was why Trevor had stayed in "the mission field," as he called it, under such deplorable conditions. "Didn't you hate God after that? For allowing such a horrible disaster to happen?"

He shook his head. "Just the opposite. I thanked God for letting me live. Also, for all the healing, and for His peace that I felt in the many months afterward. Even today."

Larissa's mind couldn't fathom it. *This guy must really be a fanatic. But he doesn't talk like one. A fundamentalist, maybe.* It would take time for her to comprehend that kind of faith, when, by all rights, God should have spared Trevor in the first place. She found her hand reaching out involuntarily to touch his in compassion. Only slightly, and only for a second, did her fingers touch his. Did he sense a connection?

"Now let me ask you something, Larissa. What about your relationship with Dean when you saw me in Barnes and Noble that night?"

She stalled for time. Her heart pounded. "I was afraid you might ask. We met over a personnel matter at MediMax, an issue involving one of his employees—my son Cody, to be exact. He'd been fired, and I went to Dean hoping to get his job back. And, as you just heard Dean say . . .well, our connection went a little beyond friendship—for a while. But it was over before it really got started. I feel dreadful about it." She stopped, not wanting to make things worse.

His eyes penetrated hers. She held his gaze, even though she wanted to jump up and run. Would he condemn her? Chastise her?

He spoke in soft whispers. "Yes ... yes, of course. ... Such things happen."

How gracious and benevolent.

She hesitated. Words failed her. Here she sat, three feet from a man her age who was insanely desirable without a wedding ring on his finger.

He leaned forward and touched her hands. His warm fingers sent an electric current zapping up her arms. He calmly closed his eyes. Perhaps he was praying. Whatever he was doing, she felt a kind of blessing wash over her, warm and deep.

"Relax," he said with concern. "If you learned from it, and if it helped advance your spiritual growth and Dean's, then who's to say God wasn't in it—and won't use it?"

God use it? She was uncertain what he meant by that, but she was glad he'd said it. "Dean had the guts to end it himself," she added, wanting to give him credit even though she figured Trevor already knew that. "He did it because he believed it was the right thing to do and because he loves Kate, and I respect him for it."

Silent, Trevor radiated gentleness.

"Thank you for not judging us," she added quietly, truly meaning it from the depths of her being. She desperately wanted to steer the topic elsewhere. "So ... what exactly do you do here, Trevor? Kate mentioned 'missions something.'"

He nodded. "Missions, yes. I'm a Jack of all trades. My title is Missions Pastor as well as a few other things. I coordinate Spirit Hills' mission activities overseas, nationally, and locally."

"Sounds like a lot going on."

"Well, let's see. Overseas, we've sent volunteers to a T-shirt ministry in India. In Romania, our volunteers have worked with an anti-trafficking ministry that rescues young girls from being kidnapped as sex slaves. In Haiti, our newest ministry works with the poor and sick. We'll be bringing them donated food and medical supplies—actually recycled equipment and unused supplies that Dean helps collect at MediMax. And in Honduras, we make tractors possible for widows and orphans of farm families."

"Whew! That sure must keep everybody busy."

"Oh, yes. My function is to organize teams of volunteers who travel from ten days to two months. Some of our lay teams have traveled on half a dozen mission trips to as many as three continents. We send them out with a team leader, often myself, and I coordinate regularly with the organizations abroad that we support."

"You mentioned Dean. Something about recycled medical supplies he collects?"

"That's right. He heads the Helping Hands, Healing Hearts ministry we created. Without him and all the volunteer hours he donates, there'd be no way for us to gather and deliver the supplies and equipment donated every year. But our main mission is not just to bring *things* to people in need. No, we bring *ourselves*, and return year after year to build relationships with the people we serve. They say we bring them *hope*. That's always our goal."

"What motivates people to volunteer like that?"

He paused. "I'd say they want to show the hurting people of this world the love of Christ. They serve the people's needs in tangible ways by sacrificing their time and energy, by sharing their wealth. And we go there because *we* need to, as humble servants who serve those whom God sees as our equals. We are an incredibly wealthy nation, Larissa. In that way, the gospel spreads, becoming real to them *and* us. Thanksgiving is an ideal time for that, of course. Our aim isn't to try and *make* people Christians; we're Christians who try to make *life* better for people. We aim to help people more—and help more people."

"Geez! Sounds like a sermon." She glanced around. "I guess that's okay … I *am* in a church, after all."

Trevor laughed. "We work with the Holy Spirit and earn the right to be heard. We go to all people, whoever they are. We follow Jesus' example of ministering to the earth's poor, sick, and marginalized. We aim to be His channels of divine love and redemptive grace."

"You make me almost want to sign up."

Trevor laughed again. She felt joy. Just what made this guy so inspiring and so disarming she couldn't say. If he were the team leader for a trip leaving tomorrow, she would jump at the chance to go, and to be *with him* for those weeks.

Hormones moved through her system as she felt swells of admiration. Doubly impressed, she felt in tune with him, body and soul. How could feeling this good ever be wrong?

CHAPTER

15

A t the local Perkins restaurant a week later, Dean sat alone eating the overly salty pot roast supper special. His thoughts drifted to Kate at home, most likely preparing dinner alone. He knew her home-cooked meal would taste far better than the meat and vegetables he was eating. Eating their meals apart saddened him, but it was one of the unfortunate consequences of their impasse. An hour earlier, he had finished his second load of wash at the nearby Laundromat and imagined Kate doing her own loads of wash at home. *Who knows? Maybe she even misses throwing my underwear and socks in the washer.*

November had arrived, and Nicole was busy cheerleading at the Burnsville Blazes' hockey game that evening until nine. In twenty minutes, he would call Nicole between periods to see how the hockey game was going—and to listen carefully for hints about the ways his absence from home might be impacting her.

Over a slice of French silk pie, he opened his briefcase and studied a stack of attitude surveys that his department's staff had collected from business units nationwide. His preliminary evaluation of the results, officially called Employee Engagement Profiles, was scheduled for a high-stakes presentation to Carl Langley's executive team later that month. Decisions about staffing and morale throughout the company's 43,280 employees in the fiscal year ahead would take shape there. Carl had gone along with Dean's recommendation to conduct the surveys at considerable expense, and Dean's ability to provide insights about the data could amount to a savvy career boost—or a high-flying flop—in front of MediMax's top brass. After eight days living in the motel, he fretted because his concentration wasn't up to par.

Back in his room at the SleepWell Inn a half-hour later, Dean watched *Titanic*, a favorite movie of the family's. On the TV screen, Leonardo DiCaprio, as Jack Dawson, wooed the lovely-but-lonely Rose, played by Kate Winslet. "Put your hands on me, Jack," Rose whispered in the scene where the two lovers kissed passionately in the vintage automobile. Dean couldn't envision his Kate ever wanting to act like that. *But how I wish! A woman like Larissa, now that's another story entirely.*

In an earlier scene, Kate Winslet's character had asked—no, insisted— that Jack draw her nude. She had then disrobed in front of him so he could sketch her—all without a hint of shame, all with passion simmering in every gesture. Rose wanted to love and be loved. Her sexual drive and sensual passions refused to settle for less. *What more could a zealous lover ask for?*

Rose's assertiveness embodied traits that Dean imagined in women whose sexuality felt comfortable to them. She represented rare women like Larissa who knew what they wanted, who stated their desires, and who acted confidently on their needs. Watching Rose and Jack make unrestrained, steamy love, Dean noticed it was Rose who took the lead and felt empowered to initiate. *What an irony! Kate Winslet compared to Kate Nelson!*

Stirred by his great longing for his Kate, he pondered: *Will* she *ever be that person? Will* we *ever have that kind of dynamic bond?* Rose's drive and boldness for romantic, as well as erotic, adventure was absent—or dormant?—in his Kate. *If only Katie would step up and claim her rightful place.*

Years earlier, he'd watched these same scenes with Kate and the girls as they huddled in their family room. Dean recalled feeling similar tensions then. While Kate sat quietly, the girls went ga-ga over Jack, and rightly so. Dean enjoyed seeing how they responded to Rose's approach to love and sex. Rose's behavior obviously impressed them, as did Jack's tender, respectful manner as her lover. When the Titanic was breaking in half and the ship's passengers scrambled into lifeboats, the symbolism of how his marriage was breaking in half also hit Dean. Kate continued watching, oblivious. On screen, the seawater flooded the doomed vessel as Jack clung close to Rose in the icy-cold water. Then, Jack's frozen fingers finally released Rose's hands, and he sank slowly into the depths of the midnight sea. Dean's heart also sank as Jack descended into the ocean's merciless oblivion. That night after the movie, when Dean turned out the light in their bedroom, he and Kate had cuddled under the covers. "Does my lovemaking match, or come near, that of Jack's?" he'd asked her.

"It's a wonderfully romantic movie, but it's sheer fantasy to think that's the way lovers are in real life," she'd responded.

He had winced in disappointment. He realized he must have failed at offering her the love she needed from him to be desired in return. "Sweet dreams, Katie. I'll be your Jack Dawson any day." As he held her, she'd slipped off to sleep without a word.

The TV screen in his motel room stared back at Dean. He paused the movie. In an instant, he knew he could switch to the motel's adult TV channel. The temptation seemed to pop into his mind on its own. He knew full well that the Adult Only listings went unidentified on a customer's room tab.

Earlier in his career, when he'd stayed in motels three to four nights a week, he'd refused many times to "catch a little skin" after a stressful workday. Occasionally he'd caved in to the temptation and felt momentary relief.

Now Dean faced two opposing choices. A memorized Bible verse reminded him, *"Your body is a temple of the Holy Spirit. You were bought at a price; therefore honor God with your body."* Also, the AA program's three-part guideline for behavior registered strongly: *Is it useful? Is it necessary? Is it kind?* Dean knew he could act exactly as he wished. Nobody was around, and opportunity beckoned—that was the second choice.

He opened his journal and scribbled: *Caving in to temptation ... Is that what's really going on? Will I be damaging my promise to God and my vow to keep Kate first in my life? Our covenant is holy and can't be treated lightly. Jerking off to X-rated videos is a lousy substitute. In what way is it useful? Necessary? Kind? How does it honor, or dishonor, my body as a temple of the Holy Spirit?*

With the remote in his hand and his thumb touching the power button, he felt the urge to flip instantly to the Adult Only listings. Instead, he could surf through CNN, ESPN, PBS, and other "clean" channels. But playing bachelor felt freeing. If he chose the former, "fun" and "release" were just one quick click away.

He could hardly count the many desolate nights in bed with Kate, denied so long with nowhere to turn. He scrawled, *Have I reached a tipping point? Although solo sex is a last resort, have I learned to want it? It's defeating to admit masturbating alone is my only outlet!*

Regardless of how lonely and disconnected it felt, the dream of sexual enjoyment and intimate connection with Kate remained dim. He wondered if giving himself some level of satisfaction meant more than intimacy with her. In years past, prostitutes, strip clubs, phone sex, and massage parlors had held negligible appeal. He'd never used these outlets, nor would he now.

He closed his eyes and prayed. *Please, Lord, help me. Your will only!*

The carnal urge reared up ferociously, stronger and sterner.

Throw down the remote, Dean. Leave the room. Spending precious solitude in a motel room indulging sinfully seemed pathetic ... yet inevitable. *But I deserve a release. Especially after playing nice so long. I deserve some excitement, some relief.*

Nobody was looking; nobody could stop him. What other choice in the past fifteen years had he ever had? He flipped to earlier pages in his journal, hoping to cool the urge.

If I understand God's law correctly, the very idea that I should feel guilty about satisfying my legitimate sexual needs makes me furious. But Jesus made it clear: " Everyone who looks at a woman with lust in his eye has already committed adultery with her in his heart." Yet a man's sex drive is divinely designed that way.

Fiery hot anger spurred a testosterone fuel-injected sexual spike deep within him. He recalled Trevor confiding to him after their breakfast at the pancake house: "When a man masturbates because there is no woman to love, it can be lonely, dismal, self-degrading. Even when fantasizing with an erotic book or sex video, the lack of intimacy can make the act sordid. The sad truth for most men, Dean, is that our imaginations run wild. Even though we believe the Bible does not specifically forbid masturbation, doing it can open one's soul and mind to a million demons."

Dean stared at the television screen, holding the remote and pondering Trevor's words. He itched to press the play button, but he heard Trevor's voice again: "Marital intimacy is the highest priority in God's divine design, because it symbolizes the intimacy between Himself and His people. God's nature and His love for people are passionate and intense, not cool or aloof. *He* is erotic and loves to express that love to those He loves."

With one click, Dean's eyes could feast on beautiful women freely exposing their nude bodies without a hint of stigma or hesitation—their willingness and readiness an aphrodisiac. A jumble of voices clamored inside him, "Just do it! No don't! Just do it! No don't!" The urge pulsated in his libido: Nudity. Beauty. Willingness. Readiness. Connection. Satisfaction. Sin.

Lord, I beg you to help me ... and to forgive.

He clicked the remote. In a flash he removed his clothes and was naked with a gorgeous young woman who walked nude along a secluded tropical beach, her full breasts swaying. Water droplets glistened on her bare body as if sea water had splashed her—or was it perspiration from tanning herself in the hot sun? Or having just had sex? Her curves excited him, especially the skin of her exposed groin.

He put his hand on his penis ...

Dean lay sprawled on the bed with the TV off, thankful for the woman who'd exposed everything she owned so willingly to the camera. He was fully aware the video fantasy was make-believe and all for show, but knowing so did little to diminish his pleasure. He nourished his reverie for several minutes until the inevitable emptiness crept in. Unable to savor the pulsing satisfaction anymore, he missed the intimacy once again with a loving, live human being … with Kate. Had he cheated on her? Was God displeased? Should he beg for divine forgiveness? How sinful had he been—or not?

BUZZ. The phone on the bedside table made its noise. He rolled over, ignoring it.

BUZZ. The phone buzzed again. The red light lit up. *Don't answer it!*

BUZZ. Again the phone interrupted. *Go away! Not now!*

He paused, uncertain if he should pick it up. *Could it be Kate? Not now! Leave me alone!*

The buzzing stopped, and the red light went out.

His cellphone beeped, then beeped again. He glanced at it and saw it was Kate texting him: "surprise! it's me. pack your bags. am here to bring u home."

Was she in the motel, he wondered, walking through the lobby to his room? He jumped to his feet and into his clothes. Seconds later he heard a knock on the door. Reluctantly, he went to the door and cracked it open. There stood Kate in the hallway.

"You said I could visit, Dean. Are you going to let me in?"

"What are you doing here?"

"You need to ask? Do you mean to make me stand out here?"

"All right, but just what is it you want?" Halfheartedly, he stepped aside.

"Your note said you were open for visitors, and so I'm visiting."

"At this hour of the night? It's pushing nine o'clock."

She scanned the room, eyeing the books on the table lying open and his laptop showing a sexuality blog. "What's all this stuff?" she demanded.

"No hello? Just barge in and make yourself at home? What does it look like?"

"I get it. So now you're playing therapist, trying to fix me."

"No. I'm just trying to understand what's going on between us. There has to be a key to the mystery somewhere."

"Mystery? Is that what you call it? How about a standoff? You've made this into a federal case, Dean. We're married, and we should be living together under the same roof. Simple. So pack up. Let's go before Nicole gets home from the hockey game. That way you can say 'hi' when she walks through the door."

"We have a problem, Kate, and I'm searching for answers."

"I see. And how do you think your slinking off to this cozy little hideaway . . ." she scanned the room ". . . to this pathetic bachelor pad, is solving anything? I'd hardly call it collaborating. Do you have any idea how this stunt of yours looks to everybody? People are talking."

"This is no bachelor pad. It's a cheap motel room."

"Cheap is right, and the way you're behaving is one big cheap shot. In case you're wondering, Nicole is beside herself."

"That's a big bluff and you know it. I phoned her between the first and second periods of the game and heard no complaints. None. She sounded great." He pointed to the books spread out on the table. "Have a seat. Take a look." He invited her to sit at the computer. "Check out this blog. There are some powerful things here you might find interesting."

Kate glanced at two or three book titles. He waited.

"Female sexuality, huh?" she snapped. "Nothing on male horniness? Nothing about your side of the street?"

"Yes, in fact, quite a lot, if you'd like to take a closer look."

"Well, I'm not really interested in a seminar right now. So when were you planning—?"

"These are *marriage* books, Katie. And if there's something 'male' that needs attention, I wish you'd tell me. It would be nice to hear what you're actually thinking for a change. You know, if you'd bother to tell me what I can do, that'd help us get through this mess."

"Actually, I'll take that under advisement. But our living apart doesn't help."

"Look, I'm only trying to meet you halfway. Here . . ." He took the book Trevor had loaned him and offered it to her. "This could be so healing for us. The catch is, it takes *two* people, working together, who both *want* something better."

She glared at him.

"Go ahead and glare all you want. Resources like this can help us, Katie. As for Nicole, I would hardly say she's beside herself."

"I'm the one seeing her at home every day, not you. As for 'two people working together who both *want* something better,' I think you're giving yourself a boatload of credit—what with your sneaking off and hibernating here."

"But I *am* working to make things better, for both of us. In all the years we've lived in the same house, when have you ever opened up about our love life or said anything useful or encouraging about it? That's hardly 'two people working together.'"

"Oh? So now you're the expert?"

"Your silence can be cruel, Kate."

She tapped her foot.

"Well? You *haven't* communicated, have you?"

"Our love life, not our *sex* life? I thought this was all about you 'not getting any.'"

He refused to dignify her sarcasm with a response.

"It so happens I'm thinking about other matters right now that have a higher priority," she continued. "Like going to church and worshiping together. People are beginning to wonder."

"Wonder what?"

"You know what I'm talking about. I have to sit alone because you've decided not to show up at all."

"And ... ?"

"And with the holidays coming, we have to be a team again. Are you returning home soon or not? I have to know, Skip. If this thing you're doing is *that* serious, then maybe it's beyond temporary."

"Katie, you know darn well I'm not abandoning you or the girls. So you can cut the drama and talk rationally. I'm here doing this for us to *stay* married, for us to get to a better place."

"Oh? I suppose next you'll tell me ... divorce?"

"No! You didn't hear me say divorce!" He pointed to the laptop screen and clicked "viewing history" with the mouse. "Look at what's on that screen. This is one of dozens of blogs about sexless marriage. It's got some interesting stories. Why would it be there if I were thinking of divorce?"

She ignored the computer and looked around the room. "You're not just here for a little hanky panky, maybe?" She stepped toward the open bathroom door, snooping like a private investigator.

"Bull shit! Hanky panky? Are you kidding?" He gestured inside the bathroom. "Take a good look. Do you see any makeup or lipstick or lady's underwear? No!" He spun around, grandly offering her a panoramic view of the confined room. "How about women's clothes or shoes? No? Why not try checking the closet. Please, go ahead."

"Stop it! I hate this! Look at what this is doing to us."

He paused. "I hate it too." He took a small library book from the table about 'the joys of menopause.' "Here, listen to this author." He read from the back cover: "'Menopause is not a misfortune that makes healthy and energetic women lose interest in sex—that old thinking has to go. Rather it's a splendid opportunity to live your second adulthood. The truth is that women over fifty are just hitting their stride, and that includes reignited passion for sex.'"

Kate looked away. "Very convenient. Well, I'm sick of it always being about me, about what I'm doing wrong, or *not* doing, or ... or ... or ..."

"Were you listening? There's an opportunity in front of you, Kate. You're forty-nine, exactly the age for the start of a second adulthood. You have no reason to be jealous, no justification. Or does my freedom bother you? Is that what upsets you? Is it because I have the guts to carve out a few days of solitude? To stand on my own apart from you?"

A bit more softly and kindly, he added, "Or is it because you're threatened I won't come back?"

She sank down on a chair. What looked like a wave of remorse crossed her face, a look he took to be for both of them, a double dose of sadness. She bit her lip. "Threatened? Yes, threatened that the wheels are coming off. Don't you see how this ... well, prank of yours is driving a wedge between us? Can it really be as bad as you're making it out to be?"

"Katie, this is our chance to push the reset button. It's half time, and we're in our respective corners of the locker room. We both need a breather to recalibrate our mutual game plan. The game is not over; it's only half time. But the playbook we've been using hasn't worked. We're not winning. Neither of us is winning. The second half is ahead of us. And we're not going to ever win unless we change. *We.* Not you. Not me. *We.*" Was this an effective attempt at *purposeful emotional agreeability?*

"You and your analogies. I don't want you getting used to 'baching' it. There. Can I make it any plainer than that?"

"That's fear talking. Where is your spirit of adventure? Where's *your* energy for *us* to grow in exciting ways?"

Kate sat at the table, slumped in frustration. She hung her head. Listlessly, she made an effort to skim the book Dean had handed her. She read the title aloud, "*The Erotic Word: Sexuality, Spirituality, and the Bible.* Where in hell did you get this? Who but you would've ever … ?" Her voice drifted off.

"Trevor loaned it to me. He thought it had some great insights. For anybody, men and women." Dean noticed her reading a passage he'd marked with a sticky note.

"What?!" She read aloud from the page: "'Our erotic selves testify to God's fire moving through us. God is the Divine Lover. His erotic energy is most evident in the love song to his redeemed people, the Song of Songs.'" Her voice rose higher. "What kind of garbage is *this?*"

"It's not garbage. Keep reading."

Words like "polygamous God" and "rapturous lover of our souls" dripped with disdain from her lips. Her voice increased to a crescendo: "'The Bible can help us bring our sexual and spiritual lives together. It's a call to a life of erotic passion.'" She flung the book down. "Crap! Nothing but crap!"

"Don't be pig-headed. Think about it."

"Humph! How can you stand this drivel? And Trevor *agrees?*"

He picked up the book, found a page, and read aloud. "You missed this part: 'The wider concept of Eros embraces not only sexual passion, but work, play, art, friendship, and many other sorts of profound pleasure. We must answer this invitation from God.'" He paused.

Kate rolled her eyes. "More crap, Skip. You're just using it to justify your position. It's heresy."

"Heresy? Oh, is it now? How can you say something like that when you've barely considered a word of the man's scholarship?"

Kate slammed her hand on the table. "Man! Yes, man! A female scholar wouldn't describe God that way. Stop trying to convert me! I don't care what some male scholar's opinion of the Bible is. And you still haven't answered my question: When ... are ... you ... coming ... home?"

Dean calmed himself in the face of her volatility. Looking with compassion into her eyes, he said, "Here, listen again. 'Married partners are created for deep connection to each other through an intimate love that is sexually erotic and exquisitely spiritual at the same time.'"

"Stop it. Enough. All my life I've heard nothing but the opposite, Dean. The flesh and the spirit are *always* at odds, *always* opposites. The Bible says so. That's why it's heresy." She stared holes through Dean.

He lowered his voice to a whisper and touched her arm tenderly. "That's only the elders of the church speaking, not Jesus. What's wrong with 'intimacy and love that is sexually erotic and exquisitely spiritual at the same time'? How does that tear you down and build me up?" He read aloud, "'We are called to settle for nothing less than a passionate love affair with God, with each other, and with life.'" He looked with kindness into her angry eyes.

"I'm leaving! I've had it!"

Dean's eye contact could not persuade her. Clearly, a truce was not possible, he realized. In time, he hoped, a fragile peace might emerge after the war between them ended one day.

Kate sprang toward the door, then stopped and spoke quietly: *"It is our light, not our darkness that most frightens us. We are children of God. Our playing small does not serve the world."*

"What's that?"

"Something I read in a devotional a few days ago."

"It's great. I like it."

"Do we have to go on being enemies, Dean?"

"Not at all. We're not enemies. We can stop the accusations right now if we choose to." He pointed to the bed. "Heck, there's what the whole debate is about right there. We could quit yapping right now, jump on that mattress, and make love. How about *that?*"

"You're bluffing."

"Am I?"

"I've got to get going. Auditions for the children's Christmas pageant are finishing up, and we're starting rehearsals tomorrow. Thanksgiving is only two weeks away, so I've hauled out the harvest decorations at home and want to get them up. Come with me, Skip. Let's be a team again."

"Now *you* are bluffing. Please stay, Kate. I honestly mean that. It would do wonders."

She hesitated, then opened the door. "I'm so sorry I bothered you. I shouldn't have dropped by."

Her sarcasm tasted bitter to Dean. "I do mean it when I say 'I love you,'" he said softly. "But I don't want my needs to define us. We're far more than sex or no-sex, Katie. A whole lot more. It may not seem like it to you, but trust it, believe it."

She plastered on a smile. "Nicole will be coming home soon. You know where you belong, Dean."

He was saddened they were parting as combatants. "I will when you are the woman I want to come home to, and when I am the husband you want to make love to."

She turned and walked out the door without a word. The door shut behind her. No kiss. No embrace.

He stepped over to the table, considering whether to go to the window and watch her drive away. *No. Let it be.* His mind reeled. *'Intimate love that is sexually erotic and exquisitely spiritual at the same time.' One day, please may it be, Lord.*

16

CHAPTER

"Just focus your breathing. Just breathe through it, Kate. Take another long inhale through your nose, then another long exhale out your mouth. Yes, that's it. Repeat to yourself, 'Relaxation helps me reach my core essence.'"

Larissa was helping Kate focus on learning ways to free up the stubborn tightness and stiffness in her neck and shoulders. She could tell Kate's rigidity was refusing to budge. Loosening up from the inside out was a goal they'd agreed on as part of their "sexual IQ/feminine freedom" sessions, as they'd come to call the private sessions.

"What stubborn emotional and psychological forces are holding you captive, Kate? Can you identify one or two? Allow them to surface in your mind, then name them."

Kate sputtered, "How much longer before we stop?"

"Five more repetitions."

"I'm not really in the mood for this. Can we stop?"

"Slowly, very slowly, open your eyes."

Kate sat quietly on the circular rug at Fitness & Flowers with her legs folded Buddha style, struggling to breathe deeply in meditative silence. Larissa sensed the elusive loosening up that Kate needed remained far off. Meditation appeared to have helped nominally. Something obstinate, something strong, held Kate back. Deeper levels in Kate's psyche seemed untouched.

"I never really drifted anywhere, Larissa." Kate gave Larissa a mournful look. "I'm not sure I even left here-and-now." Kate's eyes signaled distress.

"Then we'll have to come up with a different strategy. Does your resistance to pleasure have to do with trusting?"

"But I do trust you."

"Not me—yourself. Trusting yourself. Opening up and then extending that trust outward. Being vulnerable to Dean, for example."

"You got me there. I'm as tight as a drum. After our spat in his motel room, I don't think it will ever be different."

"It's important for you to identify what's blocking the free flow of energy within you. It may be difficult trusting the parts of yourself that have been harmed. What emotional suffering has been at the root of your sexual fears?"

"This just isn't happening. I'll never relax enough. I'm so unworthy."

"Stop saying that about yourself. Pain closes you down, whether it's physical, emotional, or sexual. Sexually, it makes you resist stimulation and penetration. So I'm curious: Do you use a vibrator? If not, it's time to turn that kind of thinking around. In order to receive love, it's essential to enjoy pleasure—and to trust being vulnerable to it."

"Right. That'll be the day."

"Doing things that allow you to surrender will open up your inner core to love, and to loving back."

"A vibrator? I have enough guilt hanging over me already. It's so aggravating." Kate slumped to the floor, groaning. "I'm not getting this, am I? Why is it so easy for *you?*"

"Well, it wasn't at first. I needed to learn a lot. But this isn't about me right now." In Larissa's mind, she agreed with Kate on both points: Kate wasn't getting it, and it *was* easier for her, because of repeated practice and the success she'd had overcoming her hang-ups.

"I do touch myself sometimes, though," said Kate, "if that's where you're headed. Probably not as often or as much as you do."

"After years without a lover, it's been my only outlet. So I've learned to let myself feel all the enjoyment I can get from it—without feeling guilty."

"It's just easier for you because you're beautiful," Kate blurted. "That's why. Because you have such a beautiful figure and awesome fitness. I'm miles behind you."

Larissa shook her head. "No. Where on earth are you getting that? Even if it were true, you are not miles behind me. Why let yourself believe that? The truth is, whatever the reason, I've basically trusted myself, and it's been that way since I was little. It had to be. I was jerked around and lied to, so I had to learn to trust myself. I'm very lucky that way."

"Lucky? I'd say blessed beyond belief. But why haven't *I* ever learned what you have? To trust. To open up and willingly surrender and enjoy? I have no idea what 'trust' means. Being female is something I've *never* trusted."

Larissa sensed that Kate's deep pain was also a clue to what held Kate captive. "You've never trusted being female?"

"I guess I haven't. Now that I just heard myself say it, I don't feel at home in my body."

"What an awful place to be. What a dreadful thing to carry around all the time."

"I guess I'm not secure in who I am, or what I am, like you are." Kate stared off into space. Larissa offered ideas and listened. Kate spoke of the ways women are often victims, how they're subject to males from cradle to grave, "in real life and in the media, objectified and put down. We're the weaker sex, Larissa, dominated and preyed upon. Face it."

"There's some truth to that. But we're *not* the weaker sex. As women, we can claim our power and not let the media or culture or tradition or religion or a perfect body image pigeonhole us as inferior. Women today have opportunities where once there were none."

"Well, I wish I had the chance to take back my growing-up years. I had no sister or brother to confide in and few girlfriends to play with. I was shy and isolated at school, an only child in an emotionally unsafe home. I was shocked when my first period came—it was a big surprise. In high school and college, I felt awkward on dates. Basically, I covered up my anxiety and went around feeling afraid."

Quietly, after she was sure Kate was done speaking, Larissa leaned closer. "Then you and I must've had opposite responses to our upbringings. I can see why it's so hard for you to trust."

"Right now I'm not sure what to think. Dean is pulling away, but years ago when we met, he was the one who coaxed me out of my shell. He boosted my confidence and made me laugh. He showed me an adventurous side of life. He took my hand, and we boldly went places I could only have dreamed of. We traveled in Europe, skied in Vermont, and went scuba diving in Florida. He coached me to put myself 'out there,' as he called it."

Kate went silent. Larissa waited.

Almost in a whisper, Kate said, "I heard somewhere that, when it comes to girls, fear has to do with their fathers."

Larissa responded, "Could be there's some truth to that. I'm not sure. Sometimes I wonder if my approach to men might be a way to discover my birth father in one of them, even though I never knew him. I had a mother I adored and loved, but she was taken away when I was four. We were torn from each other's arms, and I've never seen her since."

"What a tragedy! I'm so sorry for you. How sad."

Larissa looked at Kate, seeing great hurt and sadness of another kind. "And you?"

Kate took a long breath. "I remember my father drinking after work and marching around the house bellowing. My mother just cowered like a scared mouse. She didn't dare raise her voice or stand up to him. I've always thought it might have been more bearable if I'd had a brother or sister. But it was always just the two of us. Whenever Dad went into one of his rages, throwing things across the room or pounding his fists, she trembled in terror and squeezed me till I could hardly breathe."

Larissa nodded. "Fear bonded you and your mom together. That sounds like a recipe for not trusting yourself, for doubting yourself."

Kate sat up straighter. "It seemed normal at the time, but now I realize it wasn't."

"She clung to you, and you clung to her. A mother needing comfort even more than you, her child. Not good. And it went on like that how long?"

"Basically, my whole childhood. After I got my period, it got even worse. Not because of my father—by then he was working more hours at the office and wasn't in the house as much. But Mom preached the horrors of boys and how they only wanted one thing. 'Don't you ever fall for their tricks, Kathryn. They're only out for getting an unsuspecting girl pregnant.'"

"Sounds horrible. Say no more."

Kate stared at her, almost in tears. Larissa sensed Kate was understanding something about herself that Larissa had learned from self-help books and tapes. "You know, we all tell ourselves stories based on our experiences, Kate. And sometimes telling ourselves sad stories over and over makes us sick."

Kate looked down. "I guess that's true."

"What's the sad story you've been telling yourself?"

"Hmmm … It's been around my father and his boorish ways, I suppose. In public, everybody in the community respected him far and wide—Mr. Solid Citizen and all-around nice guy. But at home he was something else entirely. We never knew what terror was coming next."

"Were your folks lovers?"

"What?! My father and mother lovers?" Kate grunted. "Hardly! They slept in separate beds. I never saw them being touchy-feely with each other."

With a flicker of new awareness, Larissa said, "And how has that imprinting carried over to your marriage?"

"To our predicament?" Kate's eyes widened. "I guess you're right. Mom never liked being a woman, never celebrated her femininity. She buried it instead. She had me very late when she was almost forty, and she never trusted my father, and with Dean, I … I haven't . . ." Tears started to flow. Kate reached out to hold Larissa's hand.

"You're no longer a helpless child, Kate. You're an adult now. You have the chance to change your story. I know, because I had to change mine—or wallow in depression and sorrow and anger. I changed it, and so can you."

Tears trickled down Kate's cheeks. "Really? You believe I can?"

"Yes. You've been trapped. Think about it. Now you have a chance to unlock yourself from that prison. What shaped you many years ago, you no longer have to let shape you now."

Kate went quiet. She wiped away more tears. "I remember my mother and Aunt Bernice warning me to never touch myself 'down there.' They never came right out and said it, but their tone made it crystal clear that 'doing that is dirty.' They thought their warnings would help me. For them, 'the pill' made no difference because 'nice girls never have sex before wedlock.' They drummed into me the dangers of getting pregnant by an over-sexed boy, which meant all boys. Virginity was a cardinal virtue. 'Girls who like sex are sluts and whores.'"

Larissa reached for a tissue and patted Kate's teary face. "So sad. And here I thought pre-women's lib warnings like those were long gone."

"How I wish! The sixties and seventies changed a lot of things, but not in my home. And our church was very strict about such things."

"Then tell yourself a new story, Kate. Write down your new thoughts. Repeat them to yourself. Scratch out old ones like 'I've never trusted being female' and 'men can't be trusted.' Don't let those awful years keep poisoning your thoughts."

Kate sighed. "Poor Dean. This is all a rat's nest I've never wanted to unravel."

"Say instead, 'I trust being female; I trust the woman I am. Men *can* be trusted.' Say, 'I am open to pleasure and surrender myself to it.'"

"It's impacted Dean so unfairly and has fed my stubbornness with him. I know deep in my heart I haven't been fair. And I can't let it stay that way. God has to help me somehow sort through the myths and lies and misconceptions."

Larissa clapped her hands. "Hooray! Keep going. The sooner you rewrite those stories, the better. Like the story I just told you about my mom and the awful county welfare workers who ripped her out of my arms. I let that pain define me for years, even though I couldn't change what happened. I struggled terribly to accept it."

Tears streamed down Kate's cheeks. Her voice sounded scratchy. "No wonder Dean is beside himself. Look at what I've done."

Larissa patted her knee.

Kate grimaced. "Then there's the unfair impact on Nicole and Lindsay, all because of my stubbornness. I'm scared that Nicole has been affected by our intimacy troubles—how the things she's heard might be affecting her. The aftermath of our fight when he smashed the statue needs damage control, but the idea of talking with her about her own sex life feels so scary."

"That's another story you can change."

"No wonder Dean and I are stuck in such a pit." Kate's began weeping uncontrollably. She crumpled on Larissa's shoulder.

Larissa paused, glancing patiently at the clock. BONFIRE was scheduled to begin in fifteen minutes. "Are you staying for BONFIRE, Kate?"

Kate looked up through her tears, biting her lip. She nodded yes. Her eyes brightened with hope and her sobs subsided.

The BONFIRE gang—Jasmine, Claire, Annabelle, and Larissa—welcomed Kate as they sat cross-legged on the circular woven floor rug. Everyone immediately realized her emotionally stormy state. Larissa noted how the women discerned Kate's need to calm down. They waited quietly for her private battle to cease. As Kate trembled, Larissa sat beside her, steady and caring. The look on Kate's face telegraphed, *Here goes. I'm bursting to get something painful off my chest, so let's get on with it.*

"Go ahead, Kate," Larissa whispered.

"Thanks, everybody, for letting me be here today. It's time I … uh … admit something about my marriage. My side of it, that is. Forgive me if this comes out disjointed, but I've … I've refused my husband in the bedroom for months. No, actually for years. It's been completely wrong of me and has nothing to do with his being unreasonable or unlovable." Kate paused, gathered her wits. "All of this, I believe, is in spite of our genuine love for each other. We were right for each other when we got married twenty-four years ago, but I'm afraid right now he probably feels nothing like he once did. Frankly, the marriage is hanging by a thread, especially after all the suffering I've caused."

Larissa looked at Kate and squeezed her hand. "Take all the time you need."

Kate straightened up and declared, "I'm absolutely hopeless at sex. Besides being no good at it, I don't seem to need it like other people do. It just isn't something that's part of me. For years, I've thought I had something wrong with me, something missing that everyone else finds so obviously pleasurable. I'm not like normal people. And I'm sick of being this way."

Kate looked at Larissa. Larissa surmised that her new awareness of old toxic stories came to mind. "But I *want* to change, if I can. What I'm trying to say, basically, is I'm frigid. That's a horrible word, but it describes me. I wish it didn't, but it does. Don't let my two lovely children fool you. Dean and I had just enough of a normal love life for the first part of our marriage to have a couple of kids. I guess, for me, it was all an act. I haven't lived up to my vows. I promised at our wedding to cherish my husband, and I've failed. The truth is … the truth *for me* is … that sex feels dirty and disgusting. Sadly, the toll on my husband has been enormous."

Kate dropped her head, sagging against Claire sitting next to her.

The women in the circle sat silently. Claire reached for the tissue box and handed her a tissue, saying, "You and I are more alike than you realize, dear."

Jasmine put her hand reassuringly on Kate's shoulder. "That took a lot of courage."

Annabelle closed her eyes and lifted her open hands in a gesture of supplication. Larissa observed Kate's wet trickle of tears moistening her blouse. She felt privileged that her group was sharing this moment with Kate. This tiny band of women was soothing the upheaval in another woman's life, participating in her catharsis, and being her safety net, just like Larissa had always hoped her program would do.

"I'm struggling in that area of my life myself," said Claire, "so hearing you say what you did helps me."

"Don't be too hard on yourself or feel so alone," said Annabelle. "I'm sure it's more common than we know."

"We want to help you in any way we can," said Jasmine. "Let me ask: Have you ever had your testosterone level tested?"

Kate perked up. "Why would I? Don't men have testosterone and women have estrogen?"

"That's true. The thing is, testosterone regulates sex drive in *both* men and women. I've had the test done myself, and I'm glad I did."

Kate gave her a questioning look. "I don't get it."

"It works like this. Every woman has both estrogen and testosterone hormones in her system, just as every man has both testosterone and estrogen in his. And everyone, due to genetics and biology, has a natural 'set point' that's unique to that person. In your case, it might be in the low range through no fault of your own. It's a simple blood test, and it takes just a few days to get the results back."

"It could be a contributing factor," said Annabelle.

"Do you think it might explain my low libido?" Kate asked Jasmine.

"I'd sure have it checked out. Male or female, there are genetically low-desire and high-desire people."

As BONFIRE's facilitator, Larissa felt happy for Kate. She had definitely spoken her truth, and others had jumped in with helpful feedback. Larissa felt excited observing the emotional and relational openness that the women were experiencing in their pursuit of the best version of themselves. Annabelle talked about her struggles to lose weight, Claire spoke of her fragile self-image, and Jasmine confided about her attempts to curb her migraines. Each woman took sufficient time to explore her issues. It felt gratifying to hear how their fitness activities added strength to their goals for improvement, confirming her own vision for starting her fitness business. Kate's transformative experience was additional evidence.

BONFIRE is contributing to each person's empowerment. Yes! Larissa's gamble to start up Fitness & Flowers felt validated. Closing her eyes gently, she felt waves of gratitude, wave after wave after wave.

For the next hour, the women offered Kate some ideas and she offered them her own, and Larissa could tell Kate felt valued as a contributor. This happy turn of events, Larissa recognized, came about indirectly from her meeting Dean weeks earlier.

Thank you, Dean. I'm not sure how all this relates to you, but this is more than I ever could've imagined.

As the BONFIRE group ended and members departed, Kate saw Larissa approaching. "That was amazing, Kate. I'm so proud of you. You really put it out there and made a quantum leap." Kate smiled and hugged her. "By the way, I've been meaning to ask: Has Trevor said anything recently? Anything special?"

Kate didn't know what, or how much, to tell her. "Uh, he had all kinds of nice things to say about you." His enthusiasm made Kate happy for Larissa's sake, but was it her place to gossip about it to Larissa?

"Give me a little more to go on," Larissa urged.

"Oh, it's obvious you two hit it off, and he thinks you're . . ." She left the thought hanging.

"I'm what?"

"Well, I noticed the two of you having that nice little chat at the window overlooking the pond. So, let *me* ask, what do you think of *him*?"

"A true gentleman. Very attractive. But what's with a guy as handsome as he is never being married? It makes me wonder if something is off."

"Some folks might go overboard and say he's married to the church."

"You're putting me on. Like a priest?"

"Look who's talking. I happen to know someone else, ahem, who's never been married."

"Touché! It takes one to know one, I guess."

Kate sensed optimism from Larissa, yet she and Trevor seemed like an oddly matched couple. Who could say? Can a bird and a fish live together? "Look, I'm sure there's chemistry there. And I can see you have it too." She gave Larissa a small hug. "By the way, I've been meaning to ask you something. Actually it's more like an invitation. I'd love it if you'd be willing to help me with our children's Christmas pageant we're working on."

"At church?"

"Yes."

"As a volunteer?"

"Right. Behind-the-curtain stuff, like helping with costumes. I need to stay focused on choreography and training the dancers, and getting them on and off stage with the music."

Larissa hesitated. "I wish I could, but I'm not sure. I don't have the security of a home and a husband, or as much free time to volunteer.

Being a single mother and running a new business that's squeaking by, on top of working long hours and watching every penny—well, it would be a huge stretch. But I love the idea, Kate, and I'm glad you asked."

"I do understand. How about if you just think about it."

"Of course. Would it mean I'd have to pray and worship like you do?"

"You'd be free to, of course, but that's your choice. It comes with a 'no obligation' guarantee."

They chuckled.

Kate nurtured the notion that her faith might envelop Larissa in a loving community and, hopefully, provide a haven of comfort for her. "You have a great flare for design, kiddo," Kate added, "and a lovely spirit, so you'd fit right in. I hope you'll find a way to at least give it a try."

Kate saw a glimmer in Larissa's eye that hinted she was intrigued.

17

CHAPTER

"I lift my glass to you, Kate. To the finest children's choreographer ever."

"I humbly thank you, Marlene. To the finest children's music director ever."

"And to our newest crew member, Larissa," said Marlene, "our costume designer *par excellence*."

Clinking their wine glasses, Kate, Larissa, and Marlene Wilkins shared long sips of mellow merlot. "I'm so glad you accepted our invitation to lend your design talents to the pageant, Larissa," said Marlene.

"And to joining our special tradition of wine-enhanced lunches," said Kate, winking.

Kate felt thrilled Larissa had decided to join them. She'd just observed Larissa working three hours with Marlene on the preliminary rehearsal for Spirit Hills' Christmas musical, and Larissa appeared cheerful and relaxed the whole time. Now they were toasting the first dance scenes involving the six-to-twelve-year-old girls.

Kate had met Marlene years before at a statewide Faith in the Arts conference and they'd shared their love of dance ever since. "What a surprise that we belong to the same church!" Marlene had exclaimed that first day.

Today's wine went down Kate's throat smoothly, deliciously. What could compare to a fine vintage for soothing strained marital feelings and sore neck muscles? Allowing herself this small indulgence seemed well deserved. She loved eating her Waldorf salad in the shaded sunlight of Marlene's four-season porch on this cold day before Thanksgiving.

Kate offered her own toast: "To our shared love of dance, music, and design."

"I'll drink to that," chirped Marlene.

"So will I," said Larissa. The three clinked glasses.

Since her visit with Dean a week earlier at the motel, certain theological questions had triggered clashing ideas within Kate. How could sexually erotic lovemaking be exquisitely spiritual? What did God's erotic love across all cultures and generations mean? Swallowing the next sip of wine helped numb her jangled nerves. Kate sensed that their sharing a pricey bottle of merlot amounted to a sort of "bad girls" conspiracy, and she felt pleased Larissa was letting loose with believers like herself and Marlene.

"How about if we crack open another bottle and have a teeny bit more, girls?" Marlene suggested.

"I'm for that," said Kate.

When Marlene reached to add the last drops to Larissa's glass, Kate noticed her politely decline. "No more for me," said Larissa. "But thank you."

"Good thing there are no biblical taboos prohibiting it," said Marlene.

"Oh?" remarked Larissa. "I thought the Bible frowned on drinking alcohol."

"Not quite," answered Marlene. "We're not technically forbidden to drink—as long as we imbibe in modest amounts, of course." She popped open the new bottle. "Like they say, my dear, 'Everything in moderation'— *even* moderation. Ha!" She filled Kate's glass and her own.

"Well, I'd better be off." Larissa stood to leave. "With a dozen dancers to sew sequins for, and shepherds and angels to costume, I've got quite the shopping and sewing to do."

Marlene stood and graciously hugged her. "Now be sure you keep all those receipts and turn them in to Ginny, our treasurer at church. She'll pay you right back. And she'll help you with the lion's share of those costumes, too. She loves doing that."

Waving to Larissa as she headed off, Kate looked across the table at Marlene's radiant features: flowing dark hair, glowing cheeks, rainbow-striped earrings with a matching necklace of Marlene's own bold design, and a dancer's over-the-hill-but-still-in-shape figure. Outspoken and sometimes raunchy, especially after a glass of wine, Marlene's boundless energy invigorated Kate.

"So have you and Dean been trying any new positions in your bedroom? Any kinky spanking stories?"

Kate almost choked on her wine, managing to say, "Our love life is doing fine." She'd scarcely kept up with Marlene's gossip about imaginary amorous adventures she so much enjoyed telling. "How about you and Gavin?"

"Oh, my! Where to start?" Cheered by the spotlight having shifted to her, Marlene expressed mild disdain for Gavin's geekyness, but not his sex drive. "A few nights ago we … well, you could say we experimented— ooh, la, la!"

Kate kept her mouth clamped shut. Clearly the wine was getting to Marlene. Kate had carefully refrained from telling Marlene anything about Dean's leaving the house for a motel, and Marlene hadn't noticed. No gossip about *that*. Not with Marlene's loose lips.

Marlene yammered on, sipping her merlot, her tongue wobbling like a loose door hinge. "Now that our kids are busy in college, Gavin wants us to up the ante. I mean every week. I haven't found a nice way of telling him to back off, so I just go along. I do my best to fake orgasms to keep him happy."

"You fake orgasms?"

"Is that a big surprise? About once a month for the real thing is plenty for me. If I fake it, he doesn't feel like a failure."

Kate felt doubly shocked. First, by Marlene's deep level of disclosure, as though it were a new recipe she'd tried and liked. Second, by her casual way of talking about orgasms, as if they were the most natural thing ever. "And you don't think he realizes you're faking?"

"Maybe, maybe not. He doesn't let on. I look at it as a game. It's the wifely thing to do. Gavin does the husbandly thing, and we move on. But ya know," added Marlene raising her glass, "we love each other so it all works."

Kate stared at Marlene, her mind muddled by the extra wine. *What did she just say?* It seemed pertinent. And did Marlene actually experience real orgasms? What gave her that ability?

"It's all in how you manage it," Marlene went on, taking a long sip. "Men! Sex is all they ever think about. Even guys who are in a rut like Gavin—they never get tired of it. I keep hoping he'll play more golf someday, but I'm not really complaining. I sure wouldn't want him to ignore me. … Besides, it's kinda fun." She grinned.

Kate wanted to know how to feel the real thing, let alone rarely—and what it felt like. What made an orgasm so special? Since Dean's vasectomy, which should have freed up their lovemaking as it apparently did for other couples, she'd felt skittish about opening herself to him. She'd held back, unprepared to trust her own sexual energy. All she'd sensed was the dark chaos of troubling emotions—and knowing she was disappointing Dean *and* disappointing herself by her lack of response.

"D'you think men are horny becaaause it's hard-wired into their genes?" Kate asked Marlene. Had she just slurred her words?

"Their *jeans*? Ha!" Marlene burst out laughing. "That bulge in the crotch of their jeans?"

"Not those jeans. The genes they're booorn with." Kate noticed she *was* slurring her words.

Marlene laughed more, and Kate joined her. Laughing felt good.

The wine was slowing Kate's tongue and muddling her thoughts. She dimly recollected attending a six-part marriage seminar with Dean at Spirit Hills about three years earlier. Before going to bed some nights, he'd tried persuading her to experiment. "It's perfectly natural," she recalled the female seminar speaker saying, "making love leads to three-way unity with God. By divine design, God wishes intimacy between husbands and wives when they make love."

Kate brushed aside that memory and began to say something to Marlene, but the words whirled in her head. A faint memory pushed to the surface. During her newlywed days when hitchhiking with Dean across Europe, she remembered having experienced one night of lovemaking with him in Paris when her entire body responded freely, fully. Nothing like it had occurred before or since. It was a wonderfully explosive intimacy with its own Parisian flare. Exploring the City of Love with her new husband had created an aura that led to that special night in Montmartre. Did she dare believe she would ever feel as liberated again?

"Kate? Are you still with me? Kate?"

"Uh, yes, of … of couuurse."

Kate's holiday to-do list thrust aside her foggy recollection of Paris and crammed her brain with the pressure to bake cookies and decorate the house and shop for gifts. "Sorry to cut thisss short, dearie, but you and I have got a Missions meeting tonight for the team's trip to Haiti. I've gotta get going. Now."

"Well, then, it's been peachy." Lifting the bottle and pouring another slurp of wine into their glasses, Marlene declared, "Bottoms up!" As they emptied their glasses, she said, "Okay, you're free to get going now. Just don't get a DWI driving home, hear? Cheers!"

Kate parked her SUV in the garage, remembering she had promised Trevor to bring research data about Haiti to tonight's meeting. She would have to find time to squeeze in forty-five minutes of culling through info from the Internet to print off and bring along, but time was running against her. Her mind buzzed, and her feet stumbled awkwardly as she carried an armload of music scripts into the house. "Whyyy did we ever have that second bottle?" she muttered aloud under her breath, her slurred words nagging her.

Jester came racing up, wagging his tail and blocking her entry into the kitchen. "Don't, Jessster!" Her sluggish words sounded too loud.

"Welcome home," a voice said.

Kate looked up. There at the counter sat Nicole, looking bored. "Where've you been, Mom? Busy as usual?"

Struggling with the scripts, Kate pleaded, "Could you please help me with these?"

Kate heard another voice: "Hi Mom. I'm home."

Kate turned and stared in surprise at her older daughter, realizing a bit slowly that Lindsay must have driven up from Iowa without calling ahead.

"Help is on the way," said Lindsay. "Here, let me." Reaching out to take the bundle of scripts, she hugged her mother. "I hear things are a little different around here, Mom."

Kate checked Lindsay's body language and eye contact, determining how to answer. "You can saaay that again." She kissed Lindsay's cheek, carefully trying to prevent the smell of alcohol on her breath from reaching Lindsay's nose. "What brings you up here in the middle of the week?"

"A three-day weekend. My professor was sick and classes ended a day sooner than I expected." Lindsay looked at Nicole. "And Nicky thought I should get the scoop on what's going on with Dad. After she texted me, I waited to hear from you. Have you checked your texts? Is your phone on silent? So, yeah. I'm here to see what's shakin'."

This was the last thing Kate needed.

"Mom, we know you're going through a lot, that you're taking it pretty hard," said Lindsay. "We want to make it easier for you, not harder."

"Just what I need. An inquisition. Your idea of sympathy!"

Kate cringed at her overreaction. *I'm on thin ice.* She understood they had the right to know about the broad outline behind Dean's absence. That was bad enough. But feeling tipsy made her nervous because of the risk of either girl getting the tiniest whiff of alcohol. *Why did I have so much to drink? Why wasn't I thinking?*

"Sorry. Well ... thanks for driving up," she said lamely to Lindsay, whose sour face bugged her. "I think it'll be only a couple more days before he moves back, so things will be loooking up again for the holidays. And with your grandma and grandpa flying in for Christmas, everything will have to be just so. *That's* where you guys could help a lot."

"We know, we know," grumbled Nicole. "Hanging decorations, baking cookies ... "

"What about Grandma Nelson?" asked Lindsay. "Is she spending Christmas week here or in Chicago?"

"My intelligence sources tell me she's staying in Chicago this year. Uncle Mitch has his hands full and has nixed traveling in the winter since grandpa died." Kate clapped her hands, trying both to clear her head and get everyone to spring into action. "How about it, girls? Please help me get thisss house in shape."

Silence.

The two girls looked straight at her, tight-jawed.

"Mom," said Lindsay, softening her tone, "I never suspected so much tension was brewing between you and Dad. Will you please talk about it?"

Kate sighed. "We've had a couple of disagreements lately. I think he just needed a timeout. It happens. Time to think things through and all that. He's ssstill working a full schedule at work and paaaying the bills." She went to the sink and got a tall glass of water, hoping that would help clear her head.

"Think through what things?" asked Nicole. "What things are *you* thinking through?"

She stared at Nicole. *You stinker!* "You were here the night we argued. What would *you* say?"

"Mom, I think Lindsay deserves a direct answer."

Kate threw her purse down on the counter. "All right! Your father thinks we're no longer compatible in bed. There! Is that direct enough for you?"

Lindsay's shoulders sagged. "You're acting like we're judging you, Mom, or blaming you. But I'm here to help. And Nicky wants to help, too."

"Help, is it? I have the address where your father is staying right here. And as a matter of fact, I *am* seeeking help from ... from a therapist ... a specialist who knows about these things. We discussed starting some sessions a couple of days ago. And I'm asking for prayer at church." She stared at Lindsay. "Is that being clear enough?" Kate winced, having lied about getting help from a therapist—yet one more reason to harbor shame.

Lindsay stepped closer to her, reaching out to hug her. Kate grimaced as Lindsay touched her. "Mom, this is tearing you up inside."

Jerking away, Kate blurted out, "Our love life is not any of your business. Children should be spared these things."

Lindsay shrank back, alarmed. "Times aren't like they used to be, Mom. We're growing up faster and aren't little kids. We can deal with it."

"Don't give me that. Certain things don't chaaange with time."

"Okay, then what about Dad? Is he getting help? Are you both seeing the same specialist?"

Kate grimaced. *What have I gotten myself into?* "Uh … it's still up in the air. Whether he wants to, that's something you'll have to ask him yourself." Another lie. It had to be the booze talking. Steeling herself for what to say next, she snapped, "And while you're at it, you might ask him about the woman he was seeing on the sly."

A thunderclap of silence. Lindsay stared at Nicole, stunned. Kate felt a pleasurable stab of satisfaction at disarming them.

Lindsay's face reddened. "Mom, you're drunk! I can smell it! I fucking hate it when you drink."

Kate slammed her hand on the counter. "Don't you swear in myyy house! And since when did you start using filthy language?"

"Don't switch the subject, Mom. Stop avoiding. You're slurring your words. Quit trying to dodge—"

"I suppose you think your father's got it right? Has Nicole told you what he wrote me in his little note?"

"MOM!" shrieked Nicole. "STOP IT!" Moving over to Lindsay, Nicole took her sister by the hand and tried urging her to leave the room.

"Talk to us, Mom," Lindsay demanded. "We're trying to understand. Drunk or not, tell us."

"Come on, Linds," Nicole begged, tugging harder. "I know a cool place at the mall. We can check out some cute guys there. Let's go."

Toxic tension fouled Kate's thinking. Huffing, she hopped into "getting-things-done" mode. Shooing the girls out of the kitchen, she sneered, "Leave. Go see your father. Now. He's the one with aaall the answers. Go on, git."

"But, Mom, he's at work," said Lindsay. "And we're here with *you* now."

"Sorry, no deal!" Kate hollered, shoving them away. "Go hang out at his new bachelor pad. Keep him company. The weasel. Leave me be." She despised herself; the booze had wiped out her common sense and she was regressing emotionally.

Nicole rolled her eyes at Lindsay then pulled her so hard they stumbled from the room.

A fter the alcohol wore off two hours later, Kate's bitter emotions were raw. She struggled to block out the ruckus with Lindsay and Nicole. Her research needed to get done, and mentally she shoved aside her sore feelings. *What a jerk I made of myself. How the girls must hate me. Why did I get so drunk?* On her computer screen flickered Internet images from Haiti's early history of slaves being whipped while chopping sugar cane under the vigilant eyes of French overseers.

She turned and stared through the window at the previous night's dusting of snow on her rose bushes. Another evening without Dean lay ahead. The girls had told her they were eating out, so that meant a pot pie in the microwave for dinner rather than a fresh chicken stir fry for three. She envisioned the larger snowfalls that would soon smother the roses under layers of thick, white fleece. *If only I could smother my emotions like that.*

An odd question sprang to her mind: 'Who, if not Dean, will operate the snow blower when huge drifts of snow cover the driveway?'

Foggy-headed from the wine hangover and agitated about the girls' forcefulness, Kate could almost hear Lindsay blabbing to Nicky about her psychological analysis of their mother: *'All Mom's energy is a redirected sublimation of her stifled sexual libido funneled into housework and busyness at church.'*

Ugh! would their train wreck of a marriage ever get back on track?

"Only if I prove worthy of his love," she said aloud, answering her own question. She thought back to her drop-in visit to Dean's motel room. Since then, she'd had some breakthroughs in her understanding. She vowed to quietly make an effort to love and respect him, putting his needs ahead of hers, and his priorities ahead of her fears. He had valid causes for complaint, and her attitudes and actions needed to reflect that understanding, or her lifelong promise to love him "for better or worse" meant nothing. She *wanted* to love him, to see the sparkle return to his beautiful hazel eyes.

The home phone rang. Kate reached for it.

"Hey, Kate, it's Larissa. Good news. I just had a private client cancel for tomorrow. My schedule is open, so how about us doing lunch? I need some mom-to-mom insights. Oh! And right after lunch there's another BONFIRE with the gals."

"Hmmm! Let me check my calendar." Kate glanced at the calendar hanging on the wall, noting the weekly Bible study marked from noon to 1:30. Skipping a regular weekly event to help a friend work through her issues ruled. "Done, Larissa. We're on."

"Super. You have a daughter in college, and I'm hoping you can help me motivate my son. Cody may be slipping back to his old ways, sloughing off on his studies and maybe drinking too much."

"I'm all ears. We'll brainstorm, and I'll bet something useful will come up." Kate felt a twinge of guilt, knowing she wasn't exactly a role model in the drinking department.

"I appreciate that. And actually, there's another reason I called," continued Larissa. "I got this letter from my doctor today. It scared me. Can I get your thoughts on it?"

"Sure, fire away."

"It says my latest mammogram shows 'irregularities.' I've been scheduled for a breast biopsy next Monday."

"That doesn't sound very good. Best to get it checked out."

"A while back I had a strange discharge, and I'm guessing there might be a questionable lump that showed up on the mammogram." Her voice took on a fearful, shaky edge. "What do you know about biopsies?"

"Not much. A friend of mine got a letter like that about a year ago. In her case, they found the lump in her breast was benign."

"Lucky for her."

"I think most often these things turn out fine. Anyway, you sound pretty scared."

"It's not the biopsy itself, but the C word."

"Totally understandable. How would it be if I went with you to the doctor?"

"Really? You would do that? It's not the kind of thing I want just anybody to know about. Particularly Cody. But it sure would be great to have somebody to talk to in the waiting room—and when the lab results come back."

"Very wise. Let's discuss it all tomorrow."

"Whew! It means a lot to have you come with me. You're an angel. Bye for now."

Kate went to the bedroom and lay down for a nap, concerned for Larissa. Only seconds passed until her restless fears about Dean's absence resurfaced as she lay there alone. Feeling forlorn with her worries haunting her, she prayed: "Jesus, give me your peace. Take my burdens far away … far, far away. Change me into the person you want me to be, like your promises say you will whenever we ask. I want to love Dean with all of me. Come right now and help me rest. . . ."

18

CHAPTER

Dean's Honda rolled along tree-lined Minnehaha Parkway toward the Mall of America. The fallen leaves from the bare branches of oak, maple, and birch trees covered the ground in lumpy piles along the wooded parkway. He was driving Lindsay and Nicky to MOA, as Nicky called it, for a few hours of window shopping and R&R. Dean loved the hours they hung out together, like the way they had in days past when Lindsay lived at home before college. Kate was at church prepping for the Thanksgiving feast at Spirit Hills the following day.

"Being a bachelor feels super, ladies." Dean grunted to himself, feeling conflicted but wanting to appear upbeat. He winked at Lindsay sitting in the passenger seat, then winked again in the rearview mirror at Nicole sitting in back.

"Dad, you are such a bull-shitter," Lindsay said with a tone of mock disapproval.

"The Baron of BS," chimed Nicole, grinning and tapping Lindsay's shoulder. "Right, Linds?"

"Right. So, Dad, like you were saying," said Lindsay, "will you be moving back home sometime this weekend?"

"I'm not quite sure. Maybe in a couple days. What I'm still fuzzy about are the new ground rules your mom and I should agree on. I'm not trying to turn this into a tug-of-war, but it's important to keep everything straightforward and out in the open. Like, I know it's up to me to hang the strings of outdoor Christmas lights on the house, so I will. I always love doing that job anyway."

Lindsay leaned closer. "Hey, it's pretty clear what you're upset about," she said, glancing at Nicole, ". . . so understand that we're not trying to needle you."

"That's right, Dad," said Nicole.

Dean grimaced. He did not want to speak about Kate; she was their mother after all. Still, the girls needed some explanation for the seismic shift going on. "It's kind of like a dance," he went on, "but Mom and I are out of sync. We're stepping all over each other's toes and it hurts us both. I'd even go so far as to say we're dancing to two different tunes."

Lindsay frowned.

"Okay," he continued, "it's like we're trying to sing a duet but neither of us is singing the other's song. It's pretty hard singing a duet when only one person is singing."

"Gotcha," said Lindsay. "Ditto," agreed Nicole.

"I think everybody realizes how vital intimacy is in a good marriage, right?"

"Right." Both girls responded.

"So, the marriage I see your mom dancing to involves activities that are helpful and commendable, and people find all that laudable. Let me tread carefully here, but the one thing that holds a marriage together isn't a full schedule of good works, it's intimacy."

"Wait, I know the list by heart," Nicole responded. "Committee meetings, Bible study, housework, gardening, the children's Christmas musical, fitness classes, mission trips, and ... and . . ."

"Right on," said Lindsay. "And sometimes a little too much to drink."

An awkward silence descended. Dean could hear the tires crunching on the leaf-strewn street underneath the car. He kept his eyes firmly fixed on the road.

Lindsay turned and said, "You know, Dad, Mom is a closet drunk."

"Now wait a minute. Whoa, now!"

"She is. And we all know it."

"Be careful there. Don't start using your college-level analytical skills on your mother. I know you're getting A's and all that, but—"

"Why shouldn't I say it? It's true."

Nicole jumped in. "Dad, what you're doing is kinda like looking the other way, isn't it? Isn't that what you used to counsel people about?"

"You cover for her, Dad," said Lindsay. "You enable her."

"Oh, I get it. So we're hauling out all the lingo, are we? Well, I'm not so sure—"

"Dad, please! You're in denial."

He stared at Lindsay then silently turned his eyes back to the road with steely resolve. Whimpering sounds from the back seat punctuated the tension. Dean glanced in the rearview mirror and saw Nicole stifling tears. He braked and pulled over to the curb. He reached back and held Nicole's hand. "You're right, of course. Both of you are."

Dean stared through the window at joggers on the parkway trail and thought aloud, "Okay. So how are we going to handle this?" Nobody spoke. He patted Nicole's hand to comfort her. "Look, like I said, it's a dance. Mom genuinely believes in doing good works and serving others; nobody can deny that. And I believe she thinks she's leading the life the Lord wants her to."

"Daddy, shut up!" exclaimed Lindsay. "All of us know she drinks too much. So don't bother sticking up for her. And don't make everything about religion."

Dean was stunned. He'd never heard pushback like that from his children.

"It's the truth, Dad," Lindsay resumed. "It's her way of coping. She's on the go every minute, moving like a robot to the next thing. Being so busy never lets you in, into her private space … or us either."

Nicole sniffled like an injured six year-old. "Mom said you've been seeing another woman, Dad. Is it true?"

"What?! She told you *that?*"

Lindsay pressed on. "She said you've been seeing some woman on the sly. Have you been having an affair, Dad?"

Dean shut off the engine. His pulse raced. "Let me explain. You must've heard her wrong."

"It's a yes or no question, Dad," said Lindsay.

"Just like so many of my friends in school," Nicole said. "Their parents break up and everybody's unhappy. They're stuck seeing counselors and lawyers. Like this one girl on the cheerleading squad who's thinking of suicide because her folks are constantly fighting."

"Sweetie, no. No, no, no." Dean got out of the car and opened the rear door. Sliding into the back seat, he put his arm around his younger daughter. "Nicky, it's nothing like that."

"But Daddy, that's how it always goes. Somebody moves out and the next thing—"

"No, Nicky. It's not going to be like that at our house."

Lindsay leaned back. "So what about this other woman? Yes or no, Dad?"

Dean sucked in his breath. He let out a long blast, swallowed, and spoke as calmly as possible. "All right, you've got my word on this. Nothing happened. I … I admit I was getting emotionally close to a woman I rather liked. When it got a little too close, I stopped it. Period. We are still friends, sort of, but I took a big step by ending it and put a whole lot of distance between us. It's not like your mother may have let on. Nothing like your school friends' folks, Nicky. I'm happy it fizzled, and I mean that. So you can still be proud of your dad, okay?"

"Do you love her?" asked Lindsay.

"No." He paused. "Not in the way you're probably thinking."

"In what way then?"

"Well, in the way a man loves … who likes an old high school flame. That was then, this is now. It lasted a short while, and now it's over."

"Great." Lindsay paused. "You're hinting you still like her. Does that mean you're saying Mom was lying?"

"Look, Lindsay. She may be just exaggerating. I wasn't there to hear what she said."

"But," Nicole began, "if we believe you, and if you say you didn't do what Mom said you did, that means she is full of crap."

Dean couldn't believe his ears.

Lindsay looked warily at Nicole. "Hey, Nicky, you know Mom's a drunk. Drunks lie. If anybody is going to have an affair, it might be her and we'd never know it. Fact is, Dad can't get any from her."

"Damn it! That's enough! Where did you come up with that ugly talk?" It galled him that his children disrespected their mother so bluntly.

Lindsay held her ground. "But if one of you is telling the truth and the other isn't, who should we believe?"

"For what it's worth, and I really mean this," Dean struggled to calm himself, "I've never had an affair but I did feel something for this woman. End of story. Nobody asked me to end the relationship—I just did it. Because it was right. I knew in my heart God wanted me to stop."

Lindsay groaned, "Just once could you not bring God into everything?"

"Honey … ? Since when … ? That's the second time you—"

"Dad, you might as well know, I don't go to church any more. Since we're all telling the truth, I haven't since my sophomore year."

Dean felt the blood drain from his face. "I had no idea you felt like that."

"I was half-expecting you to apologize for 'lust in your heart,' Dad," said Lindsay. "Or some other sin from the Bible. You work so hard at being righteous."

Dean felt numb. "I can't believe I'm hearing this."

"You're a decent, normal guy, Dad," said Lindsay, shifting her tone and reaching back to touch his arm. "Everybody can have thoughts—sinful or selfish or whatever. You don't have to feel guilty about everything. Sorry to be so rough on you, Daddy."

Words evaded him, but he had to try. "Darling, I've always tried to set a good example, that's all."

Lindsay patted his arm, and Nicole leaned against his shoulder.

Dean stretched his arms toward each girl and touched them gently. "It'll be okay, girls. You're right. You've said some things a guy like me needs to hear—things I can learn from my dear girls. My brave girls."

"We love you so much, Daddy."

"We really do," said Nicole, hugging him tightly.

"We have to get Mom some help, though," Lindsay added. "And soon, I think."

"Mom's drinking has gone overboard," said Nicole. "We've all seen it."

"I'm fully aware of that," Dean said. "Yes, I realize she drinks too much." He shook his head. *Why have I let this go on? Why haven't I confronted this long ago?*

"What about getting her to an AA meeting?" Lindsay asked.

"There's a fine idea. Yes." He smiled stiffly. "An all-women's group would be a good start. At some point, Mom and I have to come together on this and agree. I'm tired of sucking it up and tolerating the way things are, but things have got to change between us."

Nicole spoke meekly, "What about, you know, um … the D word?"

Dean looked straight into each girl's eyes. "The D word? Evaluating that possibility is one reason I'm living on my own for a while. I can't rule it out as an option, but it's not at the top of the list right now."

Nicole bit her lip. "It's getting harder and harder at home without you."

"We want you both to be happy," said Lindsay. "That's a must. We just wish Mom would talk to us like you are talking with us now."

Dean felt pride for his daughters. "My prayers exactly, girls."

He got out of the car and back in the driver's seat, started the car, and drove on toward the Mall of America.

While his daughters shopped on their own, he sat at a crowded Caribou Coffee boutique, sipping a holiday drink with an extra shot of espresso. Gazing mindlessly at the shoppers passing by, he debated his next move. An image of Kate paralyzed in a wheelchair came to him. *How much easier and simpler it would be for everybody to understand our paralyzed marriage if they could see it that way.*

Kate was not in a wheelchair, however, and she was not physically paralyzed. Regardless of her vows, problem was he felt duty-bound to stay faithful to *his* vows. The burden of "for better or worse" and "in sickness or in health" weighed on him. His side of the vow felt ridiculously one-sided. No matter how much he focused on Kate's side of the marriage, though, he had vowed he would love her "till death do us part."

Am I in our marriage until my love *ends, or am I in it until my* life *ends?* Staring off into the distance, he slowly sipped his coffee as the shoppers continued to pass by.

CHAPTER 19

A t 9:00 the morning of Thanksgiving Day, Kate had been up since six getting ready to leave the house. Her volunteer duties today involved helping serve the annual All Souls dinner for as many as 500 guests at Spirit Hills Fellowship church. She sat in the kitchen at her computer numbed out, staring past the monitor and through the window at nothing in particular, while her heart beat like a scared child's.

The computer screen displayed her morning's "research" into Dean's "issues"—issues that had motivated him to move out and fueled his refusal to return home. Below the search bar where she'd typed "sexless marriages," she re-read a posting that reinforced her sense of self-blame.

> . . . I can count on one hand the number of times my wife and I have had sex in the past several years. Whenever she denies me, I feel like I'm the victim of a bait and switch. I get frustrated because I'm working a full-time job, being a good dad, and doing my share of work at home. All I want is to

be acknowledged in bed. How wonderful it would be if she showed me some true affection and passion. I'm feeling so devastated. . . .

It was little comfort for her that tens of thousands of couples were experiencing similar standoffs in their marriages. She felt miserable for not showing Dean more love and appreciation the past several years, and she knew it was time for her to do something radically different.

I need to act! I need to let my love for him show. And soon. Or is it already too late?

Dean's refusal to move back home scared her, although she was practicing telling herself a new, more positive story. *He and I will be together again, and we will make love better than ever.* The threat of divorce meant not only losing him but losing her lovely home and shattering the hearts of their two daughters. *Besides, I'm risking displeasing God. It's within my power to tip the balance. So what am I waiting for?*

She logged off the computer, grabbed her purse and car keys, and dashed out of the house to drive to church. Her mission? To win back her beloved husband no matter how risky or scary the obstacles were in her path.

"Welcome to Spirit Hills Church, Claire. This is God's house just like your synagogue is. We're all part of God's family."

"I'm sure everything'll be fine, Kate. No problem."

"I'll show you around. Just relax, Claire."

"Why don't you take some of your own advice?" Claire joked.

The celebratory mood energized Kate as she escorted Claire Wasserman through the throng of families already gathered for a free Thanksgiving feast. Many people were sifting through racks of clothing and talking in scattered languages as kids ran about freely. Claire seemed to enjoy the controlled mayhem in the main corridor as Kate led her through the swarm of lower-income visitors who buzzed excitedly about picking out donated clothes, household goods, and toys.

"Is all this stuff free for the taking?" asked Claire.

"Absolutely. And we make sure it's in like-new condition."

Kate noted Claire's nod of approval and her faint frown. "I realize visiting a church may be a little uncomfortable for you," said Kate reassuringly, "but we don't bite."

Claire laughed. "Nobody will corner me, will they? Or make me say fifty Hail Marys?"

"Nope. That's not going to happen. We're Protestants, Claire."

"Enough already, I believe you. Now it's your turn to relax. I'm doing fine."

Because Thanksgiving was a patriotic holiday for all Americans, not just Christians, Kate felt pleased Claire had accepted her invitation to volunteer. She gave her friend a quick hug, and together they walked into the massive fellowship hall. Immediately, both women were struck by Larissa's floral centerpieces gracing each of the forty tables.

How lovely! thought Kate. The orange and yellow mums with harvest-style grain stalks looked beautiful.

People of varying socio-economic levels and ethnic cultures mingled. One family with a mob of kids spoke in Arabic, and elderly folks in disheveled sweatshirts and jeans ambled over to the punch bowl. Teenage girls, some of whom looked pregnant, huddled together by food buffet tables, while suburban couples greeted the visitors. Curious youngsters wandered and played in clusters—mostly under the watchful eyes of parents, although many of the grownups were obviously distracted by the bounty set before them.

Banners decked the walls. Suspended over the double doors to the kitchen, a festive banner read:

Welcome to
ALL SOULS THANKSGIVING DINNER
We're thankful you've chosen to feast with us!

Another banner hung above a decorated podium:

The Bread of Life is Christ

Kate directed Claire to the lengthy serving line where volunteers buzzed making last-minute preparations. Claire's assigned spot for helping serve turkey dinners was next to Larissa. Kate smiled as Larissa saw Claire and yelped in delighted surprise. "Claire!"

"Larissa! Great to see you," said Claire warmly.

"You too. I'm thrilled you decided to join us!"

Ginny walked up carrying an armload of plastic aprons. "Here you go, ladies, one for each of you."

"Ginny! Just the person I was hoping to see," said Kate. "Take a minute, will you, and meet these lovely new volunteers. Gals, this is our kitchen coordinator, Ginny Ostrow." With a bright voice and a wink, Kate said, "Ginny's your go-to lady. She'll answer any of your questions."

Ginny smiled as she handed out plastic aprons and large industrial-sized spoons to each server. "It won't be long before the first round of families comes through these lines," she said, "so be generous with the portions you dish out. Double helpings are okay if a guest asks."

Kate stepped back, observing Larissa and Claire negotiating who would dish up the vegetables and cranberry sauce and who would serve the mashed potatoes and gravy. Kate overheard Larissa muttering to Claire, "For a while there, I thought I might be the only non-churchgoer here. Am I glad to have you aboard."

Claire poked Larissa playfully. "You can't fool me. The biggest reason you're here is you-know-who."

"What!?" Larissa swatted her good naturedly. "No way!"

"Oh, I know the truth when I see it," added Kate. "I'm with Claire. It's as clear as those green eyes of yours."

They all glanced across the room, where Trevor was dressed up like a Pilgrim preacher greeting people; he wore a brown tunic, matching breeches, buckled shoes, and an odd-shaped black hat.

"Admit it, Larissa," said Kate. "He's the most handsome man here."

"Oh, it must be his costume. . . ." Larissa paused, watching Trevor. "Although now that you mention it," she added grinning, "there is an element of truth in that statement."

"Ha! See? I told you!" Claire exclaimed.

Everyone laughed.

Helping Trevor greet visitors was Kate's friend Marlene Wilkins also dressed Pilgrim-style in a long dress, buckled shoes, and a white mob cap. Kate observed Dean standing near the podium to one side, as though ready to make an announcement. In her heart she truly did love him, and this time she *felt* that love. A warm surge of excitement rushed to her cheeks—not a blush, really, but a wave of explosive gratitude. *Look at that man, so distinguished looking, handsome, and easygoing. Why did I ever take him for granted?*

Meanwhile, young servers wearing T-shirts with the Spirit Hills logo carried stainless steel pans heaped with steaming food to the tables. The aromas spurred Kate's appetite. Her daughter Nicole was one of the servers, and she rushed out from the kitchen carrying a double armload of bread piled high in an old-fashioned basket. She almost bumped into another server, a boy who jumped out of the way to prevent the bread from flying helter-skelter. Kate and Larissa did a double take.

"Cody!" they said in unison.

"Hey, there," Kate overheard Nicole yell playfully at Cody. "Watch where you're going!"

"Well, excuuuuuuse me!" Cody responded as he and Nicole locked eyes.

"Cody—a server?!" asked Kate. "When did he volunteer?" It didn't seem like the kind of thing Larissa's son would be interested in doing.

"After helping me carry in the centerpieces," answered Larissa, "he sniffed around and decided to stay and help out. He didn't put up a fuss, either."

Kate detected a glint in Cody's eye, and Nicole's face reflected a similar interest back to him. It lasted only a split second, then Nicole moved past him, glancing backward with more than a little curiosity. He followed her with his eyes, equally curious.

Dean stepped up to the podium and said grace for the meal, then the mass of people lined up and moved along the serving lines with their harvest-themed plates and napkins. Larissa, Claire, and the other volunteers dished up heaps of food—scooping, dishing, and smiling.

Kate approached Ginny, who made sure the serving trays stayed supplied with turkey, mashed potatoes, dressing, and gravy. It pleased Kate how Larissa and Claire were getting into the rhythmic flow of the work. Their coordinated efforts made for a smooth-working, jovial team. Kate sprang into action as the serving trays needed replenishing.

"Looks like you're an expert at that, Kate," said Larissa.

"I've practiced for a few years, yes. But you're no slouch yourself."

"You never told me this would be so much fun," said Claire.

Each tray, each transfer, each glimpse of Ginny's appreciative face, each smile of encouragement from Larissa and Claire made the day more enjoyable for Kate. Dean's quizzical gaze, whenever she caught his eye, prompted a cheerful wink or benevolent nod from her. *Although he and I came separately, if we leave together it would be answered prayer. I wonder if he's playing hard to get. Maybe it's time to flirt a bit.*

Kate noticed an elderly man shuffle by. Jabbing him in the back, a crabby woman in a soiled Vikings jacket barked, "Move along, there. Move along."

The woman turned to the servers and commanded, "Don't skimp now. My belly is half empty every day, not like yours."

Larissa glanced at Claire. She gave the woman a big, big smile. "How about a double serving, then?"

The woman sneered, "Don't get uppity." Claire served her a double portion of vegetables, and Larissa spooned up extra potatoes and gravy. The woman shuffled on, grumbling.

"Our pleasure," said Claire, sincerely. She and Larissa leaned on each other's shoulders in a silent sign of solidarity.

Kate had seen it many times: volunteers engaged elbow-to-elbow in simple duties, supporting one another more than they might ever do without a common task. The value of working side-by-side in activities such as serving hot meals or chores like folding laundry in the church's clothing center had impressed her often.

As the meal was winding down and guests were coming back for seconds, Kate stepped out from the kitchen to the main hall and saw Larissa talking with the handsome "Pilgrim." *Look at that, Trevor and Larissa are mooning.* Seeing Larissa smile and laugh gave Kate goose bumps. *So this* was *why she wanted to come today.*

Delighted for both of them, Kate wished this very thing for herself and Dean. Glimpsing Larissa and Trevor reminded her of her own courtship days when Dean's eyes had peered into hers with excitement and promise. She spotted him across the hall. *I should never have let the excitement in my eyes go stale. Turn this way, Deano!* She wanted to open her heart to him, to invite him back into sharing the deepest parts of her. *I'll change in ways that will convince you. I'm sorry it's taken so long! But you'll see. We'll make love like you've been asking for one of these days.*

L arissa loosened her apron and kicked off her shoes as she served guests large slices of pumpkin pie topped with whipped cream. It pleased her to watch Kate approach Dean from his blind side and put her hands over his eyes. Startled, he turned to see who it was. Kate giggled and whispered something in his ear. Dean's face beamed with joy. Larissa smiled. *That's it, girl. More of that!*

Moments later, Larissa sat listening to Trevor preaching. The hundreds of guests eating dessert listened quietly as he stood at the podium, his voice ringing throughout the vast hall:

"We're thrilled you're here today and thank you for coming. It is *you* who are serving *us* with your humility. We hope you have enjoyed more than a delicious meal. We hope you've also received the nourishment of fellowship and community. We remember in Scripture the destitute widow whose offering of two pennies meant more to God than all the riches of the Pharisees."

Larissa felt tiny chills. Off to one side, Dean stood near Trevor in silent agreement. *I'm glad I'm here. It feels right.*

". . . Our savior Jesus said, 'Blessed are the poor in spirit, for theirs is the kingdom of heaven.' And that means all of us. Those who lack worldly riches may be closer to the Kingdom than those who have tangible riches, because the rich can depend too easily on their wealth. But in God's eyes, we *all* have value. Worldly possessions or status do not define us or make us better than anyone else. Rather, it is the common *bankruptcy* we share as human beings living in a broken, sinful world that unites us. Let us therefore celebrate God's special favor to each of us on this day of Thanksgiving."

A hush rustled through the hall. Larissa had not expected this, and she realized that her bias against God and religion had threatened to keep her from the uplifting experience she was now having. Claire put her arm around Larissa's shoulder in a show of empathy.

"Larissa, isn't this nice to be here?"

Larissa nodded in agreement. A shiver went through her as she continued listening to Trevor's resonant voice, absorbed in the passion of his preaching as well as the special connection she had with this man.

"… So let us all, on this American *holy* day," Trevor concluded, "leave here having shared a delicious meal of turkey and mashed potatoes and yummy pumpkin pie—*and* more aware of our common bond and value in the eyes of the one eternal God. We look forward to seeing you again next year. Free clothing and household goods and toys are still available as you depart. And please remember, we love you … God loves you … and we pray you will always love one another."

Loud applause rang out. Soothing twinges pulsed throughout Larissa's body. She remembered what Kate or Dean often said, "*I am greatly blessed!*"

Dean watched scores of people making their way to the exits. One family from each table won the centerpiece to take home, prompting well-pleased looks on their faces. He noted similar looks on Kate and Larissa's faces. The two women put their arms around each other's shoulders and high-fived. Dean listened to many guests saying "thank you" and "bless you" as they departed, affirming the countless hours of his congregation's efforts to contribute meaningfully to the guests. Dean reflected silently from the book of Romans, **"For we know that all things work together for good for those who love God, and who are called according to his purpose."**

He asked himself whether he had walked the path God wanted him to take regarding Kate. **"Remember not the former things,"** he heard in his head from Isaiah. **"Behold, I am making all things new; now it springs forth, do you not perceive it?"** Kate's affectionate gestures earlier signaled a shift in tone. Could he put aside his grief and open himself to her? *Starting now, I will trust You more, Lord, knowing You will make all things new.*

He watched Kate wishing guests farewell by the exit. She was unusually outgoing and unreserved, and he sensed a ray of hope. Larissa and Ginny were cleaning up tables nearby, chatting away. He savored the camaraderie they were sharing, cheered that they had become acquainted. Marlene walked up and joined them, adding to their banter. Lindsay and Nicole partnered in clearing off dishes from the tables. For one blissful moment, Dean felt suspended in an idyllic state while observing the women's friendly interaction and cooperative spirit. When Kate noticed him, she sent a playful wink that made him grin.

In so many ways, I am a blessed man. Blessed to the max.

She walked over to him and said quietly, "I'm so thankful for you. Yes, I really mean it. I've been wishing for something, Dean, do you know what it is?"

"No, what?"

She reached for his hand and held it in hers. "Can you see it in my eyes?"

"I guess I'm not quite sure." Her lovely blue eyes radiated new energy.

"I've been wishing for us to make love again. And I hope you'll believe me."

He wrinkled his brow. "That sounds, ah, wonderful. I was just wondering when God ... that is when ... I mean, you look terrific."

He felt her squeeze his hand.

"Let's just say I'm hoping wishes do come true. Especially this one. But if you need more time, that's fine." Her vibrant eyes twinkled. "Just remember I said it—and know I mean it."

She let go of his hand and he watched her walk toward the clean-up crew. Trevor ambled up to the women who were working and tipped his Pilgrim hat to Larissa.

"Look at the handsome man in that costume!" Dean overheard Larissa say, elbowing Ginny.

"Bet you never thought he could look so dashing, eh Larissa?"

"Hey!" cried Trevor. "It's a day for dressing up and being thankful. Get with the spirit."

"I think he should wear that getup every Sunday, don't you?" kidded Larissa.

"Larissa, give the Reverend a break, okay?" Kate said, putting on a fake frown. "He had a big job today shepherding his flock."

Larissa grinned. Dean chuckled watching her satirical expression inform everybody how much she admired Trevor. "Forgive me for teasing you, 'Reverend.' It just looks like you'll do anything for attention."

Trevor looked at her, amused, then at Dean and shrugged.

"His secret, ladies," said Dean as he approached the group, "is he's a flaming extrovert."

"Takes one to know one," Trevor replied wryly. "I didn't have to twist your arm very hard to get you to emcee, did I?"

Dean smiled then turned to Kate. "You and your helpers did a smash-up job today, my dear."

Kate's shoulders relaxed. "I'd say we're all pros by now. Thanks for noticing."

Nicole and Lindsay walked by carrying overloaded trays of dirty glassware and dishes. Good naturedly, Lindsay asked, "So, Mom, are you and these ladies planning to help us—or just stand there?"

"What do you say, ladies, shall we give them a hand?" Kate and the women got busy helping the girls.

Cody approached. Dean noticed him look at Nicole, who looked away in mock indifference. "So, it seems you two know each other, Nicole," Dean commented.

"Sort of … well, not really," Nicole said, trying to look none too interested.

"Pay attention to this young man, honey," Dean said. "He's going places."

Cody nodded awkwardly to Nicole. "Um, the name's Cody."

"Hi, I'm Nicole."

"Nice to meet ya," Cody said bashfully. "I work at MediMax, like your dad. But I'm just a warehouse rat. He's not."

They laughed.

"It's nice to meet you, too … uh, 'warehouse rat.'"

"Just call me Nicky."

Cody gave her a tiny grin.

Having witnessed the teens' interaction, Dean saw Kate nudge Nicole and Lindsay toward the kitchen. Cody trailed along. Dean smiled at

Kate when she glanced back. Larissa saw the exchange and raised her eyebrows, giving an approving smile. Trevor winked at Larissa and tipped his hat.

Remembering Kate's surprising new wish, Dean recalled, *"Remember not the former things. Behold, I am making all things new,"* he wondered how and when—and if—it would ever come true.

CHAPTER

"**M**alignant?"

"Yes, malignant!"

"No, it can't be!"

"Yes, damn it!"

"Oh, Larissa, now what?" cried Kate into her cellphone. She couldn't believe Larissa had cancer. Earlier in the week she had accompanied Larissa to her biopsy appointment. It was heart-wrenching to sit in the waiting room going over the pamphlets describing the alternatives facing breast cancer patients. Hearing Larissa describe her scared feelings before the doctor's exam intensified Kate's concerns.

After the procedure, Larissa told her, "I sat in the exam room in one of those flimsy robes staring at the clock for twenty minutes until the doctor and nurse came in. Dr. Myers carefully injected my breast with a huge needle."

"I would've jumped out of my skin," said Kate.

"Getting jabbed was only half of it. I'm even more anxious now, never mind the pain of the needle. Waiting for the lab results feels excruciating." Larissa gripped Kate's arm.

"The suspense must be awful," said Kate. "The results are what really matter anyway."

Larissa nodded. "They said two days, maybe three."

Kate gave her a thumbs-up sign.

Larissa's phone call with the bad news came while Kate was driving her SUV after another wine-fueled lunch with Marlene. Their hours working on the Christmas pageant had doubled now that December was in full swing. Snow was descending rapidly, clogging the streets and fogging Kate's windshield. She felt honored Larissa had chosen her to call for comfort, but saddened about the malignant lab results. The dread and powerlessness in Larissa's sobs drove Kate crazy. "I've heard enough. I'm coming to sssee you, Larissa. I'm on my waaay right now." *There I go again, slurring my words.*

"No, don't. Please don't think you have to," Larissa blurted between sobs.

"No 'buts' about it, I'm on my way, and that's that. Twenty minutes and I'm there."

Kate made a sharp U-turn and drove toward St. Paul. The slushy snowfall made driving difficult on the slippery streets. Larissa's sobs sounded desperate, and who could blame her?

"Uh ... are they *sure* the tumor is caaancer?" asked Kate. "Could there be some missstake or mix-up?"

"They said it's called *DCIS, ductal carcinoma* something. The worst thing would be if the next procedure shows the cancer is spreading. If so, besides radiation or chemo, which are awful enough, I would need a lumpectomy or maybe even a mastectomy."

"Don't go jumping to conclusions. Are you sure?" Hearing the terror in Larissa's voice, Kate felt icy pangs of alarm. Every woman's double nightmare—"cancer" and "mastectomy."

"Is there any good news, Larissa?"

"Well, they said DCIS is an early form of 'pre-cancer,' whatever that means, usually in one or more milk ducts. Hearing that gave me a tiny bit of hope."

"Thaaank goodness. Something to hang onto."

Slick icy patches on the road forced Kate to maneuver the steering wheel to keep from zigzagging. After hanging up, she berated herself for downing too many holiday drinks. Zingers of guilt hindered her driving as much as the sloppy roads. She took deep breaths and prayed, *Lord, be with Larissa right now. Give her your peace. Help her to deal with this and feel your healing power. And forgive me for drinking so much. In Jesus' name, amen.*

Impulsively, she speed-dialed Dean's work number.

"Dean Nelson," she heard him say, using his business voice.

"Skip, it's Katie. You said I could call during the day, right?"

"Yeah. What's up?"

"Well, this is reeeally important."

"Okay. Shoot."

"Terrible news about Larissa. She has a malignancy in her breast. It's been confirmed." Had Dean heard her slur the words?

"Oh, no. I'm so sorry. That's awful. What a blow." Muffled, she heard him say, "Dillon, tell the team I'll be right there."

"Are you interested in hearing about it or not?"

"Of course I am. But can you be quick? I have to head to a meeting."

"Well, if it's not the riiight time ... I mean, if ... if you don't really care to listen—"

"Look, Katie, all I said was, 'Just make it quick.' Of course I want to hear about it. Have you been drinking?"

He knows! Buck up. Switch subjects. Quick.

"Look, with my folks flying in next week from Maryland, I think it's very important for you to be living at home ... and to get to the airport on time to pick them up because I'll be busy at church. Oh, you know what I mean. Why aaam I bothering to explain?"

"Where did that nonsense about your folks come from? You're not making a lot of sense. What about Larissa's cancer? That's why you called, right?"

"I think I'll hang up now."

"Hold it. So, have you been drinking or not?"

"Aren't you ever coming home?"

Suddenly the SUV swerved on the snow-smothered pavement. The steering wheel jerked, loosening her grip. "But you have to believe me, I *am* moving in the direction you want, Skip. I haven't mentioned specifics, but I waaant you to know there's progress." She couldn't stop slurring.

"Look, if it's true you're moving in a new direction like you say, then we have a lot to discuss, Katie. So call me back later and we'll talk. Now will you get back to Larissa's cancer? … Hold it, Dillon is waving for me to hurry up. Darn it, I've gotta go."

She chewed the inside of her cheek, sensing she was about to slur her words again. How could she get her tongue back in control? Why had she stopped talking about the cancer? "The girls, Skip. They're asking about you. Can't you think of them?" She hiccupped.

"I have to hang up now. Bye." Another hiccup.

He sighed. "You're drunk. Goodbye." The signal went dead.

Oh no! I blew it!

The front wheels skidded on an icy patch as she drove across the Fort Snelling bridge, high above the frozen Mississippi River. Kate's reflexes reacted sluggishly. Her booze-fogged thinking impeded her concentration and reflexes. The SUV spun out of control. It happened too fast for her to react. Her front wheels skidded. Helplessly she slammed the brakes, making the vehicle swerve as it skidded into a curb and came to a jerky stop.

Red lights flashed in the rearview mirror. A police car's loud siren and blinking lights shocked her. She bellowed, "No! NO! THIS CAN'T BE!"

She banged the steering wheel furiously. A female police officer got out of her squad and approached Kate's door. Kate slowly put down her window. When the officer saw Kate was not hurt, she said, "Driver's license and proof of insurance, ma'am."

Kate stammered, fumbling in her purse. Muttering, she managed to pull out her wallet, open it, and hand it to the grim-faced officer.

The officer examined her driver's license. "Please get out of the car, Mrs. Nelson."

"Look, I'm sure there'sss some mistake."

"There's no mistake, ma'am. I suggest you open this door and get out. Now."

Standing inside the noisy, smelly booking station in the city jail, Kate knew she'd entered hell. The male booking officer in his blue uniform snapped orders. "Stand on that yellow line, ma'am. Now look straight ahead. Name?"

Kate gave her name for the umpteenth time. She stepped up to the yellow painted line on the floor, looked straight ahead, and heard the camera click as it flashed in her face. "Now, ma'am, turn to your right ninety degrees and look straight ahead." Another click and flash. Kate's woozy state made her unsteady. Supplying answers for the booking officer's pile of forms, she felt certain her mind had splintered to pieces. "Now sit on that bench and wait for further instructions."

The arresting officer's field sobriety test had measured .013 on the breathalyzer, nearly twice the legal limit. At the scene, Kate's finger had wobbled as she attempted to touch the tip of her finger to her nose. She'd also messed up counting backward from ten. Her comments about the nasty, icy road conditions meant nothing to the arresting officer.

Sitting helplessly in the back of the squad car, she'd watched the tow truck hook up her SUV and haul it away. During the ride to the police station, she fretted and sweated, lamenting the sorry state of her troubled soul. Nightmarish fears about Dean and the girls condemning her loomed in her mind. She imagined their horrified faces, her ruined reputation at Spirit Hills, the indignity of hiring a defense lawyer, appearing in court like a petty degenerate, the automatic loss of her driver's license, and the stigma of a police record.

Locked in the all-concrete room sitting on a bench, Kate felt like a common criminal. Her humiliation festered. A uniformed officer opened the steel door to the room, allowing her to exit. "Time for your blood test. Let's move it. Follow me, ma'am."

She reached for her purse with her cellphone. *Gone! Of course!* They'd been confiscated, along with everything that defined her.

Kate stood and staggered a bit, fidgeting and disoriented from being in custody and bossed around like an imbecile. She walked unsteadily behind the beefy male officer wondering, *When did my name become 'Ma'am'?*

The officer lifted her hand and jabbed her finger with a needle, taking a blood sample and feeding it into the blood-testing machine.

The ultimate test of her character came next—"the tank." The beefy officer opened the sliding set of steel doors and urged her inside.

"Well, look here, ladies. A fresh piece of meat!" screeched a woman's voice.

Kate turned. A fat, foul woman with crooked teeth and a bloody chin greeted her.

"Ain't she Miss Prim and Proper?" sneered a cellmate.

The officer raised his voice. "Knock it off." He turned to Kate. "You'll get one phone call after everything is processed."

"How long will that take?"

"A few hours, depending on how everything checks out. Without priors or warrants, maybe a couple of hours."

"Priors?"

"Is this your first offense, ma'am?"

She nodded yes.

"Shouldn't be too long in that case."

"What … what about getting my vehicle from the tow lot?"

He slid the steel doors shut with a slam. "Sorry, ma'am. Not my thing. Ask your attorney." He turned and disappeared.

Kate faced the half dozen women in the noxious cell. One jeered, one snored, one stared at the floor, one hummed senselessly, one babbled, and one looked straight at her like she was a newborn baby thrown into a snake pit.

"Little Miss Prim and Proper, eh?" snarled the fat woman. She shuffled toward Kate, emitting putrid breath between her crooked teeth.

Kate felt the urge to vomit. "Leave me alone. Please. Stop."

"What? You don't like us? You don't like being here? Oh, you think you're too good for us?"

Paralyzing fears rose up inside Kate, super-charging her impulse to escape. *Turn away. Ignore her. Pay no attention.*

The longest two hours and forty-seven minutes of Kate's formerly arrest-free, police-free, "tank"-free life ended when the beefy officer returned and opened the cell. "Okay, ma'am. You can make that phone call now."

She shuffled to the pay phone, dreading to call Dean. *He's going to hate me and yell at me. He has every right to be furious. I'm so scared. No, I can't ask him. But who? Who will come get me?*

L arissa's trusty, high-mileage Saturn rattled loudly. Nasty grinding noises came from the engine. Or was it the transmission? Larissa couldn't tell. The ice-packed, snow-smothered streets made driving to the police station on strange roads hazardous. She had to jerk the steering wheel often just to stay in her lane. *One more thing to worry about besides my cancer,* she groused silently. *There's just too much on my plate. I'm getting too old for this!*

Heavy snowflakes flew furiously at the windshield. Her mission: freeing Kate from jail and getting back home safely. Each moment Larissa fought off the distracting fears about the cancer harming her body. She sensed an army of marching cancer cells attacking her milk ducts, and her feeble health insurance plan was grossly underfunded.

Her aging Saturn wasn't much of a match for this weather either, and the mysterious grinding noises kept getting louder. Heavy snow kept falling and she kept fretting. Larissa finally glimpsed the police station up ahead through the frosty windshield. She parked and hurried inside, braving the freezing wind.

The officer seated in his bullet-proof glass cubicle glanced at her.

"Hello, sir. I'm here to pick up my friend Kate Nelson."

He scanned his computer screen. "DWI?"

"Yes, I'm afraid so."

"I'll need to see a valid picture ID, ma'am," the bored officer drawled through the thick glass opening. He scanned her driver's license, matching her photo with her face, giving her the usual male double take which her pretty looks prompted. She smiled curtly. He took in all he could see of her with one quick glimpse.

"Okay, Ms. Beaumont. Have a seat and fill out this form."

She sat down, unsettled by how his eyes made her feel vulnerable and exposed.

Getting Kate released took almost an hour, and by then she'd sobered up. Dusk was overtaking the daylight as they exited the jail and trudged to Larissa's car. Several more inches of snow had fallen.

"How can I ever thank you enough?" Kate exclaimed over the howling wind. She raised her arms in a gesture of freedom. "You have no idea how good it feels to get out of there!"

Larissa could only imagine what Kate had gone through. "A DWI? What's that about, Kate?" As they reached the car, Larissa scraped the windshield free of snow. They got in. Starting the engine and blasting the heater on high, Larissa asked, "Why on earth didn't you call Dean?"

"I was scared. I hated having to face him about something as awful as this, especially when things between us are so touchy. Just imagine, they hauled me in like a street criminal. I never had a clue what was going to happen next. It was terrible!"

Larissa gently touched Kate's cheek with her glove. "Let's sit quietly and regroup. The engine needs to warm up anyway."

"The shame of it. It was appalling, humiliating. How will I ever show my face to him?"

The freezing wind blew stronger, blasting the windows and shaking the car. "Breathe, Kate, just like you learned in yoga. Close your eyes. Inhale slowly. That's it. Hold it. Exhale nice and easy through your lips. Again . . ." Larissa put her arm around Kate's shoulders, helping settle her. "So what are your options, Kate?"

Kate's face puckered and she began to cry. "I feel like total crap. I've made a colossal mess for myself and for everybody."

"Your options? What are they?"

"I don't know. I've let Dean down, and my kids down, and even you down. Here I was coming to come help *you*, and now you're helping *me*. I'm so bummed about your cancer. You dear girl, how *are* you? You shouldn't have to come rescue me like this. Oh, it's all too bizarre."

Larissa gently laid her gloved hand on Kate's knee. "Calm down. Think rationally. Is this your first DWI?"

Kate nodded.

"Then shrug it off and move on. Things like this happen."

Kate shuddered. "It's all so confusing."

Larissa pictured Kate as one of those housewives you hear about who drinks secretly, sipping during the day. The extra amount Kate drank when they were eating lunch at Marlene's came to Larissa's mind.

"I just can't get my head around what's happened," Kate lamented. "How … ? How could I have let it get this far? And what will my girls say? Dean will freak out. How will I function without a car or driver's license? How?"

"Let all that go for now, Kate—let it slide. Sounds to me like the bigger issue is the drinking itself."

"Owww!" Kate caved against Larissa's shoulder, moaning. "How, Larissa? How am I ever going to deal with this?"

"Think it through. Are you worried about this as a pattern, or just this DWI?"

Silence.

"I see."

"Okay," Kate sighed. "This was not the first time I've driven intoxicated. Or, should I say, drunk?"

The harsh wind gusted, blasting more snow against the windows. Larissa put the Saturn in gear. "We can't stay sitting here. Let's get going." She headed across the parking lot toward the busy street, her tires squeaking in the fresh snow. "Where can I take you right now?"

"Oh, my God, anywhere but home."

"What about the impound lot?"

"Can't. They won't release my car without official police clearance. Twenty-four hours at least, I was told. And I don't dare go to Dean's office—not a chance." Kate groaned. "Wait! Church. Yes, church. I'll call Trevor and ask him for help."

"Okay, church it is."

Kate dialed Trevor's number while Larissa inched her way across the snow-congested parking lot. As the car approached the street, Larissa noted the traffic moving at a crawl.

"No!" Kate muttered. "It went to his voicemail." She hung up and punched in another phone number. "I'll try getting him through the switchboard."

The car lurched forward, hitting a large chunk of ice under the floorboards. A loud scraping noise occurred. Unlike the earlier grinding noises, Larissa now heard nothing. The car whimpered to a dead stop. No grinding. No clanking. No noise whatever.

"NO!" Larissa screamed. "Not now!"

"What . . .? Are we stuck?"

"What the hell does it look like? How can all this be happening?"

The freezing wind blasted harder and louder against the doors and snow pelted the windows. Larissa sank back into her seat, reluctant to venture out and assess the damage.

Abruptly, Kate's phone rang. "Trevor? Thank God it's you. We need your help!"

Trevor arrived twenty-five minutes later. His sporty MG was crusted over with chunks of ice as it crept through the ankle-deep snow. He pulled over, hopped out, and braved the fierce winds, bending down on his knees and peering under the Saturn's ice-crusted floor.

"The driveshaft is shattered!" he hollered over the noisy wind. "Have you called a tow truck?"

"Yes!" Larissa called out the slit in the open window. "But they're busy everywhere else." Larissa and Kate huddled inside without the heater on, clinging to one another like the frozen survivors of the Titanic.

"Pushing it to a repair garage with my MG is out of the question," yelled Trevor.

"Of course, I know." Larissa began freaking out. She glanced at the Saturn's odometer: 146,803 miles. *Can it be fixed? What will fixing it cost?*

Is it worth fixing? Fears shot through her about needing to buy a new car. Where would that money come from?

"You're lucky it stalled in the parking lot and not in the street," hollered Trevor. "Let's leave it sitting right here. It's safer and wiser, even if it means getting a ticket."

Kate opened the passenger door and got out, grimacing sheepishly at Trevor. "It's my fault. I'm so ashamed. All because of my stupid DWI. What now?"

"What? Did you say 'DWI'?"

"Sorry to say, yes. It was bound to happen one day, Trevor. I've been hitting the bottle. Today was the day."

Trevor whistled. "Wow, Kate. Who would've ever ... ?" The darkening sky and relentless blowing snow made him pause. "Okay, let's scrunch inside my car, and I'll get us to someplace warm. When the tow truck comes, Larissa, I'll have the guy take it to my friend's garage."

Sitting squished in Trevor's two-seater MG on Kate's lap, the three of them shivering, Larissa pondered life's travails. She resented many things in her past, yet oddly, at this strange moment, she wondered if her relationship with Trevor was genuinely serious. Despite the raging blizzard, she felt a rush of gratitude for Trevor and the Nelsons. Trevor's going out of his way for Kate was almost scary. *Hmmm, I wonder if he went out of his way for me, too?*

"Here we go!" declared Trevor, stepping on the gas. "It's getting darker by the minute and this blizzard is a beast. Hold on tight!" The car jerked forward ...

CHAPTER 21

D arkness covered Larissa and Trevor as they stood hunched in the blistering cold on the doorstep of her home. The harsh blizzard churned around them. Thirty minutes earlier they had dropped off Kate at her home, slipping and sliding through the heavy snow at every turn. As they'd waved goodbye, Kate had whispered to Larissa, "Thank goodness Dean won't discover the SUV is missing. Looks like there's a bright side to his camping out at that motel after all."

Facing Trevor in her doorway, Larissa rubbed her hands over his cheeks to warm them. He brushed off the snow chilling her face and chin. With her teeth chattering, she wanted him to read the inviting look in her eyes. "Well? Are you coming in?"

Trevor hesitated. His nose was inches away—would he try a kiss? She felt a giddy tension building within as the snowflakes swirled in their faces. She closed her eyes, half expecting his kiss.

"Sorry, I have to be leaving, Larissa."

"No such thing. I won't let you, Sir Lancelot. After everything you've done for us, won't you at least come in and have some hot cocoa?" She snuck a glance past him at his snow-smothered MG parked at the curb, wishing for the howling snowstorm to persuade him to stay.

"Uh, really, I do have to, uh, be going." He seemed to be searching for words like a nervous teenager who was saying good night on a first date.

Larissa opened the front door, tugging his sleeve for him to step inside. "Don't be shy. Come in and warm up." She stepped into the warm house, pulling Trevor's arm. "Let me show you some hospitality after all you've done."

"Well, maybe for a minute."

"Now that my car has so rudely reminded me of my finances, I need to hear your financial words of wisdom. My finances are headed for a breakdown."

"In that case, I'll try to be of help." He closed the door behind him.

She offered him the oversized easy chair, her "queen's throne" recliner, insisting that he sit down and get comfortable. "It's the best spot in the house. Have a seat." She sensed Trevor's pleased reaction to the decor and ambience she'd created; he glanced around the room, soaking in her tasteful touches.

"Sorry. It's late, I'm afraid, and I can only stay a minute." He remained standing.

She frowned in a friendly way. She hoped he liked the floral wallpaper and the restful walls painted a moss green and the antique oak bookcase.

"And where is Cody in this blasted storm?" he asked.

"He texted me and said he's stuck at a friend's house. He's going to stay overnight. In the morning, he'll get a ride here after the plows clear the streets. May I hang up your coat?"

He declined. She took off her own coat, and in doing so, she glimpsed First Lieutenant Brad Eichhorn looking out from his military portrait on the mantel. The last thing she wanted was to be under Brad's watchful eye. She wished his portrait would turn 180 degrees by magic. She was glad Cody was gone; being alone with Trevor seemed like a gift. He opened his coat, a good sign. *He might stay a few minutes longer—yes!*

"I'm afraid to say the solvency of Fitness and Flowers is precarious, Trevor. I hope you don't mind hearing about my problems."

"Not to pry, but how strapped are you?"

"Well, your forty centerpieces for Thanksgiving helped me break even for the month—otherwise I'd have been in the hole. What a godsend. That revenue meant everything."

"I'm glad it worked out so well. And you can be proud of your work."

"Thanks. It wasn't all my doing; it was Kate's, too. I'm eternally grateful to you for coming to our rescue today, and for the offer of your mechanic friend's help. You're a real lifesaver."

Trevor shrugged modestly. "Parts and supplies will eat up a couple hundred, I suppose. But don't worry; Marty will give you a good deal on labor. He's a great guy. We'll get that old clunker running again, sure thing."

"It's been my workhorse, and there's nothing in the budget for a new one."

"Like I said, I'd better be going before the roads get any worse."

"It's so nice having you here. Won't you stay another minute? I'll get the hot chocolate started. Sit down and make yourself at home." *Am I being too pushy? Needy?*

"Well, if you insist ..." He sat on a straight-backed side chair, yet seemed uncomfortable.

Walking to the kitchen, she ventured, "As I was saying, you were our Sir Lancelot in shining armor today—driving an MG no less."

"Two damsels in distress, how could I resist? And if you don't mind me saying so, I loved being that brave shining knight."

Turning on the stove, she put water on to boil. She imagined them sharing their lives far into the future. Was he the real thing? The notion of being in bed with Trevor spurred her imagination. Out of respect for him, she would never in a million years suggest anything so obvious, but she could hope, couldn't she?

As she walked back to the living room, Larissa envisioned him springing out of his chair and embracing her. The words *falling in love* and *living our lives together* ran through her mind. Would the mischievous gleam in her eyes entice him? She imagined the hair on his chest brushing her skin and her hips gyrating against his pelvis. Regardless of how much she telegraphed her willingness, however, it had to be his move. ... or did it?

She turned her head and looked toward the staircase, then up to the ceiling. "It's so horrible out, so dangerous, what if you stayed the night? You're certainly welcome to."

He caught her drift. "Unfortunately, I think we both know that's not for the best."

No surprise. He said that because of his religious values and sense of morals. "Are you offended, Trevor?"

"No."

She sighed. "Thank goodness." She admired his restraint; it made him special. She looked at him earnestly, her spirits lighter. "Thanks for having the guts to say that. I mean, thanks for pressing the hold button. I appreciate a man who can do that." *He's a man I can trust—and the invitation still stands. Someday perhaps!*

She sank back into the recliner and relaxed. She didn't have to act sexy or hot, even though her hormones were nudging her. Believing things could be heading in the right direction was enough for now.

He buttoned up his coat, saying, "Sorry, I *really* do need to be going. It's late."

A frown darkened her countenance. "But the hot chocolate! ... Look, this may be the wrong time entirely, and I'm probably speaking out of turn, but maybe we should hear each other's perspectives about religion and faith. You know, um, the way you believe, and the way I ... I don't. Is this something to get into now, or should we put it off until another time—or never go there at all?"

He knit his brow. "Heck. What's on your mind? I suppose now is as good a time as any."

"Well, hmmm, okay, here's how I see it: Your religious ideas and beliefs seem quite strong."

He nodded. "I see. And might I guess what you're thinking? That you dislike organized religion?"

"Kind of, yes. You could say that I'm aware of how we each have built our lives on different foundations, that we're from two different planets theologically."

"And you're hinting you don't care much for the planet I'm from?"

Bingo. Bull's eye. "Let's just say I see the potential for conflict." Her gaze softened with empathy. "I half expected by now you might've told me I needed to become born again … to get on my knees and beg Jesus to come into my life."

He flinched. "Not a bad idea, but have I really given you those vibes?"

She shook her head. "Well, no, not completely."

"So what do you honestly think?"

"I think *if* there is a God, he or she sits on his or her hands watching us suffer and struggle down here, then gets bored and looks for something else to amuse him or her."

"Wow, that's heavy."

"And you?"

"I believe God wants everybody to know peace and joy and grace, and never wants anyone to be alienated from His love."

"There! That's exactly my point. What if God is a *she?* And if she is loving and perfect, then why are we living in this shitty, god-forsaken world?"

Trevor shifted in his chair. "What you're describing is sin, and it cripples everyone. I agree that Christians may give non-believers a poor impression of God. As an imperfect 'believer' let me ask, have you seen any love lately? Any love from Kate, for example? Any love from the folks serving Thanksgiving dinner at Spirit Hills?"

"Yes, I'd say so."

"What other examples of love in action have you seen recently?"

"Is that a trick question?"

"Just answer it and see where it goes."

"Uh … let me see. Well, there was today when you came to pick us up at the drop of a hat. That was love."

"Okay. Good."

"You also told me you could save hundreds of dollars on my car. And you took Kate home and said you'd hold her DWI in confidence—I think that was loving. Is that what you mean?"

He smiled softly. "That's what I mean, yes. Any other times?"

"Ummm, Kate offered me the big floral job for your Thanksgiving dinner, and the dinner itself helped all those hungry people. So your point is?"

"God is love, Larissa. And we are *all* God's people, every one of us. Some of us know it, some of us don't. Of the people who follow Christ, nobody is perfect, by any means, but we try to place others' interests first, their best interests, and to allow God's love to live in us and show through us. So I'm curious: Do you honestly dislike or despise the Christians you've met lately?"

"No. Not at all. Not in the way you're asking."

"Okay. Then might there be something else that's coloring your vision? You know, some baggage from your past? Or some hurt about the way you were raised that you're carrying around?"

"Am I mad at God?"

"That's a start. Are you?"

"Damn right I am. I think organized religion is a crock. People who say they're Christians, who go to church, are hypocrites. Uh, not any of you guys, though. I've not seen that in you or Kate or Dean."

"Larissa, whoever the hypocrites were years ago who turned you off to God, where are they now?"

Even Jerry and Gladys weren't hypocrites, though they weren't perfect either. "Alright, I guess I see where you're going with this. And ... ?"

"There *is* evil in this world, and both you and I have seen it and felt it. As for today's hypocrites, they still give Christianity a bad name. That includes me and others at times when we act badly, but we still strive to live holy lives. So please don't make the mistake of blaming God. People in the church fail all the time. But God and Jesus and the Holy Spirit, they never fail. Look, I'm only trying to say that sincere Christians are never perfect, but we try."

Eeeeeee! She heard the kettle's whistle screech softly.

Larissa's mind swirled. She hadn't expected this. "You and Kate and Dean aren't like the people when I was little who wouldn't let me know my parents or tell me why I was an orphan. You're right about my being mad as hell at God. I *am*. Where was *He* when they took my mother away? If He, if *She*, is so darn powerful and loving, why didn't He or She do anything? How about my being bounced around as a kid from one foster pig pen to another? By the time Jerry and Gladys took me in, I was seriously depressed and thinking of suicide."

Trevor shed his coat, crossed to her, and knelt on the floor. "I'm so very sorry," he whispered. He knelt humbly before her, reaching out his hands. She let him hold hers as she began to tremble. Clearing her throat, she spoke haltingly. "You hit a nerve, Trev … one I thought had healed years ago."

She realized he could have chosen to parrot Scripture verses meant to soothe her with uplifting spiritual insights, or he could have preached a Pollyanna gospel message to her. She was glad he didn't. "I was a helpless little person, Trevor. Those big adults held my life, my fate, in their hands. They messed with me. They lied to me. And none of them really cared about my welfare. Do you know what lying does to a child? If God was watching, He didn't care. Or He wasn't there at all. So yes, anytime I hear 'God loves you,' I cringe."

Eeeeeee! She heard the kettle's whistle screech louder.

Trevor touched her face gently. "Being with you means a great deal to me. None of this needs to be solved tonight." He waited quietly, giving her space. He stroked her hands. The wind howled; fierce gusts blasted the windows.

"Listen to that awful wind," she said. "Are you sure you won't think about staying? It's bitter cold, and more snow is coming. Staying would be so much safer. And better."

He handed her a tissue. She blew her nose. "And would that mean we might sleep together?"

"Ummm … maybe. What do you think?"

"You brought it up, Larissa. You go first."

She giggled, now that the tone of their conversation had shifted. "Well, I guess there are two options: *A,* I sleep in my bed and you sleep down here on this lumpy old couch. Or *B,* we share the same bed."

He grinned. "Are you trying to seduce me?"

"Trying to? Well, yes, just a little."

They laughed.

EEEEEEE! The kettle's shrill whistle couldn't be ignored any longer.

She jumped up and went to the kitchen, "Regardless of what I just said about the hold button and respecting your morals," she went on, "I kind of like option B better. We'd just have to stick to our own sides of the bed." She wanted to say, *Ravish me in the most sensual way imaginable.* She reached the stove and turned down the heat under the kettle. *Saved by the whistle!*

He quietly followed her and stood in the doorway. "Once I'm next to you, though, I'm not sure how I'd ever be able to … to not . . ." He let the statement drift away. "And if we don't, or can't, stick to our own sides of the bed?"

She reached for two cups, poured in cocoa powder, and stirred in the hot water.

"If I stay, I promise to honor your virtue and remain chaste," he said. "Someday, if we make love, I'd want us both to be clear about where we're headed, where we're going for the long haul."

She shifted her feet, trembling now for a new reason. "I love that idea, and I *want* that … someday. Your gentlemanly promise to honor my virtue tonight, to wait until it's clear between us about the future, sounds like a good idea to me." Smiling, she let him see into her soul. "Meanwhile, let's have our hot chocolate."

He laughed. "But can I trust *you?*" He laughed again. "What if our emotions take over?"

"We've both agreed. That's good enough for me. One of us will have to be strong enough to press the hold button."

"Maybe we should go back to Plan A. I'll sleep down here on the couch and you sleep up in your bed."

"But I thought we just … ? I can't stand the idea of you sleeping on that lumpy couch."

"I insist. It won't be the first time I've crashed like that. Just give me a warm blanket and a decent pillow. No problem. I'll be fine."

"You've made up your mind?" She stuck out her tongue, followed by a broad smile. "Okay."

He held his thumb straight up. "Plan A it is."

She gave her own thumbs-up, then made a fist and they fist bumped.

L arissa awoke in her bed, aware the storm had stopped. She imagined the warmth of Trevor's body downstairs on the couch. The alarm clock showed 4:18 a.m. She'd just been dreaming a fantasy: *Will I ever have another baby? Will he and I have a baby together?*

She sat up, rubbed her eyes, put her feet on the floor, and tiptoed downstairs.

There he lay, asleep on the couch, one arm hanging down and touching the floor. *Should I, or shouldn't I?* She tiptoed closer. *What will be his reaction to my cancer once he knows?* This moment might be her best chance.

She crawled under the blanket, squeezing next to him. For the first time in years, her body touched a man's body. The sensations felt comforting, sublime. His masculine scent encouraged her to cuddle closer. The slim, cramped space on the couch encouraged her to squeeze tighter. Sound asleep, he responded unconsciously, cuddling closer to her. She placed her bare arm on his, letting their skin-to-skin contact excite her. His body turned toward hers instinctively. She realized at a visceral level she could not go the rest of her life without this body-to-body union, particularly with someone as special as Trevor. She felt tingly sensations in the deepest, hidden parts of herself as she envisioned their two bodies combined in synchronous unity.

In his dreamy state, he muttered, "We agreed. I'm keeping my promise," and slipped back into contented slumber.

As it should be, she thought. She lay back, drifting off to sleep, trustful and peaceful. Sleeping came easily with a man as strong in body and morals as Trevor. He'd kept his side of their bargain, and she loved him for it.

Three hours later, Cody came crashing through the back door. Jarred awake, Larissa gasped; he was home earlier than expected. Kicking off his snow-covered boots, Cody flung his jacket on a kitchen chair. She glanced at the clock: 7:21. A cloudy gray sky seeped through the windows.

Cody walked through the living room heading for the stairs, then stopped in his tracks. Larissa peeked out from under the blanket. She could tell her son noticed two bodies on the couch, two lumpy forms covered by a single blanket.

"MOM! What the hell is going on?"

Trevor lifted his head, croaking in a groggy voice, "Is it morning already? I'd better be going."

Shock animated Cody's face. He stared at Larissa. "WHAT ... ? I DON'T BELIEVE IT!"

Trevor peeked out from the blanket, looking at Cody in a daze. Larissa put her finger to her lips to shussh Cody from talking. Cody recognized Trevor and grimaced. "MOM!"

"I can explain, Cody."

Immediately Cody continued up the stairs to his room. She heard the door slam shut.

Trevor sat up, speechless.

They looked at each other.

The delicate matter of persuading Cody that everything was on the up-and-up constricted Larissa's throat, rendering it dry and speechless.

CHAPTER

The foul mood inside Dean's car got worse by the minute. Dean listened to Kate as she sat beside him in his Honda the morning after the blizzard telling him about her DWI. Fuming mad, Dean grumbled, "How the hell could you have let that happen?"

"Hey now, aren't you just making a big stink about it? Try calming down, okay?"

On his commute from the SleepWell Inn to MediMax, Dean had gone out of his way to pick Kate up at the house, all on bumpy snow-packed streets still mostly unplowed. A hefty nine inches of white stuff had smothered the metro area overnight, and Kate's phone call that morning begging him for a ride to the impound lot irked him. "Why didn't you find your own way to deal with this mess and not drag me into it?"

She stared straight ahead. "Can we just get there, please?"

Traffic was maddeningly slow despite the metro's snowplow crews doing their usually efficient job. He abhorred being late for work, especially due to her stupid drinking.

"I'm sorry, Dean. I know you're pissed off. I didn't make the blizzard happen, you know. As soon as I get the SUV released, you can be on your merry way."

"Don't get chummy," he huffed. What other nonsense about her DWI, he wondered, was she holding back.

"I wanted to call you first, instead of Larissa, but I was afraid."

"Afraid of what?"

"Afraid you'd get angry, like you are right now. Sadly, I was right."

"I'm not the one who drove drunk."

"Stop it. You don't have to be so mean about it, or rub it in. I've never seen this side of you before, Skip. I don't like it."

"Where in God's name is your remorse, Kate? What a fricking mess you've made!"

"So you think that getting arrested doesn't bother me?"

"Well, does it? You've made a big mess, and now you hope to keep it hush-hush. I haven't even heard you say you're sorry about it."

"Well, I am. I'm *very* sorry about it."

"A DWI is hardly a speeding ticket, you know. And I haven't a clue what you're going to do about your drinking." Dean knew he was rubbing it in, but everything about her DWI forced him to end his complacency. He'd seen this day coming, and here it was. Honestly, he'd been looking the other way, but he couldn't stay on the sidelines any longer. "What did you tell Nicky last night about all this?"

"I said the car got stuck in a snowdrift and that Trevor was nice enough to give me a ride home."

"That's it? Nothing about the DWI?"

"Well, it's true. Trevor did give me a ride home." She looked down at the floor.

"C'mon, Kate, that's only half of it. The reason wasn't a snowdrift, but your driving drunk. Geez! Keeping the truth from her like that is flat-out dishonest."

"Do you have to be so mad about it? I only did it to protect her."

"No, you didn't. You did it to protect yourself. Right now, it's crucial that we get a hold of an attorney. Have you tried calling Hal?"

"No!" exclaimed Kate. "Hal and Ginny can't find out about this."

"Oh, boy. More covering up. But he can refer somebody who specializes in these cases. Don't you get it? Hiring a lawyer ASAP and getting a court date is a must."

"Maybe, but I don't want the Ostrows knowing about it."

"Then I'll call Hal."

"No, don't. If you dare to, tell him it's for somebody else. Don't mention names."

"I can't believe this. You want me to lie."

"Let's try seeing the bright side, Dean. I still have forty-eight hours to drive including getting the SUV home."

"Small comfort."

Dean recalled her mentioning the forty-eight-hour grace period for first-time DWI offenders prior to the six-month, automatic suspension of the person's driver's license.

"I'm sorry my SOS call interrupted your morning," said Kate. "I do want to make you a happier man—a happier husband—and I know this is fouling up all that."

"I think a DWI is definitely ... did you say 'happier husband'?" He whipped the steering wheel around a slow-moving car ahead and hit the accelerator, spinning the tires.

"I did." She folded her arms across her chest, suppressing her temper.

Dean slammed on the brakes to avoid colliding with the vehicle in front of them. The Honda came to a skidding stop. "You're blind to the consequences of all this, Kate. Maybe getting your butt kicked will shake you up a bit. As for my being happier—*our* being happier—it would be great to hear your new ideas about how to improve things."

Kate sat mute. She stared out the window. "Remember my wish that I told you about at Thanksgiving dinner? My wish for us to make love?"

"Ah, yeah, I remember."

"Well, it's gotten stronger. But with my folks flying here in a couple of weeks for Christmas, we won't have a chance to do much about it. We can't change their plans to visit us. Everything has to go on as though this DWI never happened. And I'm going to make sure it does. The Christmas musical won't go away either, just because you might like it to."

"Oh, is that so? Now you're a mind reader? Well, maybe it's time to let your folks know a few things."

Kate stared darts at him. "Enough, Dean. By the way, are you still going to make the twinkling star over the manger? Or is that something else you're not going to—"

"Yes. Yes, I am. It'll be there. I'll make sure. The armature is half built in my room right now, and I'm getting ready to add the paper-maché, then the strings of lights. So, Kate, how about the girls? … Oh, I get it. You want us to put on a show."

"We can figure this out," she countered. "We have to come up with a new plan."

"No more dodging, Katie. No more excuses. The girls have to hear what happened straight from you—and what you mean to do about it and how it got this far."

Her voice shot up an octave. "No! We have to spare them."

"It's not a secret, Kate. They already know."

Her face fell. Dean saw fright in her eyes.

"Um, well, maybe so. They made that pretty clear to me the other day."

"They've known for quite some time. We all have. We've just kept our mouths shut about it." He glanced over at her. "Does that shock you?"

She shuddered.

"You need to tell them, Katie. They have to hear everything. The failed breath test, the handcuffs, everything. Don't minimize."

Kate's face turned red. "Before doing that, I have to know, what do *you* have to say? I have to know where *your* head is at."

He took a slow, measured breath, making sure his voice stayed calm. "I think it's all part of a larger dysfunctional pattern. The drinking is a way for you to cope, but its time has passed." His hand reached for hers. He glanced at her with softness in his eyes. "Could it be connected to your growing up? To some deep-seated scars from how you were raised?" He waited. "Let me ask: were you ever sexually abused?"

She shook her head. "Not that I know of, no. Not unless it happened when I was too little to remember."

"Whatever it is, though, the drinking is not a solution."

"I think the drinking is from guilt. Massive guilt. Do you think I need treatment? Professional help?"

Dean felt a surge of compassion. "Yes." His former training as a professional addictions counselor kicked in. "An objective, professional chem eval would be a good start. Treatment? Out-patient most likely, followed by supervised aftercare. It may have to wait until your folks leave, but you can set it up beforehand to start after New Years."

She paused. "AA?"

"Absolutely. It's always worth it. It worked for me."

"And if I don't ... I mean, if I can't ... I mean, if it's harder and more ingrained than I think it is, and I can't stop? What if the drinking ends but not what's driving it? Are you still in?"

He wasn't sure. His feelings felt too raw. "Right now, being honest and open to getting help is all that matters."

"But the timing? The holidays, the pageant, and Mom and Dad's visit? I agree it'll probably have to wait until after they leave."

He saw they were within blocks of the impound lot. The pressure to get to the office was still mounting. He stopped at a stoplight. "Getting help shouldn't wait, and you shouldn't want it to, but I see where you're headed. Getting through the cocktail hours that your folks love, and those long dinners with wine and more wine ... well, it's obvious they'll ask pointed questions if you keep off the sauce. So that's a bummer."

"It's a big problem alright. The pressure will be horrendous to go along with their cocktail hours and toasts. No such thing as stopping at two or three—not them." She looked straight up, as if seeking divine wisdom. "But more important than that, are *you* fed up? Not just about the drinking? About *us*? I have to know."

"It's hard to say. I'm trying to be patient."

"Which means? How are you leaning?"

He paused. The stoplight changed to green and he stepped a little too hard on the gas, making the car fishtail. "About our staying together?"

"Skip, it makes all the difference if you've already decided it's over between us, or if you're sticking it out only for the sake of the kids."

"Okay, if I do move home, it may or may not be to stay. We can't go back to playing the same old games. Things have to be different, genuinely different."

"What games?"

"You really don't think we've been playing games? Are you serious? Well, for starters, how about the Happy Couple Game?"

"What on earth? Do you really have to put it that way?"

"Look, it has to be more than you wanting us to look good, Katie. It'll take some convincing for me to believe you're really open about new ways our relationship can get better."

"You may not realize it, but I've been sorting out a whole bunch of things lately. Something inside me is shifting. Big time. It feels like some old attitudes are losing their grip."

"You're not just saying that?"

"Trust me, I'm changing. Maybe not much shows on the outside right now, but from the inside it feels a heck of a lot freer and more positive."

"Freer? More positive?" Dean wondered if the glacial ice was truly melting.

The turn for the impound lot appeared, obscured by a tall snowdrift. "There's the sign," he said, putting his foot on the brake. He pulled into the snow-packed lot and stopped the car. "Okay, Kate. Hop out. We'll hash this over later." Squeezing her hand and smiling, he tried to show his cooperative spirit.

"That helps," she affirmed. "I hope you'll wait here while I go inside and pay the charges. At least long enough for me to make sure I won't be stranded."

Dean knew agreeing meant he would have to sit longer, and stew longer, and he wanted to blow her off. "Just hurry. And wave when you're done."

"What I want you to hear me say," she said, as she opened the door and frigid air blew inside the car, "is that I know this would've never happened if I'd been the lover you deserved."

"What?" His head jerked toward her. "Did I hear you right?"

"Yes, you heard me right. I haven't been a willing wife to you, the wife you deserve, and that *is* changing."

He blinked. "That is the most wonderful thing you've said in ages." His frustration lessened.

"Believe it. Because it's true, Dean." She got out of the car and walked through the deep snow to the building.

Dean maneuvered the Honda to a nearby parking space. Each ticking minute delayed his getting to the office, but her words 'believe it' stirred in him. Keeping the motor running, he phoned the office, wasting no time. "Hi, Dillon. Give me the latest updates, okay? It's slow going this morning."

"Hardly anybody has made it in yet. Your meeting time with Carl has come and gone, boss. But everyone understands, given the storm."

"Gotcha. Is Carl ornery?"

"He hasn't made it in either."

Getting to work on any day after a Minnesota blizzard meant delays and rearranged schedules, Dean knew. Carl Langley, the man he most had to please, would be digging out from an avalanche of phone calls and texts, never mind snowdrifts, for most of the day.

"Flexible and adaptable," muttered Dean. It was a time-worn phrase the Spirit Hills' volunteers used during trips to Third World countries, where things rarely went smoothly. Dean felt anything but flexible and adaptable. He gave Dillon instructions about revising his schedule, then hung up and gazed blankly out the window. *How did it all come to this? But what she said about being 'the wife you deserve' ... wow!*

He dialed Hal's number and Hal answered.

"Hey there, Hal. Have you got a minute for me to run something past you—a legal question?"

"You caught me on a break. Sure, Deano. The lawyer is 'in.'"

Despite the glimmer of hope from Kate moments before, Dean felt he had to ask the tough questions that dogged him. "Look, I realize Kate wants to know when I'll be moving back home, but should I move back home for good, or is it finally time to give up and move on?"

Hal hesitated. "A legal separation?"

"Something like that. Maybe more."

"And your rationale for such options would be … ?"

"I've been debating if I have the stamina and patience for an all-out overhaul of our bed habits. Something so major could take years, even if we both worked at it, and it's a long shot that could go off track anywhere along the line." Did he really mean that? Dean heard himself speaking from long years of conditioning, almost like a stranger talking, but Kate had said, 'the wife you deserve.'

"How impatient are you? What's your timeframe?"

"Basically, I'd stick it out through the holidays, then have a divorce lawyer draw up the papers. As for now, she has a DWI she needs to handle."

"What DWI?"

"Yesterday she had a minor accident while driving, but the police officer who stopped her discovered she'd been drinking, so she actually spent time in lockup." Dean didn't feel guilty for coming right out with the facts. "Too long of a story to get into right now. I've just brought her to the impound lot to make sure she gets the SUV released. I'd appreciate it if you'd give me the name of a good attorney who specializes in DWIs."

"Sure can. But a DWI? What brought that on?"

Dean didn't care much if Kate got peeved about his telling Hal. It was unlikely he would tell Ginny; Hal could be trusted to keep sensitive information confidential. "As I was saying, I think I'm basically on hold for the short term. My gut will tell me when it's time to make the 'yes' or 'no' decision."

"Can you honestly say you'll be at peace however it turns out?"

Dean paused. "In AA, we have a saying: *Acceptance is the answer to all my problems today.* Learning to accept things the way they are helps a person feel less resentful, and to quit fighting reality. Surrendering to 'what is' without trying to change everything can be healthy. If I could discipline myself to manage my feelings like that, I'd no longer have to focus on what's missing in our marriage—I'm an expert at that. If I surrender to the relationship the way it is, then I could stand to gain some peace."

"Willingly? No conditions?"

"Yes to both."

Hal was quiet. "If you were my client, I would take each part of what you just said and put it on a flipchart. I'd ask you to drill down on each one: feeling resentful, quit fighting, how things are, no conditions, and so on. You might have differing ideas and feelings about each."

"Sounds wise. I've jotted down some ideas already and journaled about them. Debating them with someone experienced like you would help."

"Let's plan on it. How about later today?"

"I don't think that will work. I'll get back to you, and email you a few better times." Dean looked to see if Kate had exited the building. "Here I am, Hal, at the peak of my health and my career, yet so much time has been squandered and so many years wasted. Just thinking ahead to our 25th anniversary makes me shudder. Will my sanity hold up that long? Things would have to change dramatically to make me want to hang in there."

"Am I hearing that you've already made up your mind?"

"The list of negatives for getting divorced is an arm-and-a-half long. What bugs me is that Lindsay and Nicole shouldn't have to take sides or deal with the fallout. I can recite the list of ugly consequences in my sleep."

"Tell you what, Dean. I need to get back to a meeting, but consider this. Let's say you get divorced and are single, and you're living in your own apartment doing your own thing. I have a hunch what'll be going through your mind is something like: 'When will I meet an attractive woman who loves me? A woman who'll be a passionate lover, the kind I've been aching for—whom I might even marry someday.'"

"Wow, Hal, you're right on. Am I deluding myself? Will it be worth all the trouble? Considering the collateral damage, do you think it's worth it?"

"Look at what Larissa did for you. She showed you the kind of woman and lover who would make your life meaningful. She awakened the possibility that you could become the person you most want to be."

Dean swallowed. "Absolutely right."

"Have you concluded, then, that Kate will never be that woman?"

Dean remained silent. Hadn't she just said, 'I want to be the wife you deserve'? Hadn't she said the same at Thanksgiving?

"Can you keep waiting for Kate to turn her spots into stripes? Or, do you think your gambling on divorce is worth it, in the hope that the woman you need is out there waiting for a guy like you?"

"It would be nice to see a billboard from God showing me what His will is."

Hal drew in a long breath. "I'll be blunt: Are you secretly thinking that this mystery woman *is* Larissa?"

"No, not anymore." Dean shook his head. "She and Trevor … well, you know." He sighed. "Her clone would be great, though."

Hal laughed. "Okay, then instead of focusing on Kate not living up to her vow, what about *you* living up to *your* vow?"

"Exactly my dilemma."

"I read somewhere once, 'Just because someone doesn't love you the way you want doesn't mean they aren't loving you with all they have.'"

"Wow, there's wisdom in that, Hal." Dean looked up and saw Kate emerging from the impound office, waving. Dean thanked Hal, hung up, and lowered his window as Kate walked closer.

"They're getting the SUV right now," she hollered. "I'll be on my way soon. Sorry for all your trouble."

Dean put the car in gear and waved. She waved back.

"How soon will you be moving back home, Skip? Any hints?"

"I'll call you later about that," he hollered through the window.

She walked closer to the car so no one else would hear. "Believe me," she said through the open window, "I'm trying to be the woman you want to come home to—and the wife you want to make love to. And I mean it."

Dean sat up straighter. "Tell you what. When you come clean with the girls, call me. Let's make a truce and talk about my moving back before your folks get here. How's that?"

She nodded, and smiled.

He'd already taken gobs of time, and the roads were still lousy. He decided to accept her exactly as she was for the moment, to surrender and not make a fuss. *No conditions. No fighting. Let things be the way they*

are. Respect her, and leave it at that. He waved one last time and drove off, heading straight to MediMax as quickly as the miserable icy conditions allowed.

B ack home at the kitchen table hours later, Kate worked on the pile of Christmas cards needing to be signed and mailed. Signing each one, "Dean & Kate and the girls," or some variation that included Dean's name, she paused and stared out the window at the previous night's snow on the red oak trees in the backyard. Red oaks held their leaves all winter, and between the tufts of snow on the leaves, two busy chickadees pecked for seeds at the birdfeeder hanging from a branch. She cherished how peaceful it looked outside, yearning for the same peace to quell her feelings.

The evening ahead marked the twenty-ninth day without Dean at home. As she got up to warm two pot pies in the microwave for Nicole's and her dinner, the task of taking out all the boxes of tree decorations overwhelmed her. The mere idea sapped her energy. Nothing about this Christmas season felt remotely festive.

She imagined hearing Nicole whining to Lindsay, *"Mom always goes overboard at Christmas—this year just like always. Doesn't she get it?"*

Lindsay would blab to Nicky, *"Mom's energy is a sublimation of her stifled sexual libido funneled into gift-buying, cookie baking, hymn-singing, party-making, and rehearsing the pageant."*

Kate moaned, *Psychobabble!* She wrote a personal note to Hal and Ginny in their Christmas card, the next card in the stack of dozens:

Wishing you and the kids a joy-filled holiday and New Year.
Let's have a Scrabble night together soon with hot cider
and Christmas cookies.
Love, Dean & Kate

She included a family photo of the four smiling Nelsons from their summer vacation at Lake Superior. Signing Dean's name bothered her a bit, but what could she do? In the year-end letter she'd whipped out on holiday stationery, she included no hints of their discord. Setting down her pen, she let her sore shoulders sag.

A bottle of Pinot Noir on the counter caught her eye. She considered how splendid the wine would taste. She was alone and nobody would ever know. She could easily finish off the half-full bottle and say that she'd poured it down the drain. Nobody would doubt her. It was past noon, and the amount she might drink would wear off in three hours or so.

Kate went to the counter, uncorked the bottle, poured a full glass, and lifted it to her nose. The aroma aroused her nostrils. She raised the glass to her lips and closed her eyes, relishing the wine's bouquet and its power to numb her feelings, to transport her away from her turmoil. The wine touched her tongue, delivering its seductive promise.

No! I won't! I can't!

She jerked the glass away and spit the few drops into the sink. Turning on the tap water, she emptied the glass and bottle over the sink, then rinsed her mouth free of wine.

Opening the liquor cabinet, she stared at the unopened bottles of vodka, rum, whiskey, and liqueur. *All have to go.* She thought of Marlene. *Yes, give it all to her. Why pour so much good booze down the drain?* She promised herself to box up the bottles and donate them to her friend.

She thought back to her drop-in visit to Dean's motel room. Were she and Dean destined to share their bodies and souls? Was it true that a person's body is designed to experience boundless pleasure? Was *her* body designed that way? Were women over fifty just hitting their stride, the best years of their lives? Was menopause an opportunity, not a curse? What did a second adulthood mean?

One thing she knew for sure: If she continued drinking, she could never hold her head high again. She also knew she would lose Dean. And that God was looking on.

It's time to stop living small. She was tired of holding back. She understood the risks she had to take to get Dean back, and the obstacles that stood in the way of their building a fresh future. God was big enough and strong enough and forgiving enough for her to claim His divine power to help them change. All she had to do was just do it.

Just do it, girl! Just do it!

CHAPTER

Larissa sat waiting for the repairs to her Saturn at the auto mechanic's shop owned by Trevor's friend. The bright sunlight from a brilliant blue sky had dispersed the hovering clouds and now blazed through the grimy windows, raising her spirits. The oil-saturated air in the waiting room of Marty's Quality Coaches filled her nostrils. The lobby was the size of a large closet, strewn with spare car parts and posters of race cars and piles of motor mechanic magazines. Larissa found herself rather liking the smell of the oil and the sound of the industrial air compressor blasting away in the garage.

She thought about Cody's response after he discovered her with Trevor on the couch earlier that morning. While Trevor had gone outside her house to warm up his car for their trip to Marty's, Cody had walked through the kitchen carrying his college books and pulling on his parka.

"You sure know how to pick 'em, Mom."

"And exactly what is that remark supposed to mean?"

"Gotta go. Alex is giving me a ride to school." Cody jerked on his snow boots. Looking up, he said, "Are you that horny? First a married man, and now a priest?"

Her cheeks burned. "He's not a priest. He's a pastor. And don't go thinking we were screwing all night. We weren't. We never had our clothes off."

Cody pulled on a knit cap. "I'm happy for you. Gotta go." He reached for mittens and opened the back door.

"Wait." She grasped his arm. "Don't you want me to find a decent man to love and be happy?"

"Actually, yeah I do. And if he's single, all the better. Just make sure whoever it is—this guy or whoever—that he's the right one this time. Love ya." Kissing her forehead, he trudged outside.

I can't blame him. Cody's never seen me happy with any man except Brad.

Craning her neck, Larissa saw through the cluttered hallway to the garage beyond where Trevor stood helping Marty repair her car on the lift. Trevor took a good-natured swipe at his pal's butt with a shop towel when Marty bent over to pick up a wrench. The tall man with an unfashionably long ponytail swiped him back, snapping his shop towel at Trevor. She grinned.

Larissa noticed a homeowner across the street snow-blowing his driveway, digging out from the deep snow. The calm sky gave her an overall pleasant, peaceful feeling. A young woman in a parka shoveled the sidewalk in front of her house. So typical of Minnesotans to calmly deal with winter's mess, she thought.

Inside the lobby, a young twentyish man sat perched behind the customer counter entering data on a computer and answering phone calls. Metal piercings and tattoos decorated his face. His clothes signaled pride in his identity as a punker. When he reached to flip the pages of an auto parts manual, she observed his nicotine-stained yellow fingers. Except for his customary hello earlier, he'd ignored her.

Cody will be that guy if he never finishes college. My God, I hope my boy is finally finding himself.

Larissa's cellphone rang. "This is Wanda calling for Dr. Myers," said the nurse at the oncologist's office. "She would like you to come in soon, Ms. Beaumont."

"Oh? But I thought everything was wait-and-see for now?"

"She'd like to discuss the next step in your treatment."

"Is the cancer spreading? Is there something new from the lab?"

"It's a preliminary discussion Dr. Myers schedules with all her patients. She'll discuss your questions at that time. Could you come in later today?"

"That soon? Can't it wait?" Larissa's imagination went wild visualizing weeks of radiation and chemo, or worse, a mastectomy.

"Her schedule has opened up this afternoon," the nurse continued, "and she thinks it's best if you come in at your earliest convenience."

Oh, god, spare me! Larissa's ears couldn't tolerate another word. She said goodbye and shut off her phone. *Is the cancer spreading through my body? Will I lose my breasts?* The sudden news terrified her. She hung her head, holding back pangs of panic. *Push away negative thoughts, Larissa—look for the positive. Focus on optimistic thoughts. Don't let this get to you. Breathe.*

No chance. Affirmations weren't working this time. The phone call from the doctor's nurse had come while she was half listening to Christmas carols playing over the repair shop's speakers. The festive music of *Joy to the World* now jangled her nerves:

> ... *Let earth receive her King.*
>
> *Let ev'ry heart prepare Him room,*
>
> *And heaven and nature sing,*
>
> *And heaven and nature sing!*

Sing? Shit!

The carol's jubilant lyrics stirred the opposite of tender feelings in her. "Let ev'ry heart prepare Him room" plunged her into a spiral of sadness, one more reminder about God's indifference to the stormy chaos of her life.

"Your car's ready," said Marty, walking into the lobby wiping his greasy hands on the shop towel. "It should run fine for another forty thousand or so. Trevor thinks maybe longer, and anything ol' Trevor says is sanctified and holy." He winked at Trevor walking behind him from the noisy garage.

"Amen to that, Marty. Right you are. Holy, holy, holy." Trevor smiled triumphantly. "Ta-da! All done, Larissa."

Larissa muttered, "Thanks, guys ... for everything." She held back the urge to explode into tears and forced a pasted-on smile.

"Glad to oblige." Seeing her worried look, Marty frowned. "Uh, anything wrong?"

"How much did the repairs come to?" she asked.

"Just under four hundred. Trevor's labor helped keep it down."

She wanted Marty and Trevor to know her immeasurable gratitude, but the call from Dr. Myers' office was unsettling her.

Trevor elbowed Marty's shoulder good-naturedly and tossed her the keys. "It's parked on the street and ready to go. Wanna try it?"

She couldn't fight the tears any longer.

Trevor stepped over to her. "What is it, Larissa?"

"The cancer, I think it's worse. I'm sick, maybe dying, I might have to have a mastectomy. Can you believe it?" Sorrow etched her face. "Why? Why is this happening to me?"

"Cancer? Did you say cancer?"

"Yes, damn it."

"But, when did ... ? I had no idea."

"It's spreading and I ... my life will never be the same. I'll be ugly and disfigured."

Trevor sucked in air. "Ah, when did ... ? Ugly? Disfigured?"

"Please, go away."

"Go away? But I want to help."

"I'll never be myself anymore, not the woman I'm supposed to be. I'll never be who you want me to be."

"Larissa, you're not making sense. Let me help. I'll stand by you."

"No, you're just saying that." She saw Trevor glance over his shoulder at Marty, who ducked away quietly, allowing them space. The punk rocker stared, then disappeared behind the customer counter.

Larissa would never take off her clothes or let Trevor see her naked, ever. *Making love with surgical scars where my breast was, being naked together ... awful, disgusting.*

Trevor stood there, confused. "Will you *please* make sense?"

"You're being too nice," she scoffed. "It has to be an act. Go on. Leave me alone. I'll pay for the car somehow."

"You're hysterical. Stop this nonsense right now."

Over the speaker came *Hark! The Herald Angels Sing:*

> **... Light and life to all He brings,**
> **Ris'n with healing in His wings.**

Healing in his wings? That's crap. Bullshit! No such thing! She stood up and fled the smelly room. Trevor followed, trying to take her car keys. "Come on, Larissa, I'll start it for you. It's freezing out there."

Her skin felt the shock of the freezing cold without a jacket or gloves. "You have to let me handle this on my own," she sobbed. "You don't need to be involved."

"But, Larissa, I *am* involved."

"BRRRR! I need my coat," she said, shivering in the near-zero temperature. They stood by a snow bank near her Saturn. "I thought I left it in the car, but it's not there."

"I'll check in the waiting room, but first let me warm you up." He wrapped his arms around her, protecting her. Although he shielded her from the cold as best he could, they both shivered and rubbed their arms and faces for warmth.

"I'll learn more about your cancer later," he said, pulling her even closer to him. "But right now what matters is how much I care about you. When will you understand that?"

"Can you really tell me you want to get serious with a woman who has cancer?"

"Stop and listen to yourself. It's *you* I care about."

She stared in disbelief. "How can you mean that?"

"I want to love you, Larissa, but you're pushing me away. Why are you behaving like this?"

Did he say 'love'? "Why would you want a future with a sick woman?"

"Well, I do. And one day I hope that means marriage." He reached for his collar and ripped it open, popping some buttons on his shirt, brandishing his burn scars. "So what woman in her right mind wants a man like *this*?" Pointing to his burn scars, he said, "See? Look for yourself. They run down my back and ribs."

Larissa stared, gaping at the jagged brown wrinkles on his bare skin as his muscles rippled from the cold.

"Listen. If you can accept me, I can accept you," he said, his teeth chattering. "We're both wounded, Larissa. Don't you see? Our gift to each other is our brokenness, our wounds."

She crumpled against him, speechless, her lips turning numb. "The nurse said the doctor wants me to come in as soon as possible."

"When do we go?"

"*We?*"

"Yes. What are we waiting for? Let's hurry."

"You mean *we* are going? Going to the clinic together?"

"Absolutely. I'll drive." He pointed to his MG parked a few spaces away.

Taken aback, she stammered, "But my car is fixed … and I … I can drive on my own. So you don't have to go."

"Not a good idea. You shouldn't be driving as riled up as you are." Taking her arm, he guided her back toward the shop. "Come on. We'll get our jackets and go."

She resisted, but he was too strong. She gave herself into his care.

"Hurry!' he said, tugging her. "There's no time to waste."

"Yes … okay … I'm coming." She felt lighter on her feet already.

CHAPTER

"Hey there, gals, can you give me some help?"

Kate was struggling to get through Marlene's back door as she carried the box of wine and liquor bottles she'd packed. Marlene and Larissa sat at the kitchen table sewing costumes for the pageant.

Marlene sprang up. "Hold it, let me get the door."

"What's in the box?" asked Larissa.

"Think of it as an early Christmas present," said Kate, setting the box down on the counter. "Some libations for your holiday festivities, Marlene. Yours too, if you like, Larissa."

"What on earth?" exclaimed Marlene. "You've got over a dozen bottles here. So generous, Kate? How come?"

Kate smiled. "I'm making it official, Marlene. My drinking days are over." Both Marlene and Larissa looked surprised. "It's time I give up the grape. Every other kind of alcohol, too. Forever. So enjoy!"

"You've got to be kidding. I had no idea. Were you having problems?"

"Well, that's what a DWI and a stint in jail . . ." she glanced at Larissa, "will do for you—or rather someone like me. These are all yours now."

"A DWI? When?" asked Marlene.

Kate sat down next to Larissa for moral support and spilled out the entire set of events, applauding the much-needed help Larissa had provided. "So, after I thought about quitting for good, I couldn't see wasting all this fine booze. Now it's yours, Marlene. And if you'd care for some, Larissa, help yourself."

Grateful, Marlene fist-bumped with Kate. "Fine and dandy, if you insist, kiddo. But it sure looks like you've bounced back pretty well from your arrest. Good for you."

"I'm proud of your decision to quit," said Larissa. "I'm behind you one hundred percent."

"Me, too." Marlene clapped her hands. "I want to hear more about it. But I think we need to get cracking on these costumes. Dress rehearsal is coming up fast."

Equipped with scissors and needles and thread, the three women plunged into the detailed work of finishing costumes for each angel, shepherd, wise man, and dancer. Kate observed Larissa plugging right along, cutting fabric and sewing on sequins in stride. "It's great to have you on our team, Larissa."

"Thanks. It's fun to do something without dollar signs for a change. By the way, Kate, did you get your testosterone test results back yet?"

Kate paused. "Late last week. Why?"

"And … ?"

Kate looked at Marlene, presuming she had no idea what Larissa meant.

"That's okay, dearie. Larissa and I have been chatting. I've heard a bit about what's happening between you and Dean. Your ears must be burning. So why haven't you told me?"

"I thought I'd keep it to myself—you know, damage control. I hoped it might blow over." She glanced sheepishly at Marlene, who reached over and patted her hand warmly.

"So what did the test results say, Kate?"

"Basically, my hormone levels came back low, very low. The nurse said normal is usually around 25 to 75 for women, and my hormone level was 14."

"Were you surprised?"

"I wish I could say so, but no. A number that low tells me what I've known all along—my libido is in the basement."

"And you're feeling bad about it?" Larissa asked.

"Yeah, wouldn't you? Who wants to be 'low-desire'? I admit I just didn't care for a long time, but now I have many good reasons to want my number to go up."

"Well, at least now you have some biological basis to explain things. It's not all psychological." Larissa leaned closer. "My theory goes like this. We can reasonably predict Dean is a mid- to high-testosterone person with a corresponding high level of desire. Do you agree?"

"I think that's pretty obvious."

"Okay. So when you were falling in love years ago, Kate, nature made it easy for you to look, act, and feel like a higher-libido person because you were in love. New love does that. Think of all the love songs and how crazy and illogical falling in love feels. My hunch is you both thought it would stay that way. But your biological 'set point' was, and has been, in the low range genetically through no fault of your own. The problem developed when the infatuation phase ended. That's when your hormones returned to your natural low set point, but neither of you realized it."

"Oh boy. That explains a lot. Maybe I was even born that way. Over the years, Dean got tired of less and less sex until he finally couldn't put up with it anymore. That's when he started making a big fuss."

Larissa nodded. "When you wanted to have children and start a family, you ratcheted up your low desire. It was all very natural and typical in the child-rearing years, until your desire dropped back down."

"I get it. And his high set point stayed high?"

"Think about it. His libido, through no fault of *his* own, never changed. And he couldn't fathom why you weren't feeling excited about making love, because for him it's so pleasurable and natural."

Marlene spoke up. "Larissa, I wonder if it's basically the same for men with low desire and wives with high desire?"

"Yes, I'm sure it works both ways."

Kate paused, setting down her needle and thread. "So, are you saying that's why he's been so angry and resentful?"

"Well, doesn't it make sense? After you had Lindsay and Nicole, did you notice your motivation for sex dwindle? You probably clicked straight into mom mode—and the less sex, the better."

Kate's eyes widened in recognition. "Oh, boy. You've got *that* right! For him, though, it's been the total opposite. He can get revved up in the blink of an eye. But he keeps saying he wants to feel closer to me. ... I guess we *have* been living more like roommates or siblings."

"Right."

"So the hormone thing is a reason it takes so long for *my* 'on' button to light up?"

Marlene jumped in. "Kate, he *needs* it. What *you* need is to make sure he understands that you know that. Getting aroused is easy for him, so you have to meet him halfway."

Kate looked down. "Okay, so I'm a moron. That's why it's hard for him to be refused. There must be a book out there for people like me called *Sexless Marriage for Dummies.*"

Larissa smiled a sympathetic smile. "It's science, Kate, and nothing to be ashamed of."

"He has misunderstood you, and you've misunderstood him, Kate," said Marlene. "It's easy to see how you're feeling embarrassed. Forgive one another and move on."

"Like always, it's so complicated!"

"Do you want your marriage to go to the next level, or not?"

"What next level?"

"Sustainable, pleasurable intimacy," said Marlene, smiling.

Kate looked uncomfortable and squirmed a bit in her chair, giving her a skeptical eye.

"Or you might call it 'erotic monogamy,'" Marlene continued. "Marriage by definition is monogamous, right? Basic principle number one: total fidelity to your partner. There's nothing like eroticism to nurture a marriage and keep it growing and exciting. We talked about that, remember? ... Having orgasms?"

Kate slammed her hands against her ears. "Yes, Marlene, I remember! Can we end the inquisition now?"

A long silence.

Marlene looked at Larissa, "Can you see by her face that it's time we all go 'exploring'? I think the time is ripe for that big surprise you and I talked about, Larissa, don't you?"

"Yes indeed, our friend needs our help. We can leave all this here and come back to it later."

"*What* big surprise?" asked Kate. "What the heck are you two talking about?"

Marlene stood up and reached for her coat hanging on a peg. "Oh, just a little idea we cooked up before you got here, right Larissa?"

"Right. It's a place where we both love to shop, Kate."

"Huh? Shopping? Where?" Silence. "What sort of secret plan have you two hatched?"

"Think of it this way," said Marlene, putting on her coat and reaching for the door handle. "We're kidnapping you. For your own good, I might add. Now let's go."

Kate stayed seated. "But ... but ..."

"No 'buts' about it," said Larissa. "Just go with Marlene and I'll meet you there. I'll be right along after stitching this hem."

S nowflakes flew in Larissa's face and icy patches made her feet slip on the frozen sidewalk outside Adam & Eve's Fantasies shop. She stepped inside. Displays of male and female sex toys greeted her: vibrators, lingerie, dildos, videos, and lubes of every style and color. Every item invited customers to indulge in sensual pleasure.

"Welcome to Adam and Eve's," said a well-dressed woman behind the sales counter. "Let me know if I can answer any questions or be of help."

Larissa smiled, "Thanks. It's nice to be back again." This was her first visit in months. Having discovered it was also one of Marlene's favorite boutiques had made her giggle. She approached a display of men's devices and saw Kate at the end of the aisle.

"See something you like there?"

"Oh, hi, Larissa," said Kate, who was looking wide-eyed and a bit in shock. Marlene waved, winking to Larissa.

"How's the novice doing, Marlene? Enjoying her initiation?"

Kate's eyes narrowed. "So *this* was your little secret plan? Don't tell me this store is old hat for you too, Larissa. Both of you seem pretty acquainted here."

"We hope you are getting a heck of an education," replied Marlene. She ushered Kate to a display of vibrators.

While Larissa watched Marlene accompany Kate down the aisle, her mind drifted. A solo sex life had been her only feasible option for years, a source of reliable pleasure and sex play. *How often toys like these have substituted for the real thing!* But intimate body-to-body, soul-to-soul, being-to-being unity was the biggest prize of all, and Trevor clearly fit the bill as a potential lover. Making love with him could lead to so much more than imaginary excitement and self-generated play.

"Look," she heard Kate say, "this thing has adjustable settings." One of the rechargeable vibrators intrigued Kate, and Larissa noticed her holding it gingerly.

"So what do you think of that one? Like it?" Larissa saw Kate hesitate. "Are you worried about pleasuring yourself?"

"It can do wonders," suggested Marlene. "Uh … you do masturbate, don't you?" Marlene backed away as Kate went silent. "Well now, sorry. Should I not talk about it? Or are you game?"

Kate looked at the floor. "I guess it's finally time, isn't it?"

"Think of it as a tool, not a toy. It's a tool to stimulate feeling good. And it's your right as an enlightened woman to use it, and to feel *good* about using it."

"Well, okay, I'm open to trying it."

Marlene and Larissa smiled. Marlene patted Kate's shoulder. "That's the spirit."

Straight-faced, Kate asked, "How do I get lessons?"

Larissa and Marlene laughed.

"It's best for you to start finding out what it does for you all on your own," said Larissa.

"You can always come to either of us with your questions," said Marlene.

Kate wiped pretend sweat from her forehead. "Whew! I was beginning to worry."

They all laughed.

"So why don't you give a few others a good look and see which one you like best?" asked Larissa.

How wonderful, Larissa thought, that Kate was open to experimenting and stretching her boundaries. As Kate and Marlene checked out other "tools," Larissa envisioned Trevor's athletic physique, his long, dark swept-back hair, his quick open smile, his strong broad shoulders, and his stiff erection. His burn marks, repellent though they were, somehow were strangely exotic. Could she enjoy both satisfying couples sex with him as well as solitary sessions with herself using her battery-powered boyfriends?

A decent man like Trevor was replacing her memories of Brad. *It's about time!* As much as she loved Brad, it was past time to say goodbye. *Brad, you were one wonderful lover and hunk of a man. I thank you for being the love of my life … but now, goodbye! I'll never forget you!*

Visions of frolics with Trevor teased Larissa's libido. She recalled how much she'd wanted him to make love to her the night of the storm, yet how he had honored her virtue by keeping his promise to stay chaste. Despite his self-discipline, his ardor for her was anything but weak. She wondered, though, whether he would view her solo-erotic activities as "sinful" and become intolerant if they ever married.

But in all his years of singlehood, wouldn't *he* have developed his own affinity for self-pleasuring? She laughed to herself. *Of course! Ha! When we're "doing it," I wonder if he'll insist on the "missionary" position.* She giggled. A wave of gratitude washed over her for his accompanying her to the doctor's office the day after the snowstorm. They had heard *together* Dr. Myers's recommendation for a lumpectomy, and they'd learned *together* that the procedure was the least invasive and most effective next step in her treatment.

Yes, he is my man.

Five minutes later at the cash register, Larissa and Marlene congratulated Kate for purchasing the vibrator.

"Now the fun starts," whispered Marlene. Kate blushed, but showed her glee at the same time. Larissa congratulated her for taking the first step in the direction of her new goals.

"Now you're on your way, kiddo," said Marlene.

Larissa winked with impish amusement. "Erotic Monogamy 101!"

"I think 'sustained pleasurable intimacy' sounds better to me," Kate replied.

Larissa and Marlene shared a knowing glance.

"Whatever," chimed Larissa. "You have the first tool in your toolbox for your 'new you' right there in your hand."

CHAPTER

D ean sat sipping a vanilla mocha latté at a neighborhood coffee shop with Colton and Mel, his companions from the Loving Husbands marriage group. He was processing his feelings with them about his decision to return home after checking out of the motel.

"So, let's see. … " began Colton, the lean accountant-type fellow. "You're heading home from here, but you're not sure what the new guidelines are?"

"That's about it. We just haven't sorted out our expectations for intimacy, and it's a very fragile area," replied Dean. "When I get there, I'll have just enough time to drop off my things and say hi to Kate before driving in traffic to the airport to meet her folks. They're flying in from the East Coast for a week."

"And you've agreed to pick them up because she can't?" asked Mel, the leader of the men's group.

"Right. Her driver's license is suspended. That, and the fact that the tech rehearsal for our church's Christmas pageant runs from five to nine this evening, and she's a huge part of that."

"Basically, then, you're unsure about sharing a bed with your wife?"

"That's the crux, Mel. You nailed it."

"Meanwhile," said Colton, "Christmas is around the corner and everything has to look 'normal' to her parents, like nothing ever happened?"

Dean nodded to Colton. "Looking good matters a lot to Kate."

"Let me come at this from a different angle," said Mel, licking his fork while finishing a strawberry cream puff. "Sex during marriage has three phases. There's kitchen sex, bedroom sex, and hallway sex. Kitchen sex is the spontaneous type that married people have at first. Bedroom sex is the routine lovemaking that sets in after a few years. Hallway sex is when a husband and wife pass each other in the hallway and say, 'Screw you.'"

Colton and Dean laughed, but less than wholeheartedly.

"Guys, I want nothing like 'hallway sex' for us," Dean said. "Actually, I'm sick of the whole sex-or-no-sex issue. It's defined our marriage too long. Two people coming together in marriage means so much more than that."

"Granted," said Colton. "But without sex—or does 'making love' sound better?— marriage is like an old-fashioned wagon wheel with a broken spoke. When one of the spokes is badly cracked or missing, every time the wheel rotates, the place on the rim without support weakens. Over time, that part of the rim gets weaker and weaker until it collapses and the wagon grinds to a stop. Unless the wheel gets a new spoke, or is fixed, the wagon stays stuck."

"Or," said Mel, "the damaged wheel gets tossed and a new wheel with good spokes replaces it." He glanced at Dean for his reaction.

"In that case, our marriage is still at a dead stop," said Dean. "I'm tired of hoping that our 'broken wheel' is fixable, when I don't have the power to fix it." Mentally he recited: *'Delight yourself in the Lord, and He will give you the desires of your heart.'* Lord, you know my desires! And hers!

Colton frowned. "I hate to admit this, but I'm considering a replacement wheel myself."

The men looked at one another.

Dean put his hand on Colton's forearm. "Sorry to hear that. But I'll pray for both of you." Mel appeared already informed.

Mel cleared his throat. "Have you fellas ever tried writing out things you'd like to hear your wives say to you? You know, what you'd like them to tell you that would change everything?"

"In a letter, you mean?" asked Colton.

"On paper, written out, yes. I've jotted down a few things, putting myself in my wife's place as if she were talking to me." Mel unfolded a piece of paper from his pocket. "Here's what I'd like Lisa to say: 'I recognize the years of suffering and loneliness you have endured, Mel. I know you're weary of having to bring up this troubling subject and having me shut you out. But those days of waiting for me to open up to you are over. Let's enjoy being in bed together, and start making love again.'"

"Here, here!" cheered Colton and Dean.

Dean believed Mel's statements expressed what was positive and effective for his own marriage. Dean spoke aloud some statements he intended to jot down later in his journal: "'I want us to be lovers and excited about life again, Dean. … I want to reward you—between the sheets—for all the waiting and grief you've been through. … I want to become the fulfilled woman you want me to be because I love you and I'm learning to love myself more.'"

"Right on. That says it," confirmed Mel.

Colton nodded vigorously. "Couldn't have put it better myself."

"For me, words like that really hit home," Dean continued.

Mel smiled then looked at his watch and Colton checked his smart phone. "Time to run," said Colton. "I hope we'll do this again."

"Let's count on it," replied Dean.

"I'll see you guys at the next husbands' meeting," said Mel.

"See ya, Dean. Take care."

Dean sat back and gazed vacantly at his laptop. *'Delight yourself in the Lord . . .'* ran through his mind. Something Trevor had said earlier while they were eating breakfast with Hal stuck in his memory. "Do you really believe in miracles, Dean? Do you? Are you convinced that God is the God of big miracles? If you are, stop doubting and believe."

Dean sighed, then went to close his laptop but stopped. A new blog post from *Forlorn* appeared on the screen where Dean had posted his thoughts the day before using the moniker, *Hanging On*:

> I wish I had the answers you are looking for, Hanging On, but I'm like you. I crave my wife's touch. Living like we are is so painful that sometimes I can't breathe. Like you said in your post, hanging on much longer seems futile. It's a heavy burden to carry, and I'm glad I can connect with people like you who are going through it.

Dean saw another new entry, a reply from *Fed Up*:

> Those who do nothing to stop the misery tearing at your heart, who insist sex doesn't matter, who refuse to be a true husband or wife, they aren't your friend, they aren't loving and kind. Ask yourself: Could you live with yourself in a marriage where your partner was desperate and sad and fed up because of YOUR behavior? Or would you expect your partner to run to some lover or to a divorce lawyer? Pardon me while I get on my running shoes!

Dean felt a jab to his gut. A sour urge to act on his own behalf gripped him. *Screw it all!* he wanted to shout. *Oh, how I want to be selfish! To stand up for myself and be done with all this!*

Dean slowly lowered the laptop lid, while every molecule of his being commiserated with his fellow bloggers. *Mitch certainly thinks I should 'run,' that I'm a fool to keep hoping. Is it time to replace the 'broken wheel'?*

Kate waited for Dean, expecting him to arrive home in the next half hour. The clock in their bedroom showed 3:35. On the phone that morning he said he'd arrive about 4:00, leaving enough time to bring home his luggage and laundry from the motel before driving to the airport. *Finally! He's coming home! Can't wait!* The tech rehearsal at church was starting at five, and she could find no way to avoid being present at church to direct the dancers. As she opened the closet door, she looked at the empty space where Dean's clothes would hang again soon. *Yay!*

She went to the bathroom and turned on the water to fill the tub, expecting a bath would help her smell fresh and appealing for when he arrived. She undressed and reached for a towel from the linen cabinet. Tucked away in a far corner was the vibrator she'd purchased, still in its box, unopened. She reached for it, slowly opened the box, and removed the vibrator: ribbed, rubbery, and ruby red.

What an amazing thing! Should I try it now?

Glancing at herself in the mirror, she froze—the image of a beautiful woman caused her to marvel. She "saw" her body with its comely shape and curves in an altogether new way. *Why didn't I ever notice before? Hey, I'm gorgeous!* Her figure had changed little since getting married except for a few pounds around her hips after giving birth, but since her workouts at Fitness & Flowers she realized she looked better than ever. A smile of delight curved her lips.

Turning off the water, she cupped her breasts and gently ran her fingers along her nipples and around the areolas. Flashes of pleasurable energy shot through her body straight to her genitals. The tingly shudders felt surprising and satisfying.

"Well now! Just what have I been missing?"

She reached for the long-unused KY Jelly in the drawer. She'd purchased batteries, and inserted them now into the base of the vibrator. Rubbing a generous amount of jelly along the shaft of the vibrator and down to the base, she flipped the switch that adjusted the intensity of vibrations. Abruptly, the vibrator slipped out of her hands.

"What the … ? Never expected that!"

She picked it up from the floor and saw that it was set on 'five', the highest setting, so she adjusted it to 'one' and the vibration slowed to a gentle buzz. Spreading a dab of the KY Jelly on the tip, she lowered the vibrator, touching her clitoris and lightly rubbing it. *Much better.* The pink bud began emerging from under its hood and stiffened as she gently rubbed it. More flashes of stimulating energy shot through her system. Her awkward use of the unfamiliar gadget made no difference.

I'm learning as I go. So what? Get over it.

She flipped the switch to 'two', and more intense waves of pleasure radiated through her torso. Shifting the vibrator in a circular manner, experimenting with areas where it felt most enjoyable, she risked a bit more and flipped the switch to 'three'. The force of sensations multiplied. Moving the vibrator downward to her vaginal area, she inserted it slowly and gently, feeling a fresh set of tingly sensations. Inserting it another inch, she felt another burst of pleasure. *Yes, that's more like it.* She inserted it two more inches and lifted the shaft, then lowered it and inserted it more until the vibrations came into contact with her cervix. *Ooooh!* She pulled it out and pushed it back deep inside, then pulled it out and pushed it back in again, repeating the motion. *Wow! Unbelievable!*

Her reproductive organs felt energized, super-charged. The vibrator poked and stroked and thrust from the tip inside her to the base in her hand. She grasped the edge of the sink to steady herself. Sliding it back and forth, the feeling of a volcano within her gradually rising to a ferocious eruption grew stronger, fiercer. She perspired. She moaned. The pleasure felt so intense, beyond any limit she'd ever allowed.

She stopped and let the device slip out. Glancing in the mirror, she was amazed by the self-portrait of a passionate woman she'd never known who looked rapturously happy. She began to reinsert the vibrator, knowing it could send her to new places. She could flip to settings 'four' or 'five' and experience wave after blissful wave sweeping her away. Or she could relish her excitement and savor her victory of self-exploration, knowing more victories awaited her. She paused, uncertain what was appropriate or wise.

"Hi Katie, I'm home!" Dean's voice came from downstairs.

Oh, my! Her ramped-up energy subsided, and the thinking part of her brain went into red alert. "Hi, Dean!" she called out. "I'm up here in the tub."

It seemed normal that he should find her taking a bath in their master bathroom. Quickly wiping off the vibrator and jamming it in the box, she stashed it in the corner of the linen cabinet and slid her body into the tub. Perspiration covered her face and upper body; dunking herself in the steamy water hid all signs of it. Only the redness in her cheeks and forehead remained, but she knew that could be explained by the hot bath water. She lay back, letting the heat from the water soothe her.

Yes, excellent!

Dean poked his head in the doorway. "Hey, there. Nice to see you, Katie."

"Hi, honey. Welcome back. Good to have you home." She saw him place his suitcase on their bed and carry his shirts to the closet. "I'll only take a minute to throw a few dirty clothes down the chute, then I'll get my lazy butt to the airport."

"You've never heard me say you've ever been lazy a day in your life."

He lifted his eyebrows. "Thanks. You're right. It's good to be back."

"I think deciding to come home is the right thing to do, Skip. It's been five long weeks. The girls will love having you around. Not half as much as I will, though."

She blew him a kiss. He smiled.

She wondered if it might be a turn-on for him to see her naked. As a test, she arched her back, lifting up her breasts and subtly extending them for his viewing pleasure. She could tell he welcomed the sight. Why should she be guilty about showing off her body or using a vibrator? Free-thinking women like Marlene and Larissa used theirs without blame or shame.

"Before you run off, Skip, would you mind sponging my back for me?"

"Sure, glad to." He paused. "But I think I'd better stay on schedule. Your folks would hate it if I'm late."

He seemed distracted, busily unpacking and putting his underwear and socks away; otherwise he would've heard her not-so-subtle hint and let it register. *Having him home is enough for now. Let it be.*

"Come here, then, and give me a kiss."

"Sure." He walked into the bathroom, bent over the tub and became more aware of her feminine assets. He gave her a juicy kiss on the lips.

"That's better," she said, reaching up and holding his head, kissing *him* on the lips. Could he see her love for him? "I'm so glad we'll be sharing our bed again."

He pulled back.

"What, Skip?"

In a flat tone of voice, he said quietly, "Maybe, maybe not."

"What's that supposed to mean?"

"I'm home and that's what we agreed to, and it does feel good to be back. But for a while at least I think I'll be sleeping on the couch in the den. I've taken naps there before and—"

"Hold it! You're home to stay, but you're going to sleep in the den?"

"I think so. For a while."

"Why not our bed?"

"The couch in the den will do fine for now, and once your folks leave, we can reevaluate."

"Reevaluate? What's to reevaluate?" Kate felt a jab of panic, her angst about divorce reawakened. He would be ninety-nine percent home—and ninety-nine percent was good, but not good enough.

"Look," he said, kneeling to her eye level, "I've promised you to be a model husband and father, so your folks won't notice a thing and the girls can relax. And I'll even laugh at your dad's dirty jokes and smile whenever your mom makes excuses for him. After they leave, let's talk about it when there's more time."

"But you'll have to sneak in your pajamas to the den. And what if someone sees you going back and forth? It'll be a huge red flag if Mom or Dad does. I think it's a ridiculous idea."

"Well, that's how it's going to be for now at least."

"Oh, boy. I'm getting the feeling you're not really back permanently. Am I right?"

"Look, I'm here until after the holidays, and we can reconsider any time before that."

"Reconsider?" Kate pouted. Was this some kind of trick? "Do you have plans to move out again?"

"No, but our love life is still on life support, Katie."

Damn! Now Dean was finding new reasons to leave her. If they divorced, her sense of failure would flare up again, and his leaving yet another time would mean losing face at church with everyone. She'd heard quiet rumors spreading already about his staying in the motel. Never mind the harm to the girls. "Okay. Has this got to do with my drinking? Because if it does, I've quit. I haven't had a drop. You have to believe me."

"No problem. I believe you."

"I don't get it, then. We're back together, but just not completely?"

"If you must know, and I'm sorry about how this may sound, I'm still not entirely certain of where we stand." He paused. She sank lower in the tub. "Please, Kate, your being lovey-dovey and making hints about changing ... that's all good. But is that because you don't want to lose the marriage? Is it for real? Or will it go back to being the same old, same old? I'm in the dark. I'm not exactly sure you're ready to take on being a committed lover long-term."

Kate sagged down to her ears in the tub. "That was cruel. Very cruel."

He exhaled. "Not if it's true. If having sex—excuse me, making love—is a way of keeping me here so we'll still be married in the eyes of the world, or keeping me around for the girls' sake, or so my bringing in a nice income will continue, well then—"

"Shut up! I hate you!" Kate splashed water on his face and clothes. He staggered backward.

Regaining his equilibrium, he said, "I guess I deserved that. All I'm asking, though, is that you give this new start a bit more time while the holidays are in full swing. Don't pressure me, or yourself. Let's focus where we should ... on the Lord."

"Oh my, so pious, are we? And I suppose you want me to promise it will all be worth it. Is that right, dear Deano?"

Wiping his wet face and dabbing his shirt with a towel, he said, "I think we've talked enough about this for now. I need to go."

She put her hand on the edge of the tub, reaching for him. "Please, I'm so sorry. I didn't mean that. I don't want to hurt you, ever. I just want to *love* you. But you have to believe me; things *are* changing—slowly but surely." Hadn't he heard anything she'd been telling him?

His eyes reflected ambivalence, not anger. He could have shouted at her, she knew, but he stayed composed and unruffled. His eyes searched hers. "I don't want to make this any harder than it has to be. The plane is landing soon. I've got to go now."

She noticed him run his eyes over her naked figure, and she suspected he liked what he saw.

"I don't want your folks unhappy because I missed meeting them on time, Kate. You asked me for this favor, and I'm doing it." He turned and walked out.

She lay back in the warm water, but it no longer felt soothing. Her stomach clenched at his words. *It's high time I told myself a new story, not the stale old one about Dean being oversexed and our love life being out of my comfort zone.* Instead of thinking about Dean acting like the tame husband she had once wanted, it was time she started acting like the bold wife *he* wanted.

Yes, it's time.

CHAPTER

Kate arranged the plate of scrambled eggs, crisp bacon, and charred toast exactly the way her father liked it and brought the plate to the breakfast table. "Just the way you like your eggs, Dad. Scrambled in heavy cream. Enjoy."

"Where's the Taylor's Ham?" he croaked. "Do you think we brought it all the way here not to eat it?"

Kate glanced at her mother as she sat down. "It's in the fridge. Mom and I thought we would save it for Christmas morning."

Frowning, Fredrick Barcourt mumbled an objection and sank his fork into the eggs, chewing like a goat. Dean and Nicole stifled giggles, amused yet annoyed. Muriel, Kate's mother, clamped her jaws shut and smiled apologetically at her daughter, making sure her husband didn't notice her rueful look. Everybody at the table understood how dearly the Barcourts loved their prized Taylor's Ham, an East Coast specialty sausage that was a holiday tradition stretching back decades.

The evening before, Dean had done his son-in-law duty and picked up Kate's parents at the airport on time. But they were disappointed because she wasn't there to greet them. "You mean your rehearsal for the children's pageant meant more than we do?" was how her mother had put it.

Kate shuddered watching her father eat his food. His coarse way of chewing, along with his uncouth attitude—*I'm king of the castle, even my daughter's castle*—set her stomach churning. He displayed better table manners in public, but his true colors came out in private. Everybody in the family knew this. Today he wore a pressed white shirt over his bulging waistline, reminding one and all of his executive status, even though he was retired from Capital Bank. Her mother's frail demeanor, meekly subservient to her husband, accentuated her hopelessly out-of-date hairstyle, a tight nest of sprayed curls commonly worn by elderly ladies. Her face reflected a permanently pinched scowl that went well with her cigarette-ravaged, gravelly voice. Each time Fredrick boomed a complaint, whether about Kate's cooking, or Lindsay's absence from the table because she was sleeping in, or "Minnesota's ungodly winters," Kate flinched.

"The eggs are overcooked," Fredrick grumbled.

"Really, Dad, how about thinking of something nice to say?" Kate glanced at Dean. "We're glad you and Mom are here, but would you brighten up the mood a bit?" She noted Nicole rolling her eyes and Dean choking uncomfortably on his bacon.

"Yes, well," said Fredrick, "you had the good sense to invite us this year."

Even when he tried to say something nice, it sounded blaming, Kate thought. The Nelson family hardly ever sat down to a cooked breakfast at eight. Seeing Dean and Nicole seated at that hour to please their visiting relatives was a minor miracle. Not good enough for her dad, though. Lindsay had refused to get up so early, accustomed as she was to setting her own wake-up schedule at college.

"Mom, I'll bet you're raring to go shopping with us girls after we clean up?" Kate knew this offer gave her mom a way to free herself from Fredrick's imposing presence.

"Why yes, I think that would be lovely, dear," Muriel replied. "Santa needs some gifts for under the tree, and he needs helpers, doesn't he? I've heard so many things about the Mall of America. Is it all it's cracked up to be?"

Nicole spoke her first words of the day. "You mean you know about MOA back east?" Touching her grandma's arm reassuringly, Nicole added, "Don't worry about the crowds, Grandma. I know my way around. You'll see. I know the shortcuts. Wait till you see what Santa's little elves have picked out at Victoria's Secret." She giggled.

Kate grimaced. Muriel blanched. Fredrick choked on his toast.

Dean offered, "I'm sure you have others on your list you're buying for, right Nicky?"

"Of course, Dad. I'm just excited to show Grandma my latest gift wish."

How could Nicole have made such a blatant *faux pas* in earshot of her grandparents? Still, Kate enjoyed an amusing giggle rather than fretting about it. *Hey, dropping my disapproval of Nicky is a new reaction. Another chance to tell myself a new story. Way to go!*

"So, Katie," Dean asked, "what time did you say today's dress rehearsal gets over? I was thinking about dropping by for a few minutes with the star I made."

"Really? That would be wonderful." Kate looked at her father. "Maybe you'd like to go along with him, Dad."

"Nah. The flight was tedious, so sitting around staring at your Christmas tree is about all the thrills I need," Fredrick quipped. Nobody was amused. Kate figured her father thought he'd made a merry jest, albeit solely to his own acerbic taste.

Ignoring her dad, Kate took note of Dean's relaxed manner. He looked like he belonged right at home, like always. He played the role of devoted husband and loyal son-in-law perfectly. She loved him for it. Absolutely nothing in his actions hinted that he had lived away from home for over a month, and the girls hadn't let on either. She'd even allowed herself to be fooled for an instant, choosing to forget the trial separation. *If I step up and make him feel special, he'll be sharing our bed soon. He is special, and I want him to know that.*

Kate had to chuckle. So far, Dean's plan to sleep in the den was working. It involved keeping out of sight of the adjoining stairway that connected to the guest bedroom on the ground floor. Anyone looking up the stairway could see or hear a person entering the den.

"Looks as though you're good at playing cat and mouse, Skip," Kate had said privately.

"Well, I'd say it's bringing a little adventure to our home life. Risk not, gain not."

Risk not, gain not? I could use a dose of that philosophy myself.

After breakfast, Dean drove Kate's dad to MediMax's headquarter offices for a tour while Kate and the girls headed off with Grandma to MOA. Dean had a hunch Fredrick, being a corporate veteran, would like a familiar office setting and feel at home there. His father-in-law was true to his glad-handing ways as Dean introduced him to staff members. But he groused when Dean left him on his own to sit in the lobby because Dean's boss needed to spend a few minutes with him.

After Carl left his office, Dean took fifteen minutes for a breather. With his office door closed, he asked Dillon to hold his calls and to freshen his father-in-law's coffee while he sat in the lobby. Swiveling in his chair, Dean leaned back and looked out his office windows.

Kate's parents are hopeless. Stupid me. It took their visit to remind me how their awful home life caused her unhealthy outlook and behavior.

On a whim, Dean phoned his brother Mitch.

"What's up, Deaner?" Mitch was driving his car to their mother's memory care facility in Chicago. "It'd be great if you could get down here to visit. She misses you, Deaner. Whenever she has a few lucid moments, she asks about you."

"I miss her too, Mitch. Next summer looks like it'll be a good bet to drive down. What you're doing for her means a lot, believe me. You're my hero. Is she doing okay?"

"More or less. Now that she realizes Dad passed, well, it's been more downhill."

"I get that you're carrying a big burden. Caretaking is tough. I'm sorry I'm not there to help. I moved up here eight years ago for this great job, not to get away from you and Mom's Alzheimer's."

"That's cool. You've got it good up there, I get that. So what's up?"

"Well, I need some of your wisdom, Mitch. I'm deep into some tough crap."

"Okay. Shoot."

"I've just had an *aha!* moment. Now that her parents are visiting us, every time they talk—her father especially—it's obvious she was victimized. Geez! I feel so much for her! No wonder she … I mean, it's clear she had to survive somehow and keep sane in an alcoholic environment that was so dysfunctional and toxic."

"So it just hit you, Skip? Just like that?"

"Yes, dummy me. I should know better—being a former counselor. But it's hard to see what's right in front of you when you're so close to it. Now it's as plain as the nose on my face why she judges herself mercilessly, why she's super responsible and so busy. She tries so hard to be the perfect wife, mother, friend, and model Christian. It exhausts her. The pressure she puts on herself, geez, she can be her own worst enemy. But knowing that only makes me love her more."

"Wow, you haven't been this worked up in ages. But I like it."

"Think about it, Mitch. Because she had to protect herself as a child, she had to build up walls to defend herself, to keep the craziness at bay. Those eventually became walls of silence, but they also made her more of an observer than an active participant in life. They provided safety, but she 'went inside' herself and learned to keep her head down."

"I'd say that syncs with what I know about her."

"I think it explains why she's afraid of expressing her thoughts and feelings. Her mom and dad fed her and made sure she had financial security and an education, but they didn't feed her heart or show her the love she needed. And being an only child she got through it all on her own."

"Hey, what if we'd never been brothers? How would we have ever managed? Right?"

"Amen to that. By the time she was an adolescent, it affected her natural sexuality. It got skewed unfairly, and my guess is much of her energy as an adult has been trying to avoid making any sexual choices at all."

"That reminds me. As your brother who loves you—and you know that's true—does any of this help you get closer to calling it quits and getting your own place?"

"She's still trapped and I can't abandon her, Mitch. I don't know what exactly that looks like right now, but I've got to try. Maybe God is the only one who knows, and I just have to learn to trust. …Yeah, to trust Him more. And trust her."

"I hate seeing all this happen to you—you're being hurt and getting rejected and shoved to the sidelines. I love you, man. If you're not ready to ditch her now, if you think you can hold onto your sanity, then what does your 'trusting more' do for *you*?"

"Well … I guess … it makes it all less personal. She's just acting the way she's been conditioned. Look, she's been showing up recently in all kinds of new ways and saying things that are closing the gap between us. Years ago, she stuck by me through some pretty tough times, remember? It could be that I'm supposed to love her through this whole mess with no strings, no 'buts,' no off ramp for me to take."

"You've held back a long time already, man. Are you able to forgive her? 'Cause I'm sick of seeing you miserable, and want to see you stop rationalizing and get on with it."

"I see your point, but Scripture says something else. 'Love does not keep a list of wrongs; it does not bear any grudges; it does not insist on its own way. As you have been forgiven, so you should forgive others.'"

"My divorce from Shelly was horribly messy, but it's worked out great for me. No regrets. I'd do it all over again. If it's impossible to forgive her, then cut the cord. Just do it."

"Kate's a wounded soul, Mitch, and so am I. Leaving her now would ruin all chances of … Dang! It's been ages since she and I just sat down together and had fun relaxing like reading a book, or doing a jigsaw puzzle, or watching some silly comedy on TV for no reason other than being together. No agenda. Nothing heavy."

"Are you dodging the issue?"

"It's time for more than a truce. What about the ninety-five percent of living that's been pushed aside? Does it have to only be about sex anymore? What if we played Scrabble or went out to a play? We have tickets for the Guthrie Theatre that we still haven't used."

"Well, use 'em. If that's what makes you happy."

"And I know Kate wants to visit her favorite national parks next summer, just like I want to get back to tinkering in my workshop. Did I tell you I'm making a paper-maché star for our Christmas musical?"

"Well, then go for it. Stick it out. Hey, right now I'm pulling into the parking lot to see Mom. Gotta run."

"Give her my love." Dean took a deep, satisfying breath. "This has really helped, Mitch."

"You asked for some wisdom, right? So here goes: 'What we are is God's gift to us. What we become is our gift to God.'"

"Hmmm, I like it. I'll ponder that one."

"I saw it on a restroom wall over the urinal." Mitch hooted.

"Ha! Give Mom a big kiss for me, okay? That goes for you, too, bro." He hung up.

Dean looked out the window, feeling pounds lighter.

Kate monitored Nicole's steering of the SUV on the freeway to Mall of America. "Nicole's practice driving is developing her driving skills, Mom. Isn't she doing great?"

"Right now the only great thing would be a cigarette."

"Gosh, Grandma," Lindsay said, "that sure sounds affirming."

Kate had told both her daughters the full details about the DWI. The only surprise was how little *they* were surprised. Any hint that Kate's mother might learn of the DWI or her suspended driver's license rattled her, but so far her 'Nicole's practice driving' cover story was working, thanks to the girls' cooperation.

Muriel opened her purse and took out a pack of Newport cigarettes. She started to light one. Kate insisted, "No, Mom, we don't smoke in here."

Nicole echoed, "We don't smoke at all. Anywhere."

"Well, I guess you've made that clear enough." Muriel cleared her throat, coughed, and put the cigarette away, none too pleased.

"Kids today, Mom," said Kate, filling the silence, "they're so different. They hardly smoke anymore. Can you believe it? They have all kinds of options and opportunities we never had, like texting and tweeting and Facebook and Pinterest. Isn't that right, girls?"

"Texting while driving—horrible!" Lindsay bellowed. Her sarcasm dripped.

"Absolutely horrible," Nicole added, swerving into a faster lane.

"Slow down, Nicole! Stay in this lane," Kate commanded. "Our exit is right up ahead."

The kids' sarcasm, Kate speculated, came from the generation gap between digitally saturated teens and analog-bred parents. Or, perhaps the girls might be fussing about their coerced cooperation to play along with Kate's "practice driving" fib. Kate could only guess.

At the mall, Nicole took the lead and deftly maneuvered the four of them through the dense crowds of holiday shoppers.

"There's a rumor going 'round that Nicky has a new boyfriend on the hockey team," Lindsay tattled. "That's why she's so gung-ho to wear what she's picked out at VS."

"You traitor," Nicole yelped, punching Lindsay's arm.

"VS? What's that?" Muriel asked.

"Victoria's Secret, Grandma." Lindsay giggled, sticking her tongue out at Nicole.

"Okay, girls, cool it," said Kate, good-naturedly. "Let's go and see what this excitement is about, shall we?" She took her Mom's arm. "It's okay, Mom. They're Millennials, and they're inviting us into their world. Time to go with the flow."

At Victoria's Secret, Nicole appeared from the fitting room wearing a lacey, form-fitting, low-cut camisole. Muriel looked offended. Already put off by the brightly lit gaudy displays of low-cut bras, flimsy garter belts, and tiny pink panties, she sucked in her breath loudly, enough so that nearby shoppers turned their heads.

"Sh ... shame!" Muriel sputtered.

"Sexy! Over-the-top sexy!" Lindsay exclaimed.

"Get back in that fitting room," Kate demanded. "And shut the door."

Nicole paraded defiantly in front of the full-length mirror, wiggled her shoulders, and with an amused smirk animating her face, slowly walked into the fitting room. Lindsay ran to join her, yammering her approval.

"I've never ... seen ... something so horrid," Muriel wailed.

Kate whispered to her mother, "Quiet down, Mother. People are noticing."

"Oh, are they? Well, is that right!" she declared too loudly. "Is this where the prostitutes shop?" Muriel picked up a frilly string panty, more lace than cloth, and shrieked, "Forty-nine dollars for *this*?"

"Mom, I totally get it. You're right. Nobody said we're buying anything here, just looking. All Nicole was doing was trying it on to get a reaction."

Kate took her mother's elbow and shuffled her toward the exit. Muriel balked, jerking her arm away. Kate's voice remained low, stern. "Outrageous, Mom. That's what I think, too. Like I said, it's today's kids. … But you and I both know this is not a store for prostitutes. The way you're behaving is making things worse."

Muriel looked at her, befuddled.

"It also brings up something that you and I have needed to get straight for a long time."

"As her mother," Muriel declared, "you should give that girl your two cents, Kathryn. What in heaven's name are you talking about—something we need to get straight?"

"Mom, we both know Nicky went too far. Didn't I say so? But she's acting her age. Think of it as experimenting. She's trying out new boundaries."

"Listen to you talk. Bah!"

Kate escorted her mom out of the store to an out-of-the-way bench and urged her mother to sit. "Like I was saying, Mother," Kate stated, sitting beside her, "you have your opinions and your standards. But it's time you heard about how those standards made *me* feel growing up." Kate pushed closer to her on the bench.

Muriel stared at her. "Are you sticking up for them? Do you think Nicky prancing around like a slut is okay? When you were that age, you did exactly what you were told."

"Yes, I did. Often to my regret."

Muriel's face changed from defiant to confused.

"Have you any idea what your stuffy standards did to me, Mom? I hated the way you warned me about my body, and sex, and boys—always boys getting girls pregnant. Your warnings made me afraid, Mom, and they've screwed up my life ever since."

Shock etched her mother's face. Muriel's eyes looked down, then back up with defiance. "Screwed up your life? *I* screwed up your life? You hate me that much?"

Kate drew a long breath. "I didn't say I hated *you*. You're always turning things around. You know that's not what I said. I hated your *warnings*, Mom."

Isolated in their tiny private world, Kate gripped her mother's wrists, amazed at how weak her mother was, and leaned closer, eye to eye. "Be honest. I'm going out on a huge limb here … a *huge* limb. Have you and Dad ever made love since I was a baby?"

"My God, *what?* That's no business of yours! What makes you think—?"

"You haven't, I'm guessing, have you?"

"I heard you the first time. I need a cigarette. This has to stop. Now!"

Kate held her Mom firmly from moving, keeping her voice low. "Is that why he gets so mad and nasty, to get back at *you* for depriving *him*? Why didn't I ever have brothers or sisters, Mom, when so many kids I grew up with did?"

Her mother's eyes turned fiery irate. "Oh, aren't you all high and mighty? You're not so great, you know. You little fool. Remember how we had to drag you to church? You didn't want to ever read your Bible, did you? And then all that feminism drivel. Bah!"

Gritting her teeth, Kate barreled ahead. "Were you afraid? Were you ever comfortable in your body? All those girdles and garter belts and sneaky ways you hid your body—why?"

"Now you listen to me, and listen good. I never existed in your grandpa's eyes. To him, I was invisible. He put my brother Earl first no matter how much he messed up. No matter how many A's I got, or how often I helped Mom, my father did nothing but criticize every little thing I did. Earl always got his way. It made me want to wring both their necks."

"I asked about Dad. You're dodging, Mom. You're avoiding what I asked you about." Kate softened a bit. "Mom, I'm so sorry. I didn't know all that. I don't remember you telling me things like that. But just now, I asked about you and *Dad*."

Muriel looked down at her feet. "Your father? I married him thinking everything was going to be different. Ha! He was a carbon copy of your grandpa; even worse—a beast. Why I didn't see it when we were courting, I'll never know."

"Did you refuse him in bed?"

"Watch it, young lady. You're crossing the line." Abruptly Muriel sagged. "Why do you think we've slept in separate beds all these years? I told him we needed to because he snored so terribly and thrashed around in his sleep tangling up the sheets, but . . ."

"I see." Kate loosened her grip, offering a tiny smile. "Did you have to keep him off you? Did you use a diaphragm? The rhythm method?"

"So personal! Where are your manners?"

"I've been wondering a long time about how you kept from getting pregnant."

"That is not up for discussion." Muriel clamped her mouth shut, folding her arms harshly across her chest.

Kate lowered her voice. "Hear me, Mom. It's important. I've wanted to ask you this for ages. Remember the time I walked into the bathroom when I was nine and saw a pinkish blob in your hand?"

"Stop right there. It was only a diaphragm."

"Yes, Mom, that's exactly what I figured out later." Kate paused, taking a long breath. "But, as usual, we never talked about it. Eventually it made sense as I got older, but it would've done a lot more good had we talked about it then." Kate put her arm around her mother's shoulder, leaning gently toward her. "Mom, I'm sorry to keep bringing this up, but didn't you and Dad *want* more children?"

Muriel stared straight ahead.

"Mom, did you hear me?"

Muriel ground her teeth. "He did. He wanted sons. Oh, how he went on and on about having sons. I vowed he would never get the satisfaction. As the years piled up after you came along—thanks goodness, you were a girl!—he finally demanded I go see a doctor. The short answer is that the doctor pronounced 'us' infertile."

Kate sighed, deeply affected. Feeling sympathy and great sadness for her mother, she soothed her with a tiny hug. "That was very brave, Mom. Thank you. Why didn't you use the Pill? He would never have known."

"Oh, my, my! The Pill wasn't easy to get, my child. Even if a woman wanted to take it, you had to have a prescription. Nobody could just waltz in and get it for the asking. Besides, why would an infertile woman ask for a prescription to keep her from getting pregnant?"

Kate sat quietly. "You're right." Kate clenched her jaw. "So did that lead to all your warnings about me, my body, my sexuality?"

Her mother swallowed slowly; her chin quivered. "Woman to woman?"

"Woman to woman."

"I would like to say no. But as I think about it, and the way you just asked about it, now that I see how you've struggled, I'm so sorry you had to pay such a high price."

Her mother gripped Kate's arm, but tenderly. She leaned against Kate, almost like a child. "Please don't hate your poor mama. I did what I had to do to get through the day. Yes, dear, I wish it had never been like that. Everything I harped about to you. And now, I need a cigarette."

Kate hugged her firmly. "I love you, Mom. Bless you." Kate realized how her fingers felt stiff from gripping so intensely.

Muriel patted her arm, stood up, and gestured to the row of large glass doors at the entrance to the parking ramp.

"Okay, Mom. Go have your cigarette, and I'll corral the girls. We'll still have a jolly, merry Christmas, starting right now. How about it?"

"Whatever you say, dear." Her mother speed-walked as best she could to the "smoking allowed" area in the entryway. Kate walked back toward Victoria's Secret. Emerging from the store, the two girls were all giggly. Kate plastered on a happy face. Nicole and Lindsay acted buoyant and giddy.

"We're all set, Mom. Let's go."

"Hi, girls." Kate renewed her determination to make their outing festive again. "How about us all getting a Ho-Ho-Latté while Grandma puffs on her cancer stick?" As they walked to the nearby coffee shop, Kate raised her voice brightly. "So, Nicole, just who is this new boyfriend of yours? I'm dying to know."

"Oh, Mom, Lindsay was just putting you on."

Lindsay held up a Victoria's Secret gift card. "Hear you go, Nicky," she said, rubbing it in for Kate to hear. "I'm sure that sexy camisole will be much cheaper at the after-holidays sale when we come back for it."

"You two!" Kate cried pleasantly. "What am I ever going to do with you?"

L arissa glanced out the church window and saw Dean park his car in the Spirit Hills parking lot. Getting out, he carried a large papier-maché star about the size of a bicycle wheel spray-painted gold and studded with strings of electric lights.

"Look at what Dean's got," she said to Ginny. "That star sure is big."

Ginny was kneeling next to her, pinning up the angel's gown worn by a junior high girl who was texting on her phone. "My, it sure is," said Ginny, looking out the window. "I'm excited to see how it will look lit up over the manger."

Larissa was pinning the hem of a shepherd's cloak worn by an antsy eight-year-old boy. "Hold still a few more seconds, Tyler, please."

The girl in the angel costume asked Ginny, "Will I be standing next to the star or in front of it?"

"I'm not sure," she replied. "That's up to Mrs. Wilkins."

"In any case, be sure to keep your wings out of the way, sweetie," said Larissa. To the boy, she said, "There you go, Tyler. That'll do for today's rehearsal. Now remember to keep practicing your line, 'Look, ye! An angel descending from the stars.'"

The boy ran off carrying his fake shepherd's staff, shouting, "Look, ye! An angel descending from the stairs! Look, ye! An angel descending from the stairs!"

"Not *stairs!*" Larissa hollered after him. "*STARS!*"

Ginny howled with laughter.

Kate was instructing the dancers in their sequin-trimmed tunics twenty feet away. She turned to Larissa and Ginny. "Kids and dogs, right? They always steal the show."

"*He* would be *perfect* for the cast of the Best Christmas Pageant Ever," Ginny said. Larissa added, "I haven't had this much fun in ages."

"That's the spirit. That's what I like to hear," chimed in Marlene, walking up. "Are we all ready for lights and music? I promised our parents we wouldn't let this rehearsal drag on." Marlene clapped her hands, getting everybody's attention on stage and at the sound-and-lights board. "Okay, gang, full dress rehearsal with lights and music in five minutes. Find your marks and get ready."

Larissa marveled at everybody's collaborative energy as they scurried about. Kate grabbed her elbow and corralled Larissa and Marlene into a spontaneous huddle. "Hey, girls," Kate lowered her voice conspiratorially, "I tried out my new vibrator." She smiled a huge smile.

Larissa felt a twinge of joy. "And ... ?"

"And it worked!"

They squealed with delight, giving Kate a collective hug. As Larissa turned, she caught sight of Trevor. He held a clipboard and paced near the back of the auditorium, talking to technicians who worked at the sound-and-lights board. She sent him a flirtatious smile, and he smiled back playfully. Larissa felt a warm tingle.

Dean entered the auditorium carrying the large gold star. He brought it straight to a teenage stagehand, instructing him where and how to position it. Larissa watched as Kate joined Dean and put her hand on his shoulder approvingly. Kate clearly liked his handiwork, and the way he casually smiled at her, and she at him, told Larissa they had restored some of their customary ease with each other—a thankful sight indeed. Larissa hummed softly to herself, pleased she could be a part of this homegrown theatrical effort.

What a great thing, volunteering for all this.

As she walked back to say hi to Trevor, a stinging sensation in her left breast startled her. Since her lumpectomy procedure the week before, the one-inch incision on her skin stung occasionally. Trevor noticed as she winced. "Hey, Larissa, what was that about? Is something wrong?"

"Um ... well, nothing serious. I'm not quite myself lately, as you might imagine. But it's nothing really."

"Any bad news?"

Larissa shook her head. "It partly has to do with the cancer, but I'm also stretched too thin right now. I have a four-thirty class today that I don't want to be late for. I haven't heard from Cody the past few hours, and he usually texts me. I have errands to run and groceries to pick up." She felt grateful to be talking with Trevor, and she didn't want to come off as needy.

"Would it help if I said, 'I love you?'" he whispered, putting his arm around her. They stood in the back, out of the bustle of activity, as the others busied themselves with getting into place. Larissa's tough exterior immediately softened.

"Thank you *so much,* Trev. I'm putty in your hands!" she said, beaming at him. "I can't thank you enough for going with me to the doctor's office. It meant so much having you there that day, and again when we went together to same-day surgery."

"I'm glad I was with you to hear the doctor's comments. You're one brave gal."

"It was such a relief hearing Dr. Myers say that ninety percent of women like me with DCIS have a normal life expectancy."

"You bet—along with not having to endure radiation or think about having a mastectomy."

"Your being with me made it all the more wonderful to hear. Especially when she talked about the lower risk of recurrence." By sharing all this good news, Larissa felt her confidence in her health was bringing them closer together.

Another sting troubled her left breast. She grimaced slightly. "Sorry, I'm having a bit of discomfort right now. I'm sure it'll pass."

He reached out for her again. "Come here and let me hold you. Nobody's watching." He squeezed her gently, and she loved feeling his touch. Putting a happy face on her struggles, she stepped away and swept her arms in a wide circle. "I love what's going on here, doing all this with Kate and Marlene and the others. And with you. It's a whole new world for me."

She pointed to Kate and Dean on stage helping the stagehand, who was having trouble hanging the star. "Look, they're both even joking around. Isn't it nice how they've found that spark between them again?"

"Sure is. ... but I'm afraid Dean is still teetering."

Silently, she and Trevor observed their friends.

"I've seen Kate make good progress opening up recently. I think she's getting to a new place, Trev."

"That's super, but at times Dean feels discouraged, like giving up."

"Before they do anything drastic, let's make something constructive happen."

"Hold it—I know," she continued. "I've got an idea. What if you and Dean come to my fitness class the week after Christmas? Other men will be there too, so don't think it's just for women. That way you guys would get a workout and get to see my world. Afterward, we could all go hang out somewhere like Sacred Grounds—like a double date."

"Sounds great. I'm all for it."

Abruptly, Marlene's voice rang out: "LET'S GO, PEOPLE! PLACES, EVERYBODY!" Marlene looked toward the back of the room. "Larissa! We need you backstage. Our angel needs one of her wings hot-glued."

"Yes—coming!" Larissa answered. She kissed Trevor's cheek, squeezed his hand, and hurried down the aisle.

"OKAY, TROOPS … LET'S LOOK SMART!" Marlene yelled out. She turned to Kate, assembling the dancers. Kate nodded, then gave Dean a thumbs-up as she admired the beautiful gold star, all lit up and shining over the manger. In the wings, kids dressed as Mary, Joseph, and barn animals stood poised to make their entrance.

"ALRIGHT, EVERYBODY," hollered Marlene. "ACTION!"

CHAPTER 27

Dean always enjoyed Christmas Eve at Spirit Hills. The green pine trees twinkling with tiny white lights and the sparkling gold garlands adorned with red ribbons added splendor to the crowded sanctuary. He picked the fourth pew from the front for his family members to sit, an advantageous view of the rustic Nativity scene on stage.

"I think we'll get a good look at everything from here," he said to Fredrick and Muriel as they sat down alongside Lindsay and Nicole.

"Seeing Kathryn up close when she comes in with the dancers will be wonderful," said Muriel.

Dean wedged himself between his in-laws and Lindsay and Nicole, who showed minimal interest. He knew they'd attended, or played parts in, a string of similar Christmas pageants.

"Such a fuss," Fredrick muttered. "Too bad her time has been eaten up working on this thing."

"Hush, Fred," said Muriel. "This will be a lovely play, and we'll get to see her creativity." Dean appreciated his mother-in-law's standing up for

Kate. "Remember, Fred," Muriel added, "she loves doing this, and we should be happy for her."

"Yes, yes." Fred cleared his throat. "It won't last more than an hour, will it?"

Dean had heard enough. "Look, let's be thrilled for her, okay? She's worked weeks on this project. This is more than entertainment; it's sacred, so let's be reverent. How about if we all genuinely tune in to the music and the wonderful message?" For twenty-four years of their marriage, nothing he'd done had succeeded in changing Kate's parents' downbeat view of him, nor had his record as a committed father and husband meant much to them, as far as he could tell. Now, he didn't feel like holding back his opinions.

"I, for one, think Mom deserves lots of credit." Lindsay added, with a tinge of boredom. "Don't you, Nicky?"

"I sure do. And, Daddy, I like your star hanging over the manger."

Lindsay leaned toward Dean and whispered in his ear, "Yes, Dad. I like it, too."

Dean replied, "Do me a favor, Lindsay, okay? How about if you run up afterward and throw your arms around Mom? She'll love it. It might also distract Grandma and Grandpa just enough to get them to end their pity party."

"Gotcha." Lindsay slipped her arm under her father's elbow. "Have I told you lately how much I love you, you dear sweet man?" She kissed his cheek.

Lindsay's words moved Dean to his core. He squeezed her arm, smiled, sat back, and let the next few minutes float by.

"Hey Dean," a voice called behind him. "How ya doin', guy?"

Dean craned his neck. Arriving two rows behind him were Hal and Ginny. "Yo, Hal—great. Nice to see ya, Ginny. How are you guys?" They exchanged holiday pleasantries, and Dean introduced his in-laws to the Ostrows. "Hal and Ginny are our mission teammates, Mom and Dad."

"Mission teammates, what a joke," Fredrick rasped to Muriel loud enough for Dean to hear.

"Oh, Fred, stop it," Muriel said, smiling her typical stiff, embarrassed smile.

Dean ignored the dig. Several rows back, he spied Larissa sitting in an aisle seat. Ordinarily, a current of high energy would have passed through him, triggered by Larissa's stellar looks. *But those days are over. Her beauty hasn't changed, but I have.* He was glad she could enjoy the show as an audience member, now that her work backstage on costumes was completed. Because Trevor served as tonight's host of the pageant, Dean didn't have to guess *he* was another a reason for her attendance. Dean knew of the creative teamwork between Larissa and Kate, and it cheered him. Their influence on one another was a marvelous thing. Next to Larissa sat Cody, who looked alert and curious, not bored or blasé. Dean surmised he might have showed up because of Nicky as well as to observe his mom's artistry and hard work.

Perhaps due to her cancer scare, Larissa looked a bit somber. Dean had sent her a get-well card weeks earlier and phoned her expressing his encouragement and support when he'd heard about the scary news. He wished to comfort her now without it seeming inappropriate—strictly as a friend. Should he stand up and go greet her? Doing so minutes before the start of the production, though, was poor timing. He wondered if she still felt a tug of desire for him, however faint. What he would give to see in Kate's eyes the same impassioned look he'd once seen in Larissa's eyes.

Trevor walked on stage wearing a flowing, majestic white robe. He lifted his arms high and prayed: "Holy Father, we are your people, the sheep of your flock, here to praise you for reaching out to a hurting world with the arrival of the new life that Jesus brought, and still brings, to all the world." Dean felt God's quiet, steadfast, uplifting presence in his own life as Trevor concluded the prayer.

The first melodic chords of "Hark! The Herald Angels Sing" filled the auditorium. The house lights dimmed. Hordes of children whispering to each other and stumbling on their costumes entered the stage. A spotlight shone on the girl playing the angel, with her arms spread wide and a halo dangling above her head. She stood elevated under the unlit star above the manger scene as the music paused. "Behold, for unto you a Child is born. I bring you great tidings of glad cheer, of … ah, great joy!"

The star lit up, beaming rays of bright light.

"Look, ye!" shouted Tyler, the shepherd boy. "An angel descending from the stairs!"

"*Stars. Say, stars!*" called a hushed adult voice from the wings.

"Look, ye!" shouted Tyler again. "An angel descending from the STARS!"

The audience erupted in laughter. Dean and many others enjoyed the performance all the more. Meanwhile, dozens of children's voices continued singing ...

> *Peace on earth and mercy mild, God and sinners reconciled,*
>
> *With the angelic host proclaim, Christ is born in Bethlehem!*
>
> *Hark! the herald angels sing, 'Glory to the newborn King!'*

The carol's uplifting proclamation of "*Peace on earth ... and sinners reconciled*" touched Dean's heart. He listened intently, allowing the glad tidings of Christmas to sink in: how almighty God arrived as a humble baby and entered messy human history to offer unmerited, grace-filled eternal life.

Children in bathrobes and wearing flip-flop sandals moved about on stage reenacting the centuries-old drama, lifting his spirit. He checked to see if his family members were as inspired as well. All appeared to be entertained; even Fredrick showed mild delight.

Dean's mind drifted as the pageant gained momentum. He'd slept in a motel bed for five weeks and wondered if his retreat had made much difference. Praying more, journaling more, and reading his Bible more had filled his time, along with extended work hours at MediMax. He'd poured himself into the year-end rush at the office, and the value of his advisory role had ratcheted up after his high-profile meeting with Carl Langley's executive team. He recalled stopping once at a book store after a long workday where he found himself browsing in the erotic book section. A handful of lusty tales piqued his attention, fantasies about sex partners pushing the limits of carnal pleasure. He envied the intensity and mutual passion that the partners showed for each other—but he'd not dallied too long.

Huddled around the cardboard manger, children from four to fourteen dressed as cows and sheep tended by shepherds gathered to worship the baby. One boy sang a solo, his voice high-pitched and pure. The carol's melody and message, "... Born to raise the sons of earth, born to give them second birth," reflected Dean's own personal rebirth, a transformation of spiritual change he'd experienced nineteen years earlier.

The scene came back to him with crystal clarity—a lakeshore in Minnesota's Superior National Forest, where he'd collapsed in despair one April afternoon while hiking alone. It was there he met God's merciful eternal acceptance. He felt too weak in his own strength to alter the course of his then-chaotic existence, and Kate, too, was stressed to her own breaking point. There, alone in the forest, Dean pushed aside his non-belief in God, who in his mind had always been a sham, and prayed to this invisible spirit in the form of His Son. He begged Christ to enter the deepest core of himself, calling out, "Jesus, save me!" Impossibly, a cleansing, transcendent transformation occurred deep in his being.

At that moment the Holy Spirit had entered his being. His hatred and bitterness because of the abuses he'd endured in his youth from his overbearing mother and absentee father were washed away. In a burst of deliverance, he exchanged his spiritual bankruptcy for the Lord's supreme sufficiency. Forgiveness and grace flooded his heart—both for his own wayward actions and his parents' failings. Ailments that once plagued him—depression, a stomach ulcer, obsessive nail biting, months of insomnia, and torturous headaches—dissipated over time until they were completely gone. New attitudes activated new behaviors and gave him, and Kate, hope for the future. Having seen his dramatic changes, Kate made her own decision months later to commit her own life to Christ.

". . . *Glory to the newborn King!*" The carol ended on a triumphant chord.

"Here they come, Dad," Lindsay whispered. Nudging Dean, she pointed out the dozen child dancers who entered the stage with Kate leading them from the wings. They danced in time to a modernized musical arrangement of *O Little Town of Bethlehem*. Muriel elbowed Fredrick, pointing out Kate's energetic direction of the children. Dean realized anew Kate's skills as a choreographer and her talent to inspire the kids in her charge.

As youthful Mary and Joseph reenacted the centuries-old drama of the unlikely circumstances of a peasant mother giving birth to the Christ child in a smelly barn, the singers sang on key and the dancers kept in step to the hymn's rhythms. He hoped that the story's power got through to everyone. If so, the untold hours Kate and her colleagues spent away from home and family surely would be worth it.

Yet, as he watched Kate, Dean bristled at the vast investment she made every year planning and rehearsing this exceptional event. Although justly proud of her, he questioned the cost that Kate's volunteerism played in their daughters' lives and his own. Her many roles—mother, homemaker, deacon, volunteer choreographer, prayer intercessor, short-term missionary—displayed her obedience to Christ and earned public accolades. *If only 'lover' were one of her roles, too! It would certainly earn her private accolades—mine!* Petty or not, Dean had to admit he felt jealous at times of her passionate love for children, which seemed to displace her passionate energy for him.

I'd love to see her gorgeous blue eyes shine again when looking at me, he mused. *I've seen glimpses already.*

Loud applause stirred him from his dreamy state. The children took their final bows as Trevor stepped forward and lifted his arms for quiet.

"We thank you all for coming tonight, folks. We trust the story of divine love being born in human form moved you, and that your hearts will celebrate our Savior's birth on that chilly night more than two thousand years ago. Let us praise the great God of Abraham, Isaac, and Jacob for this new covenant and magnificent blessing. We lift up Jesus' coming to Earth to bring healing and redemption. Our entire offering tonight will go to support the people of Haiti who are still devastated from the great earthquake and by diseases like cholera and AIDs. Like us, they are desperate for Jesus' love, and we aim to help satisfy our Haitian neighbors' deepest needs in His name. Many thanks, and may the Lord of All bless you tonight, and always."

Trevor gave the benediction, and the audience flocked to the exits.

Fredrick and Muriel made their way over to congratulate Kate. "Lindsay and Nicky, why don't you go with Grandpa and Grandma?" suggested Dean. The girls trailed Fred and Muriel obediently, and Dean saw Lindsay give Kate a big hug as he had suggested. Hal and Ginny wished Dean "Merry Christmas" as he looked for Larissa among the crowd but couldn't find her.

"Hey, Dean," Hal said. "That pageant sure rocked."

Ginny smiled broadly and nodded. "So are the in-laws driving you nuts yet?"

"Close. Very close."

"I'll bet." Ginny ambled toward Kate and the dancers.

Hal pulled Dean aside. "So how's the home life now that you're back?"

Dean sensed Hal's empathy. "Well, not so bad, not so bad at all. Eating with the family again feels great."

"Good to hear it. Otherwise?"

Dean shrugged. "I'm trying to see all the positives, Hal, and there are some. I've turned it over to God and believe He has a plan that neither of us can see right now."

Hal frowned. "Well, look … best of luck while Kate's folks are here." He punched Dean's shoulder.

"I need it!"

"Ginny's waving to me. I'd better go. See ya before New Years when you and Kate come over for another get-even Scrabble match."

"Good, see you then." Dean hadn't heard about being invited to Hal and Ginny's, but it sounded great. Several rows away, Larissa drew Dean's attention. *A minute for a friendly check-in can't hurt.* He walked over to her.

"Hey, Larissa," he called. "So good to see you." Their eyes locked. "How *are* you?"

"Never better. And you?" The recent stress weighing on her showed, even through her cheerful smile.

"I'm good, thanks. And does that 'Never better' include your health?" Dean avoided the "c" word.

"Yes, overall. The tumor's contained so far, fortunately, and that's a lot to be glad about."

"I'll say. Great news. Like a welcome Christmas present."

"Sort of. You know, there are a lot of other wonderful things to be happy about tonight, too. I loved the show, didn't you?"

"Absolutely. Everything—the dancing, the kids, the music—it all came together. Oh, and the costumes looked terrific."

"Thanks."

Being an arm's length from Larissa, he sensed the same open look in her eyes, but the seductive energy was gone. That was all right, and it didn't dampen his gratitude for her role in reviving his faith in the possibility of a passionate partner. "Sounds like you're working hard to be brave," he said.

She looked pale. "Trevor's been a huge help. And Cody's on good behavior."

"If I can support you in any way whatsoever, please let me know." Dean wondered where Cody had gone.

She offered a weak smile. "You sound like you really mean it."

"I do. Of course I mean it."

"Sorry, Dean, I'm a little touchy. It probably has something to do with the lumpectomy."

"Given your level of stress, you've been a real trooper."

People's voices rang through the church, joyous and buoyant. Larissa looked over toward Kate.

"Enough about dreadful topics, Dean. I'd like to let you in on something. Your dear wife is making great strides in many ways, and I'm not sure you're aware of it."

"Oh? What strides?"

"The kind you've been waiting for. She's doing it in her own way and own time, which you probably know means she's staying quiet about it and not being as dramatic as you'd like, but she *is* making progress."

Again—words. Words of encouragement, words of promise, but still just words. He could choose to doubt and be resentful, or to believe and be trusting. "Well, right this minute, I'll take your word for it. I've had hints. I'm sure your being friends with her has made a big difference. And what a kick it's been, seeing you two hanging out together. I love it."

She perked up. "Keep the faith!" She blushed. "Gosh, was that me talking like that? But do have faith. She's worth it." Larissa gently touched his arm. "Keep trusting, and don't give up."

"You seem pretty certain." He paused. "I guess I'll pay more attention."

Her eyes held his. "Before you go, I want you to know how immensely thankful I am that you linked me up with Trevor. He's one great guy." A smile animated her face.

Without warning, her smile sparked his old romantic stirrings for her. *No, I'm deluding myself. Get real, Dean.* His amorous leanings toward Larissa, he judged, had morphed into a wider-ranging, expansive, more charitable friendship. "You and Trevor make a great match. I feel genuinely happy for you."

"Thanks! Oh, by the way, we have an invitation for you and Kate. Would you like to join us for a fitness class right after Christmas? That way you'll get a chance to tone up, and we could all go someplace afterward like Sacred Grounds, then on to Hal and Ginny's for a Scrabble tournament." Hal's mention of Scrabble now clicked.

"Uh, yeah, that sounds like a fine idea." *Yes, indeed. We're friends now. Just friends, as it should be.*

"Great. Then it's a date."

L arissa stood observing Dean in a fresh way as they chatted. Here was the man who had generated so much excitement in her life, and now he seemed more like a big brother or uncle, and she didn't have to feel awkward or shy around him.

Children ran by, chasing and hollering, happy and free. From nowhere, Cody ran up the aisle in a whirlwind of excitement. "Hey, Mom. It's a go. I asked Nicky, and she says I can drive her home. You said I can have the keys, right?" Behind him, Larissa noticed Nicole walking up with an eager look on her face.

"Yep, that's what we agreed to." Larissa had let him persuade her earlier to drive the Saturn if Nicole said yes to Cody's invitation to give her a ride home. His record of no pot-smoking and less drinking on weekends played a part in her willingness. Now that Nicky had said yes, it was official. Larissa guessed she would find a ride home somehow—with Trevor, her first wish, or with Kate and Dean, perhaps. In a pinch she'd take a cab.

"Does Nicky have her dad's permission?" Larissa asked Dean with a touch of humor.

Dean looked at Nicole, playfully hesitant. "And what time did you say he should bring you home, Nicky?"

"By midnight."

"Hmmm. Make that before Santa comes down the chimney, say eleven-thirty . . ." Dean drew out the pause like a TV game show host ". . . and you have a deal."

Nicole let out a squeal like contestants on game shows do, lifting her arms as if leading a cheer. "Eleven-thirty it is!"

Cody grinned. "I promise she'll be home on time, Mr. Nelson."

"Oh? It's back to 'Mr. Nelson,' is it?" Dean grinned and nodded okay.

Larissa felt a tiny bit squeamish about Cody's overconfidence. "No joyriding, hear?"

"I promise, Mom. Nicky, we'd better split before they change their minds."

"Hold it, Cody," Larissa ordered. "Hang around a few minutes, will you, and check with me to make sure I have a ride before you go, okay?"

"Sure, Mom. I'll bring back the keys if you need me to."

Cody and Nicole sprang away. She watched her son's shaggy head of curly hair disappear down the aisle. Glancing at Dean, she saw he was as amused by Cody's exuberance as she was.

"Since the Thanksgiving dinner," Dean said, "I've noticed Nicky and Cody getting along pretty well."

Larissa grinned. "So it seems, 'Mr. Nelson.' So it seems."

Larissa noticed Kate looking tired standing on her feet, chatting with kids' parents who were congratulating her. "I think I'd better get over and congratulate Kate."

"Go right ahead. I'll keep her folks company so you can have her all to yourself."

"Great." Larissa approached Kate as Dean peeled off to talk with her parents.

Kate perked up. "Larissa! I'm so glad you were part of this. Did you enjoy it?"

"Immensely. Loved it. The dancers did so well. Everything went off without a hitch." She felt real joy for her friend.

"And those costumes were so colorful. Are you glad you came on board?"

"Absolutely. Wouldn't have missed it for the world." She hugged Kate with all her strength, being careful not to squeeze her left breast. "Everything came off beautifully, Kate. You should be very proud."

"I think it did, too. Say, are you feeling better now that you've had a few days to recover from your surgery?"

"Thanks for asking. But this is your night, Kate, and I don't want my stuff to mess it up."

"Stop right there. Come on, Larissa. Don't be a martyr."

"Okay, I'm feeling some twinges of pain now and then. But I do have a tiny bit of news, and good news at that. With the daily monitoring of everything, I'm told the chances of a recurrence are quite low."

"Terrific. Super. No bad news?"

"None really. But I have to say it bothers me how I'm depending more on cosmetics to feel good about myself. This whole thing has made me stop and think about how much I'm aging, Kate. So, guess who's using more makeup?"

"Oh, sweetie, don't go there. You look gorgeous, like always."

"It kinda scares me. It's like I'm trying to hide behind my makeup."

Kate waved her hand. "You have to let crap like that go. I promise we'll do a girl date soon. How about it? Right after my folks leave, let's do a long lunch."

"That would be awesome."

"It's a date, then. I'll be in touch."

More excited parents walked up and saluted Kate. "We loved the show so much. . . ."

Larissa stepped aside, realizing Kate was the stronger of them currently. Something about their brief conversation soured her. *Is it envy? Is it because I miss the blessings of a loving family?* Kate had her handsome husband and a fancy house in the suburbs, with spare time to volunteer and kids doing well in school. Plus, Kate and Dean had the assurance of an afterlife that Larissa knew they believed was real.

Time stopped. She recalled how the slow, pious notes of *O Come, O Come, Emmanuel* had stirred her inner being. Growing up attending Jerry and Gladys's church every Christmas and hearing the same hymn, she recalled the word "Emmanuel" meant "God with us." *How far I have distanced myself from God!* The melody and words of the hymn came back to her.

... *Cheer our spirits by Thy advent here,*

Disperse the gloomy clouds of night,

And death's dark shadows put to flight.

She sensed no assurance, but her soul experienced an unexpected tug beyond her understanding. She'd carefully watched the teenage girl dressed as Mary on stage, holding a live baby in her arms, rocking it gently. Larissa's mind dismissed the notion of a virgin girl being impregnated by divine force. How could a baby be both human and divine? She felt pity for people who believed in such far-fetched myths.

". . . He came to the lowly, the poor, the sick, the outcast," Trevor had prayed on stage, "to bring healing in his wings, to bring hope for the hopeless, to bring comfort for all who suffer, to bring salvation for every soul afflicted by sin in this fallen world."

Larissa's afflictions felt very real. Watching "Mary" hold the newborn baby, she felt the fleeting desire to be held and rocked and comforted as well. Earthly evil and madness marched on as usual, and people just endured it. She reasoned her own history, exacerbated now by cancer, offered personal proof.

It's all a big fairytale!

Her trials in life were no fairytale, however. Watching the pageant, she'd addressed God silently. *Are you there? I'm in your church. Are you listening? If you* are *the loving God everyone says you are, when will you remove people's suffering? My suffering? Are you really there?*

The girl playing Mary then laid the baby carefully in the cardboard manger, cradling him in a fake feeding trough with light beams from Dean's star radiating overhead. Jittery, tremulous, Larissa felt a deep ache for the godly love that the characters on stage and the people in the pews seemed to feel so personally. *I need a miracle. Right now would be great timing!* Nothing. Her faith in miracles hit an all-time low. *God with us. God with* me? *No, I won't be fooled.*

Strangely, ignoring her skepticism, an amazing inner tenderness returned now as she stood in the aisle where the rough-hewn Nativity set commanded her view. She felt a stirring of feeling whole, an uplifting sensation she could not explain. A calm beyond all logic visited her, an assurance that her needs would be met. Peace and freedom from grief about her life warmed her.

Behind her, someone walked up quietly and she felt a strong set of hands around her waist pulling her close. "Guess who?" a deep masculine voice whispered.

"Trevor?" Larissa turned and there he stood, smiling.

"The one and only!" He now wore a dark suit and colorful Santa Claus tie. Sporting a smile to match, he looked dashing.

"Wow, the pageant was really great."

"We're majorly blessed, aren't we? Especially thanks to volunteers like you, with all you did, along with Kate and Marlene and their team and everyone's hard work."

"I don't suppose you have time to give someone a ride home tonight, do you?" she asked. "I mean, I'm sure you have other things you're busy with, and—"

"A ride? Let's see." He furrowed his eyebrows. "If that someone is who I think it is," he looked carefully into her eyes, "what else could be better? How could a lonely bachelor like me enjoy anything better than spending his precious time chauffeuring a lovely lady home?"

"Well now, I know that certain someone would *love* to spend *her* precious time with just such a lonely bachelor on this cold Christmas Eve."

He cleared his throat. "In that case, my chariot awaits, m'lady. You have your ride. But on the way, how about a stop at my place?"

"Oh?" She wavered, then pointed to the Nativity scene. "Will there be room at the inn?"

"Ha! Touché. Why don't you come up for a toast and see?"

A wide smile brightened her face. "Fantastic. It's a deal."

"Let's be away then." Taking her hand, he walked with her toward the exit.

She grinned, feeling her worries and cares fleeing. "I'll just need a minute to let Cody know what's up, and that I'll be late getting home."

"The night is young, my dear, and sharing your company will be the finest of Christmas presents ever."

C H A P T E R

Trevor's apartment in South Minneapolis overlooked Lake Calhoun, one of the five popular lakes in the city. As she walked inside, Larissa discovered an open-space layout. The apartment was tidy but not too neat, as befit a bachelor pad. Perched on the top floor of a three-story older brick building in the trendy Uptown district, it had a lived-in feeling, large windows, functional furniture, two walls of books, and some manageable clutter.

"I like the view," said Larissa, stepping over to a front window.

"I'm glad you're here to enjoy it. This place doesn't see many visitors."

She looked out at the mile-wide lake, frozen over with snow like an immense frosted cookie. She took in the pale moonlight on the lake's windblown surface. Larissa could barely make out the walking path that circled the lake. In the summer, the path was shaded by trees and enjoyed by masses of people. Now the trees were stark and snow-covered.

Trevor rummaged in the refrigerator, removing a bottle of champange for a festive toast. She felt nervous energy about being alone with him in his home. Should she set a time limit?

"I have an invitation for you, Larissa, my sweet," he said, walking over with the champagne and two stemmed glasses. "Let's sit down here." Both sat on the sofa; he poured. "I admit this is coming out of nowhere, but is there anything stopping you from staying over?"

She hesitated. "Well, that's quite an offer. But don't you have to be back at church tomorrow morning?" She actually felt delighted about the idea.

He toasted her with his glass. "I do, yes. But I won't have to leave until nine-fifteen for the ten-thirty service. That means I can make us a dandy little omelet with buttered toast and fresh-squeezed orange juice before I leave."

The idea appealed to her. She would need to call Cody and tell him she wouldn't be home until morning. "Does it also mean you wish us to share sleeping arrangements?"

He sat up straighter. "All options are on the table."

"Such as?"

"Well, there's option A, I sleep on the couch and you sleep in my bed. And there's option B, vice versa. And C, we share the same bed. What are your druthers?"

What did she want? She instinctively wanted option C, but would they keep to their separate sides of the bed all night? Or did she even want them to? "I defer to you. You made the invitation, you go first."

"Well, there's a strong case for A. We spend the evening sharing this champagne and chat to our heart's content, and each of us gets a full night's rest while your virtue and mine remain secure and intact."

"Sounds good. I can go along with that."

"Okay then, option A it is."

"Or . . .? What about, um, option C?"

"Interesting. Let's consider the sub-options. One: We share the same bed yet I will honor your virtue and remain chaste all night long, Scout's honor. That's because I wish to love you only when the timing is right for both of us, when the future for both of us is clear."

She waited. "Or … ?"

"Or, sub-option two: If you choose to not stick to your side of the bed, I will be tempted to ravish you in the most sensual, sexual way possible—

devouring you with my love." He paused. "It's your turn to weigh in. You've heard my choices."

She shifted on the sofa. He was being so formal. She wanted both, to be ravished *and* to have her virtue honored. "I like the idea of being devoured by your love, truthfully." *That would be over-the-top wonderful.* "And I want to give you all the love *I* have." She knew that in seconds after taking off their clothes, they could be passionately entwined. But the pain in her breast from the surgery might mean putting off sex until she was fully healed.

"Or?"

"Or, I will accept your honorable, gentlemanly offer for option C-one until the future makes clear to each of us whether we are in this for the long haul."

"Exactly as I see it. Well said. And no doubt God is pleased, too."

She wrinkled her brow. *There he goes again, slipping God into the conversation.* It made her pause. Marriage was the single greatest thing that had eluded her in life. The idea of waiting to make love until some far-off day made her appreciate all the more his willingness to wait until the right time. That attitude felt empowering and reassuring. The God part—well, that was her hang-up.

"Another toast," he offered as they clinked glasses. "To togetherness tonight. C-one!"

She sipped, then sipped again. The hope of marrying a man like Trevor made her want to say, *Okay, I see us well matched and mates for life, and we both deserve each other.* But could she inflict her cancer predicament on him? Was her defective self her best offer? And how could she, as his wife, deal with this God issue? Then there was …

"As two bodies in the same bed," he said, sipping his champagne, "I'm sure one day we'll make beautiful music together."

"Ha! What a come-on line. But . . ." she began, "my history with men has always amounted to sex first, love later. Frankly, I no longer want it that way. It has to be different this time. It's got to be love first, sex later. I'm telling you this to convince myself as much as you. I have to be upfront about my past."

"I'm glad you brought it up. That's being honest."

"But you're not like other men who want sex before love. Does my wanting love first and sex later make me sound frigid?"

"Not a bit. It makes you irresistible."

"I haven't turned you off?"

"No! I'm turned on. To me it means we have to hold off on the final act. As long as it's mutual, nobody suffers or gets fooled. But all this brings up another thing—something that's probably too soon to discuss, but I want to get it out there."

"Oh? What's that?"

"Okay." He took a deep breath. "I've never been a father … and I'd like to be."

She laughed, then laughed again. Her immediate thought was, *It's too late. What's he doing talking about making babies? But who cares—I'd love to!* "For the sake of argument, Trevor, I'll go along. It seems kinda late in the game for both of us, don't you think?"

"Does it?"

"Well, I'm less than a couple of years away from turning forty, Trev, and you're a couple of years ahead of me."

He nodded. "But, are you saying you wouldn't want to have children with *me*? Or, are you saying a woman's biology when she's in her late thirties, like you are, isn't conducive to having babies? Or, that it's too late for a woman with cancer who's your age to have babies?"

She paused. "Oh my gosh, so many layers. Let's see. With you? Yes, I'd like that. A woman's biology? Not sure. A woman with cancer? Hard to say. You heard the doctor."

"May I speak freely? … Good. As for a woman's biology, you look lusciously fit and capable of a successful pregnancy. Certainly there are women in their thirties and early forties who have healthy children. As for the cancer, the doctor said your chances of living a full life are ninety percent. Unless you're not sure about marriage in the first place, or marrying me, what's to think about?"

Oh, my! Having you as my husband … and the father to our child!

She leaned forward and kissed him. "I still don't see why you're not running the other way as fast as you can." She kissed him again. "The whole cancer thing is still a mystery to me. Children? That means creating a home together and being *parents*. I mean, I have a college-age son. My days of changing diapers are over, or so I've thought. A baby would mean a heck of an adjustment."

He smiled and set down his glass. "Certainly, yes, it would mean major adjustments for us both. And now we've come full circle. First of all, are you staying tonight?"

"Uh … well … yes."

"Good. Option A? C-one? Or C-two?"

"Um, eeeny, meeny, miney, mo … option C-one."

"Excellent. Virtue, not ravish—correct?"

"Correct." A sharp tingle went up her spine. "But as long as you understand what I *really* want is ravish, for now I think virtue wins. It has to."

"Done. Virtue it is. At least we can cuddle under the same covers, trusting each other."

"I do trust you, Trev. But what if our emotions take over—like mine did when I crept downstairs at my house and crawled in beside you on the couch?"

"You'll have to ratchet up the resistance, I guess. Both of us will have to be strong enough to press the pause button."

"At least nobody will barge through your door tomorrow morning and catch us."

"Unless Cody dresses up like Santa and can squeeze through the crack under the door."

They laughed freely. By the look in his eyes, she felt convinced he was trustworthy yet felt a tad uncertain of her own fortitude. She stuck out her hand and shook his. "Which reminds me about Cody. He texted me saying that he wanted to stay over at his friend Alex's tonight after dropping off Nicole. So now I can text him back saying it's okay."

"Hey, then you won't have to worry your pretty little head about it, right?"

"Right. You know, I'll need something to sleep in, of course. I 'forgot' my PJs."

"Let slumber time begin," he said, heading to his bedroom closet.

"Any old baggy T-shirt will do. Don't make a big fuss, Trev," she called after him.

From the bedroom, she heard him say, "Coming right up. Aha! I have just the thing." He walked back in the room carrying two oversized T-shirts—one sporting a Minnesota Wild hockey logo and the other a scripture verse: "I am the Lord's, and the Lord is mine."

"Perfect!" she exclaimed.

"Which one?"

"The Wild one."

"Am I to read anything into that?"

"Uh, I don't think so. It just came out that way."

He grinned "So you say." He flung it to her.

She caught it. Big enough for a professional hockey player, it was the manly gray athletic kind she could curl up in—clean but scented with his smell. It looked like it would almost reach her knees. She couldn't recall the last time everything seemed so delightful, when she'd felt so harmonious with a man. This night of all nights could be her happiest in ages.

L arissa awakened during the night in Trevor's bed, feeling the warmth of his body. The sublime sensations of his presence felt comforting and invigorating. She cuddled closer. Deeply asleep, Trevor responded unconsciously, reaching across her body to encircle it with a strong arm. She placed her bare arm on his bare arm, letting the skin-to-skin contact boost her sense of connection. When she put her bare leg on his leg, his body turned toward her instinctively. Glancing at the clock, she saw it was 3:37. Slipping her hands under his T-shirt, she felt the rough texture of his burn scars trailing down his neck and back.

He awoke. He opened his eyes and looked directly into hers. In the dim light, only a small glint of arousal appeared visible to her. But her conscience wanted to keep her own promise, despite a stronger part of her wanting him to make love right then. She pulled off her T-shirt and tossed it across the room, which left only her bra and panties on.

"We promised each other to wait," he muttered in a deep, sleep-drenched voice.

That was all it took. She stopped, rolled back, and let her desire cool. "Thank you," she whispered, feeling like she needed to scold herself.

He grunted, rolled over, and slipped back to sleep.

Blushing, she felt a rush of gratitude because here was a man who valued her person over her body, and valued his own morals highly, and a man like him was worth waiting for.

B eams of sunlight streaked through the bedroom curtains. Gently awakened by the beckoning aroma of bacon sizzling in the pan, it took a few, groggy seconds for Larissa to remember where she was as she basked in the glow of love.

She opened her eyes and peeked out. The bright sunlight jarred her. Rolling out of bed, Larissa noticed the Wild T-shirt across the room, hanging halfway to the floor off a table lamp. Crumpled on Trevor's side of the bed was his baggy "I am the Lord's" T-shirt. She went to slip it on, but first removed her bra and examined the cut from the lumpectomy. It was healing fine. Yawning, she peered at her face in the full-length mirror, eyeing her reflection, and rubbed the sleep from her eyes. Sounds of Trevor cooking in the kitchen filled her ears along with his jovial humming of "I'm Dreaming of a White Christmas." Today, she decided not to count the aging wrinkles she perceived emerging around the corners of her eyes and mouth. She banished the insecurity about her fading beauty.

If he doesn't notice, who cares? If he does, he'll have to take me just the way I am.

Before stepping out to greet Trevor in the full daylight, she walked to the bathroom and washed off any hint of makeup, deliberately looking as plain and as "down home" as possible. It was time Trevor saw her exactly as she was. He could take her measure that way without any enhancements or props, and, if necessary, reconsider his commitment to her.

Trevor stood at the stove mixing a cheese and scallions omelet, wearing only his pajama bottoms. Larissa walked to the counter and perched on a stool where the rectangular opening looked into the kitchen. Toasted English muffins topped with butter sat on a plate. With no makeup and her hair pulled back, she allowed the over-sized T-shirt to expose the cleavage of her braless breasts. She almost laughed to herself, because his eyes alternated between the scripture verse and her boobs. She must have looked the worst, yet she detected no change in Trevor's eye contact—he seemed to still see her as beautiful. She noticed him glance twice at her uncovered legs, the same twinkle lighting up his face. She blew him a kiss.

"So . . ." she mused, laughing, *"one* of us kept our promise."

"Indeed! Actually, we both did. Not that it was easy."

"Amen to that. Do you think God was looking down and helping you stay pure?"

"Ha! Maybe so. He has been known to do that, so I'm happy to give Him credit. I, for one, am in heaven."

"It *was* rather heavenly as far as it went, wasn't it?"

He adopted a playful elevated tone. "One of the finest Christmas presents ever! Heavenly indeed."

"For a few seconds there, I didn't like having to stop, but that changed when I thought about it."

"Close call."

They laughed.

Trevor flipped the sizzling bacon in the frying pan. "I'd sure like us to cross that line someday."

"Me, too—after, you know … the wedding bells ring, *if* that's meant to be." The room became still. The ugly, "I'm not enough" feeling reemerged in Larissa from stabs of physical discomfort in her left breast.

"Trevor, I'm sorry to be laying this on you, and I don't want to ruin a wonderful morning, but I have to confess something you'll have to live with if you want there to be an 'us.'"

"Are you hinting there's not an 'us'?"

"No such thing. What I want to tell you about is this: Right now is one of the worst times of my life. I have a tricky health diagnosis *and* a messy past."

"Your past doesn't matter to me."

"I had an abortion. It was *awful*—in every way you can think of. Besides ending the life of a human being who had no say in the matter, I lost a ton of blood and went into major shock."

He raised his hand like a traffic cop. She ignored him.

"Maybe you've seen those bumper stickers that say, *Abortion: One Dead, One Wounded*. Well that was the baby—and me."

He objected again. She ignored him.

"I've also had some one-night stands, although not in years. I even tried to seduce Dean not so long ago. So if you think of me as a floozy or a slut, as a loose woman, I can see where you're coming from."

He just stared at her. "But I've already said it doesn't matter. As for other men, including Dean, I assume, as my wife, you'd be faithful to me. And I would trust you."

"And I, you. Absolutely." She wanted to show him with her eyes how trustworthy she was. "There's more. I may have an ugly future up ahead. Cancer kills. And there's no guarantee where that scary road will take me. So here's your chance to—"

He reached and placed his hand over her mouth. "Stop. Enough." He glanced down the front of the T-shirt at her breasts, then peeked at her legs. His eyes told her he found everything satisfying, and it pleased her that he was trying to look respectable and gentlemanly, but his eyes kept running over her curves.

She cracked up laughing. *Yay! He likes what he sees!*

"You are the sexiest woman ever. And here you are, a Playboy centerfold any guy would give his left nut to take to bed and make love to all day and all night, right here with little ol' me. How do I rate?"

"How can you say that? Looking the awful way I do?"

"What? I think women are too self-conscious. Relax. You're the only lady who's ever graced the doorway of this apartment, and I've already sworn to God and myself to cherish you no matter what. You're gorgeous, whether you're wearing makeup or not. And I mean that about the inner you, too. Don't you get that?"

She composed herself. "Yes, I think I do." He had a good point, but part of her still wanted to go hide her flawed body forever and never bother him again. All she had to do was chit chat through the next few minutes, smile as she said goodbye, and forget him forever once the door closed behind her. But there was something else she felt torn about telling him.

"You need to know there's still something between us, Trev, and that's the whole religion thing."

A startled look remolded his face. "I thought we'd covered this. One of these days I'd like the chance to separate religion from spirituality for you, things like the tangible church and its doctrine from the intangible Spirit and its freedom. Then, perhaps—"

"But, I have some major issues with God. Period."

"We were just speaking about love. What happened? If I'm tracking with you, it's clear you don't believe in a loving God who is real, or who comes first in your life." His attempt to put on a happy face fell flat.

"God is love, you say? You believe in a loving God? Look around. All kinds of people get all kinds of diseases. People get cancer, people like me. Kids grow up fatherless, like Cody. Babies are taken from their mothers' arms and never learn why. Decent guys like Dean can't get laid, and women like Kate drink secretly. You get burned as a boy and thank your 'loving God' for the scars. Can you see how screwy this seems?"

"Yes. Yes, I can."

"Why didn't God prevent you from being burned? He could've. But no, you praise him. Why not snub him for letting suffering like that happen?"

Trevor's defenseless gaze showed no urge to argue, no anger—only love. "I'm sorry for your pain, Larissa. Truly, I am. If I'm hearing you right, you believe this is too big of a barrier and we might never make it?"

Tears began to form. She took a kitchen towel, wiped her eyes, and grabbed a tissue to blow her nose. "Yes, I guess that's what I'm saying."

"But where you see a barrier, I see a bridge. Can we try looking at it that way?" He turned down the heat under the omelet.

She looked down.

"With time, with love, Larissa, I believe we can find a way to work out all our concerns. My hope is that you see the bridge in our future."

"Oh, boy. Do you mean, let's go tiptoeing down the primrose lane holding hands and singing *Jesus Loves Me?*"

"Look, you're in pain. I see that. People say things they don't always mean when they're hurt. And we all hurt. We all get hurt. And we all hurt others. When we do, we get blinded to possibilities. But God is never blind, never unkind. The very thing blocking you and me, that you think is a barrier, could bring us to a new place. Bridges don't separate people; they bring people together."

Something in his steady way of speaking, besides the words themselves, calmed her. He was so self-assured, so unruffled. "I don't know," she sighed, feeling frazzled. "How can our two lifestyles ever be compatible? How can it ever make sense for me to live with a missionary when I don't even go to church?"

He sprinkled paprika on the omelet and sliced it in two.

"This is vital, Trev. So let's say we're married and you go off to church— not to 'work' like most people, but to church. Of course you have a job there and you work hard at it every day like most professionals, but your heart and soul *and* your paycheck *and* health benefits come from your vocation to serve God and how you perform as a minister. Sundays you go to church to worship. But me? I don't. I never expect to. How can I actively support you in your career when my heart and soul aren't in it? We're not on the same page, Trevor, and if I did join you at church functions and make appearances, I would be an outsider. Do you see where I'm coming from?"

"Yes, completely. So let's turn it around. What if I resigned as missions director, stopped worshipping on Sundays, and we never bothered with church again? Would that make you happy? Us happy?"

"I doubt it. No. You'd be faking it. It wouldn't last, and we'd end up on the ropes because you'd be miserable." Her appetite for debate was fading. "Look, it's Christmas morning, and this conversation is going in circles. I'm getting dizzy. Are we going to eat?"

"Trust, Larissa. Trust. What we need to know right now is whether it *can* be worked out in time." He placed the omelet on a plate and served breakfast with a gallant flair.

She sensed his earnestness, felt his tolerance, appreciated his passion. Someday she might understand. Every word from his lips flowed easily and smoothly, like a sweet flowing river. She might not know how to work this issue out but what she did know was, *He loves me!*

The advice she'd offered Kate just days before about telling a new story came back to her, reverberating in the deepest part of her. *Yes, a new story. A better story.* A new truth glimmered faintly in her heart: *If Trevor can overlook my cancer, my skepticism, my ugly past, and still love me and be my lover, I can find a way to overlook this Jesus stuff.*

"But for now," he spoke again, chewing the omelet, "if you're saying my career in ministry is a major wedge between us, then let's both think about it a while. Next week I leave for Haiti to prep things there. We can look at this again after New Years when I get back."

"Okay—deal. I guess a break might be good for both of us." *But I'll miss you!*

Realizing how hungry she was, she ate heartily. Good sex, even in one's imagination, did that to one's appetite. Tackling his half of the omelet, he mentioned his need to leave for church in twenty minutes.

"If it's my career, Larissa, and not my actual beliefs, then I'm open to an alternative. I've been thinking about it lately anyway. I'm open to doing something else, as long as I still lift up God in my life."

"You're open to other careers? You're not just saying that?"

"I've asked Dean for his advice about it already. He has a bunch of contacts."

"He does? So, if you did something else, would you still believe like you do?"

"Yes. I'd have to. It's my life. For me it *is* life." He stopped chewing and looked at her directly. He smiled, returning to a breezier tone. "How's the grub? Like it?"

"Yummy! Love it! Better watch out, or you just might win me over with your cooking."

"You know," he said, cleaning his plate and licking his fork, "I've been on this missionary track since I was a little boy. Just because my father spent his whole life as an apostle doesn't mean I have to automatically follow in his footsteps. Who's to say it's not time for me to reconsider?"

She clapped her hands. "I like that. But last night, you looked so official up there in front of everybody saying that prayer and presiding over the pageant."

"It's worth giving it some thought, though, right?" His eyes sparkled.

She knew exactly then what she really, truly, utterly wanted most: For Trevor to be hers.

CHAPTER

Kate placed the beef tenderloin on a baking pan and pre-heated the oven to 425 degrees. With her in the kitchen were Lindsay, shelling fresh peas, and Nicole, preparing the puff pastry dough for Beef Wellington—the royal centerpiece of the Barcourt family's traditional Christmas Day feast. Jester wagged his tail, hoping for a taste of meat scraps.

Outside the window, shivering in the freezing cold, Muriel stood puffing a cigarette. Kate watched her mother, aware of how she disliked the Nelson's no-smoking house rule. She wondered when and if her mother would ever stop enduring the degrading consequences of her tobacco habit, of ruining her lungs and lingering like an outcast in uncomfortable places puffing away. Then Kate remembered how much her father hated her mom's smoking, and she realized it helped her mother to keep her distance from him.

She watched Dean sitting in the family room on the sofa reading the newspaper, tolerating Fredrick's complaints about congressional gridlock. Her dad stood up and poured a stiff cocktail—a dry manhattan with two olives, his first drink of the day—and she regretted it would not be his last. Fredrick had purchased a costly supply of liquor when he arrived: liters of whiskey and vodka, three brands of wine, four bottles of champagne, and a case of beer.

Kate felt her own ongoing battle against alcohol cravings, minute-by-minute struggles against the gnawing urges to drink. Resisting was harder than she'd expected. The shame and remorse of her DWI and its aftermath had kept her sober so far. Having seen how her father's misbehavior could spoil a fancy dinner, she wished she could numb out with a drink right now. *No!* She actually looked forward to getting her diagnosis from the chemical dependency evaluator who had interviewed her days earlier. She'd largely accepted the humbling truth: *I am an alcoholic.*

Jester was drinking water from his bowl when his weak legs collapsed.

"Somebody help him get up," said Kate, alarmed.

"We've got to get him to the vet," replied Lindsay, helping the dog stand. "He's been like this for days."

"You know," said Nicole, "Cody has this crate he's made for injured and sick animals where he cares for them. Maybe he could find out what's wrong with Jester."

"Jester needs the vet," said Lindsay. "You're just head-over-heels for that boy. Anything to spend more time with that hunk, eh Nicky?"

Nicole stuck her tongue out at Lindsay. Kate noticed Nicky blush, and she wondered how much Nicky and Cody liked each other. "I thought he was very polite when he walked you to the front door last night," Kate had told Nicole. "It was nice of him to step inside and say good night to us all." Lindsay made a face at Nicole.

When Muriel came in the house and saw Kate rolling out the Wellington dough, she announced, "It has to be rolled to a half-inch, just so. No thinner."

"Mom, it looks right to me," said Kate, sticking her finger in the bowl to taste it. "Ummm, and it tastes right, too."

"It's too thin, Kathryn. You'll have to start over. Here, I'll show you."

"But, Mom, the thickness should be a quarter-inch. Not more."

"No, a half-inch and no less."

"No, Mom, a quarter-inch. No more."

Muriel's face reddened. "I know how your father likes it. Don't you try—"

"But that's not how *we* like it."

"Listen, today *his* way is how it's going to be, and I'll hear no more about it." Muriel jerked the rolling pin from Kate's hand. "Now stand out of the way."

Both Lindsay and Nicole looked shocked and irritated. Kate was in no mood to quarrel over getting her way. Offended, she turned away. *Am I being too touchy? What's making Mom so testy?*

Kate noticed her negative feelings and, rather than losing her temper, switched her attention to more positive energy. *Take a break. Walk away. Be forgiving.* She entered the living room and sat down by the Christmas tree, quietly recalling the opening of their gifts that morning. It had gone smoothly for once. There was the usual overkill of her father's expensive presents: a $400 watch for Dean that he probably would never wear, the $300 sweaters for each of the girls, and the $1,000 diamond pendant for her, "his princess." *So much money, and it could've been better spent on people in need.* Since her childhood, costly gifts had been her dad's way of showing his appreciation. Perhaps it was sincere because he failed in so many other areas. She questioned if his expensive gifts were "peace offerings," subtle bribes for tolerating his pain-in-the-ass behavior all year long.

Dean's gift to her—five prepaid full-body massages by a female professional masseuse—made her love him all the more. "For your neck and shoulders especially," he'd said lovingly. "Just think of me while you're zoned out on the table all relaxed."

"Yes, sweetheart," she replied with a wink, making sure her folks could hear. For the moment, it seemed that she and Dean were back on comfortable terms again. It was refreshing to instinctively say something pleasant to him, and mean it. *I hope he feels honored.* For her special gift to him, Kate hinted, "It's a secret, but I have something very special for you. You'll just have to wait a little while until New Year's."

The big surprise came when he gently cornered her by the Christmas tree and gave her a six-inch square box tied with gold ribbon. "Here's something extra special I wanted you to have," he said, grinning.

"Something I want only you and I to share." He even had scissors in his hand to cut the ribbon.

Totally taken aback, curious yet cautious, she cut through the ribbon and lifted the lid. "Oh, how wonderful!" Inside was a chocolate éclair on a lacey white doily. Instantly she knew what it meant—*He still loves me!*

She hugged him. It was a tradition they'd started as newlyweds. During their travels in Europe, they'd stopped one day at a patisserie in Paris and discovered they had only one franc between them to purchase a treat. Buying a single éclair, they sat together and ate it from both ends, each one taking small bites and savoring the exquisite taste of the creme filling inside the pastry shell topped with chocolate. When they reached the final bite in the middle, their lips came together in a kiss—a passionate, open-mouth, tongue-swirling kiss. Giggling and laughing, they kissed again, prompting applause from the patisserie's owner and several customers.

Standing by the Christmas tree, Kate saw Dean's face lit by the tree lights as he kissed her the way he had in the patisserie. "I want you to know where my heart is, Katie. It's with *you.*"

"So romantic! I'm thrilled!" Her lips pressed his again. It seemed to her that a lifetime had passed since this tradition had brought joy to their faces. The timing couldn't have been better, and the symbolism cheered her. *There's hope! Real hope!*

She looked into his bright hazel eyes and cooed, "Let's share it later. I know just when we should eat it. Leave it to me."

Dinner at four started out with everything perfect—fine china, polished silver, linen napkins, lit candles. Sadly, Fredrick was well on his way to getting drunk already.

He lifted his glass of champagne. "Everyone, let's have a toast to thisss great occasion."

"Good idea. Please pass the ginger ale," said Dean.

"Ginger ale?" whined Fredrick. He poured champagne from the bottle into Dean's empty glass. "Here, haaave some of this."

"No thanks, Fred. I think you know I've been sober for some years now."

"Aww, forget that sobriety crap. Go ahead for once. Haaave a little."

The girls sensed trouble was brewing, but Muriel barely seemed to notice. Having hit the bourbon hard since noon, Fred's mean streak emerged. "You're not gonna haave a tiny sip? One teeny weeny tiny sip? I s'pose that means you're better than the ressst of us?"

Kate resented her father. Pompous and prideful, he lacked the expected polish of his status as a corporate executive and church elder. Out of the public eye, he was a pig. She despised how he threatened and bullied his family, as if it were his birthright. He never felt ashamed of the nasty things he said or did. No matter how outrageous or preposterous, he spewed drivel whenever he wanted. Kate had learned the safest strategy was to let things slide, to never make a fuss, because that only escalated his temper.

"Awwright, have your damn ginger ale."

"I really don't need your permission, Dad," said Dean.

"Dad? Who are you calling Dad?"

Fredrick noticed Kate was only sipping. "You've been drinking kiddie cocktails all during our visit. Haaave you become a teetotaler like him? No? Then have another, Princess. Bottoms up. We're juss getting sstarted. Time to celebrate!"

"Dad, getting drunk is hardly the right way to celebrate Christ's birth."

"Whass that s'posed to mean? He turned water into wine, didn't he? Where does it say he banished wine?"

"Okay, but he never condoned heavy drinking. Back in those days, wine wasn't the same as it is today, and nobody drank hard liquor."

"I don't see whaat you're getting so upset about. I only asked if you wanted aaanother."

"No, Dad, you didn't ask. You insisted."

Kate felt the pressure building within her. Her exhaustion from the children's musical and the chaotic week leading up to it, besides being forbidden to drive, had frayed her patience. Memories of her disrespectful father in her childhood years crowded her mind. She had survived those long years yearning for justice, experiencing it rarely in *his* house. She'd come across a profound phrase in her daily devotional: *The opposite of poverty is not wealth, but justice.* Hadn't Ginny spoken about

Kate's "poverty of pleasure?" Justice had been hard to find; her father had impoverished their home life. She'd always wanted to stick up for the truth, but that instinct had been crushed as a child. Well, no longer.

Her dad bellowed, "Bottoms up, I say! Whooo here objects? I want some cooperation!"

The girls dropped their forks. Dean sat up straighter. Kate, having lost her appetite and her fear, shouted, "Stop, Dad! You need to stop drinking. Now. Everybody here deserves an apology." Silence. "Dad? We all want to get back to our Wellington. So apologize. Now."

"Who are you to tell me what to do? You just button your lip."

"Dad, you're out of line," said Dean. "Don't talk like that. Apologize. Please."

"Loser! You don't know your place! Zip your lip!"

"This is my home, Dad," said Dean. "This is our house. We deserve better. Your 'Princess' deserves better. I'm going to ask you to behave and stop making a scene, and quit insulting my wife."

Fredrick downed the wine in his glass and growled, "Muriel, fill me up."

Kate leaned forward. "Dad, you're drunk! I fucking hate it when you drink! Stop! Stop now! Or go home!"

Fredrick slammed his hand on the table, rattling every dish. "I'm your father! Don't you swear at me! You little shit! Go home, you say?"

"Kathryn! Since when did you start using filthy language?"

"Mom, don't switch the subject. You're always trying to stick up for him. You married a pig, Mom."

"Oh? Is that so?" her father spouted. "I deserve respect, but nobody around here seems to think so."

"And what a pathetic father you are. And always have been!"

He bared his teeth. "I'm not going to puuut up with your insssolence." He threw his buttered roll at her, aiming for her head.

She ducked. "You don't deserve any respect. And, no you won't get any. You're a brute and a bully. Face it, Dad. Face the truth for once." Her heart raced but she stood strong.

Fredrick slammed his fist again, making two dishes fall off the table. "I *demand* an apology. NOW!" He stood up, making a violent effort to charge toward her.

"Never, Fred!" Dean rose and blocked his way. "You've been one son-of-a-bitch since I've known you. Now, sit down and be quiet."

Kate screamed, "Yes! All my life, Dad, you've been a bully, and I'm sick of it."

"Stop it! Stop it, both of you!" screamed Muriel, collapsing in a nervous fit. Nicole used her napkin to wipe her grandmother's face, and Lindsay waved her napkin to cool her down.

Kate stared in horror, remembering something Dean had said: *"Arguing with a drunk is like wrestling with a pig in the mud. You get filthy, and the pig likes it."*

"Muriel, look at your sorry-ass daughter bitching about nothing," Fredrick said, glaring at both Kate and Dean. "You've gone and ruined everything!"

"Shut up, Dad. I'm in my late forties, and I've still never gotten over growing up with you. I've always hated your drinking and bullying, and yelling your drunken profanities. You're a tyrant. And Mother is coming apart because of you. That's your doing, Dad. You've scared the living daylights out of both of us so many times. Except in public. There you made sure people saw you as a saint, a pillar in the community. Nothing but bullshit!"

Kate saw Dean looking at her, his eyes full of pride.

Muriel stammered, tears flowing, "Calm down, dear. Get control of yourself."

"You're a fake, Dad, a total phony, a hypocrite. You and your religion—elder and deacon of the church, ha! Everybody had to be perfect and never tattle on you. I hated you for it. Mom had to be perfect. I had to be perfect. Wherever we went as a family we had to kowtow to you. And now I'm making my husband and my kids try to be perfect. I'm sick of it. If people had only known how you screamed at Mother and made her cower. How you pounded your fist on the dinner table demanding your way, exactly like you just did. I hate you."

"Kathryn, dear, calm down. Please! Show some control!"

Kate turned to her mother. "And you! You put up with all his shit like a scared little mouse, never standing up to him."

"Quiet! You don't know what you're saying."

"Oh yes, I do, Mother. You were always cowering, always shaking in your boots trying to please him, never standing your ground. I absorbed all that like a sponge, day in and day out. You were the woman I modeled my life after. *You!* You taught me how to cringe!"

"What the hell is she talking about, Muriel? What does she mean?"

"Enough, Dad," shouted Kate. "I want you two to leave. You are no longer welcome here. Yes, I said *leave*. Go pack up your things this minute. Now."

"Fly back to Maryland? Are you serious?"

"Dead serious. This meal is over. Fly back home. Go." Kate threw down her linen napkin and turned to Dean. "Skip, would you start the car and drive them to the airport?"

Her father swung his fists. "You take that back! I'll wring your neck! And I damn well mean it!"

Dean intervened, holding back his father-in-law's flailing arms, but Fredrick wrenched free and swung at him.

Nicole screamed, and both girls jumped up and ran from the room.

Fredrick shouted louder. "Shame on you! Shame on both of you!" He flung down his napkin and sputtered, "We don't haaave to put up with this, Muriel. We're leeeaving, and it's *our* decision to leave this god-forsaken house. Right now!"

"No, Fredrick … please no," Muriel blathered between sobs.

Fredrick stepped over to her, grabbed her arm, and jerked her toward the stairs. "I hope you're haapppy, Kathryn. I'm ca-calling a cab!"

Kate was silent.

Fredrick stomped down the stairs, hauling Muriel behind him. "Dammit, Muriel, move!" In his drunkenness, he wobbled and missed a step, collapsing to his knees. Dean rushed to help. "Stay away, you. Don't you dare touch me. I blame *you* for all this. YOU!"

Dean stood mute, unshaken by the insult. Kate noticed the girls peeking around the corner, astounded and speechless, but they appeared quietly delighted, which lifted Kate's spirits.

"Dammit, Muriel!" Fred swatted her. "Get moving! Let's go!"

Kate and Dean rushed to the kitchen. Dean got his car keys and put on his coat. He headed to the garage and started the Honda, amid howling curses and slurred profanities from Fredrick. Kate hoped the liquor's sedative effects would finally take over.

Returning to the kitchen, Dean hugged her. "That's my girl! That's the girl I married!"

She glowed. "I'm so happy to hear you say that." She hugged him tightly, snuggling her head on his chest. "But Dean, I could sure use a stiff drink."

Dean laughed, a deep belly laugh. "Katie, no wonder. Hey, in the good old days I would've even poured one for you." He put his arms around her, kissing her. "I've never been so proud of you, Katie."

"But I just blew up at my folks. Don't you think—?"

"No. You finally spoke your truth. I love it."

She bit her lip. "But it wasn't very Christian, was it?"

"It was honest. And long overdue."

Kate's self-esteem soared. The girls tramped into the kitchen, their faces flushed with astonishment. They helped carry their grandparents' luggage to the garage.

Looking at Kate, Lindsay exclaimed, "That was awesome, Mom."

"You really laid it out there," echoed Nicole. "Wow!"

Dean loaded the luggage in the Honda and came back inside, ready to drive to the airport. While the Honda was warming up, he hugged Kate again as the two elderly parents passed by, tight-lipped and fuming. He ushered them out and loaded them in their seats, over Fredrick's garbled protests. Dean got in, backed out of the garage, and they were gone.

It's over! Dear Jesus! I hope that was You speaking through me. Was I speaking Your truth? I hope so. I really hope so.

An hour later, Dean called to say her parents had successfully booked the first plane to Maryland, thanks to his infinite patience switching tickets for them. A half hour later, he called saying Fredrick had sobered up enough to board the airplane.

CHAPTER

"Okay, ladies *and* gentlemen, lift those thighs, arch your backs, and hold that pose five more seconds. That's it. You can do it. Breathe, remember to breathe."

Kneeling on a floor mat while extending his arms and legs, Dean listened to Larissa give yoga instructions as he glanced over at Trevor and Hal in their workout sweats. The two men were exerting effort and perspiring to hold their poses just like him. *This is harder than it looks.* For all his regular workouts, Dean was stretching muscles he never knew he had. Near Dean on floor mats were Kate and Ginny and regular clients exerting themselves to hold their poses. The women were making it look so easy. He was getting a taste of the lengths women went to in order to get trim and stay fit.

"Okay, everybody, Table Top … that's it, hold it, hold it … and now Plank, good … good, and … rest. Excellent!" Larissa clapped her hands, ending the late afternoon class. "Namaste."

Dean felt a rush of energy. Wiping his damp forehead with his sleeve, he said to Kate and Ginny, "Now I understand the kind of work involved in yoga."

"There's more to it than meets the eye," said Ginny, wiping off a sheen of sweat.

"I'll second that," added Trevor. "And this was a *beginner's* session?"

Kate laughed. "Yep. Intro to Yoga 101."

Larissa walked up. "Glad you boys could join us. It's good to have a few guys around, isn't it, ladies?"

"Very challenging," said Hal, breathing hard. He reached over to Ginny and put his arm around her. "Are we all set for the get-together this afternoon at our house?"

"The Scrabble board is ready," she replied. "Only the players are missing."

"Then let's head over from here," said Trevor. "That way we'll get an early start on New Year's."

Dean and Kate had accepted Larissa and Trevor's invitation for a game date. After playing Scrabble, they intended to celebrate New Year's Eve two days early because of Trevor's flight to Haiti the next morning. Dean noticed the relaxed way Kate mingled with everyone, especially the women he'd just met—Claire, Jasmine, and Annabelle.

"You're wonderful, Larissa," he overheard Claire say. "It helps so much to learn new ways to de-stress and leave behind the old rules I've lived under all these years."

"I'll gladly second that," said Kate.

"I'm so happy your migraines are improving, Claire," said Larissa. "It could be those old rules were messing with you somehow. And Kate, it's clear you're trusting your intuition more. It's great getting out of our heads and into our body's natural wellness, isn't it gals?"

They agreed. The men agreed too.

"By the way, Kate," said Claire quietly, "I've checked my calendar and I'll be able to give you a ride to AA tomorrow. I think you'll fit right in with the group."

Dean liked overhearing that.

"That means a lot, Claire, thanks." Kate put her arms around Claire's shoulders then turned to the men. "And how about our new guests today? Wasn't it great having the three new guys here?"

"You don't have to answer that," said Trevor, kiddingly. "I, for one, think a class like this should be on everyone's priority list."

"Kudos to you, Larissa," said Jasmine, stretching at the barre with skilled ease.

"That's overly kind, but thank you. When I came up with Fitness and Flowers, I thought the fitness part would naturally enhance physical well-being, but I didn't imagine how much it could also affect our mental and emotional lives."

Cody walked in the back door. In his arms, he was carrying Jester. Dean did a double take.

"Mom, I need to talk to you about bringing in this new dog for my shelter."

"Whose dog is that, Cody?"

"It's ours," said Dean, stepping closer. "That's Jester. He's got arthritic legs."

"Nicky!" Kate exclaimed, startled, as Nicole followed Cody in the door.

"Hi there, everybody," said Nicole. "Dad, can you help us out? Uh, I thought you and Mom were on a date."

"We are." Jester noticed his master and wagged his tail. Dean crossed to the crate and helped Cody place Jester inside it. "Hey there, young man. Nice to see you."

Cody looked as surprised to see him, "Uh, Mr. Nelson, I'd like to keep Jester here a couple of days and see what I can do for him."

Dean liked the idea—and Cody's calling him Mr. Nelson. "Okay, let's give it a try."

Kate noticed Nicky was wearing her cheerleading outfit and asked, "Do you have a hockey game tonight, Nicky?"

"Yep. And Cody's taking me, once Jester is settled. Lindsay went out with some friends and couldn't give me a ride to the rink."

Dean and Kate looked at each other, then at Larissa, then in unison they said, "Well, now … !"

Laughter rang through Hal and Ginny's house as the fiercely fought Scrabble tournament peaked. "Hold on, Trevor," shouted Hal. "Kate only has two tiles left. Don't put your Z there, or she'll use it to beat us all."

"Don't even *think* of making it easy for her," urged Ginny, bluffing.

"But I need to get rid of it, or ten points will go against me," protested Trevor. "Where else do you expect me to put it?"

"Stop telling him what to do," cried Kate.

"Oh, go ahead and see what happens," insisted Larissa.

"Easy for you to say—you're on Kate's side," chided Dean.

"Go on, Trev," said Kate, smiling ear to ear. "No risk, no gain."

"Okay, here goes." Trevor placed his Z tile on the board and declared, "Z-E-N-I-T-H, 36 points, double word."

"HA!" exclaimed Kate, clapping her hands in victory. She placed her last two tiles with a flourish. "Z-E-P-H-Y-R, 69 points. Triple word score, plus I'm out. Game over!"

"You *did* let her win, Trev!" bellowed Hal. His voice rose, intensely competitive yet in the tone of a good sport.

"Not again," lamented Dean. "She always wins when we play. Just this once I wish . . ."

Amid banter and sips of hot cider, each player counted their point totals. "Too bad Marlene and Gavin couldn't make it tonight," said Ginny. "We could've had two tournaments."

"And Kate would've won both somehow!" kidded Hal.

"Try being a good loser for once," she said, faking a frown. Dean howled in mock agony at his buddy's loss.

Hal announced, "Okay, everybody, we've still got an hour before we toast the New Year and say *bon voyage* to Trevor. So how about if we check out some of the video clips of Haiti that Ginny found on YouTube, then celebrate?"

Moving to the computer, Ginny cued up YouTube as the Scrabble players assembled around her. "Here's a taste of what's going on there, gang," Ginny said, locating several panoramic photos of the countryside: lush green fields with pristine ocean beaches and denuded forests with eroded dirt roads trod by impoverished villagers carrying bulky loads.

Video scenes of the 2010 earthquake damage followed: crumbling old-style colonial buildings, downed telephone poles jammed with snarled wires, scores of barefoot people treading dusty and garbage-strewn streets teeming with noisy marketplace activity. The group viewed vendors hawking figs and mangos, native women chasing away mangy dogs scratching for food, and idle men sipping native tea near rotting waste in ditches.

Kate turned to Dean and whispered, "And you're considering going with Trevor on his next trip?"

"Yep. And Hal is too."

"Good luck leaving our nice, comfortable home for a place as desperate as that." She shuddered.

Video footage showed a contemporary cluster of native drummers beating out African-based rhythms, a far more upbeat look at the country, thought Dean. An impromptu gathering of local dancers assembled, cheered on by locals chanting Creole-inspired songs. The spectacle of the native dancers brimming with athletic energy fascinated Dean. The native spectators stomped their feet and clapped along.

Dean's eyes focused on one of the female dancers, who threw her considerable weight around. She appeared to be working herself into a state bordering on religious ecstasy. Piercing shouts erupted from her as she twisted and twirled.

"The voodoo influence seems pretty clear, doesn't it?" said Trevor.

A slimmer female dancer's mu-mu flew about wildly as a male dancer spun her around rapidly in circles. The male dancer's shirtless torso rippled, his every muscle stretching and bulging on his superb body.

Dean glanced at Kate. It surprised him that she looked mesmerized instead of grimacing or looking away. The dancers' hypnotic movements reflected in her pupils. She put her arm through the bend in his elbow, pulling him close to her. He looked at her strangely as she whispered, "Powerful, isn't it?"

He stared at her, unsure what to think.

"Things are changing, Skip, believe it. *I'm* changing and glad of it."

I want to be glad too whenever words turn into actions.

The dancers' frenetic movements reflected a wilder form of religious fervor—freely shared by the boisterous bystanders. Kate's face radiated fascination, even enjoyment, the kind Dean hadn't seen in years. *No frowning or making a face? This is new!*

The raucous drum rhythms supercharged the dancers' sensuous energy to orgiastic levels. Cheering louder, the bystanders of all ages were swept up in the free expression of all-out abandon. Dean was enthralled watching Kate swaying *with* the music instead of stiffening *against* it. The dancers' exultation turned hypnotic for everyone but Dean, who felt the fire of the dancers' moves but stayed detached. *What is with Kate?*

The male dancer lavished more attention on the women, wooing each one as he rubbed their bodies and pressed his chest against their slick skin. His body glistened with sweat.

Kate had told him that she was feeling freer, yes, and that she was letting go and opening up more—but this? Since telling off her parents at the dinner table, she was acting more like when they were newlyweds. Before her parents' visit, he recalled how she'd told him, "But something inside me is shifting, Skip. My old attitudes are losing their grip. Trust me when I say I'm changing."

His sense of hope quickened. Her promises echoed in his mind. He felt his heart opening up to her, to forgiving her. His resentful feelings faded—*Yes! I forgive you!* The drumming ended and Kate's trancelike focus ebbed away. Pleasantly mystified, he returned her look.

Ginny clicked off the Internet. "Okay, everybody," she announced. "I'm sure this has made a huge impression on all of us. Let's debrief what we've seen, then you boys can start packing the duffle bag of medical supplies for Trevor's trip. Gals, let's go to the kitchen and break out the snacks and bubbly." Dean felt pleased Kate had made sure to bring a fancy bottle of sparkling fruit cider for *their* bubbly.

In the kitchen after the group's discussion about the video clips, the three women took out bottles of champagne and the Nelson's sparkling cider from the refrigerator. Kate and Larissa perched by the counter, where stemmed glasses were set out on a tray.

"Hey girls," said Kate, "I'd say our little problems are miniscule compared to those folks in Haiti. Can you imagine what it must be like living in such wretched conditions? And what about those dancers, weren't they amazing?"

"You looked mesmerized," said Ginny.

"I was. Something was certainly going on inside me."

"What 'something' do you mean?" asked Larissa.

"In the past, I'd have been hyper-critical and judgmental, making catty remarks in my head if not out loud."

"What was different?"

"The dancers were so free, so uninhibited. I grew up all prim and proper and stuffy in a world of puritanical formality and etiquette. It reminded me of how different my upbringing was."

"It made me think we Midwesterners are uptight, too," said Ginny, popping a cork. "All that Scandinavian and German heritage. You know, 'Minnesota Nice' and all that."

"That says it, Ginny," replied Larissa. "Instead of repressing their sensuality and stifling themselves, those dancers got into being passionate and wild."

"They were letting everything hang out for sure," Kate added. "And it didn't seem like such a terrible thing."

"No blame, no shame," said Ginny.

Kate thought about how she'd put her arm through Dean's elbow, pulling him close as they watched the dancers, and how surprised and appreciative he'd been. The feeling between them felt like a delicate new bud beginning to open.

"Ladies, I'm tired of feeling bad about not having sex with Dean," announced Kate, "and feeling like a whore if I go to bed with him. Those dancers moved their bodies shamelessly and nobody judged them. It's what I've always seen in you, Larissa. How I'd love to just let go like those dancers and open up like you."

Larissa looked flattered. "You can. You will. And being loose and open is healthy."

"I've even thought of being the one, you know, who initiates. Who gets things going."

"Hurray! It's time, Kate!"

"Isn't that what my vows say, Ginny? To love and to cherish, to think of my husband's needs before my own?"

"It's what we promise our guys and what God wants for us," she replied. "And it's what our bodies want. God wouldn't have created us to have those feelings otherwise."

Kate relaxed. "That's what Dean has been trying to tell me for so long. For me to show my desire and let him know I *want* him."

"You go, girl," said Larissa. "Claim your right to pleasure and intimacy."

"Being sexual feels good when it's right," added Ginny.

Kate realized her excuses about staying busy with her many to-do projects had sapped her energy for being Dean's lover—had shriveled her interest in loving him. She could see how being a lover was altogether different than being a wife, a mother, or a church volunteer. Those other roles were public ones and could elicit praise, or criticism, but they paled compared to the vital expressions of love that she and Dean could share in the marriage bed.

"I noticed him watching the dancers and wondered what *he* was thinking," Kate said. "I'm sure he felt their heat."

"The 'old you' would've never said that," Larissa replied. "It sounds like you allowed yourself the freedom to identify with the dancers' energy, and I'll bet that's what he noticed."

"I can see that, yes." Kate quietly grinned to herself. "Did either of you get a little turned on, too?"

"Fired up, that's how I'd say it," Ginny replied.

"Fired up enough to jump into bed with Hal?"

"Absolutely. I learned something a long time ago: If I wanted a happy husband, sex was the surefire way to make him—make us both—happy. Happy husband, happy wife. Happy wife, happy life."

Larissa reached over and slapped Kate's knee. "Stop analyzing. Start doing. Quit thinking. Analysis paralysis—forget it."

A strong tingly feeling moved up Kate's spine. *It's time to risk it. But how will Dean react? Can I risk* not *risking it? Is it already too late?*

Ginny said, "It's time to embrace all your gifts, Kate. So get on with it."

"If you don't *take* a chance, you don't *stand* a chance," said Larissa. "Didn't you say you've made secret arrangements for something special with Dean?"

"Yes. He doesn't know it yet, but I've booked a three-day getaway to our favorite ski resort up north this weekend."

"Nice going!"

"Whooppeee!"

Kate smiled like she hadn't smiled in ages—until her cheeks hurt.

Trevor peeked through the kitchen door. "Hey, when are you guys coming?"

"Would you two mind giving Trevor and me a little time together," Larissa asked as Kate and Ginny got up to join their husbands in the living room. "Once you get on that plane in the morning, Trev, I'll sure miss you."

Trevor looked at her fondly. "If you're hinting, there's still time to reconsider going with me. We've been over all that, I know, but I want to remind you that you're still welcome to come."

She put her arms around his neck and kissed him. "Sorry, but I've got a business to run and a son to feed. That doesn't mean, though, that I don't admire your courage to go and scope things out there."

"Very nice. So, while you were thinking of going, what were your pros and cons?"

"Pros? Well, for starters, I'd get to see you in action doing your missionary work. That would tell me volumes. Also, you and I could have spent time learning a new culture. It would be a great travel adventure, in any case, just going to a completely new and different part of the world."

"Great. And the cons?"

"Well, there are the cancer appointments and my follow-up tests here. Keeping Fitness and Flowers going and my clients happy is a biggie, plus I wouldn't be bringing in any revenue. And leaving Cody at home unsupervised, not to mention the money it would cost to travel, well ..."

"Yep. Con wins, I'm afraid."

"This time it does."

Trevor paused. "Speaking of Cody, one of these days I'd like to sit down with him and really get to know him better, to make a solid connection."

"That would be great. I'd love it. I think he would too."

Trevor put his arm around her and pulled her close. "After this trip, I promise Cody and I will do something special together, just us guys."

"I'm sure he'd like that. That would be awesome. Frankly, I also see a plus side to our not going together. We both could use the time to sift through our options and consider the direction we want things to take."

"Hmmm, you're probably right."

"And we can always be in touch. That's why they invented smart phones, you know."

"Good idea. Texting each other every couple of days or so—does that sound like a plan?"

"Sounds like one to me." She leaned toward him, giving him a bear hug, carefully using less pressure on her left side. "Dang! I'm going to miss you soooo much, you gorgeous man, you!"

"Hey, you two," hollered Hal. "What's up out there? We need you in here to toast the New Year."

"Coming!" yelled Trevor, looking into her eyes with love.

She felt his gaze and reflected love back to him. "This New Year feels happier than any other in a very long time, Trev." Her eyes twinkled as his lips touched hers. Their kiss deepened, lasting longer and longer. She held him close ... not wanting to ever let go.

CHAPTER 31

The hard metal folding chair made Kate squirm. Beside her in the circle of sixteen AA members was Claire, her companion at the women's-only meeting. In Claire's car while she drove to the meeting, Kate had listened to more of her story about her ex-husband's heavy drinking. "It was the main reason I divorced him, Kate, and I never would have had the guts without the support of my Al-Anon friends and the AA women you'll meet."

"I really appreciate you driving me there. So a few of the women attend both groups?"

"Yes, it's fairly common. Think of it as two sides of the same coin."

"I only went to Al-Anon a couple of times back when Dean first got sober. It was more of an experiment. But I've forgotten—do they both use the same twelve steps?"

"They're quite similar. You'll see how it flows after a few minutes. There's nothing to worry about, so just relax."

Kate spoke up when her turn came: "I'm Kate, an alcoholic." She winced. "That's the first time I've ever said so in public."

The women applaused.

Although shame and blame jabbed at her emotions, the burden on her nerves lessened as she realized no one was judging her. An odd sense of relief moved through her. An alcohol-free New Year's Eve had come and gone, her first in a dozen years of excessive drinking, and her fragile "sober self" still felt very new and embryonic. She still experienced some intense cravings daily, at times only hours apart, and fighting them off took effort. A quiet confidence was slowly building within her to face down these cravings, propelled by her fury over her dad's drinking. *I will never let liquor own me like it does him.*

"As a new person to AA," said the spokeswoman, a casually dressed professional woman in her fifties, "we're here to help you get off to a good start. We were all where you are now once ourselves."

"Thank you for that," Kate replied. "It's really awful to have to admit that. I just don't know whether I'll stay clean or end up having another binge."

The women in the circle ranged from twenty years younger to twenty years older than Kate, and they offered fragments of their stories. Kate noticed a poster on the wall showing The Twelve Steps, and she read Step One: "'We admitted we were powerless over alcohol—that our lives had become unmanageable.' I would agree that my life has become unmanageable, but I'm not sure about being powerless over alcohol. It seems like such a black-and-white thing to say."

"Very few people like to admit they're powerless over *anything*," said the spokeswoman. "It goes against our pride and desire to be in control."

Kate looked in the faces of the women who looked much like herself, and felt less alone. "Mainly, I've been sneaking drinks a lot, and pouring myself doubles when nobody will catch me. I even drank when my husband was at work or the kids were at school."

"That's exactly how I drank," a woman in her mid-thirties said. "Whenever I was by myself, I felt I could let my guard down because nobody was watching. But the minute my husband or kids were around, I'd hide the bottle and pop gum in my mouth, or I'd go someplace where they couldn't see me."

"That's called isolating," Claire explained to Kate.

A white-haired woman with stooped shoulders and a harsh voice spoke up. "We say 'I-solating.' It's all about the 'I.' It's a pretty strong indicator you've made the right choice to come here."

Kate listened closely. Her pride had fought hard to prevent herself from being compared to her father, and the fear of having inherited her addiction from him had nagged her. Admitting defeat—being powerless—felt humbling.

"At first, drinking solved a lot of things," she said, "or so it seemed. Then one day a couple years ago I woke up—with a nasty hangover—and realized it had definitely become a problem. Like my marriage, I shoved away the truth month after month and year after year, until things reached a crisis." She looked at Claire and patted her hand. "I realize now that I have an alcohol problem that's making my marriage worse."

"Great to hear you talk like that!" chimed in Claire.

"I once drank exactly the same way," said the spokeswoman. "I thought my drinking would numb my feelings about my husband, but the booze and wine became my 'best friend' and trapped me. I gradually moved away from him, unfairly I might add, until divorce became his only option. Thank goodness I stopped in time. Now we're much happier, and I see that alcohol was my 'worst enemy'—not my 'best friend.'"

The frankness of the discussion touched Kate in profound ways. Ninety minutes zoomed by until the meeting adjoined. As everyone held hands and recited the Serenity Prayer, the phrase from the prayer—"the courage to change the things I can"—resonated in her conscience. Instead of a scary evening among total strangers, Kate felt she'd allowed these people to glimpse her real self.

Spending time with the girls that evening, Dean realized the wisdom of his decision to move back home. He was hanging out with Lindsay and Nicole in the kitchen, not in the silence of his room off on his own at a motel. As he stirred the shrimp in the frying pan for his specialty, "Cajun Shrimp ala Deanetto," he added garlic, peppers, and Tabasco sauce to the spicy mixture. Lindsay unloaded the dishwasher and handed plates and silverware to Nicole, who set the table in the breakfast nook for three.

Lindsay made a sad face and nestled her head on her father's shoulder. "I'm disappointed Mom had that darned AA meeting to go to and couldn't be here with us."

"You can say that again," chirped Nicky. "On top of committee meetings at church, now it's AA."

"Hey, girls, let's be glad for her, okay? She's taking sobriety seriously. And she's doing something constructive about it."

Suddenly, Nicole bolted over to Lindsay and tugged her arm. "Come on. You've gotta see this, Linds."

"See what?"

"I'll show you. Just come!"

They dashed off to Nicole's bedroom. Soon Dean heard them giggling, their voices exclaiming about some guy's photo on Nicole's computer. "He's sooooo cute!" Then he heard Cody's name.

Grinning, Dean thought, *Let them have their sister time together. They're going to be apart as soon as winter semester begins.* Sadly, Kate was missing out on enjoying their fun.

"After AA," Dean heard Lindsay say, "I bet Mom's heading for church to save the world from sin."

"No she's not," said Nicole. "She's coming straight home. Don't be so snippy."

"Save the world from sin?" Dean hollered. "You're overdoing it, Lindsay. Enough of that." He knew Kate's committee meeting was the next day, not that evening.

"All I meant was . . ." answered Lindsay, returning to the kitchen, "I wish she could be here for dinner tonight with us. I miss her, Dad, like we all do. I'll be heading back to Iowa early next week, and now she's gone again."

"Well, young lady, don't you think she would be here if she could be?"

Nicole popped back into the kitchen. "It's hardly her fault, Linds. When push comes to shove, I think Mom and Dad aren't to blame for acting on their faith, even when it pinches. In fact, I admire that."

Lindsay grimaced. *"Mea culpa!* Sorry!"

"But I hear you, Lindsay," Dean offered. "Our lives *are* fragmented. You're right. And it's something I regret, too."

"Okay, okay. I guess I should never have said anything." Lindsay inhaled deeply. "Can we just dish up dinner now, please?"

Dean felt the biting truth of Lindsay's throwaway remark. Serving and sacrificing for God's Kingdom was his and Kate's way of glorifying God, of making their faith real. He believed in Kate's dedication even when it "pinched" and was proud Nicole had stood up for her.

Kate deserves a warm welcome when she walks through the door.

"It'll be so good to get back to dorm life next week after all the drama around here," sighed Lindsay, sitting down at the table.

"My, my, a teeny bit sarcastic, are we?" Nicky scolded.

"What's up with your snide remarks?" Dean asked.

"Sorry. I guess I'm just missing Jester terribly."

"I think we all are, Linds," Dean said. "Nicky, what have you heard from Cody?"

"He's doing everything he can, and he says Jester is walking with less pain, but we'll still need to get him to the vet. Oopps! I forgot. I have to go Facebook him now." She ran to her bedroom.

"Hurry back," Dean shouted. "Dinner's getting cold." He looked at Lindsay, shrugged, then reached for Divine Delight decaf grounds and loaded the coffeemaker. He looked at Lindsay and sighed. "Just imagine all four of us eating the same meal at the same time. That would be a real miracle, huh?"

Dean sat with Kate in the den later that evening watching television. The news story about state legislators in gridlock over tax policy made Kate yawn.

"Not again," she grumbled, sipping decaf coffee. "Let's watch something else, Skip."

"Here's the remote. Help yourself."

Kate clicked through a half-dozen channels and stopped on a preacher speaking to hundreds of people in a large church. An attractive woman stood beside him, smiling. The camera panned to a double bed next to the pulpit as the preacher pointed to it. "Since when was it okay for us in the church to kick God out of the bedroom?" the preacher asked. "My wife Karen and I asked for this bed to be placed here because that's where we believe it belongs—in a holy place."

Dean jerked straight up. Kate gaped at the screen, and almost dropped her cup of coffee.

"While society has taken sex too far, the church hasn't taken it far enough," continued the preacher, a handsome middle-aged man. "That's right. God *wants* married couples to make love with passion, with purpose, and with pleasure."

"And with Him as part of a three-way love fest," said his attractive wife. "A healthy sex life is more than just sex. When couples ignore it, it's like a house without heat in the winter; you might survive in it, but it's not enjoyable."

The crowd laughed.

Dean sat dumbfounded. He checked the channel; it was a nationally televised network news program. The on-camera reporter said, "Yes, you heard correctly. There's a surprising trend sweeping evangelical churches across the United States like Reverend Roger Marston's here in St. Louis. They are embracing an ancient code of sexual freedom—some even say, long forgotten theology."

Kate turned to Dean as if he had magically made the program appear.

"It's not a lack of love that makes marriages monotonous; it's a lack of focus," continued Reverend Marston. "Instead of fleeting moments of pleasure, God wants our marriages to experience greater depths of pleasure and ongoing intimacy that lead us to true inner joy."

His wife nodded. "This is not just a gimmick, folks. Far from it. What we're suggesting is a balanced and biblical view of sex that's real, but not raw."

Reverend Marston took his wife's hand and they sat on the bed. "The truth? God wants married couples to experience the powerful gift of sex. We recognize that many Christians believe there's no place anywhere for even a discussion of sex. But we also recognize the millions of folks out there who are dying for answers to their intimacy dilemmas. Our chief aim is to remove the stigma and confusion around this vital issue and spark frank discussions about a universal human act that's ordained by God."

Inflated with hope, Dean wanted to shout, *Yes!* Kate gave him a dubious, but friendly, how-did-you-do-that look. "I had nothing to do with you finding this, Kate. You clicked the remote. I had no idea this was on at all."

"We have no idea who in blazes these people are," Kate said. "At least *I* don't. What they're saying seems … well, I like it but they could be kooks for all we know."

The phone rang.

"Then let's get their information, go online, and check 'em out."

The preacher's wife continued, "We don't believe God thinks sex is evil, it's only the mind of mankind that makes it so."

The phone rang again.

"Let one of the girls get it," Kate said, turning her attention back to the TV.

The phone rang again.

"Oh, boy," said Dean, glancing at the caller ID. "It's Trevor. I'll get it." He leaped for the phone. "Hey, Trev. Good to hear from you."

"Hi, Deano. Glad you picked up. I need to get a message to Hal but couldn't reach him. First, let me tell you what's going on down here. Got a minute?"

"Okay. Let's hear it."

"Well, Pastor Pierre's field clinic is operating out of a tent in a remote area where people need a lot of medical help and very few get it. So he was gung-ho to get our donated supplies. You're going to enjoy meeting him some day. The scenery here is brown and sparse, and the view of the ocean is hardly like any travel posters you've seen. And this Caribbean heat is a shocker. The humidity hovers in the high nineties. Besides all that, the people down here are desperate. I've met someone in particular who could *really* use our help."

"Sounds interesting. What's going on?"

"Her name is Zafora, and she lives with four little kids in a nearby slum. As you can guess, being a female in a male-dominated society, she never went to school, and now she faces physical and verbal abuse from her unemployed husband almost daily. Zafora has to feed her four children, but she lacks job skills and, most of all, the confidence to even look for a job. Not that there are many down here to find. It's hard to stomach how much poverty there is here."

"So how can we help this woman?"

"Essentially the culture here tells her that she's inferior, and the sad truth is, she believes it herself. Now here's where it gets ugly."

"It gets uglier?"

"Wait till you hear. She decided to get a micro-loan and start a business selling charcoal at the local market. Unfortunately, the loan shark came by her hut sooner than they'd agreed and he demanded that she repay the entire loan—about sixty dollars. She had zero money to repay it. Here's the kicker. She's one of dozens of other vendors also selling charcoal, and that keeps her prices miserably low, and, even worse, nobody cares. Not the government, not her husband, not relatives, not neighbors—nobody.

"Sounds terrible. What a crime. If she's looking for money, sixty dollars isn't a fortune, so what if we gave—"

"Hold it, it gets worse. A couple days ago, she was frustrated, so she went to her local voodoo healer—you know, a kind of witch doctor—who told her the difficulties in her life were due to her ancestors' angry spirits. In order to appease them, he said she had to sacrifice a bull, a huge expense that requires money she just doesn't have. All the while, she's caring for her children and fending off her out-of-work husband who rants and raves at her."

"Sounds awful."

"You got that right. Her suffering is endless. And she's trying to believe what we're telling her, that God will meet her needs and answer her prayers. Pastor Pierre has encouraged her to pray and believe, but it's tough, real tough."

"I hope we can be the answer to her prayers, then. So what ways do we have to help her?"

"Well, we can come alongside her in this crisis and build a strong relationship with her over the long haul. Hopefully that will allow her to feel Christ's love and, rather than using voodoo healers and loan sharks, she'll have the chance to experience how God's power can improve her life."

Dean's sense of excitement for this ministry shot up. "Count me in. I'm on board, Trev. Can't wait to get there and join you."

"Fabulous. Look, I'm calling from a pay phone because I couldn't find a way to recharge my phone battery. So I gotta go." They hung up.

Moving back to the couch to watch the preacher on TV, Dean looked at Kate and understood how the dilemma of their sex-impaired marriage paled in comparison to the hardscrabble desperation of the Haitian people. Theirs was a Third World predicament of life-and-death stakes compared to his and Kate's First World predicament of wouldn't-it-be-nice stakes. The obvious gap in intensity between the two worlds pricked his conscience.

A commercial was on the TV and Kate, sitting quietly, turned to Dean. "We could be that preacher and his wife someday, you know. What a powerful couple they are."

"Yep. Just like we're going to be," he said, hugging her. "What we're going through is peanuts, though, compared to the kinds of trials and tribulations Haitians are dealing with."

She rested her head on his shoulder. "I'm sure that's true. But let's make the rest of tonight only about us, okay?"

He squeezed her tight. "Well said. I can agree to that."

CHAPTER

L arissa sat at Sacred Grounds going over her account books. She had extended credit to three clients who now appeared they would never pay. Heating bills for the studio had doubled due to the harsh winter, and she had two months' rent due on her lease still to pay her landlord. Keeping flowers in stock was more expensive this time of year, and her website needed a makeover estimated at $450. Cody's next tuition payment hung over her head, and the cost of groceries had crept up. Regrettably, Sacred Grounds' cozy atmosphere and the charitable people sitting around her brought no comfort. Large flakes of snow descended outside her window seat, possibly the start of another big snowfall. Not much to be jolly about.

Beep! Beep! Her phone signaled a new text from Trevor. She opened it:

"am sitting in my tiny room here in this ghastly heat, wishing i had u in my arms. hav you given mom-hood more thot? i want to be the father of our children. am convinced we would raise beautiful babies and be a great family. love, trev."

She held the phone to her heart. *What a guy!* She knew what her gut wanted to reply: *Yes!* But starting over as a new mom and never-before-wife seemed overwhelming now that cancer was part of the picture. What pregnancy risks might her cancer, or a possible recurrence, bring? Launching into married life thrilled her, but at the same time scared her, especially as a pastor's wife. So many marriages ended in divorce. Even Kate and Dean's had teetered on that brink. She wanted to text back: "am ready. would love to get started being the mother of your children. sounds great."

But am I ready? Am I the right wife for him? Would I risk being abandoned again? Yet who else but Trevor could ever be my quality guy?

She closed the ledger and reached for her mittens, cap, and down parka for the icy drive home in the 10-below-zero temperature.

Thirty minutes later, Larissa heated homemade beef stew on the stove while Cody got ready for work. "Be sure and eat plenty of stew before you leave, Cody. You need healthy protein to give you energy before you rush off."

"Aw, Mom," he drawled, buttoning his blue work shirt. "You worry so much."

"Actually, I worry about what you don't eat—fruits and vegetables, and you need more dairy."

"The way I eat is fine. But it's nice that you care enough to nag me." They shared a quick smile. He crammed a handful of potato chips into his mouth and chugged a high-energy drink from the fridge.

"It's *your* stomach, Cody." Shaking her head, she handed him an official-looking envelope from St. Paul Community College. "This came today for you."

He tossed it on the table. "Gotta run."

"No you don't. We both know it's your grades. Open it. Please."

"Do we have to go through this? Really?"

"And just who is paying your tuition? I have a right to know what my money is paying for."

"I'll open it if you tell me when you'll pay your half for my car like you promised. You've been stalling, and I've proven I can hold a job."

"I've just gone over the Fitness and Flowers books. It'll be tight, very tight. Somehow I'll find a way. But you have to promise me you'll drive more carefully."

"I will, I will. Whatever. You know my driving record's clean."

"Except for running a stop sign and a speeding ticket. And what about that icy patch when you ran that red light a month ago? You slid right through the intersection and could've hit somebody."

"Driver error, yeah, yeah."

"Lucky there wasn't a cop around. It would've been a violation if you'd been pulled over."

"Look, Mom, why are we arguing? You said I could have a car months ago." He smiled. "It's a good thing you got yours fixed, though. It's been running a whole lot better."

"Don't thank me, thank Trevor."

"Uh, just how tight are you guys getting?"

"If I said tighter and tighter, would that be okay?"

"Maybe. For a church dude, he's not so bad."

"And ... ?"

"No major red flags so far."

Larissa smiled, accepting that as a positive sign. She pointed to the envelope on the table, giving Cody a stern look.

"All right!" He took the envelope and ripped it open. His poker face showed no hints. Then, slowly, a broad grin curled his lips into a smile.

She snatched it from him and scanned the grades: one A, two Bs, and a C. She threw her arms around his neck. "These grades are great, Cody!"

He looked as shocked as she was. "I had no clue. Really, Mom. I thought I'd bombed the English final."

"Two Bs and an A. I'm so proud of you. It's a good start. I'll bet Nicky will be psyched about your grades too."

His chest puffed up. "She thinks college is really worth it and says you get back what you put into it."

"Good for her."

At the mention of Nicole, a small smile touched the edges of his mouth. Larissa was tickled to see Cody show interest in such a fine girl.

In the next three minutes, Cody gobbled down the bowl of stew, put on his jacket, borrowed the keys for the Saturn, kissed her cheek, and bounded out the door into the snowy afternoon. Other than her 4:30 fitness class at Fitness & Flowers, she planned to enjoy curling up with a good book until bedtime that night.

She opened the Fitness & Flowers's ledger and once more realized the need to invest more time and money into marketing her studio. Where would the hundreds of dollars for Cody's car come from, never mind the funds for rent, tuition, groceries, and the website makeover? Reaching for a calculator, she tabulated the profit-and-loss figures once more, hoping the numbers on the troubled balance sheet would improve on their own.

Outside the window she heard the wind blowing stronger as snow swirls blurred the darkening sky. Turning on the radio, she heard the radio announcer interrupt the program: "This just in, the latest Weather Service storm advisory. Officials are warning metro residents that unusually frigid temperatures are making driving conditions hazardous. Roads are turning icy, and drivers are cautioned to slow down on the slick roadways and to take special precautions on slippery ramps and bridges."

Larissa felt a stab of concern for Cody. His drinking and recreational use of pot had tapered off recently, so that wasn't so worrisome.

She walked upstairs, pondering Trevor's text about wanting to be a father. If married, would her feelings of never belonging, of being an orphan and having only herself to depend on, finally fade away? If she married Trevor, would they run the studio together some day? Did she want that?

Two hours remained before the first client walked into Fitness & Flowers for class. Wearily, she climbed the stairs to her bedroom. She sat on the edge of the mattress, yawned, and stretched while settling back in bed for a few seconds—only a few seconds, she told herself—just enough time to close her eyes and allow the stresses and worries to leave her body and her misgivings to drift out of mind.

When Larissa catapulted out of bed, the clock on the bedside table read 4:02 p.m. Rubbing sleep from her eyes, she scurried downstairs and out the door, jogging to the studio in the driving snow while trying to make record time. As she reached the alley, a passing city snowplow sprayed jets of flying snow all over her. Frozen stiff, she reached the front door where clients were waiting, and she apologized to each one for being tardy.

Ninety minutes later, her phone rang while she was bidding clients goodbye. It was Cody, and she let it go to voicemail. As the last client, Claire, headed out into the snow-clogged evening, Larissa waved. "Goodnight, Claire. See you on Thursday. Get home before another foot of snow buries us."

Larissa's phone rang again as she waved to Claire. The phone beeped, signaling a voicemail. As she prepared to lock up, the phone rang again. Irritated, she picked it up.

Immediately she heard Nicole's panicky voice: "You have to come quick! They've taken Cody to the hospital! He crashed the car!"

"WHAT? Slow down. Crashed the car? What hospital?"

"HCMC. Hurry! They're not sure he's going to live! I'm with him now, but I'm injured, too."

"Where? Where did you say?"

"HCMC. Hurry!"

Larissa felt the floor drop out from under her. Nicole's words echoed: *Cody ... they're not sure he's going to live!*

But Larissa had no car. How could she get to HCMC? Waving madly out the door through the fresh falling snow, she hollered, "Claire, stop! CLAIRE, PLEASE STOP!"

Claire had pulled away from the curb in her Volvo but was stuck in the deep snow. She saw Larissa through the frost-covered windshield and lowered the window.

"I need a ride! Can you help? It's an emergency!"

"Of course, hop in." Larissa was sure Claire could see the panic in her eyes. "But first I'll need a push!"

"Okay!" Larissa moved to the Volvo's rear bumper and shouted, "On three, step on it. Ready? One, two, three!" She shoved with all her might. The car budged. Larissa shoved harder. Working in tandem, they maneuvered the Volvo into the street. Cars skidded and honked their horns. Larissa opened the passenger door and hopped inside. The Volvo's wheels plowed straight ahead into the line of traffic, moving the car steadily forward.

"Cody's been in an accident. He may be dying!" Larissa cried. "We have to get to HCMC. Quick!"

"Oh my gosh! Where did you say?"

"Hennepin County Medical Center. Can you go faster? You'll have to turn around and go back toward downtown Minneapolis."

"Did I hear you right? Cody may be *dying?*"

"Yes. He crashed the Saturn."

"Oy vey!" Claire glanced down at Larissa's feet. "Where are your boots? Your coat?"

"No time. All that matters right now is getting to the hospital—fast."

Shivering, Larissa rubbed her bare arms. In her frenzy, she could still hear Nicole's panicky voice shouting, "They're not sure he's going to live!" *Cody, my only child, dying?* Losing Cody would mean … she stopped. *I will NOT think negative thoughts.* Her mind flipped to, *Cody will live. He has to make it. He* has *to!*

The car's heater blasted warmer air. Larissa rubbed her arms and hands, bewildered by a torrent of questions: Why Nicole? Why wasn't Cody at the warehouse working? Why were they together when the car crashed?

Larissa leaned back, trying to calm herself. "Please hurry." She speed-dialed Cody's number, but it just rang and rang.

Outside the emergency operating room thirty minutes later, Larissa paced like a tiger. Cody lay on the operating table, tended by doctors scrambling to save his life. So little about what was happening made sense. She was worried sick that a nurse would come any minute and announce, "I'm sorry, ma'am, we couldn't save him."

Nicole lay slumped on a gurney a few feet away. Her head was tipped to one side and blood and bruises discolored her skin. A splint held her right leg so it jutted straight out, and a sling cradled her limp left arm. Drugged heavily, she moaned and sobbed.

Larissa stepped over to the gurney and put her hand gently on Nicole's good knee. "There now, Nicky. You'll be okay. Hang in there. Everything will be all right."

"No, it won't!" Nicole blurted, abruptly awakened. "Nothing will ever be okay again!" Heavy doses of pain meds slowed her speech.

She held Nicole's free hand, hoping the calming effect of wordless, gentle touch would soothe her. She winced seeing Nicole's facial bruises, and lamented the responsibility of being the only parent within hundreds of miles. "I phoned your mom and dad, Nicole, but they didn't answer. Then I remembered they were out of town skiing."

Nicole didn't seem to hear her. Larissa guessed Dean and Kate were out on the snow-packed hills, or they had simply turned off their phones.

"What is *taking* so long in there?" asked Nicole. "I'm so afraid ... so afraid he won't make it."

Please don't talk like that. "We have to be positive."

"The longer it goes, the less chance he has . . ." Nicole's voice trailed off.

Larissa glanced at her phone, checking to see if Trevor had replied to her text a half hour earlier informing him of the accident. Nothing. She feared the digital signal from the northern United States to the Caribbean was unreliable. Her texts had failed before. She pressed the resend button, gritting her teeth as if that might help the message get through.

From what Larissa pieced together, the Saturn had skidded on black ice and crashed into a bridge abutment, totaling the vehicle. The heavy snowfall and unplowed streets were major factors. Cody's chest had slammed into the steering column, sending his head against the windshield. The paramedics who arrived on the scene had to pry the car open in order to lift him out of the wreck, while Nicole lay severely banged up on a stretcher in the ambulance.

"Ma'am, I'm sorry," a husky masculine voice told Larissa, "but you'll have to clear the hallway."

She turned and saw a black nurse carrying a clipboard, a kindly Somali immigrant by his facial features and closely cropped black hair. "You may sit there in the waiting area, if you like."

"Yes. Okay. Thanks."

The male nurse moved Nicole's gurney next to an empty seat where Larissa sat down.

As she faced the loss of her son, her fears combined with her own cancer-related uncertainties—and now the loss of her car. *How much can one person handle?* Her life felt cursed. All her troubled life she'd faced stiff odds. Her anger flared. *So where is Trevor's mighty, all-powerful, loving God now? I'm sick of this life! This is all unfair!*

Larissa had nothing with her but her phone—no money, no purse, no coat, no ID. It seemed symbolic, how much the little things in life mattered when they were gone. Thank goodness for Claire, who'd dropped everything to drive her to the hospital in dangerous conditions, insisting on going back in the storm to retrieve Larissa's purse and a warmer set of clothes, and to lock up the studio. *What a friend! What do I have in this life except great friends like her? And Trevor. At least for now I have Trevor—but he's so far away ... and Cody ... oh, I hope, hope, hope I still have Cody!*

Emerging from her drugged state, Nicole mumbled, "Cody was playing hooky."

"Hooky? Why wasn't he at work?"

"His shift never started because of the storm, so he drove over to my house. He was so excited about his grades and re-enrolling in classes." She struggled to speak.

"Why did he drive to your house instead of returning home?"

"We wanted to go to M.O.A. Hanging out together at the mall seemed like a great idea." Nicole drifted back into a semi-stupor.

Larissa looked upward, seeking some kind of help. *If You are there, and if You are a god of justice, then Cody has to live. Do You hear me?* She ached for comfort and solace, for everything to be better. How could she go on living without her only son? Surely God must know what *that* meant. *I wish Trevor was sitting here holding me. But no ... I'm alone. I always am. Trevor, I need you! Trevor, come back home!*

Panicky, she dialed Gladys and Jerry's phone number; it rang and rang, then went to voicemail. "It's me, Larissa. Terrible news ..." She told them the basics and asked them to call her back.

Nicole moaned. Larissa gently stroked her neck where the strap from the sling rubbed her skin, hoping her fingers brought some comfort. *What's taking so long in there? Is he still alive?*

"Are you Cody Beaumont's mother?"

Larissa looked up. The same black nurse with the clipboard stood there.

"Yes ... Yes, I am." She was shaking.

"The surgeons want you to know it will still be another hour. But he's hanging on, ma'am. They've finished working on his head injuries, and now a thoracic surgeon is working on his chest, repairing his lung injuries."

"Is he going to make it?" She tasted salty tears.

He gave a reassuring smile. "They're doing everything they can, ma'am. Everybody wants him to live." He spoke a few words in his native Somali tongue that sounded prayerful.

"Will he be paralyzed?"

"How about if I check back with more news when we know more?"

Larissa nodded mechanically, wiping her eyes with a tissue from a nearby box. She whispered, "Thanks," then went silent. *Keep hoping. Keep believing. Be grateful. Trust.*

Nicole stirred. "Cody wanted to steer around a stupid snowplow. I was afraid and told him not to. But he wouldn't listen. Then, boom! We hit the bridge."

Larissa swallowed hard. "Was he speeding? Being reckless?"

Nicole wavered. Whether due to the painkillers or the pain of violent memories, Nicole went quiet. Then ... "I can see how much you love your son. And I really care for him, too."

Nicole's words could not have sounded sweeter to Larissa's ears. She took out her phone and texted Trevor: "please, please answer. have u checked ur messages? i need u here badly."

Larissa wondered if a disrupted signal or faulty connection had blocked her text messages. Waiting. More waiting. Slowly, the minutes ticked by.

CHAPTER

S now blew in Dean's face from his skis as he shooshed down the steep hill. Kate watched from the bottom of the hill near the chairlift. It was a happy sight seeing her beloved husband cutting loose and having fun. He came to a stop near her, making his skis spray loose snow. She enjoyed seeing the icy crystals covering his face and his ruddy cheeks.

"So how did you like that Black Diamond?" she asked.

"Lovely. Absolutely lovely. One huge mogul almost got me, but here I am." He smiled in a natural, stressless way—something she hadn't seen in months—as they herringboned to the chairlift line.

"Okay, Mr. Ski Bum. One more run, then it's the bunny hill for this kid—or the chalet. My legs are like rubber."

"Be that way if you have to," he kidded. "Okay, one more run will do it."

The snow-packed hill and the brilliant sapphire sky surrounding them looked like an award-winning landscape calendar. She felt him leaning closer to her as they reached the lift area, preparing for their turn to ride up. She couldn't remember a merrier time when just the two of them had spent free time together like this away from home.

An hour later, they opened the door to their deluxe suite with north woods decor and knotty pine paneling. They shed their ski clothes and put on white terrycloth bathrobes. Kate reveled in knowing they still had two more days of "couple time" at their favorite resort, three hundred miles north of the Twin Cities. She'd taken charge of making a "winter wonderland" getaway happen, and now a pastel-tinted sundown heralded a blissful evening—just for them.

Dean ran bathwater in the Jacuzzi and removed his robe. His physique was still fit, and even more pleasing than she remembered—in fact, he was sexy. She readied herself to join him, her heart beating faster. Was this her moment or would she chicken out? Now was the perfect time for the chocolate éclair she'd saved for them. She opened the box stowed in her luggage, took out the éclair, and held it up for him to see. "Remember this? Are you hungry?"

"Ah, yes, looks yummy. I was wondering when …" Fully naked, he stood there smiling, a big grin on his face. "Well, as soon as you get in the tub, let's go for it."

She caught his double entendre. Unfortunately, her cellphone rang.

She sighed. It rang again. She saw what appeared to be a strange foreign number pop up. "Dang. Hold on, Skip." It rang again. "Something tells me I should take this." She answered.

"Hi, Kate." Trevor was fuming mad. "Guess what? My smart phone got stolen today!"

"Oh, my. Oh, no. What the heck happened?"

"Pastor Pierre and I were in town bargaining with a contractor to repair the broken water pipe to the clinic. We were haggling over costs, and I took my eyes off my things for a second—for *one* second—and a thief grabbed the phone and got away. I ran after the bugger, but he slipped into the crowd."

"Did you get a look at who took it?" she asked, startled by the fury in his voice.

"Not very. I should've known better."

"No description at all?"

"Some kid, probably ten years old. Screw it. I'm so fed up."

This hardly sounded like the Trevor Kate knew. She looked at Dean, bending naked over the Jacuzzi as he got in, and tried to think of a quick way to hang up. "I remember you warning us that this kind of thing could happen."

"I know I did, Kate, of course. But now it's happened to *me*. Look, I still have to get a hold of Larissa, and—"

"Larissa? It's nice to hear you mention her. Are you missing her?"

He sighed.

"Let me guess. There's someone in your life now who was never there before."

"There's never been anyone like her, Kate, never someone back home waiting for me. Now I can't even text her or get her messages. I'm going bonkers." Trevor paused. "I'm overreacting. Sorry." He sighed again. "I think it's because I miss her so much. I can't live without her, Kate."

"The way you're talking makes that pretty clear. So whose phone are you using now?"

"Pastor Pierre's. Will you pass the number on to her?"

"Of course." Kate looked through the window at the fading pastel orange sky in the distance.

"Listen, I just can't let this golden opportunity with Larissa slip by," he said. "How often do people get a second chance at love?"

Kate flinched at the thought of Larissa as *Dean's* second chance at love not so long ago.

"She's the one, Kate. I know it."

Kate laughed for joy. "Sounds like you've opened up your heart to her, Trev. I'm sure she's opened up her heart to you, too."

They covered a couple more details and hung up.

Kate entered the bathroom where Dean was soaking in the hot, bubbly water. "That was Trevor. His phone got stolen, and he's all tied up in knots about it, *and* over Larissa." She unfastened her robe, taking her time to get into the Jacuzzi. She wanted Dean to appreciate her unclothed figure. He did, and she basked in his enjoyment.

"What's the scoop from Haiti?"

"We'll talk later about it. It can wait." She stepped in and lay back in the soothing, churning water, closing her eyes in a swan dive of pleasure. "It's so much easier relaxing away from home. No chores, no schedules, no kids to think about."

"Agreed. So let's have that éclair now."

She reached for it. "Ooopps. It's on the nightstand. You know, I wonder sometimes if the very things we spend our time caring about at home are the things that dampen our energy for playing like this."

"When do we ever take time to play at home, Katie?"

"Exactly. Always the next thing to do."

"Yep. Going to work, errands, parenting, shopping, church."

"Right. Take out the garbage, rake the leaves, drive here, drive there."

"All the more reason I'm hyped that you arranged this little getaway," he said.

She splashed water at him. He splashed back. They giggled, and splashed each other. He reached over, put his hand on top of her head, and pushed her completely under water.

She came back up, gasping. Covered in froth, she sputtered, "I'll get you for that!" They giggled and began a water fight. Shoving playfully, Kate tried to dunk Dean. Pushing, pulling, tugging, jostling, they splashed and sprayed and squirted. Coming up for air, spitting jets of water, she laughed and he spewed suds. They looked at one another and smiled … two wide smiles.

After they toweled each other off, they plopped on the king-size bed. Side by side, free of clothes, she waited for her heart rate to slow. Dean slid his hand next to Kate's, intertwining his fingers with hers, and she stroked his brow. "I loved seeing the way you skied down that Black Diamond today, my love, just like when we were dating. You made it look so easy."

"Are you trying to flatter me, Katie Nelson? Are you weaving some kind of north woods spell on me?"

If she meant to do something, the moment was at hand. Whatever might happen, she wanted it clear that she was the one initiating and not merely allowing something to happen. "Let me answer that without words," she said. She took the éclair from the nightstand, bit into one end, and offered the other end to him. *Now we're lovers as much as husband and wife.*

Their private little game began as they both chewed toward the center. Tasting the vanilla in the creme with the bittersweat chocolate topping satisfied Kate like never before. As they devoured the pastry, their lips touched and kissed—slowly at first, then more passionately, more fervently, more feverishly. Within Kate a tiny spark triggered rapturous feelings that were long buried as she kissed him hungrily. She stroked his shoulders and back, but he rolled away slightly. Placing her hand on his chest, she stroked his chest hair and allowed her fingers to gently drift across his pecs. Although his skin felt hot from the Jacuzzi, she sensed hesitation in his actions. Had his fire for her gone out? He seemed less responsive. If she was right, she wanted to rekindle it. Her own small fire was building within her. At last she was finding her "on" button! She wanted him to know it was *her* desire driving her actions, that she *wanted* him—truly wanted *him.* Wasn't that what he'd always asked for?

She delicately touched his skin as far as his belly button. He asked, "Are you hinting, Katie? For real?"

"Yes, I am. Isn't it obvious?" She glided her fingers along his skin toward his groin.

"Well, yippee!"

"We're alone, we're away from home, and we have time. It's been a *long* time, Deano. We deserve it."

He turned and looked straight at her in wonder. "I'm all yours." He lay back and closed his eyes.

Swallowing her anxiety, she traced her fingertips along his shoulders and ribs down to his thighs. She wanted to offer him the same energy as the Haitian dancers. "Remember those dancers on YouTube?" she asked. "Didn't I say, 'Things are changing—believe it'?"

"You did, yes. And now I do."

Kate's mind whirled. She looked into his eyes and recognized the deep hurt he had lived with, sensing his history of unrelenting disappointment. The pain she saw in his soul made her pause.

D ean sensed her rekindled fire for him, but had he any left for her? Clearly her libido had reawakened. As her fingers drifted across his thighs, his arousal felt frozen in ice—the ice she had shown him for so many years. Was this new Kate for real?

He felt her delicately trace her fingers along his skin back up to his belly button—and back down to his genitals. Still, he did not get aroused.

Kate stopped. She gazed at him, sat up, and stepped over to the bathroom sink. He watched her naked form backlit by the window. *Lovely. Exquisite.* Her curves and figure were every bit as appealing as when she was a newlywed, even more so. Entirely natural in its beauty and relaxed movements, Kate's body was exactly everything he'd ached to enjoy for ages.

That was all it took for his body to respond.

Kate returned to him with a wet towel and folded it on top of his forehead, as if to soothe him. He gently brushed it away. His erection became prominent.

"Well now, look at that!" she said.

He felt clumsy and out of practice. Having sat on the bench so long, he wasn't sure of his own capability. Kate touched his erection and they both laughed as it wiggled.

She took her time. He wondered if she might wrap her hand around it, and she did, smiling and looking eager. Her face turned earnest as she whispered, "I've thought through very carefully what I'm going to say next, so hear me out. Lie back and listen."

He blinked, bewildered.

"We'll get right back to the play-by-play, I promise." She kept her hand where it was and snuggled next to him. "Because this is a big moment for us, I want it to be extra special. For many years I've ignored God's urgings to be intimate with you. Basically, 'mommy madness' took over, and that went on far too long. I didn't take seriously our becoming 'one flesh' like God meant us to be. I focused so much on the kids and the house and church that making love with you seemed bothersome. Our intimacy was my lowest priority. I never even thought about your pleasure, or my own. You've been more than patient and you've been upset for good reason. While I was trying to please everybody and save the world, you were trying to save our marriage."

Of course he had realized all this, but it felt extremely gratifying that she was saying it and was willing to admit it. He started to speak, but she touched her finger to his lips and showered kisses on his bare chest. "I just want you to know this is a new beginning for us and I'm grateful for it."

His heart cried out: *No more delays. No more time to waste. Finally!*

Dean shed his regrets and turned playful and fun-loving. Kate wiggled her breasts and brushed her erect nipples against his chest, behaving like a new lover. Her energy felt fresh, assuring him that his endless waiting was over. He sensed she wasn't experiencing pain or just doing her duty. His arousal intensified. Daring and joyful, she seemed determined to tip the scales. She was truly going for it, and he reveled in her bold behavior.

Looking into her eyes, he trusted her. He was seeing the new Kate. She generated both emotional warmth and physical heat, melting the deep freeze between them. His erection got harder. He was clumsy, but he knew that smoother lovemaking would come in time. He rejoiced in how she opened herself and received him fully. Thrusting inside her, he felt waves of bliss that he'd waited so long and so desperately to experience. As they embraced, he felt uplifted. Although without finesse, their intimacy seemed palpable. Pleasing sensations flared through him, energizing his inner being in a rhapsody of fireworks.

In Dean's embrace, Kate felt deep appreciation for her husband like never before. Her evolving sense of self now warmed to Dean's longing to embrace her and welcomed his "deepest wish and desire to be closer." The impulse to loosen her grip on her modesty meant she and Dean could be real lovers now. Modesty had been her badge of honor, and once had meant being free from vanity and ego and self-indulgence. But it was also an obstacle to pleasure and ecstasy and intimacy. What, after all, was an orgasm other than ecstasy—and with the soul mate she loved?

As Dean moved rhythmically within her, she understood God wanted to free her to approach life with abandon, trusting herself to be vulnerable. Her past, although rooted in fear and conformity and timidity, no longer held her captive. Now she could sing a new song.

He moved deeper inside her. His arm curled around her shoulder, reminiscent of the tender embrace of Rodin's naked lovers. Experiencing these feelings while making intimate love was her baptism. Like the statue's male lover, he enfolded her in his loving caress in response to her signals of openness.

She gently ran her fingers along his cheek. "I've hardly had half a minute to say how much you mean to me, Skip." She pulled him toward her and kissed him, offering a full, tongue-touching kiss. She smiled, and responded like she had in their courtship days. Hadn't her entire body responded freely back then when they'd made love in Paris? Why not now? Why not right here? *Yes, here.* They plunged into the wordless dance of love. The excitement of a wild ride aroused her, and this time she wanted her own soaring flight to ecstasy.

In his arms, she allowed Dean to be in charge. He wanted to bring her pleasure, she knew. So she could let herself go, trusting him, permitting herself to feel exhilaration, leaving the responsibility for her own pleasure in his care. *Inhibition be damned! I am safe!*

Skin-to-skin, she stroked his hips and thighs. "You stud, you. Bring it on." Emotions deep and suppressed burst forth. No longer did she feel like a whore or a slut for feeling sensual and sexy. She tingled as he responded; her lessons with Larissa and Marlene were paying off. She thanked the Haitian dancers in her heart—and the vibrator stored in the linen cabinet.

Whether Dean decided to leave or stay in their marriage, she felt committed to making love to him right then, with no strings attached. Her love did not depend on keeping him at home or looking good. She was ending her captivity and breaking her chains. Her willing vulnerability drew him closer.

Dean affirmed her assertiveness with powerful thrusts of his hips. This resurrection of desire was what she wanted to define their marriage from now on. Goodbye to fear and false dread. Her avoidance of sex would no longer imprison her. Fear of losing her husband, fear of divorce, fear of alienating Lindsay and Nicole, fear of fracturing her own sanity—all gave way to a fearless freedom.

She opened herself to him, wanting more of her inner being to reach him. *Yes, bring on the adventure.* In Dean's embrace, she let herself revel in the riches of her unlocked sensuality. She loved her dear Deano with her *body.* She wasn't going to stop until he rolled off her exhausted, spent, and happy.

Dean's eyes sparkled as he looked into her soul. She put more into giving of herself without bargaining or extracting promises. Together, they gave each other the pleasure and intimacy that invited transcendence. Orgasm was within reach, and she wanted it. She lavished her new passion on his body, steadily dissolving his inner pain. A newly discovered erotic imp came alive inside her. Her "on" button was on.

Carefree, she writhed, and his rhythm matched hers as carefree and overjoyed as her own. "Yes! Yes! Yes!" Her orgasm exploded in waves. Real, not faked, it flooded her being and her deepest core with elation and delight.

"More! More! More!" She welcomed his love as a sign of God's grace. God was willing this pleasure for her, for Dean, for their marriage, to make it whole again. In that instant, a third essence came into being generated by their unity. They became one in three parts—the feminine, the masculine, and the Sacred.

CHAPTER

"Cody, you're going to make it," whispered Larissa in his unbandaged ear. "This is Mom talking. Believe it. You're going to come through this."

She looked at the bandages covering his face and body as he lay in the ICU hospital bed. Minute by minute, she wondered whether all the plastic wires and rubber tubes could prolong his life. She felt shiverish. The slow-moving minutes dragged by as the sounds from the machines monitoring his vital signs made intermittent beeps. At times the beeps got fewer and farther apart, and she held her breath. She kept looking at the clock, dreading the final—inevitable?—beep.

But he has to make it. God, are You there?

Larissa trusted medical science only so far, and trusted God less. Cody needed a miracle. The skin around his eyebrows and the tip of his nose were all she could see of his face. Splints covered his arms and legs, except for one uninjured hand. It frightened her how he looked like a mummy. *A mummy wrapped up for burial!*

Nicole, still quite groggy, lay in her hospital bed down the corridor on the same floor. Larissa's eyelids drooped from constant watching. She thought of retreating to the adjacent family waiting room where she could rest and peer through the large observation window, steadfast in her vigil.

The emergency doctor walked into the ICU unit accompanied by a female nurse, and Larissa's ears perked up. "Your son has lost a lot of blood, Ms. Beaumont, and he's in a coma." The young surgeon's solemn expression ratcheted up Larissa's alarm. "It's lucky the EMTs got him here at all in this snowstorm," said the doctor. Larissa glanced at the nurse taking notes on an electronic tablet.

"Is there any hope he's improving?" she asked anxiously.

"Well, he's sustained multiple injuries. There's been a huge blow to his chest and abdomen. His spleen was ruptured and there's damage to his esophagus. We've removed the spleen, but there's considerable internal bleeding. We're replacing the blood loss right now, but it'll take more time. His sternum and upper ribs are fractured, and he took a big blow to his head when he smashed into the windshield. There's no sign he was wearing a seat belt, and the driver's air bag didn't inflate."

She gasped as tears came to her eyes. "But … is there hope?"

"Well, we've put him on a respirator, which does his breathing for him, and so far so good. That's hopeful. He's on meds to calm him so he won't try to pull out the breathing tube. Unfortunately, some of his autonomic brain functions may be impaired."

Her tears flowed. "So there *is* hope—or not?"

"I'd say there is. He's suffered tremendous trauma, though. He's got youth on his side, and no alcohol or drugs were involved."

"Thank God!"

"But until his blood volume goes up and stays up—and until we find out how he'll breathe on his own once he's off the respirator—there's not much more I can tell you, Ms. Beaumont."

"Will he be paralyzed? Will he sit in a wheelchair and just drool, or will he be able to walk again and use his hands and legs?"

"I'm sorry, there's no way to predict that right now." The doctor directed the nurse to adjust the I.V. drip. "Fortunately, his head trauma isn't as serious as we first thought. That's a plus."

"Is there some sign to look for? Some way to know if he hears me?"

The doctor cleared his throat. "Well, if you see his eyelids flutter, or feel him squeeze your fingers, those are good indicators."

"Okay ... okay, thank you."

The doctor forced a smile, then he left the unit. The nurse checked Cody's instrument readings and adjusted a timer, then left with his electronic chart.

"I love you, Cody," Larissa said softly, leaning toward his exposed ear. She waited and watched. *What's left other than to hope and pray? Did I say, 'pray?'*

Dean nestled closer to Kate as they shared the afterglow of love. "You know, Kate, that was the greatest gift you could've ever given me."

"I'm so glad—so so glad. It was a gift for me as well."

He wanted to flood her with compliments. Instead, he just let his fingers trace meandering circles on her skin, which stirred sighs of pleasure from her.

"Dean, I love the way you're touching me; it feels great." He kissed her bare belly and the tender skin under her breasts.

She nuzzled closer. "Wait! Can I assume that we're sleeping in the same bed when we get home?"

He nodded. "From now on, yes."

"Yay!" Kate laughed and kissed him. She settled back and held him close, savoring their rapport.

Buzz! Buzz! Kate's cellphone rang.

"Don't bother," said Dean.

Buzz! Buzz!

"No, we go through this all the time. I'll get it." Kate peeked at the the LED display. "It's Larissa. Something must be going on. She wouldn't keep calling otherwise."

Kate answered the phone. "Hi, what's up." Her face dropped. "No! It can't be. Oh my God, NO!" She shoved the phone at Dean. "There's been a terrible accident. Larissa says Cody may not live."

"WHAT?"

Kate put the phone to Dean's ear. They both heard Larissa say, "There's more. Nicole was in the car with him."

"Dear God!" Kate gasped. "Is she all right?"

"She's banged up and has a lot of bruises, but she's talking."

"Can you hand the phone to her?" asked Dean.

"She's sleeping in her room. I'm keeping a close eye on her."

"We're on our way!" Dean exclaimed.

He and Kate jumped out of bed, got dressed, and threw their things in their bags. They rushed for their car and drove as fast as they dared back to the Twin Cities.

H ours had passed. Larissa stood at the observation window staring at Cody. It was after twilight, and an update she'd recieved from Trevor minutes ago was discouraging. He'd texted her using somebody else's phone from the Port au Prince airport, saying that his phone had been stolen and explaining he'd heard the news about Cody and was waiting to board a flight to Minnesota. He'd texted: "nelsons got thru to me about cody's accident. am stuck here, hassled by delays and jacked-up ticket prices. had to bribe a ticket agent to get a boarding pass. am hurrying home as fast as i can and praying every minute for cody. love you, t."

Larissa struggled to blot out the chaos Trevor must be facing in Haiti, while pushing away the fear of Cody dying before her very eyes. *Why haven't Kate or Dean called me? They could've let me know they'd gotten through to Trevor.*

She looked at her phone, and two messages were unchecked—one each from Kate and Dean. "No wonder!" she said aloud. She hadn't checked her messages in hours. Perhaps she'd dozed off, or had mentally blanked on monitoring them.

She heard voices, and turned to see the Nelsons walking into the observation room still wearing their ski jackets. "Kate! Dean!"

"Is he going to make it?" asked Kate, hugging her. "Fill us in on everything!" She was shocked to see Cody smothered in bandages.

"Any good news?" asked Dean, peering at Cody with obvious concern.

As Larissa talked, she walked from the observation room to the ICU cubicle while Kate and Dean followed closely behind. Approaching Cody's bedside, Dean held Cody's free hand and spoke quietly, whispering prayers and attempting to make a special connection with him.

Kate hugged Larissa even tighter. "We came as soon as we could. We just peeked in on Nicole. She's dozing in bed, and we didn't want to disturb her, poor thing. We talked to the doctor, and it seems she'll be okay eventually. Have you heard anything from Trevor?"

"He's on an airplane, at least I hope he is. It's crazy down there, I guess. Last I heard, he was waiting to board, and I haven't heard anything else since. That was two light-years ago. Claire, dear Claire, offered to pick him up at the airport and bring him here. Can you believe it? A friend like that?"

"I can believe it. Claire is a dear. So she's there waiting right now?"

"Yes. In her car, standing by."

Will Trevor ever get here? Larissa did not fully trust that Cody would last long, even on the respirator. Or that he would breathe properly after they removed it. *Hurry, Trevor!*

The respirator began beeping erratically. Cody's vital signs plunged down, back up, back down, then stayed down. The veteran nurse dashed in and rushed to Cody's side, checking the monitor screen. "I'm sorry, folks. You'll have to clear the unit."

Larissa felt nauseous. The nurse worked rapidly, adjusting settings and tubes, while Larissa and the Nelsons moved to the observation room to watch. Fretting desperately, Larissa stared at her son through the window. Kate cradled her and Dean squeezed her hand. Slowly, slowly Cody stabilized.

Larissa's phone rang. "Trevor?"

"Hi, it's me. Yes, I've just landed in Minneapolis. What a nightmare. Is Cody doing okay?"

"It's so great to hear your voice! He's hanging on, but hurry! How soon can you get here?"

"As soon as I get a cab."

"No need for that," Larissa declared. "There's someone waiting, ready to drive you here." She told Trevor about Claire and a few details about Cody's condition. "Please, hurry! Look for Claire—she's in a tan Volvo waiting by Arrival Door 3. She'll drive you straight here."

"Gotcha. Hang in there, Larissa. I love you."

"I love you, too. I totally, totally love you."

Larissa hung up, cheered by Trevor's arrival. But it didn't last long. In a heartbeat, she felt nervous again about the roads, still clogged with heavy snow. She ached for him to arrive safely—and fast. The Nelsons had gone to check on Nicole and Larissa was alone.

A wave of depression, as much for herself as for Cody, reminded her of how sick she was of having the world on her shoulders. *I never knew my own birth family. There's only me, alone. Is there a god for orphans?* Then it occurred to her: Had the god of orphans connected her with the Beaumont family? How else had she come to be rescued? Clinging to frayed hope, she laid bare her innermost grief to Whatever or Whoever might be 'up there' or 'out there.'

Staring through the window at her only child whose life force might be ebbing away, she lifted her open hands in a gesture of supplication. *Heal him! Whoever You are, if You are there, if You care, please heal him.* Had she been heard? *Please, please, heal him!*

An hour and twenty minutes had passed since she'd talked to Trevor, and the foul taste of mortal fear filled Larissa's mouth. The ICU nurse and a technician arrived in the unit to remove the respirator. Larissa stood out of the way by his bedside as they scrambled to shut off the machine and test Cody's ability to breathe. Glancing through the observation window, she saw Kate and Dean slumped in the family room's lounge chairs, dozing.

"Please step back," the nurse stated. "Doctor's orders, Ms. Beaumont. Now we'll see how he does." She patted Larissa's arm in a kind gesture.

Come on, Cody, breathe! You can do it!

The nurse slid the breathing tube out partway. If Cody failed to breathe on his own, that would mean severe swelling of the brain and, potentially, an indefinite vegetative state. The machine stopped. Cody's chest remained static. The technician rechecked the dials and hookups still connected to him. Larissa's own breath stopped. Cody's chest moved. His natural inhale-exhale response returned and became rhythmic; so did hers.

"Oh my god that was scary!" Larissa said to the nurse, who closely monitored his pulse rate. "So, are his lungs functioning properly again?"

The nurse gave a thumbs-up. "For the moment. He's taking in oxygen on his own now."

"Does that mean he will come to?"

"That's the next development we're looking for, if the coma lifts."

"And if it doesn't?"

"I'm sorry, but that's something only the doctor can discuss with you."

Larissa's fright meter shot higher. "So he's *not* out of the woods yet?"

Silence. The nurse and technician concentrated on several indicators beeping on the electronic monitors. "One victory at a time, ma'am. I'll be looking after your son now and the doctor's been notified, so why don't you go sit in the family room and give yourself a rest?"

Larissa left the unit and, just then, noticed Nicole entering the family room in her wheelchair. Pushing the chair was another girl Larissa didn't know.

"Larissa, this is my sister Lindsay."

"Oh, hi—it's good to meet you, Lindsay."

"Nice to, ah, meet you, too." Lindsay did a quick scan of Larissa, down to her dance shoes, then added, "As soon as I heard, I drove up from Iowa."

Larissa offered a quick smile and said, "I'm sure your family appreciates you coming." She turned to give Cody her full attention through the window. In her peripheral vision, she glimpsed the Nelsons huddling around Nicole and Lindsay in an impromptu family reunion. For one piercing instant, Larissa imagined herself at the center of a loving family like theirs.

Her mind refocused on Cody. He was breathing stronger, she could tell, but other risk factors came to mind. Complications from his head wound and the hazards of a seizure troubled her. The doctor entered the observation room, his face flushed with relief.

"What will it mean, doctor," she asked, "if Cody stays unconscious in a coma?"

"If the coma lifts and he revives reasonably soon, his chances for a favorable recovery will improve greatly. If the coma lingers, his chances will be less than favorable."

She winced. Kate and Dean now huddled around her, listening carefully. "And just how long might a coma like this linger?" Larissa asked.

"For hours, for days, sometimes for weeks."

Larissa went pale. "That long? And what would that mean?"

The doctor hesitated. "That would mean the patient remains in a vegetative state."

Larissa swallowed hard. "Indefinitely? Are you saying he might *never* come out of it?"

"Medicine is as much an art as it is a science, and right now we don't have the science to discern when a coma like his will lift."

Despair attacked Larissa. She excused herself, went into the bathroom, and closed the door, sagging on the toilet seat lid. *If only I could give my own life for Cody's!* Powerless, bereft, emotionally bankrupt, she sobbed.

The sobbing made her nose run and tears streamed down her face. *I'm sick of going it alone. Sick of having nowhere to turn, no anchor in my life, nobody to lean on. I can't handle it any more. I'm done. If Cody dies, my sanity goes with him to the grave.*

A silent sob punctuated her flurry of heart cries. She looked up, daring an invisible Power to take pity on her. "Look, I'm not going to sugarcoat this," she declared aloud as she looked up. "If you care even one tiny bit about Cody, or me, help us now. Please. Heal Cody. Heal *me*. Please! If you have the power to heal like Trevor and Dean and Kate believe you have, then bring Cody back to life now. Do something ... !"

She opened her eyes. A small movement within her, similar to the kind she'd experienced on Christmas Eve during the pageant, calmed her. "Trevor says you are the bridge, Je-Jesus. Is that true?" Saying the name Jesus was difficult, but a feeling of peace came with the strange utterance. A feeling of being whole and complete infused her, inexplicably separating her from her worries. Cody's fate, whichever way it went, was beyond her control. Yet, even so, an inner calm soothed her. For the first time since the car accident, she felt the weight of worry and doubt and anguish lifting, and in its place came serenity and calm.

"Be real to me," she spoke aloud. "Be real, Jesus. I want what Trevor and Dean and Kate and Ginny and Marlene and the others have."

She heard a commotion. Wiping her tears, she bowed her head in deep reverence and whispered, "Thank you, God." Saying that felt awkward, but she realized she'd addressed God directly for the first time as though God were really there. She opened the door, preparing herself for whatever came next.

Gladys and Jerry Beaumont had entered the family observation room. With them was Russell, the stepbrother she once felt closest to in high school. Her heart leaped; he was so handsome in a rugged, wind-blown way. Gladys used her cane to walk toward Larissa while carrying her Rosary beads. Jerry was his usual tall and sinewy self, wearing down-home barn jeans and his Seed Co-op baseball cap. Larissa recalled asking her client Jasmine, standing now to one side, to keep calling her farm family until she reached them. *And here they are.* Jasmine smiled at Larissa, trying to appear hopeful.

"Our baby girl!" said Gladys as she gave Larissa a big hug. "We're so sorry about Cody." Russell looked at Larissa with special affection. Jerry kissed her cheeks and muttered, "Have faith, Sweetie," then gave her one of his famous bear hugs. Gladys began repeating verses of the Holy Rosary, bowing her head and entreating God for a blessing. Larissa heard her invoke the ageless prayer for supernatural healing, "O Holy Lord, blot out our sins; O Master, pardon our iniquities; O Holy One, visit and heal our infirmities."

Larissa felt a wave of comfort seeing them again, especially Russell. "Hey, stranger, no hug?" she chided him affectionately. He approached her, smiled, and without a word lifted her off her feet with his powerful farm-strong arms. Larissa yelped with as much glee as she could muster at the moment. She took Russell's hand and left the room with him, heading straight to Cody's bedside. "Here's your favorite uncle, Cody. Russell, say hi to your nephew."

"Hey there, kid," said Russell into Cody's ear, holding his good hand. "You'd better perk up pretty quick, hear? Your mama needs you. An' I want to see you back on the farm milking cows again. Don't let this beat you, kid."

With all her soul, Larissa wanted Cody to keep fighting. Suddenly another strong set of arms wrapped around her, squeezing her tightly but gently and sending a profound feeling of security through her body. She turned and there was. ... "Oh, my God! Trevor!"

Trevor's arms held her to him, his sky-blue eyes shining with love and strength. Claire waved from the corridor, smiling broadly and offering a bright thumbs-up.

"I made it at last, Larissa," Trevor said. "Sorry it took forever. But I'm here."

She collapsed against his chest. "I'm so relieved!" Her spirit soared. "And glad, so incredibly glad!"

"How's Cody doing? Any better?" Trevor saw Russell holding Cody's good hand. The two men silently shared eye contact, each nodding respectfully to the other. Russell stepped aside and left the room.

"There's no telling when he'll come out of the coma," she told Trevor, "or even if he ever will." She told him what the doctor had said.

"That doesn't sound very good. He either comes to—or he doesn't? That's it?"

"Basically. That's what it all comes down to. From here on, it's a waiting game. No one knows how long, or how soon, or even if ... "

She pulled him closer to her, putting her arms around his waist, blissful one instant yet anxious the next. Although Cody's breathing remained steady, she knew the many people who'd arrived to support her must be feeling as overwhelmed and powerless as she was.

"God can heal him, Larissa," said Trevor quietly. "Believe it."

She wanted to tell Trevor that she'd prayed for Cody's healing, and even that she'd thanked God for it, and how she'd felt a strange assurance come over her. Before she could get a word out, she realized he interpreted her pause as doubt.

"Just because you don't believe in something like divine miracles, Larissa, doesn't mean they don't happen."

She tucked her head into his shoulder. "But if I *do* believe in them, does that mean I have true faith?"

Startled by her response, Trevor was tongue-tied for a second. "Are you saying you *do*?"

"I do, yes." She smiled.

He smiled joyously.

She guided Trevor to the family waiting room, where she sensed everybody saw something special about her and about the two of them. She introduced Trevor to Jerry and Gladys and the others, then signaled people to gather around in a circle. Turning to everyone, she said, "Let's all pray," then looked at Trevor. He responded with surprise, but collected himself and reached his hand out to Dean, who reached out to Kate, and soon the circle was complete.

Trevor bowed his head. "Dear Lord, we lift up Your child Cody in this time of crisis. He needs Your healing, and we ask for Your touch to powerfully heal him, so he will return to full health. His life is in Your hands, yet we know that You both give and take away. Our prayers are for Your good and perfect will to be done here today."

"Yes, Lord," prayed Dean, his voice quiet as well as commanding. "We ask for Cody to regain consciousness and have a full life. We dare believe it's Your purpose and in Your power to do this. We pray he becomes the man You have created him to be, and that this accident may somehow become a necessary, positive step in that process. We recognize You as sovereign and believe You will do what is wisest and best for all."

"And we pray for our dear Larissa, Lord," said Kate. "Show Your great power to her and Cody, and how You can accomplish immeasurably more than we ask or imagine. Wrap her in Your loving and comforting arms this very minute as she faces this trial. We know You have wonderful plans for her, as You do for Cody. Help him awaken and come out of this coma."

"I need to butt in here and say my piece," said Jerry, clearing his throat. "Hey, Lord, I see a fine young man ready to step into life, into his best years, ready to do good things. Show him mercy, Lord, please, and bring comfort to his mother's heart. Heal him now, we pray."

Silence followed.

Larissa wiped her wet face and runny nose. She wanted to go back and feel Cody's hand squeeze her fingers, to see his eyelids flutter. Unexpectedly, a quiet cry escaped her lips. Everyone turned to her as she cried out again, her head bowed.

"Bring him back to me, please! Do not shame these people by refusing their prayers. If you are the God of justice, the God of mercy and grace, then show us your stuff. All my life I've waited for you to act, so please act now. These nice people believe you love them and care deeply for them, and Cody and I need your love and care, too. Amen."

Seconds went by. Nobody spoke.

Larissa glanced at the faces in the circle. Each person loved her, she knew, and wanted the best for her. She sensed a strong yet soothing energy. She could not explain it, yet something special was happening. An inner calm was visiting her. She understood beyond all logic that Cody's destiny was safe and unshakeable, and that her own deepest needs could be—would be—met fairly and fully. With Trevor's muscular arms supporting her, she felt free to rest securely in the center of the loving family members and friends surrounding her.

The quiet stillness of midnight brought welcome tranquility to the ICU unit. Larissa stood at Cody's bedside holding his free hand, allowing the quiet to soothe her nerves. Trevor stood with his arm curled around her waist, providing closeness and comfort. Everyone had left and gone home except for Kate who sat in Nicole's room at her bedside. Cody's eyelids had fluttered twice moments before, boosting Larissa's sagging hopes for his coma to subside. The nurse had just notified the doctor and checked Cody's vital signs, then given Larissa the okay to stay a few extra minutes. Sleepy and spent, she rested her head on Trevor's shoulder, allowing the restful quiet—punctuated methodically by the electronic beeps of Cody's respirator—to settle her fears.

Trevor leaned closer and whispered in Larissa's ear, "I have something very important to ask you, and I can't wait any longer."

Mystified, she turned and looked into his warm eyes. She watched as he bent down on one knee and looked up at her. His face shone with love.

"What on earth—? Why are you on the floor?" *His doing that must mean…!* Her heart raced with excitement.

Softly his words reached her ears. "Miss Larissa Beaumont, love of my life, will you do me the great honor of marrying me?"

Time stopped. Could she speak? She must! Lightheaded and breaking into a wide smile, she swooned. "Y-yes!" Then louder, "Yes! Absolutely!"

Trevor's face beamed with delight as he stood and embraced her. "I love you with all my heart. We'll find a way to make everything work out, I promise."

"Yes. Yes, I think we will too." Her heart sang.

"All those long days and lonely nights in Haiti, all I could think of was you," he said earnestly.

"Oh, Trevor, you have no idea!" She hugged him with every ounce of her strength. Nothing in all of Larissa's life had ever felt as affirming and uplifting. Tears trickled down her cheeks.

She turned and looked at Cody. *Now if only ...* His eyelids fluttered a few seconds, longer than moments before. *Oh, Cody, you have to wake up and hear my good news—our good news!* She lovingly took his hand—and thought she felt a tiny squeeze.

CHAPTER

Dean handed the TSA agent the heavy duffle bag loaded with medical supplies. As the brawny agent placed the bag on the conveyor belt, Dean watched it move through the scanning machine. He glanced up at the rows of national flags displayed high above the ticketing area of the Minneapolis-St. Paul International Airport, wondering if Haiti's flag was up there as well. The agent gave Dean the all-clear signal, "Good to go, sir."

Dean headed for his fellow travelers at the security checkpoint, Trevor and Hal, where they were inching through the line, completing the clearance process before boarding at the gate. Kate walked beside him, holding his hand.

"I'm really going to miss you, Skip. As things get back to normal here, I'll keep in touch."

"I'm counting on it." He pulled her close and kissed her—a solid I-really-love-you kiss. "I'm glad you'll be helping Nicky get back on her feet."

"It's a no-brainer to be there for her. And I'll have good company with Larissa. She needs lots of help with Cody, so I'll be able to support her while she spends those long hours at the hospital during his rehab sessions."

"Thank the Lord he's over that hurdle and bouncing back. You and her will be good company for each other."

"I hope you're not fretting about my going back to the bottle while you're gone," added Kate.

"Not really."

"Are you sure?"

"As sure as I can be. It's been about a month without a slip. You got through your folks' visit and New Year's just fine, and you're going to AA meetings twice a week." He looked at her with a bit of concern. "But do *you* feel you might slip back?"

"Sobriety does feel very new, and the cravings haven't stopped. But I'm seeing my old drinking patterns in a much larger context, so it all feels different than I thought it would. With Claire and Ginny and Larissa around, I'm sure I'll manage just fine."

As Dean and Kate approached the security gate, he noticed Trevor and Larissa fawning over one another. "Well, now, look at those two lovebirds in their own little world. How sweet." He made a "tweet-tweet-tweet" sound.

Kate smacked his arm playfully. "Now cut that out. They might be saying the same about us," she said, giggling. "Besides, any girl would be head over heels getting the beautiful engagement ring he gave her."

"Well, it's sure nice seeing how happy they are." Dean felt deep satisfaction. He was also pleased that Cody's coma was lifting gradually and that the prognosis for a favorable recovery looked good.

Hal waved to Dean to hurry up. "Come on, guy, let's go. You too, Trevor. Get your passports and boarding passes ready. Let's move it."

Standing near her husband, Ginny winked at Dean. "Give your lady a big sloppy kiss and get going. Time's up."

Dean swept up Kate in an embrace and kissed her as zealously as good manners permitted. He watched Kate open her pretty blue eyes, and they were shining. *Yes, we're connected again, more than ever.* He turned and saw Trevor and Larissa in a similar embrace.

"Like I said," Hal repeated, raising his voice, "move up in line now, Dean. That also goes for our fearless leader, Trevor. Ahem!"

Trevor slowly broke away from Larissa and stepped into line alongside Dean and Hal. Larissa ambled over to Kate, who asked, "Are you and Trev still deciding on a date?"

"We thought of October when you first introduced us," Dean overheard her say, "but sometime this summer is more like it. Of course, we still need to tell Cody when he's ready, but overall we're raring to go. And we're so grateful that you and Dean will be our best man and matron of honor."

"*That's* an honor for *us*," replied Kate, giving Dean a quick wink.

After clearing security, Trevor flung his arm around Dean's shoulder.

"Ready to go, Deano? All set?"

"Sure am. How about you?"

Trevor smiled. "This time is different. I have somebody special to come home to."

Hal walked up behind them, clamping his hands on each of their shoulders. "Wave to your sweethearts, boys, and let's hit it."

Dean turned to walk toward the boarding gate, then glanced back at Kate and Larissa standing shoulder to shoulder, waving and blowing kisses. *What a sight! I guess there's such a thing as big miracles after all.*

Acknowledgements

Every book requires the caring efforts, insightful critiques, and encouraging comments from cooperative people. I wish to acknowledge: Connie Anderson, Dara Beevas, Jeff Donovan, Norm Hauer, Peggy Henrikson, Karen Johnson, Diane Keyes, Ian Leask, Jane MacCarter, Ed Newman, Alan Pranke, Rick Sanders, Laurie Scheer, Emily Shaffer Rodvold, and Paul Walker.

Thank you one and all.

About the Author

J. Z. Howard sees life through the eyes and hearts of people who strive for the very best in their lives. As a father, husband, professional counselor, and spiritual seeker, he champions women's equality and empowerment in every sphere of life. He also invests heavily in his male characters so they will radiate robust yet caring masculine virtues.

His chief goal in his fiction, as well as real life, is to develop both male and female qualities in ourselves so we are more balanced and motivated to contribute selflessly to people. His optimism and positive actions are inspired by God, the rock of his Christian faith.

Besides his 10-year career in Hollywood's TV industry, J.Z. has directed award-winning videos and published three addiction recovery books. He lives with his charming wife and true love in Minnesota.

Visit him at jzhoward.com, or jz@jzhoward.com.

2ND EDITION

JUNE 2014

Made in the USA
Charleston, SC
15 June 2014